Liliana's Voice Hit the Air Like a Jet Engine.

"I am not just going to kill you!" she screeched. "I am going to tear your chest open and drink the blood directly from your beating heart!"

"That's just gross, Liliana. Didn't your poor, dead mama ever teach you any manners?"

I slipped to another section of the roof as she tracked my voice. Hopefully I could play mouse to her cat long enough to find the twin to the door she'd just destroyed. Then I'd run some more. The thought made me want to break something.

I could confront her, of course, maybe even smoke her if she wasn't too fast or too strong. If my aim was true. But I realized, though I wanted to kill her, I couldn't. Vayl should be the one to finish her.

I found the door, framed by hanging baskets, and gently depressed the handle. Nothing happened. It was locked. *Okay, Jaz, you are now trapped on top of an eight-story building with a homicidal vampire. Time for Plan B.*

"Rardin's lively, fast-paced urban fantasy debut features a host of characters and a plethora of plot twists."

—*Library Journal*

JAZ PARKS NOVELS

Once Bitten, Twice Shy

Another One Bites the Dust

Biting the Bullet

Bitten to Death

One More Bite

Bite Marks

Once Bitten, Twice Shy

A JAZ PARKS NOVEL

Jennifer Rardin

www.orbitbooks.net

NEW YORK • LONDON

Orbit
Hachette Book Group
237 Park Avenue
New York, NY 10017
Visit our Web site at www.orbitbooks.net

Orbit is an imprint of Hachette Book Group. The Orbit name and logo are trademarks of Little, Brown Book Group Limited.

Printed in the United States of America

Originally published in trade paperback, October 2007
First Orbit mass market edition: July 2009

10 9 8 7 6 5 4 3 2 1

For Kirk, my inspiration, my joy, my love.

Once Bitten, Twice Shy

Prologue

Fear sucks. Because you never know when it will attack. Sometimes it sneaks up behind you, giggling like your best girlfriend from seventh grade. Then it whacks you on the back of the head, takes you straight to your knees before you realize what hit you. Other times you can see it coming, just a dot on the horizon, but you're like a canary in a cage. All you can do is hang in there and hope you don't get motion sickness and puke all over the newspapers.

I already felt pretty queasy as I perched on the single wooden folding chair my boss, Pete, kept for visitors to his office. In fact, I hadn't been this scared since I'd started working for him. Not even when, about ten hours into my first mission, I'd walked into my hotel room to find a vampire standing beside the bed, holding a crossbow. *My* crossbow. The one I'd meant to use to eliminate him.

Unlike that scenario, this was not a case where I could just go away and try again later. Or, as I had actually done, kick both shoes into his face to throw him off balance, blast his kneecaps with the .38 I wore under my skirts for insurance, then finish him off with the crossbow he'd dropped when his bones shattered. In this instance I was forced to sit absolutely still and try not to ralf all over the top-secret files stacked in rows two and sometimes three deep on Pete's green metal desk. Because, despite the fact that I'd successfully completed every mission he'd assigned me so far, Pete was about to fire my ass.

There could be no other explanation for this call-in. The man, notorious for his penny-pinching, had phoned me at 3:00 a.m. direct from Ohio to London for the express purpose of informing me I should buy a first-class ticket back to headquarters as soon as my job there was finished. He was probably looking at the receipt now, along with all the other expenses of my latest trip abroad. He ran a hand across his head, making his three remaining dome-hairs stand on end as he studied the open file in front of him.

I couldn't bear it any longer. There is only so much you can take of staring at blank turquoise walls, rows of black metal file cabinets, and white slatted blinds that have never been opened (which would explain the dead plant sitting on the table by the window). I sat forward, the chair creaking alarmingly beneath me. *No doubt about it, I am the only item in this office under the age of fifty.*

You wouldn't know it to look at my clothes, though. I'd come straight from an American Airlines flight during which an aviophobic widow had wadded various handfuls of my blouse and jacket into her fists the entire trip. I looked like a homeless woman. Holy crap. If I lost this job I'd soon *be* a homeless woman. And that was the good news!

"Look, Pete, I know you told me to cut out the car hits.

The repairs are too expensive. You told me that. So I stopped. I haven't caused an 'accidental' crash in three months—you know that! But this last one just couldn't be avoided."

"I understand you took out my counterpart in MI5."

"Well, yeah, but only because his driver was in on the plot. He'll be fine. You heard that too, right? His back will heal in, like, six weeks."

"I heard there was a bomb."

"It didn't go off."

"But it could have."

I shrugged. "Better there than at the coronation." *Wait, that sounds a little casual for somebody who should be begging at this point.* "But I am sorry about the car. I took out extra insurance."

"This has nothing to do with the car. In fact, I'm glad you put that bastard in traction. Self-righteous twit. No, you're here because I have a new assignment for you."

Thank you, God. I still have work! I nearly relaxed. Which, considering my current state, would've sent me right to the floor. But Pete had started cracking his knuckles. In my time with him I'd seen pencil chewing, furniture kicking, file throwing, and a short bout with scented candles. But the knuckle cracking was new. I sat back carefully and waited.

"You've heard of Vayl?" Pete asked.

"Well . . ." Only whispers. You could almost call them rumors, their subject matter seemed so implausible. If you bought the stories, Vayl had built himself a legendary career, and not just because he'd become one of the 15 percent or so of vampires to gain acceptance among humans. He was also supposedly the best assassin our department had ever fronted.

"I'm partnering you with him." Pete's eyes darted away from my face, so I guess I wasn't hiding the *What the hell!* very well. Long silence during which I tried to make my head stop spinning and Pete cleared his throat a few times.

"Pete, I . . . When you hired me, you promised I could work alone." My previous job had involved an entire crew, of which I had been the leader. It had ended badly.

"Jasmine, Vayl has requested a partner. You fit his specifications. You're smart, tough, resilient . . ."

My lips had gone numb. "Uh-huh. And?"

He sighed. "And increasingly dangerous." He rushed on before I could interrupt, which was a good thing, because I think my first response might've ruptured his eardrums. "You've been taking bigger and bigger risks. You're a loose cannon out there, and I'm starting to think I can't trust you to work alone."

Bullshit! Stop feeding me lines from cop movies, ya wanker! I know when I'm being jerked around!

He rushed on. "I know how furious you must be—"

"I don't think so! I've kicked ass all over the globe for six months, Pete. I haven't botched a single assignment. Not one. Show me another agent with that kind of record."

"Vayl—"

"Needs me like he needs a suntan!"

Pete gave me a get-hold-of-yourself stare that worked like looking in a mirror. Shit, was I actually frothing at the mouth? "Do you recall the job in Cuba?" he asked.

I'd hit Castro's most trusted adviser, a general named

Miguel Santas. In the middle of a crowded market. In broad daylight. Within arm's reach of his lieutenants. But I'd gotten away clean. Didn't that count for anything?

"And the one in Colorado?"

Aaah, sweet. A pedophile named George Freede had started a church called International Brothers of the Light. Their main focus seemed to be kidnapping children from the United States and selling them to the highest foreign bidder. I'd tracked him to a resort and pushed him off a mountain. Okay, we'd both fallen off, but I'd landed on my skis in nice, fluffy powder. He'd dropped on a rock.

"It's my responsibility to make sure my agents survive," Pete informed me.

"So you got me a babysitter."

He laughed, deep in his belly where it sounded the most real. "Hell no. I hooked you up with a guy who's been alive nearly three hundred years. I was hoping some of his levelheadedness would rub off on you."

It was the laugh that got me. I took a breath, then another. I thought, *Okay, maybe he's right. Maybe I have crossed the line a couple too many times. And he doesn't even know about the blackouts.* Plus it was kind of nice to be looked after, cared for. I had only been alone a little over half a year. But it had felt like thousands.

I sighed. "You said he requested me? Why?"

"He's got his own reasons, which he says he'll reveal to you in his own time." Pete and I shared a cynical raising of the eyebrows.

"Quite a mysterious character, isn't he?" I noted.

"When he wants to be," Pete agreed.

"So what can you tell me about him?"

Pete pulled a two-inch-thick folder off the top of a short pile and opened it. "He's been with us since the early 1920s. Full name is Vasil Nicu Brancoveanu. Born November 18, 1713, in Mogoşoaia, Rumania, which is near Bucharest."

"Oh, for chrissake, can we skip the birth certificate and get to the dirty laundry?"

Pete shook his head at my impatience, but he closed the folder and gave me an indulgent smile. "He's a power, Jaz, and I thank God every day he chose our side. I've read this file four times and still don't think it covers all his abilities. I can tell you he's got pretty well-developed hypnotic powers. He's a helluva swordsman, skilled also with ranged weapons but prefers to fight up close and personal. Vampire strength and speed, of course, along with a finely honed ability to just disappear."

"And?"

Pete nodded. He knew I was waiting for the biggie, the core power around which the others revolved. "He's a Wraith."

So the stories were true. His touch could actually freeze a man to death.

We talked for a while longer, which was when Pete revealed that, while he wanted me to stop taking crazy chances, *his* bosses appreciated the fact that I was willing.

"Our government looks at Vayl as a national treasure, Jaz," Pete said. "On paper you're his assistant. In reality, you're his bodyguard. You've met the members of our oversight committee."

And how. Senators Fellen, Tredd, and Bozcowski had pretty much cured me of ever wanting to vote again.

Pete went on. "They've asked me to drive home the importance of your primary mission, which will always be to make sure he comes back in one piece."

I'm five-five. I weigh one-twenty when I remember to eat, which isn't regularly. No question this guy Vayl could snap me like a twig anytime the urge hit him. Plus, you don't live that long without honing some major survival skills. I laughed. "Pete, lay off the bullshit, will you? Vayl needs a bodyguard like I need a pet poodle. You and I both know you're not being straight with me about this deal. But you know what? I'll go along for now. Because I'm curious." And because, God save me, I loved the job. It had kept me alive. It had kept me sane, after . . . after.

Pete looked embarrassed enough that I thought I'd give it one more push. "Come on, boss, really. Why me?"

He smoothed those three hairs and dropped his hand to the desk. "Because Vayl wants you. And around here, what Vayl wants, Vayl gets."

Chapter One

Six Months Later

"Get outta my way, you old bat," I muttered under my breath as an elderly woman who shouldn't have been driving a golf cart much less a Lincoln Town Car at this time of night putt-putted down the street in front of me, her blinker announcing she meant to make a right turn sometime before she reached the ocean.

"Are we a little testy tonight, Lucille?" Lucille Robinson is my usual cover and my alter ego: a gracious, sweet girl who always knows the right thing to say. Vayl invokes her when I step out of line. I nearly flipped him off, but since he's still got one foot mired in the 1700s, I thought better of it and stuck my tongue out at him instead. I wasn't sure he'd see me making faces at him in the rearview, but of course Vayl sees everything. I realized I'd come to count on that as much as I sought his approval which, at the moment, had ditched me.

"Do not be distracted by menial events," he reminded me in his stern baritone. "We have a job to do."

"But if you'd just let me ram this old biddy into the next electric pole I'd feel much better."

"You would not."

I sighed. Six months. Scary how much Vayl had

learned about me in such a short span. In my defense, given time he could worm the true ages out of the entire cast of *Desperate Housewives.* Still, the only living person who knew more about me was my sister, Evie, and she was just that nosy.

"It's New Year's Eve for chrissake," I grumbled. "There's supposed to be snow on the ground. It's supposed to be freezing." I guess the natives of Miami would've disagreed. And to be honest, all those palm trees would've sent me skipping around in circles if I'd been on vacation. But we Midwesterners have a thing about winter holidays and snow, and this year I had yet to experience either one.

Vayl went still, a sight that will creep you out big-time if you've never seen it before. He sort of resembles a statue anyway, as if da Vinci had chiseled his square forehead, high cheekbones, and long, straight nose from smooth, pale stone. His curly black hair was cut so short that right now I'd almost swear someone had painted it on. The temperature inside our silver Lexus suddenly dropped ten degrees. A breeze ruffled my red curls, playing them across my shoulders as if they were harp strings.

"You make it snow inside this car and I swear I'm going to park your butt in the middle of the next retirement village we come to and take the first plane I can find back to Ohio," I warned him.

Strange to think of Ohio as a base for any operation more dangerous than cataract surgery. But that's why we're still doing the government's business. Of course, people know we kill bad guys. They just don't want the gory details. But if you asked them in a dark room where their neighbors couldn't hear, they'd tell you we're not nearly as proactive as they'd like. Witches, vamps, weres . . . some would vote to throw them all on a gigantic bonfire and have done. But there's good sorts among those *others* who have earned—and deserve—the same rights and protections we humans get.

Vayl is one of them. And after six months of partnership, I was glad I hadn't pulled a diva and stomped out of Pete's office when he'd suggested our pairing. We'd clicked like checkers from the start. At this point I couldn't imagine working without him. But he did have his eccentricities. And, okay, some of those quirks made me want to dangle him from the Terminal Tower from time to time. His intense interest in my so-called Gifts. The fact that he'd flunked out of the School of Positive Reinforcement. And especially his adept avoidance of any subject related to the why of our hookup sometimes annoyed the hell out of me.

He sort of came alive again, catching me off guard, as it would if, say, I was strolling through a botanical garden and the cherub in the fountain suddenly started flapping its wings. He sat forward, his smile just a twitch of the lips.

"How can you miss your sleepy little state when I have brought you to one of the most exotic spots on earth?"

"Okay, I know you're too old to be taking lessons from a young punk like me—"

"Jasmine"—(he pronounced it Yaz-mee-na, which gave me the biggest thrill, though I'd never let on)—"while I agree that twenty-five is quite young, you can hardly call yourself a 'punk.' "

Yeah, but nutcase is just too close to the truth. "Dammit, you old fart, would you turn right already!" The white-haired wonder leading what had to, by now, be a blocks-long parade must've turned on her hearing aid. Because she finally pulled into the United Methodist Church parking lot, praise God, leaving the rest of us free to party until some other octogenarian found it necessary to take to the streets after dark. In Ohio, old folks know better than to drive at night. Yet another reason Cleveland rocks.

We drove straight to our very old, very exclusive hotel. Called Diamond Suites, it towered above the pink stucco wall that surrounded it and its gardens, rising nearly twelve stories before reaching its peak with a steep, red tile roof. The windows all wore black metal bars, decoratively scrolled top and bottom. The gated parking lot required a key card for entry. We'd retrieved ours along with the car we now drove, part of the privacy policy with which Diamond Suites attracts its reclusive, generally famous, clientele.

Vayl's eyes were the icy blue of an Alaskan husky as he took in every detail of the scene before him, his brain cataloging it for future reference. Parking lot full of high-end rentals. Check. Automatic, key-card entry door with bulletproof glass. Check. Lobby full of complimentary goodies from fluffy white towels to imported shampoos, all graciously displayed on the shelves of antique armoires. Check. Not a single soul in sight. Excellent.

His hands full of bags, Vayl leaned over and whispered, "According to legend this inn is haunted."

I snorted. An unladylike habit, I know, but one which,

like swearing, has its place. "Probably your old poker buddies waiting around to even the score." This was not as far-fetched as it sounded. Rumor had it Vayl had won his cane and his first gold mine in a game of five-card stud.

Vayl's lips twitched again. Not for the first time I thought, *If he ever truly smiles his face is going to shatter.* But I tried not to think it too loud. On the plane he'd overheard the flight attendants discussing the pilot's stun gun from the back of the plane as he sat beside me in the front row. A man with that kind of ability only needs to listen slightly harder to hear my harsh thoughts.

Vayl had reserved the penthouse, so we took elevator 6A to twelve. At that point I did a little soft-shoe—the semiclaustrophobic's version of the I-gotta-pee dance—until Vayl figured out which way to slip our key card into the metal slot on the elevator's control panel so the door would open. After I'd leaped out and regained a somewhat steady pulse, I took stock. We stood in a small enclosed entryway decorated with a massive flowery mural that involved all four walls, including the elevator doors, and half of the ceiling. Tiles in the pastel pink so common to Florida covered the floor.

I wrinkled my nose at the color. Something about pink makes my stomach churn. Maybe it's the resemblance to Pepto-Bismol. Personally, my taste runs toward bolder colors. That's why I currently wore an emerald-green silk shirt under my black jacket. Unlike Vayl's coat, which reached his knees and looked like it could comfortably hide a shotgun, or a sword, or possibly a small pony, mine stopped just below my waist and, because it had been tailored to mask my shoulder holster, fit superbly. My black slacks felt a little loose, probably because I'd missed lunch all month. And since the Weather Channel had warned of a cold spell hitting Florida at the same time we did, I'd worn my new boots. Hopefully they'd hold up longer than the last pair, which had fallen apart the first time I'd stepped in a puddle of blood.

I tugged my trunk through a set of white French doors that opened into a sunken living room furnished with flowered couches and chairs, glass tables, and Pepto-pink carpeting. On the opposite end of the room, next to ceiling-to-floor curtains in Elvis velvet, sat a bigger glass table surrounded by chairs. I noticed it mainly because the chairs had rollers, which keyed a memory from my childhood.

My brother, sister, and I were staying with our Granny May at her farm for the summer. Her kitchen chairs had wheels, so we spent part of each day either pushing each other around the room or having spinning contests to see who fell off first. Good times. I felt a throb of homesickness for those few golden moments when my sibs and I were friends, teammates, and coconspirators. Why couldn't it have lasted forever?

"Never mind," I whispered. "It's over now. Move on. Move on. Move on." I caught myself in the litany and clamped my lips shut, imprisoning the words before they could betray me.

Still carrying a suitcase, our laptop, his garment bag, and cane, Vayl strolled into the room and took inventory. His eyes rested momentarily on a cut-glass vase full of white orchids and moved on to a silver bucket filled with ice and a bottle of champagne.

"Nice," he said, nodding with approval.

"Yeah, it's uh"—I struggled to put some of the expected enthusiasm into my voice—"grrreat!" I skirted the rim of the living room bowl, rolling my trunk after me. I liked it because it looked the way I felt most of the time, battered and old. Right now it appeared sorely out of place, and if the furniture could talk I was sure it would shame my low-class luggage right out of the building. The pack on my back wouldn't score any points either. Despite the fact that it dressed in basic black, it too had seen better days. But it worked, carrying my weapons in well-padded pockets along with my ammunition and cleaning cases. So rather than run to the nearest Motel 6, I just kept walking, taking my most treasured possessions toward another set of French doors to my left, which no doubt led to a grossly sumptuous bedroom.

"Come now, Jasmine," Vayl chided me. Already across the room, he set the laptop on the table and moved to the curtains, which I expected him to stroke like a pet panther. Instead he flicked them back, peered out the window. Satisfied, he looked over his shoulder at me. "I bring you to the most exclusive hotel in Florida and the only reaction I get is your Tony the Tiger impression?"

I felt like slumping against the wall, at which point I would bang my head repeatedly until I passed out. But no, the bell had dinged, forcing me back into the ring for Round Fourteen of the Never-Ending Battle. Nope, no blows traded, damn it all. Our struggle was just a continuous conversation during which Vayl tried to figure out how I'd grown to adulthood without acquiring the slightest refinement, and I continued to be baffled that a man old enough to remember when bathrooms were windowless shacks built above deep stinkin' holes could be fooled into thinking that ugly flowers and crappy-tasting liquor *meant* something.

"Look, Vayl, we've got a *really* big night ahead of us. Can't we just agree that I'm a cretin and you're a snob and move on?"

For a minute I thought he was having convulsions. Then I realized he was laughing. Depositing his stuff on an end table, he collapsed on the nearest couch and heaved with barely suppressed merriment. He looked . . . Now, why would the word "yummy" come to mind? Under his coat he wore a dark blue sweater that hugged his torso as if they'd been reunited after a long separation. On the plane he'd mentioned his gray slacks had been tailored by a guy named Nigel Clay who spoke with a lisp and sewed like a savant. His shiny black shoes had come straight off the shelf—in Italy. Since he'd assumed the identity of a high-end antiques dealer named Jeremy Bhane, his elegance was called for. It baffled me that such a thing could come so naturally. Or that I should find it so . . . delectable.

What is the deal with these food metaphors, girl? I asked myself. *Miss too many entrées, did you? Or are you hungry for something a little more—no, no, no, don't you dare go there. For damn sure not with your badass vampire bossman. He could never replace Matt anyway. No one could.*

"Jasmine?"

"Huh?"

"Are you all right? You suddenly look . . . haunted."

"Oh, yeah. I mean, no." Short, fake laugh while I fished for something to say. "I was just wondering why you don't smile more. And I thought maybe it's because your fangs would show."

"Would that bother you?" he asked sharply.

"Not at all. We had two vamps on my Helsinger crew. Stellar people." *Now dead, dead, dead . . .* Feeling a guilty sort of pride that I'd been able to say that last bit without breaking down, I opened the bedroom door. Surprise, surprise, it had a huge round bed with a fuscia duvet and a mirrored headboard. I'd call the carpeting a nauseating mix of Pepto-pink and cherry-flavored NyQuil. I liked the Whirlpool tub in the next room though, and the shower was big enough for me and the cutest six guys I could round up on short notice.

"I suppose you find this room a bit over the top," said Vayl, making me jump and squeal.

"What is the *deal* with you tonight?" *And how come you keep showing up just when I'm trying not to think of how long it's been since I've had sex?*

He shrugged. "I am, how do you say, feeling my oats, perhaps?" He'd let a trace of his original accent creep into his voice. His left eyebrow moved upward a couple of notches. I forgot to breathe as I wondered just how many women had lost themselves in those blue eyes. *Over nearly three hundred years? Don't make me laugh. And don't think about him that way anymore. You're his assistant. Period.*

I sighed, feeling a whole new level of bummed. "Well, I'm not. I was supposed to hang out with my sister tonight, not hop a flight to Miami. She's already mad that I missed Christmas, and if this trip triggers her labor I'm never forgiving myself. Or you. So can we just start the briefing? The quicker this is over the faster I can crawl home." *And grovel. At the knees of my kid sister. Oh, how the mighty have fallen.*

He checked his pocket watch. "All right," he said. "The party is in two hours and, knowing women as I do, it will probably take you at least half that time just to get dressed."

I knew Vayl wasn't complaining, but since I already felt vulnerable, the comment cut me. And when I bleed, I get pissed. *It's like he's implying a tough girl like me needs a miracle to transform herself into a beautiful lady and, as we all know, miracles take time. What an ass!*

His touch, bare fingertips on my cheek, startled me. I could tell by his feverish warmth that he'd eaten when he woke at sunset. The decent vamps, the ones who were trying to blend, all fed without killing. Many had willing donors. Others bought their blood from one of two government-licensed suppliers. More would likely pop up as vamps like Vayl made obvious the advantages of integration.

He said, "I have offended you."

"Actually, yeah, you have." I shook my head to dislodge his hand. It felt a little too . . . nice. "It's okay, though," I said, my anger deflating somewhat in response to his stricken expression. "People ought to be able to point out the truth, or at least give it a nod on the way past without other people getting all freaked out about it."

"I have no idea what you just said."

"Good. Now, let me unpack and I'll meet you in the pit, um, living room in five minutes."

He left me alone to empty my trunk. I didn't. I sat on the bed, fished a pack of cards out of my bag, and began to mix them. Blend, bend, bridge, over and over I shuffled the dog-eared pack until Evie's tears, my ghosts, Vayl's unintended insult, and the immense suckage of the holidays, which I'd spent equally between blacking out and melting down, receded beneath the steady thrum of the cards.

Vayl had already draped himself across one of the couches by the time I came into the living room. All he needed was an ivy crown and some half-dressed bimbo fanning him with palm fronds between bites of grapes and he'd have been a dead ringer for a gorgeous Julius Caesar. Aw, who was I kidding? He'd probably palled around with the man before Cleopatra showed up and ruined all their fun. I sank down on the couch opposite him, curling my feet underneath me. "Getting into character?"

"We are going to a five-thousand-dollar-a-plate charity dinner/dance. Our target has invited only the crème de la crème of society. He will expect both of us to behave with a certain amount of savoir faire."

"Let me see if I can translate your bullshit, um, I mean French. We're supposed to be a couple of big spenders?"

"Yes," he replied, raising his eyebrow a disapproving tick at my language.

"So who's the target?"

"A plastic surgeon of Pakistani origin. His name is Mohammed Khad Abn-Assan and he has either lifted, tucked, or liposuctioned half of Hollywood. I understand several of his celebrity clients will be there tonight."

"And here I left my autograph book in my other purse. So what's the charity?"

"It is called New Start. It brings in millions of dollars a year, allegedly to pay for reconstructive surgery for child victims of disfiguring accidents."

"Cool. Only I'm guessing the kids will never see a dime."

"That is highly doubtful when you consider the fact that Assan is diverting most of those funds into the Sons of Paradise."

"Whoa, hang on just a second. The Sons of Paradise? Are you telling me we're going to hit a financial bastion of the most extreme of the extremist terrorist groups?" Vayl nodded. "Awesome!" *Those assholes will be dining on sand and pisswater by the time we're finished with Dr. Bankroller.*

Perhaps my delight could be explained by the fact that the Sons of Paradise had, among its most recent atrocities, blown an army Pave Hawk out of the sky over Burma, murdered its five-member crew, and released the footage of how they'd mutilated the bodies to the entire world. Referred to by journalists as the "Mother of All Cults," Sons of Paradise members worshipped a mythical creature called the Tor-al-Degan, which, as a chaos beast, didn't have a face or a place to call home. But the Deganites didn't seem to need statues or heaven. Just an excuse to vent their hate and havoc.

"But you said they're only getting most of the money. Why not all of it?"

Vayl's eyes hardened, obsidian, even the most penetrating stare couldn't break. "Sources say he uses the rest to perform surgery on members of the organization who cannot afford to look like their Most Wanted posters anymore."

That got my motor running. "What a creep."

"The world is full of them."

"You're telling me. It's good there's people like us around to balance things out."

"What is this optimistic talk I hear coming from your mouth?" Vayl asked. "Are you Jasmine's evil clone, come to lull me into fluffy white thoughts so you can stake me in my sleep?"

"At best your thoughts are pink. Kind of like this carpet." Vayl's eyes lightened suddenly, a trait that will make you do a double take if you're not used to it. The vamps I'd known before him didn't have that particular ability, but then it wasn't really fair to compare. Vamps have their individual gifts and weaknesses, just like humans. The one sitting across from me, for instance, wore his eighty-odd-years' string of successful missions like a mantle. He had infiltrated the most exclusive factions, beaten the highest tech security systems, faced the most powerful supernatural forces ever seen on earth and won. So why did he need me? I really should have a clue after six months, shouldn't I? Well, shouldn't I?

"Anything else you want to tell me?" I asked.

"Assan has never before been more than a link in a chain. How do you say . . . a yes man. But he has suddenly gained great power within the Sons of Paradise. We understand he has brought them a new ally, one with the money and clout to rock this country to its core. There is not much chatter about this person, but when you listen to the whispers, you hear scary things."

"You mean scarier than usual things?"

Vayl nodded. "This ally brings more than financial backing. He brings *others*, from nests, covens, and packs."

Uh-oh. Cinch your seatbelt, Jaz. Things are about to get bumpy. "That sounds like the Raptor." Only the Raptor had been able to make such traditionally quarrelsome sects cooperate long enough to work together toward any common goal.

"Precisely. Thus our mission tonight is to case Assan's home, mark his security arrangements, and return in the wee hours of the morning. We will remove Assan from the premises, interrogate him back at Diamond Suites, and then terminate him." Well, didn't that just shine a whole new light on this job? If we could stick it to the Sons of Paradise *and* make Assan identify the Raptor, maybe give us a location, we'd be rockin'.

The Raptor had been our department's number-one target for nearly a decade, as more and more evidence had surfaced against him. His lethal mix of charisma and savagery had raised him high among the ranks of the Vampere from the start. But apparently vampire domination hadn't been enough. He'd learned to consolidate power globally, accepting fealty oaths from a dozen large U.S. nests, two covens of black witches in Scotland, and several packs of Spanish weres. His tactics were brutal, his intentions vicious.

Vayl ran his fingers across the black cane that lay beside him on the couch. A museum piece, it had been hand carved in India and had inspired almost as many whispers around the office as its owner. A procession of intricately detailed tigers marched around the leg of the cane up to a gold band, which separated it from the multifaceted blue jewel that topped it. When you twisted the head, the tigers shot away from it, revealing a hand-hammered sword whose maker had been dust for centuries. It was unusual for Vayl to carry it with him here, where he should've felt safe. Where I'd felt pretty cozy myself. I sat up straighter and looked around the room.

"What aren't you telling me?" I demanded.

"We are going to have to be extremely careful. While we believe the Raptor to be Assan's new puppet master, we think there is also at least one U.S. government official dancing from the same strings. This is no simple hit, Jasmine, far from it. And . . ."

"What?"

Vayl shook his head. "Just keep your eyes and ears open. Something about this feels . . . wrong."

And that was really saying something, coming from the CIA's number-one assassin.

Chapter Two

Half an hour later I'd rediscovered my femininity. It's fun occasionally, sort of like an archaeological dig without the sweating. I stood before the bathroom mirror resembling the pale, regal daughter my mother would've preferred, wondering how I was supposed to hide my modified Walther PPK, which I called Grief, underneath material that clung like an obsessive ex-boyfriend.

I'd gone for an Asian look and discovered the red mandarin collar and short, half-moon sleeves suited me fine, especially with my hair pinned up and swirled around the way I'd seen it done in *Cosmo*. Fake diamonds dangled from my ears, and though no one could see, they matched my belly button ring perfectly. The hilarious bit was that Pete had been the one to give it to me.

His face had slowly flooded with color as he'd handed me the case. "I understand this is an appropriate item for your, uh, I mean that since you've got that, uh, piercing—"

"What's it do?" I'd asked as I'd taken the case and pulled out a faux diamond stud.

"It's a homing device," he'd said, obviously relieved

that I hadn't made him stutter through the whole setup. "You activate it by breaking the gem off the post. If you don't have a way to keep it on you once it's signaling, it has been tested safe on the digestive system, so you can swallow it."

Oh goody. "What happens after it's triggered?" I asked.

"We have a team standing by in Miami. Once they receive the signal, their orders are to try to contact you and, failing that, to coordinate a massive search and rescue."

So with my jewelry firmly in place, I gave myself one last critical look. I'd been careful with the makeup, so my eyes looked larger, greener, more soulful than usual. I had fine, fragile features that fooled almost everyone I met, a real advantage in my line of work. And the fact that my body leaned harder toward bony than athletic didn't hurt either. My legs were by far my best feature. They occasionally peaked through the side slits of my calf-length, red satin skirt. I wore red, low-heeled sandals I could actually run in, and I'd chosen a sequined handbag to match, so that's where I finally stowed my weapon.

When I came out, Vayl's bedroom doors were still shut. I rapped on one.

"Yes?"

"I'm going scouting. Back in thirty."

"All right." I took off to find the address on our cleverly faked invitation.

Diamond Suites was situated about fifteen minutes from Assan's place. The Lexus purred under me like a snoozing lioness as I drove there, but I resisted the urge to wake her up on the interstate. Pete's blood pressure tended to spike when he thought I'd done any excessive spending, and I figured he'd stroke out if I showed up with a speeding ticket on the way *to* a location.

I took a leisurely tour of Assan's digs, trying not to gape too much at the enormous, brilliantly lit mansions fronted by country-club-style landscaping. The lawns were so well manicured you could've used them for putting greens. What a hoot if Dave and his buddies had lived here, because they actually would have. I could imagine them all, full of that eighteen-year-old cockiness you wish guys would never lose, drinking our dad's beer and calling their shots like it was a game of eight ball.

I spared my twin one more minute, wondering what part of the world held him tonight, hoping he was okay. Like me, Dave's pretty high up the hush-hush ladder. Like me, he'd started in a different part of the Agency, but now he's a Special Ops stud, so he spends the majority of his time overseas. It's an excellent excuse not to keep in touch and we use it like a dustrag. If we were careful we'd never have to speak to each other again. A hell of an accomplishment for people who used to complete each other's sentences.

"Enough," I told myself. "Enough, enough, enough—" I bit my lip, stopping the loop with pain. *You're working Jasmine, so work. Focus on the work. The work will keep you sane. At least in everybody else's eyes.*

I took a deep breath and let it out with a laugh when I saw the fancy, scrolled metal sign on the gate in front of Assan's house. Anything with an entrance right out of *Jurassic Park* and enough fencing to contain a herd of Brachiosaurus demands a name, and Assan had chosen Alpine Meadows. Without a mountain in sight. Nor were there any cute Austrian kids running around singing "Do, Re, Mi." Who was this guy really kidding? The name might trigger thoughts of *The Sound of Music*, but it looked like *The Haunting of Hill House*.

Driving on, I discovered the area contained more dead ends and cul-de-sacs than a game of Clue. But I did find a couple of quick routes out just in case. I cruised the neighborhood five more minutes, soaking in the ambience, picturing myself looking like I belonged inside one of these six-bedroom, four-and-a-half-bath monstrosities. Then I went back for Vayl.

I didn't see him when I pulled into the parking lot, but I could feel him waiting for me. Although it was more than that. It's an extra sense, one I've only had since . . . well, for about fourteen months. And I'm not the only one who's fascinated by it.

During our first mission together, Vayl had betrayed his interest in the fact that I can smell vamps. Not literally. Still, it's almost a visceral scent, something near the back of the nose and just behind the eyeballs that whispers *immortal* to the base of my brain. Different vamps make me react different ways, but that's the basic idea.

We'd been stalking a renegade named Gerardo, whom the Italian authorities had asked us to bag before he decimated yet another university residence hall. Apparently he'd run through so many in Europe he'd felt the need to emigrate. Having trailed our quarry to the hushed corridors of Vassar's Noyes House, we'd hoped the undergrads had enough brains to keep themselves barricaded in their rooms and that my inner alarm would sound before one of them needed to escape for a quick pee.

"Do you feel anything yet?" Vayl had asked.

"Nope. And I'm not sure it would help if I did."

"Why not?"

"It's not like I could give you coordinates. The Sensitivity doesn't work that way. Best-case scenario, all I know is he's in the same room as us."

Vayl had stopped me, his fingers so warm on my shoulder I would've suggested a trip to the emergency room if he'd been human. "I believe this Gift is just the tip of the iceberg, Jasmine. If we nurture it, develop it, I think you will be amazed to discover what lies deep beneath the water."

Ironically, that was where we found Gerardo, hiding under the lily pads in the fountain in the building's courtyard. I'd seen vamps fight before. Fought beside them, in fact. But Vayl surpassed them all. He attacked Gerardo with the ferocity of a starving crocodile, his lips drawn so far back from his teeth I could see his rear molars without squinting. They both fell back into the fountain, slamming the statue of Emma Hartman Noyes that stood in the middle hard enough to make her wobble.

When they emerged, blood bubbled from a huge gash in Gerardo's shoulder. He broke free of Vayl's grip and tried to jump out of the water. Vayl caught him halfway and he fell hard on the concrete rim. Like a lion on a zebra, Vayl latched on to the back of Gerardo's neck, the look in his eyes just as fierce and nearly as primal. Suddenly I knew why the Romans had packed their coliseum on a regular basis. I wanted to roar with approval. My gladiator was kicking ass, baby.

A sound to my right distracted me. A ponytailed coed shuffled out of the shadows. I ran toward her. "Get back to your room. You don't want to see this."

She'd jumped me almost before I realized she smelled undead. But the newbies are sloppy. Lack of training, maybe, or an overabundance of hunger. My crossbow bolt pierced her heart before she could even form a decent snarl. When I looked back at the fountain, Vayl stood alone as well. We'd smoked both our vamps without sustaining any major personal damage. Always a cause for celebration.

Vayl had pointed to the little bits of ash and dust that had fallen where the girl had stood moments before. "That is why you must hone your skills."

"I'll have you know I'm a helluva vamp killer," I replied hotly.

His nod barely stirred air. We locked eyes and I didn't bother to hide how much his comment annoyed me. "I never questioned your lethality," he said. "However, that weapon in your hand will do you no good if you die before you get the chance to use it."

Six months later, while I'd accepted his logic, I hadn't made much progress. I often felt like yanking my hair out by the roots, but Vayl maintained his cool. He just kept saying, "Easy is for fools and the truly dead, Jasmine. Remember that."

I looked around the lot, wishing I could ping some sort of radar off him. After all this time, I still hadn't figured out how to narrow my search. I'd learned only that if I paid attention to the awareness, it might alert me when he moved. Leaving the car running, I turned off the headlights and turned on the night vision. It was easier than it sounded.

One of my roommates in college was a techno wizard named Miles Bergman. The tall, skinny son of a Russian dissident and an environmental biologist, his paranoia prevents him from working for the government outright. But he does sell us the rights (sometimes exclusive) to use his gadgets. Pete loves the arrangement, because it means he doesn't have to put out any extra cash for pesky items like health insurance and vacation days.

One of the many cool inventions Bergman developed for me was a set of night-vision contact lenses. I squeezed my eyes shut for a couple of seconds and when I opened them the interior of the Lexus looked like it had been parked under a green streetlamp. The cars surrounding me could've come straight from Enterprise of Emerald City. All lovely shades of lime, they lined up like contestants at the Miss Oz Beauty Pageant. Only one wasn't what she seemed. One hid a dark, long-lived secret. But which?

I scanned the lot quickly, never letting my eyes rest in one place for too long. And I still nearly missed him. He stood between a Toyota Tundra and a Jeep Cherokee, an inkblot in the shadows, tapping his cane on the side of his shoe.

"I see you," I whispered. As if I'd shouted, he stepped forward. I unlocked the doors as he made his way to the car, just another well-to-do gentleman going out on the town. He looked like an Oscar winner, handsome and elegant in his black tuxedo. Even his cane worked, an integral part of the affluent man's evening clothes rather than an assassin's tool.

He slid into the car beside me, which shook me more than I let on. I preferred him sitting in the back, like a boss, rather than in front, like a date. I moved to change gears and nearly yelped when his hand brushed against mine.

"Wait a moment," Vayl said, looking at me steadily through his predatory eyes. I tried not to fidget while he took stock of my hair, dress, shoes, though every passing second squeezed at my nerves, as if he'd wrapped them in barbed wire and turned a crank that pulled it tighter until they screamed. I wanted to thump him. Didn't he know he was being rude? And unsettling? And rude? I opened my mouth to tell him exactly what I thought when he said, "You look incredible. Like a goddess. I take back everything I said earlier."

The attention-starved teen in me melted. Even my brain reverted. All I could think for a second was *He likes me! He really likes me!*

Okay, so he'd never complimented me before. Still. Gag.

I squeezed my eyes shut, took my vision back to normal. It helped restore my equilibrium too. "Thanks," I said. "You look pretty sharp yourself." I paused a second. "I was just thinking about our first mission."

"You were?"

"It reminded me of a question I've been wanting to ask for a while." One I apparently only felt brave enough to pose while in goddess mode.

"Oh?" His tone buttoned up like a Victorian collar. But, being temporarily divine, I barreled on.

"I noticed you always bleed your vamp targets before you take them out."

"That is true."

"Well, for cripe's sake, don't go all frosty on me. I

don't give a crap about that part. I just saw a pattern and wondered—"

Vayl sighed and the whole car filled with the sound, like a mournful wind bouncing off the walls of an empty canyon. "It is my fail-safe. I do not want to kill innocents, so I take their blood during battle. I can taste whether or not the donor gave it willingly or with his last gasp."

"Wow, I didn't know you could do that. Cool." I glanced at him. Not much changed. But the easing of the lines around his eyes and lips told me I'd said the right thing. Which was when I realized it mattered to Vayl what I thought of him. Wow. When had that happened?

Probably during your last blackout, spat a bitter, scared corner of my mind.

I regarded it as if it stood separate from me, a flat-chested freshman wearing too much eye shadow and the confidence of a lame-duck president. *Shut the fuck up*, I told it. Then I drove my boss to the job.

We arrived at the gates of Assan's mansion behind a short line of vehicles that included two limos and a gleaming black Jaguar. One by one the drivers showed the guards their invitations and were allowed to enter. I hadn't seen any guards on my scouting trip, though intel had informed us Assan kept anywhere from ten to twelve on staff. These two shopped in the big-and-beefy section and still their suit coats barely buttoned, maybe on purpose, so all the guests could see the outline of the guns riding underneath.

One looked to have some Chinese ancestry. He wore his black hair pulled back into a ponytail. His partner reminded me of Schwarzenegger in his bulkier days. If he spoke with an Austrian accent I'd struggle not to laugh in his face. Unprofessional, I know, but the more stressed I get, the more likely I am to bow to inappropriate hilarity. I could already feel the giggles tickling the back of my throat.

"This had better be a damn good forgery," I said as I took the invitation from the seat beside me and rolled down the window.

"What?" Vayl whispered. "Are you finally nervous?"

Is the Pope Catholic? "Shh, it's our turn." I pulled up to the gate and handed the invite to Arnold Jr. Up close he overwhelmed the eyeballs, built like a tractor with the confidence that came from knowing he could mow us flat without breaking a sweat.

"Welcome to Alpine Meadows," he said in an American accent—*whew*!

Vayl sat forward. "Thank you," he said, his voice more melodic than usual as his eyes met those of the guard's. I felt the magic cross my skin on its way to Arnold Jr., a scented breeze of power so purely Vayl, I would have recognized it in a perfume factory. "In five minutes you will not remember our faces or the fact that you admitted us." Junior's jaw went slack and his pupils dilated like he'd scored an instant high. He nodded, handed the invitation back to me, and stepped away from the car.

"Can you do that for me next time Pete wants to wring my neck?" I asked as I moved the Lexus toward Assan's minicastle. The rumble in Vayl's throat could've been anything from a growl to a burp. I stole a look at his face, and from the way his lips were quivering decided it was a chuckle.

The valet had a hard time understanding why any high-society dame would want to park her own car. Then Vayl spoke to him and made it all better. He directed us around the side of the house, where I backed into the space closest to the front door. I sort of specialize in quick getaways. Too bad I wasn't driving a Hummer. It would've been fun to pull straight in and then mow over the perfectly trimmed hedges and gigantic urns on the way out.

Like a good little blue blood, I waited for Vayl to stroll around and open my door. We took a path lined with Japanese lanterns around to the front of the house—uh, mansion—um, pretentious freaking monstrosity posing as a home. Yeah, that's more like it. At the top of white marble steps that led to doors the size of rocket silos, a barrel-chested, pock-marked man with the eyes of a scorpion took our invitation and added it to a lace-lined basket at his feet. I had a sudden image of him skipping through the woods holding that basket in front of him like Little Red Riding Hood, and laughed out loud. He and Vayl both looked at me strangely. I tucked my left hand into the crook of Vayl's arm and patted him with my right.

"Oh, honey, I finally got that joke you told me on the way here. Hilarious!"

Vayl nodded as if he understood and led me indoors. "You will explain that one to me later, I hope?" he whispered out the side of his mouth.

"I'll explain it to you now." Then I forgot what I was going to say as we entered a massive, marble-lined hall lit with five—count 'em—five sparkling chandeliers. So many candelabras lined the walls that even if the lights winked out you still could've seen well enough to read the fine print on an iffy contract. And the art! I smiled up at Vayl as if I belonged among people who thought nothing of owning paintings bigger than my apartment. I had never felt so sorely out of place. Even my teeth felt fake.

"You are looking gorgeous tonight, my dear," Vayl said.

Somewhat reassured, I said, "Thank you, darling. And may I say you grow more handsome with each passing day?"

He nodded graciously, every bit the self-assured multimillionaire we wanted our host to think he was. Speaking of the devil, here he came, greeting his guests with the slick friendliness of a tiger shark at a daily feeding. His white tuxedo set off his dark hair and skin to perfection, and the gold rings on six out of ten of his fingers highlighted his remarkably slender, blunt-nailed hands.

I managed not to flinch as he came at me, all teeth and glittering black eyes. Sometimes things would be so much simpler if you could just pull out your gun and shoot the bad guy. Reason number seventeen why Indiana Jones is my hero.

"My dear lady," the little snake was saying as he took my hand from the top of Vayl's arm and kissed it—yuck. "I am so pleased to make your acquaintance."

I smiled brightly as his mouth continued to move, but I no longer heard the words. *Oh God, not now.* But God had taken a coffee break and my senses had gone along for the donuts. Another sound had replaced Assan's prattle in my shivering brain. A loud buzzing, like an oven timer on steroids, gave warning. Next my vision would narrow to a speck and then—poof!—disappear. I might come back to myself in five minutes. Or it might take a couple of days. Afterward, if I asked the right questions, I might find out what I'd said and done in the meantime.

This can't be happening! but it was, and I felt like I was dying, drowning in the flooded hull of my sinking sanity. I looked at Vayl, hoping he'd throw me a life preserver as I tried not to blow it, not to panic. He met my eyes briefly, just part of a second when, without a single word, he was somehow able to communicate that he knew something had thrown me and that I'd find a way to rise above. I couldn't betray that trust. I wouldn't. I took a deep breath and the darkness retreated.

"Lucille Robinson," Vayl drawled, introducing alias-me to Assan, "and I am her"—he paused, allowing our host to jump to any nasty conclusion he wished—"associate, Jeremy Bhane. We are, of course, staunch supporters of New Start and delighted to finally meet its famous founder."

Assan shook Vayl's hand. "So good of you to come," he said. He reached back and pulled a Jessica Simpson clone to his side. I'd been so distracted I hadn't noticed her join us. She stood at least three inches taller than me, which gave her a good half foot on her husband. "This is my wife," he said, "Amanda."

I held out my hand with some difficulty. My little brownout had taken the oomph from my muscles and deposited the whole seething mass in my stomach. If she shook too hard I'd puke all over her Vera Wang. But Amanda wasn't up to heavy lifting either. She squeezed my hand as if it were made of porcelain, did the same for Vayl, then dropped her arm like concrete encased it as she murmured, "Pleased to meet you."

One thing about feeling miserable, you instantly recognize it in others. Amanda Abn-Assan, I knew, was giving almost everything she had to the task of just staying upright. I looked at Vayl quickly, to see if he'd noticed the puffiness under her eyes. The look he gave me said he had. *Now why would the wife of a brilliantly successful surgeon have been crying recently?* Several reasons came to mind, but none that totally satisfied my gut feeling about her. It was a mystery worth solving. Later.

Assan excused himself and Amanda, leaving Vayl and me to stand around trying to look natural. Vayl snagged a couple of champagne flutes off a passing waiter's tray and we toasted each other. My face started to hurt from all the smiling. Vayl bent down to lay a pretend kiss just below my ear. Even though it didn't land, I still felt it clear to my toes. *Okay, Jaz, don't hyperventilate now. We're just faking out the party guests, that's all. The fact that your knees feel a little weak is probably just an estrogen spike. Yeah, that's it.* He whispered, "Let us begin."

I nodded, relieved to be done with the standing around. Ready, in fact, to sprint from my current position if it would distance me from these highly inappropriate feelings. I would concentrate all my efforts on identifying the security measures and memorizing the layout of the place. Then, after all the guests had left, we'd return for Assan. That was the job, and God help me, I loved it.

My whole body buzzed with anticipation. I lived for this. This was what chased away the looping thoughts and the nerves and the nightmares. Only the work allowed me to manage a conversational tone as I said, "I'll be right back, darling. Make sure you miss me!"

"I have already begun," said Vayl, giving me a look so mushy anybody who weighed more than a marshmallow would sink up to their knees in it. What a load of bull. And yet it was reassuring to know if Pete ever dumped us we could always write dialogue for *Days of Our Lives.*

I gave him my biggest, phoniest smile and turned toward the grandest staircase I'd ever seen that wasn't plastered across a movie screen. Red plush carpeted the steps, which would hide the blood nicely if anyone ever got shot on them. They split halfway up at a landing that held an ornate golden bench on which to rest should the hike have left you winded. Since I needed to scope out the second floor, I made like Scarlett O'Hara in reverse and swept up the first flight.

A discreet little sign with a Southern belle printed on it encouraged me to take the next flight to my left and another sign posted at the head of the stairs suggested I try the first door I came to. I reached down to adjust my sandal strap and get a good look around. At the top of the stairs a sitting area with couches draped in white silk and a matching oversized ottoman separated the ladies' bathroom hall on my side from the men's bathroom hall on the other side. The hall on my side narrowed, running past the bathroom and four other closed doors, two on each side, before turning the corner. A quick stroll to the other side as I pretended to enjoy the view showed the exact same layout.

I walked back to the ladies' bathroom. As I opened the door I looked over my shoulder. I'd already identified which of the guests were actually Assan's goons in disguise. None of them were looking, because Vayl had chosen that precise moment to drop his glass. So I moved down the hallway, trying each door as I passed, finding them all locked. At the end of the hall I turned right, because a left would've taken me downstairs and, from the sound of it, into the kitchen.

This hall contained a long bench on one side and a bank of windows on the other. The view must've been spectacular during the day as, I supposed, it looked out on several acres of lawn. The wall behind the bench held a rectangular, spotlighted painting of a whole passel of naked Egyptian serving girls bringing gifts of gold, food, and wild, caged animals to the pharaoh, who looked ecstatic to see them all.

There were no stairs at the other end of this hall, just a huge oval mirror with a fancy gold frame. I shared a troubled look with myself as I recalled the brownout I'd just experienced. The thought made me nauseous, so I tossed it away, forced myself to concentrate on the job.

"The job, the job, the job, the job," I whispered, until I realized what I was doing and bit the inside of my cheek. I turned right at the mirror and, as expected, found myself in the men's bathroom hallway. Again I encountered two sets of locked doors. At the men's room I made as if to go in, pretended to realize it wasn't the room I wanted and feigned embarrassment as I hurried past the front sitting area to the women's bathroom.

This time I went in. The room consisted of a small lounge decorated with diamond-patterned wallpaper, a red velvet chaise, and a massive potted fern. The commode sat in its own little claustrophobic's nightmare of a closet, and the claw-footed tub and floor-to-ceiling shower shared another room with an entire wall of *four* sinks.

Looking to waste the expected amount of time, I washed my hands and fiddled with my hair. Someone else came in, so I turned to leave, a polite smile fixed on my face. It must've fallen right off in my shock at finding I was sharing the bathroom with a man, who looked as shaken as I felt.

"Sorry," he said, raking his fingers through his thick, blond mop of hair. "I know the guys are supposed to use the toilet across the way, but I was sure they'd find me there."

"Well, they'll probably find you here too as soon as the rumor gets around that a guy is hiding in the ladies' room." I studied his face as I spoke and immediately liked what I saw. He had that fresh-out-of-college look that makes you think maybe the world's not such a pit after all. He wore a black tux with a red bow tie, red cummerbund, and matching red canvas high-tops. And he was chewing bubblegum.

I'd seen smiles like his a few times before. The message was clear—*if you don't love me yet, you will soon.* But such honest humor accompanied it that no way could it offend me. "Aw, come on," he said. "I can tell you're not a gossip. Help me out here. I'm not a pervert, just a party crasher." I almost believed him. But his eyes darted away from mine at just the wrong time. He hadn't been lying nearly as long as I'd been catching liars.

"So what's the deal? Do you fill up on olives and cheese cubes and then run?"

"Something like that."

"Bullshit." The shock on his face was comical. Apparently he'd never heard a grown woman swear. "Tell me why you're really here before I bypass the guards and call the police."

He took a moment to ponder the wisdom of telling a

total stranger, no less one with a potty mouth, the truth. "You know, most people buy my shtick."

"I'm not most people."

"No doubt." The look he gave me combined equal parts respect and flirtation. Yeah, I was flattered, but I didn't let it show. I was too busy hiding a bemused smile as he blew a perfect purple bubble, popped, and retrieved it. He gave me an apologetic grin. "My last girlfriend was a smoker who thought it would be fun to corrupt me. The gum helps kill the nicotine cravings."

"Good idea. Now quit trying to distract me and fess up."

"Okay, here's the deal. I'm a private investigator. Mostly I look into insurance fraud. But I know Amanda Assan from way back. We were friends when she still had a gap between her front teeth and permanently scraped knees. That was before her mom decided she'd never be happy until Amanda had won every Little Miss Beautiful pageant from here to Tallahassee." His disgust for Amanda's mother made me see her clearly. A bitter, middle-aged divorcée with more chins than sense. Poor Amanda, she'd probably thought she was breaking free when she married Assan.

He went on. "Anyway, Amanda called and asked me to investigate the secret doings of her hubby. That is, who he's doing secretly."

"Isn't this kind of a public forum for a private investigation?" I asked, mostly to cover my disappointment in him for trying to put one by me and in me for thinking anyone over the age of ten could survive this world with any part of their innocence intact.

"Yeah, but you can learn a lot about a guy by watching

him at an event like this. People who have stuff to hide never think they're giving themselves away, but it's often obvious to anyone who pays attention."

"And I take it someone's been paying too much attention to you?" I couldn't help but laugh at the face he made. It belonged on a five-year-old who's just been caught drinking Mountain Dew for breakfast.

"I screwed up royally," he admitted. "Assan noticed me having a conversation with his wife a few minutes ago, and now his goons are chasing me all over the house to find out why."

"It must've been a pretty intense conversation."

"She was crying."

Amateurs. "All right," I said. "Let's get you out of the house, shall we?"

His eyes lit up like I'd just promised to buy him a pony for his birthday. "You're going to help me? That's great! Oh man, I can't thank you enough!" The grin resurfaced. "You like me, don't you?"

Good Lord, he must have more first-date sex than George Clooney! "Yeah, that's why I'm helping. I find you absolutely irresistible." *That, and some instinct is telling me to get you the hell out of here.* "What's your name?"

"Cole Bemont." He held out his hand, so I shook it. At least his grip was firm.

"Lucille Robinson," I said. "Now, here's what we do. You and I will find a back way out of this place. If we come across someone else, we make like a couple of lovesick teenagers. People generally hurry past heavy breathers. I get you to the parking lot, you vanish. Got it?"

He nodded. "There's just one thing I've got to do before we go," he said. Before I could inquire, he grabbed me and planted a kiss square on my mouth. It was short but fiery, despite the grape flavoring, and when he let me go I was panting.

"Holy crap!"

He smiled, not at all apologetically, and said, "I've wanted to do that ever since I saw my first Bond movie."

I nodded. "Well, you have excellent timing. Now, shall we go?"

He gave me a courtly bow. "After you, Madame."

I opened the door, scanned the area, and closed it again. "Goon at the bottom of the stairs making his way up," I told Cole. "Change of plan. You wait here while I divert him. As soon as his back is turned, go down this hall, take a left. Go straight down the stairs to the kitchen and outside. Got it?"

To Cole's credit he stayed nice and calm. "Got it."

I wrenched the door open and stepped into the hall. Cole's goon was at the landing. I started toward the stairs, timing it so he'd be two steps below me when I tripped into him. Will Ferrell couldn't have done it any better. I squealed to get his attention, my hands flew up, though I made sure to keep a tight grip on my bag, and I fell right into his arms, turning him as he caught me so his back was to the bathroom. I gasped and babbled long enough for Cole to sneak out of the bathroom and down the hall.

"Oh, thank you *so* much," I told the guard, straightening his jacket and dusting him off as if I'd dumped a bowl of baby powder on his shoulders. Though I kept my focus on the guard, pouring on the charm so thick you'd need a foghorn to navigate it, I still kept a peripheral eye on Cole. He'd nearly made it to his first turn when a door opened beside him. Cole paused, said something, and the door closed immediately. He shrugged, went on his way, and I blessed the guard's heart one last time before heading down the rest of the stairs.

I found Vayl in the room adjacent to the front hall. It might've been called a parlor in another century. He held my drink with one hand while he nibbled off an appetizer buffet with the other.

"Darling," he said, "you must try this pâté. I think it is the best I have ever tasted."

I smiled, took my glass from him, and headed toward the end of the cloth-covered table. Vayl followed closely. Too closely. I stopped short and he nearly mowed me over. Turning to face him, I laughed lightly, but under my breath I said, "Are you *sniffing* me?"

His expression could've been chipped from granite for all it gave away, but his eyes had gone a stormy grayish blue. "I cannot scent vampires," he said icily.

What a weird thing to say. "I know." I turned to get a plate, fork, and napkin, then walked to the opposite end of the buffet, forcing Vayl to dodge several couples and a white-coated caterer to keep up with me.

"But humans are an entirely different matter. I can smell them so clearly at times it is like driving down a newly tarred country road." He stood so still that when he didn't speak I could swear I was shoulder to shoulder with Madame Tussauds's reproduction of the world's deadliest good guy. Only he didn't seem so good right now.

"What's your point?"

"Two distinct scents cover your own," Vayl said as I spooned minisausages onto my plate. "Both of them are male. And what is left of your lipstick is smudged. Would you care to explain?"

I smiled coldly as I wiped my lips clean with my napkin. "It's a long story," I said, "and we have a job to do." I added more snacks to my dish while Vayl waited for a couple of B-movie stars to clear out. He piled on more stuff as he continued our murmured conversation. He kept his voice even, but his eyes, the only windows I'd ever found to his true feelings, began to change again. *Uh-oh.*

"Yes, as I recall we did agree to some sort of plan earlier this evening." Vayl and sarcasm went too well together. The mix made me want to punch something. I settled for stabbing a bowl of caviar repeatedly with a serving spoon. Vayl watched me beat the fish eggs into submission as he continued. "The security system will be easily compromised. We will have to watch the guards longer to get a sense of their movements even though the party will take them somewhat out of their normal routine. That is, unless you would prefer to pull out an Uzi and mow them all down right here?"

I glared at him. But I was madder at myself. I did seem to be developing a tendency to jump first and hope for a parachute later.

"Tell me you have not compromised this mission," he demanded.

"You know me better than that!" I retreated to a corner beside a tall, potted ficus and stuffed sautéed mushrooms down my throat while I tried to figure out how to make what I'd just done sound remotely logical. I shook my head. Once I'd been a sensible person. Now, well, there's just no explaining me. At least not without using words like "insane," "stupid," or "Nighttime NyQuil." But I'd hidden that me so well. Until now.

Vayl came in close, towering over me like a grade-school principal. I looked up at him and swallowed a grape in one guilty gulp. "Can we have this conversation never?"

"What. Happened."

So I told him everything, start to finish. And damned if it didn't come out sounding like an episode of *Nancy Drew.*

"So, do you make a habit of kissing strange men in bathrooms?" Vayl's eyes had darkened to jade with swirling gold flecks that made me slightly dizzy. When I didn't immediately reply he added, "Because it certainly was not mentioned in your file."

What is it about the people who know you best? You never reveal to them the secret location of your make-me-crazy buttons and yet, like toddlers at preschool, they root them out and push them repeatedly. Mine are directly connected to hand grenades. So as soon as Vayl finished speaking I heard the telltale clatter of a pin rattling to the floor. *My file? I wish it was in my hands right now. I'd smack you over the head with it so hard your bell would still be ringing for church next Saturday night!*

Then I'd clonk myself, bang on the frontal lobe. Maybe that would cure me, and I would never again have to be embarrassed by what we in the CIA like to call my PDD (Previous Dumbass Decision). However I was not done digging my grave.

"I don't make a *habit* of kissing *anybody*, thanks to you!" Realizing Freud would have a field day with that statement, I rushed on. "It was a spontaneous action, something I'm sure you have no experience with, and though as my boss I can see how you might be upset that I helped him considering what we're here for, you might also congratulate me for defusing a situation that might've interfered with our plan." And truly, part of me wasn't sorry. Cole safe was a good thing. For him and, though I couldn't explain why, for us. As for the kiss, I hadn't just allowed it. I'd participated. Enthusiastically. Because . . . why *would* I do such a thing? The answer came into my head like the soft wail of an old widow. *Because for just a second Cole reminded you what it was like to be pretragedy Jaz. Remember how much you loved being her?*

"Do you think these two men you encountered will recall you?" Vayl asked.

"I sure hope so!"

"So when the police investigate Assan's disappearance and his eventual passing, and they question everyone whose invitation lies in that lacy little basket and cannot find Lucille Robinson, these men will be able to describe you quite easily?"

My stomach clenched and all the food I'd just wolfed down spontaneously combusted. "Hey, when you're done lecturing me, could you speak to my ulcers? They seem to be misbehaving as well."

Vayl took my plate in one hand and my elbow in the other, marched us both to the garbage can, where he dumped the plate (though I'm sure he considered leaving me there instead). Then he escorted me out of the parlor, into the dining room, and out an ornate metal-framed screen door to the pool area.

"Uh, Vayl, I know you haven't lived in America long by your count, so I'd just like to point out that bosses don't generally drown their assistants when they've screwed up royally."

He shoved his hands in his pockets. The corners of his mouth dropped; on anyone else it would be described as a grimace. "You have jeopardized our mission and my high opinion of you." He frowned harder. "This is completely out of character. Tell me what possessed you."

"Look, it seemed like the right thing to do at the time."

"Kissing a perfect stranger seemed right to you? Do you realize how ludicrous that sounds?"

His eyes caught me, and though I wanted to say, "I know you expect absolute professionalism from me. And I have delivered. But I'm human, Vayl. It was inevitable that I would eventually screw up," I didn't. You can only try to explain yourself so many times before you start to sound like a whiner.

"I blew it, Vayl. I'm sorry." And now the hammer would fall. I'd been so careful, but he'd finally caught on to spaz Jaz. I should've known my run with the Agency couldn't last. But the hope of sticking the broken pieces of my career back together had been the only thing that kept me from jumping under a train after my, uh, incident. Guess I should've used brand-name glue.

Vayl backed me into the shadows between the house and a wrought-iron dining set. For a minute I thought he'd snapped and I was going to find out firsthand how much it really hurt to be vampire-bitten. "I can smell your desperation," he whispered. "It is like burnt metal on my tongue. But above that I sense determination.

Courage. The instincts of a predator and the skill of a master. It is a confusing combination, Jasmine. Can I trust it?"

What? It doesn't take me long to move from any strong emotion to pissed off. Mom used to blame it on the red hair. I guess a shrink would have a different theory. But suddenly I felt like wadding up the last six months and shoving them down his throat. I'd sweated blood to get where I was today. I'd fought the nightmares, brought the heat, nailed every mark. I'd buried my past and part of myself and tried to live up to the incredible demands of a goddamn legend. I'd been perfect—until this mission.

I glared at Vayl, mostly to give the tears that threatened a big, fat nuh-uh. He responded with his most inscrutable look. I thought of Cole's sparkling eyes and love-me smile and wondered how many times a man would have to smother his own feelings to get to the expression on Vayl's face. "My life for yours," I snapped. "If that's how it goes down, that's how I go. No questions asked." *And you* know *that. So just shove your, "Can I trust it?" right up your—*

"That is not what I mean," he said.

Okay, now my brain's going to melt. What else could we be discussing?

We heard a bell ring and noticed people begin moving into the dining room. Though I felt like I'd been shoved off a train in Siberia during a blizzard, Vayl's short nod signified he'd made up his mind. "Will you join me?" I knew he wasn't just talking about supper.

I wanted to say, *No, let's do this another day, when I'm not shaking like a strung-out crackhead.* Instead I nodded, tucked my hand into the crook of his bent elbow, and allowed him to escort me inside. Lucille's smiling face met those of the guests who'd begun to gather in the dining room. And not one of them guessed that behind the facade lurked a hired killer.

Chapter Three

I'll say this for me, even when my insides are twisting like a contortionist in the Cirque du Soleil, I do know how to focus. By the time we reached our seats Lucille Robinson had taken charge. She took real pleasure in her surroundings, enjoying the granite-topped table, the gold-rimmed plates, the enormous vases (pronounced vah-zes, my dear) bursting with pink and white tulips. My seat-mate told me the nurseryman got them to bloom so early by faking them out, making them think they'd spent an entire winter underground when in fact they'd only spent about six weeks in the cooler. The word for the process, she said, was "forced." Those gorgeous forced flowers reminded me of Amanda Assan as I watched her negotiate her way through the meal.

She ate five thousand dollars' worth of French onion soup, Caesar salad, chicken Parmesan, and coconut-cream pie, all the time making pleasant conversation with my tablemates, who, after a word with Vayl, would never remember me in the morning. Not long ago she'd been crying on an old friend's shoulder. Now she wore a catalog-model smile.

When the white-aproned servers cleared the last dessert plate, Assan suggested we all move into the ballroom. Vayl leaned in and murmured, "I saw it when I was looking around earlier. This is where you get to guess what is behind Door Number Four."

"A new Corvette?"

"No. But probably just as expensive."

We moved out of the dining room, across the hall, and to a pair of custom doors decorated with intricate scrollwork and generous amounts of gold leaf. Two muscle-bound doormen let us into a room that made the guests gasp. The ceiling set the theme for the entire space. Half-dressed nymphs danced across fields of flowers while studly young princelings looked on from beds made of silvery-white clouds. I suspected the artist to be a direct descendant of Michelangelo.

The burnished gold walls sported enough detailed trim to keep an army of plasterers busy for six months. The wood floor was so dark it was almost black. Two long tables set with punch bowls and crystal glasses sat along one wall underneath oversized windows dressed in black velvet. Another wall backed a miniature orchestra, its members dressed to match the curtains. As soon as the door opened they began to play, and the song lasted until all the guests had entered. Amid applause for the musicians, Assan stepped up to a microphone.

"Notice the dark-haired man in the shadows just to Assan's left," Vayl whispered.

I nodded, and we shared a moment of unspoken communication. When the time came, taking out Assan's personal bodyguard would be my responsibility.

"Thank you all for coming," said Assan, his voice

echoing weirdly in the enormous room. "You are the reason so many young children have been given a second chance at life." He went on, but I stopped listening, so steamed by his BS I'd begun to consider how I'd kill him if Vayl gave me the chance. But those daydreams ended abruptly as my nose twitched and my scalp began to tingle.

"Jeremy?"

"Hmm?"

I tugged on his sleeve so he'd lean down, bringing his ear within an inch of my lips. "There's another vampire in the room." It seemed weird to be the one—of the two of us—who could sense this. But vamps are completely closed to one another. I imagine it makes for horrible relationships.

"Find him."

I focused on the scent, a rotten-potato kind of odor that made my head ache. Most vamps who aren't trying to blend smell vaguely of the grave. Those who do attempt to live by society's rules gain something extra. Some call it a soul, though I don't see how you could prove it. All I know is Vayl's scent reminded me of an Aspen ski slope. This other guy—decay.

When the vamp slithered his way to the front of the crowd I knew it was him. He wore his nutmeg-colored hair long, past his shoulders. His eyes, a piercing sapphire as cold as the Bering Sea, kept him from looking girlish. His blue pin-striped suit fit so well at least half the guests would be asking him for the name of his tailor before the evening ended. But it didn't look as if he meant to stay. He caught Assan's eye, signaled him with a slight nod, and suddenly our host couldn't get away from the microphone fast enough.

"Excuse me," he said. "I am afraid that duty calls. Please enjoy the rest of your evening knowing that, even tonight, your generous donations have helped to make an unfortunate child whole again."

I caught myself short of a full-blown snort. I murmured, "If he's going to put some poor kid's face back on straight tonight I'll do the hula."

"Lovely dance, that. The story is all in the hands. I did not know you knew—"

"Vayl, I was kidding."

"Oh." Tightening of the lips. Translation—crap, when am I going to leap into the twenty-first century and get with their damn humor? Jerk of the head. Translation—obviously not today, so let's get on with the job, shall we?

Vayl's power generally hovers at the edge of my senses like the fog above a mountain peak. When he kicks it into gear I feel it in different ways, depending on his intentions. Just now it slid over me like silk pajamas. *Yummy, we're going incognito.*

Vayl moved to follow the men. I dogged his heels, staying within inches of him in order to fully benefit from his magical camouflage. No one even glanced at us as we passed, and most of them couldn't have seen us if they'd tried. We trailed Assan and his vampire friend into the part of the foyer that wandered underneath the stairs. Assan's vamp wouldn't sense me here either, not as long as I shadowed Vayl.

We crouched behind a huge statue of a naked guy and listened in. Okay, the gleaming black marble butt in my face distracted me slightly, but I'm still a pro, so I did hear the highlights.

"—well?" Assan was saying.

"Yes," the vamp replied. "The virus is nearing its third stage."

My stomach clenched at the word "virus."

Assan bobbed his head happily. "So we are ready for the final test?"

The vampire nodded, pushing his hair away from his face in a way I found chilling, because it was such a graceful gesture. The worst monsters are always the prettiest.

"I wish we could do it tonight," Assan ventured, but the vampire shook his head.

"No, we must follow the plan. We must verify the lethality of the virus before we make the final transfer."

"And then?"

"You know," the vampire said indulgently.

Assan's grin would've fit better on a shark. "And then the purge begins."

The vamp flashed his fangs in ecstatic agreement. He looked at his watch. "Svetlana and Boris arrive in thirty minutes. We should go."

Vayl and I traded looks of dread. I jerked my head toward the surgeon and his undead friend, raised my eyebrows. *Let's take them now. Try to make them talk before this virus can be unleashed.* I badly wanted to grab the bastards and bang their heads together.

Vayl shook his head. I knew what he was thinking. *What if they clam up just long enough for this virus to be released into the populace?* Though it chafed to admit it, he was right. Only God knew what vital information we'd miss if we hit them now. So we followed the men toward the back of the house. When we knew they were headed for the garage, we shifted into high gear.

Vayl took my hand, his power surging through me like I'd just chugged a Frappuccino six-pack. We dodged into the dining room, slipped out the poolside doors, and raced to our car. Together we swept through the night like a couple of phantoms, Vayl's power pushing us so our feet barely touched the ground. I'd never felt so strong, as if all the complex systems that allowed me to exist were working with such perfect precision I could perform miracles if I wanted to. *Nifty Gift*, I thought. If Vayl's ferocious grin was any sign, he agreed.

I'd left the car unlocked just in case. My keys were in my hand almost before I thought of it, and within seconds we were rolling down the driveway.

"No lights in the rearview," I said.

"Good. Do you know where you are going?"

"Yeah. One of the neighboring houses is vacant. The drive's open, but there's a row of pine trees near the road that screens the rest of the yard and the house. We can wait there." Vayl nodded his approval of the plan.

The guards at the gate waved us through without a second glance. I made a left as if I was headed for the interstate. When the gate had disappeared behind us I took the next right and killed the headlights. After some high-speed, highly illegal driving, I hit the driveway of the empty house, drove into the grass and behind the trees. With my night vision activated I could easily see Assan's mansion and, moments later, the headlights of a vehicle began to close the distance between the house and gate. Vayl didn't tell me it was all in my hands now. Even though I'd screwed up less than an hour before, he still trusted me to know my job. It hadn't always been that way.

Usually our missions abut one another so closely if one ends at breakfast another begins before lunch. But we actually had a two-week break between our first and second assignments. Which was when I learned Vayl didn't appreciate my driving style.

"We will practice," he'd announced, when he'd discovered we'd have some downtime. *Crap. So much for visiting Evie.* "Every night you will meet me at the parking lot beside the office building and we will drive."

"I'm an excellent driver," I informed him, trying hard not to sound like Dustin Hoffman's character from *Rain Man*. "I finished top in my class at—"

"Class is never the same as life," Vayl said, his voice level but his eyes snapping. So we drove. Every night. Everywhere. Unlike some of my training experiences, we didn't tail other agents. We followed the mayor. We deliberately ran red lights and stop signs and then lost the cops who chased us afterward. Vayl identified a couple of local vamps who needed to be taken down a peg, and we practiced the old pit maneuver on them and their drivers. I had been good. I got better. And the intensity with which Vayl approached every aspect of his job began to rub off on me.

That intensity fed my awareness now as I pulled back onto the street. Following taillights is easy in a low-traffic area like Assan's neighborhood. It gets more challenging on the interstate, but Assan's vehicle, an extended-cab Dodge Ram the color of strawberry Pop-

Tart filling, was tough to miss. Too bad this virus bombshell had blown our original assignment to shreds. I could've taken his truck out on the interstate and no one would ever have known it wasn't an accident.

Twenty-five minutes later we'd followed the Pop-Tart truck to an abandoned air force base. As soon as we could, we ditched the car and headed toward a congregation of forlorn buildings gathered in the empty compound. A hundred yards from Assan's truck, we grabbed cover among the jungle of shrubs and tall grasses that edged one of the base's old helipads and watched the two men exit their vehicle. The vamp leaned on the hood while Assan went to an electric pole, where he fiddled inside a large gray box. Seconds later a ring of red lights came on and less than five minutes after that I heard the rhythmic thump of helicopter blades spinning overhead.

I tensed with expectation as the copter touched down and a couple, one large, one small, wearing black jumpsuits hopped out. They crouched low as they hurried toward Assan's truck. Moments later the helicopter flew away and our four subjects made their own exit. I sat in the weeds and watched them go, trying to come to some practical conclusions.

Okay. So we have two new vamps named Svetlana and Boris arriving the night before the final test of a virus that mutates and is capable of purgelike deaths. Hey, maybe it's not all that bad. Maybe the Russians are computer geeks and the virus is just a big, bad worm. I wish. I really, really do.

We gave Assan, his buddy, and the Russians just enough lead time that they wouldn't see us pull out behind them and hoped their next stop would lead us to some answers that didn't include the phrase "end of the world as we know it."

Chapter Four

One of my worst childhood memories is of sitting at the kitchen table of our tiny house on the base at Quantico. I was crying so hard my favorite Mariah Carey T-shirt had wet blotches on it, and snot bubbles kept popping out of my nose, which Dave thought was "way rad!" I remember that bothered me even more, because I thought *he* should be crying too. Mom sat across the table from us, smoking a cigarette and patting a howling Evie on the back. Evie always cried when I cried. It was one of the reasons I finally stopped.

Mom looked at me with what I took to be an utter lack of sympathy. And she said, "I know you were expecting your dad to come home today. I know you were planning to share a piece of your birthday cake with him. But you've gotta remember, Jaz, nothing ever goes according to plan. Nothing. Not ever."

I believed her. What I couldn't tell her was that I also believed Dad hadn't made it home because he'd been killed in Desert Storm. My neighbor had told me so. The twelve-year-old daughter of a staff sergeant who ruled us all with her advanced training in name-calling and dirty fighting, Tammy Shobeson got her kicks from torturing me when Dave wasn't around to back me up. And learning it was my tenth birthday had inspired her. She'd buried her claws deep too. I spent the rest of my childhood dreading the news of Albert's death. Despite his long absences. Despite our chilly relationship. And then, *bam*, Mom keeled over in the shoe department of Wal-Mart. A massive heart attack had proven once and for all that nothing ever goes as planned. Nothing. Not ever.

I carried that lesson like a compass. And most of the time it got me where I needed to go. This once, however, fate caught me by surprise. When I glanced into the rearview not a mile from where we'd pulled back onto the interstate, I found an SUV flirting with the back bumper of our Lexus.

"This was definitely not part of the plan," I murmured.

"What?"

A spine-shuddering thump was Vayl's answer. "What the—?" He turned in time to see the SUV hit us again, crumpling the trunk upward so far it looked like we'd grown a spoiler.

Suddenly my hands were full trying to keep my wounded car between the white lines. The SUV had to veer off as well, but it was back fast, crunching into my fender like we were playing bumper cars.

Had Assan pegged us? Had he called in backup to pull us off his tail? No more time to wonder. After another meeting with the SUV our rear end had more wrinkles than an Agatha Christie novel.

"Son of a *bitch*!" I floored it, but speed was only a temporary solution. We didn't have the horses to outrun him, and if he took my bumper at the wrong angle, I'd go spinning off the road like Jeff Gordon after a run-in with Tony Stewart.

"All right," said Vayl, "I have had it."

"What are you thinking?"

"I am thinking it is time we find out who is trying to kill us."

"Can we do that without dying?"

"Perhaps."

"Then I'm for it." I watched in the mirror as the SUV closed in on us. Geez, but he was coming fast. "Hang on," I told Vayl. I slammed on the brakes. Taken by surprise, he swerved, caught my back bumper with his side panel and continued his spin on into the median.

The impact triggered our air bags, and for a while Vayl and I fought to get our eyes uncrossed. They may have slowed those bags down, but when one goes off in your face it still feels like you just got your neck sprung by a Rock 'Em Sock 'Em Robot.

I was debating whether the ringing in my ears was a product of the blow to my head or a sign of imminent mental breakdown when the doors opened. A red-faced, gray-bearded man blocked my exit. He towered over me, wearing faded blue overalls and a Dolphins jacket, looking like he could flip the car over without breaking a sweat. His eye had swollen shut.

"I hear raw steaks work wonders on shiners that size," I offered.

"Shut your mouth before I do it for you." He grabbed my arm and yanked me out of the car. I stumbled, fell against him, felt the hard outline of a pistol jam against my ribs.

"What do you want?" I asked. Good. I sounded brave.

"Just think of yourselves as a stain and us as bleach."

O-kay. Maybe these guys weren't with Assan after all. Maybe they'd just escaped from some understaffed, underfunded psych ward.

I turned my head to check on Vayl. They were taking him very seriously. He stood among the brush and scrub that passed for a shoulder on this part of the highway, leaning on his cane as he traded stares with three men in their late twenties.

Two held him at bay with silver crucifixes. One had JESUS SAVES emblazoned across the front of his gray T-shirt in big orange letters. The other wore a black sweatshirt that framed two praying hands surrounded by a beaded necklace with a silver stake hanging from it.

The third man, who'd come straight from a funeral judging by his three-piece suit, aimed a cocked crossbow at Vayl that would've made me laugh in different circumstances. It looked like he'd built it in his seventh-grade shop class.

"And don't try any of that mumbo jumbo on us," Jesus Saves warned Vayl. "I'll tell them if you do, and you'll be smoke before you can blink."

As Graybeard yanked me around to Vayl's side of the car, two big lightbulbs went off in my brain, which probably meant I was flirting with an aneurism. But while I still had my faculties I figured Jesus Saves was a Sensitive, like me. He also must've been present at a staking to know vampires do leave trace amounts of dust and ash when they're vanquished, but the biggest part of them goes up in smoke.

We were down on numbers and weaponry. Never a good place to be, even when you're a pro. I admit, dread had sunk its claws into the back of my neck, and it wasn't helping me think any clearer. Then Vayl met my eyes—and winked. Suddenly I could breathe again. Because in that moment I knew no two-bit operation run by a bunch of yahoos was going to beat us. Not tonight. Not ever.

As soon as my mind cleared, I noticed two things. An undeniable affection for my partner whose survival meant a lot more to me than mere job satisfaction. And the identity of the organization fronting this one-night event.

"Hey, Vayl." I jerked my thumb at Graybeard. "This one's into cleanliness and that one"—I nodded at Jesus Saves—"is into godliness. What's that make you think of?"

"God's Arm." Vayl's instant reply pleased our captors. It's always nice to have your ultrafanatical religious affiliation recognized.

"Let's walk," said Graybeard, gesturing toward a grove of trees in the distance with the .357 Magnum he'd pulled from his front pocket. Vayl's slight nod encouraged me to cooperate, for now. So I walked, my sandals protecting me so poorly from the rocks and weeds I considered kicking them off. Only the possibility of stepping on shards of glass or metal deterred me. It had gotten colder too, and my party dress wasn't providing much protection against the wind that kept brushing against me in an endless, winter-borne tide. The full moon lit up my goose bumps and the pseudo-path ahead of me. But I squeezed my contacts into night vision anyway, preparing for a trek through the deeper brush ahead.

Nobody talked during the walk, which only took us about two hundred yards off the highway, but seemed endless. Something about the march seemed eerily familiar to me. It was like the entire store of knowledge I'd built around criminals and their victims had coughed up the ghosts of those who'd walked ahead of their murderers, sometimes cold, sometimes stumbling, leaving glowing footprints for me to follow. Only they were angry that I'd consented to follow that trail. "Fight!" they whispered, their wild, haunted memories sharpening their voices. "Fight now. Fight hard. Die, if necessary, only die fighting!"

I never meant to go another way. And I think . . . yeah, now.

I sucked in my breath and screamed, "Oh, God! Something bit me!" I grabbed my right ankle, hopping around as much as Graybeard's grip allowed.

"What do you mean?" he demanded, looking from my pain-contorted face to my ankle and back again.

"A snake," I gasped. "Look, there it is!"

I pointed at the feet of the Suit, who immediately backed up and looked down.

"It's too cold for snakes," Graybeard was saying, but too late. Vayl had seen his opening. He shot his scabbard at the Suit, knocking him sideways. The bolt from his crossbow flew off into the bushes. Vayl's blade flashed and the Suit dropped, holding his left arm and groaning as blood spurted from it in steady bursts. I didn't wait to see how Vayl dealt with Jesus Saves and Praying Hands. The confusion that had delayed Graybeard's reaction was clearing. In moments he'd be putting his Magnum into action.

Holding my hand rigid like a knife, I hit him so hard I could almost see the nerves in his elbow curl up into a ball. His fingers stopped cooperating and the gun fell into the brush. I followed up with a punch to the groin, but he blocked it, blocked the hard high front kicks I tried next that should've at least knocked the breath out of him. He'd been trained, and well.

I threw a whole series of punches and kicks at his torso, moving so fast he started to gasp trying to keep up. The second I could tell I'd locked him onto defending his chest and abdomen I jump-kicked him, striking him solidly in the temple. His head snapped sideways and he staggered backward. I closed in fast, but he recovered more quickly than I expected. The punch he threw would've broken my ribs if he hadn't been backing up. Even so, I'd be feeling that blow for a week.

I spun and hooked him behind the knee, swearing inwardly as my ribs burned in protest. Graybeard landed with a crash that sounded like a tree falling. He tried to roll away, but I nailed him with two more hard kicks to the head. He stayed put after that, quietly bleeding into the brush.

I'd warmed up, by God. Fully in my element, steaming straight ahead, I was ready to kick some more ass. Not only had the adrenaline slowed time until I could've captured the moonlight in my fist and used it as the ultimate flashbang, it had given me rearview vision too. Somehow, even though my back was turned, I knew Praying Hands had broken away from the standoff with Vayl to come after me.

I spun to face him. He ran hard, intending to bowl me over with his impetus, overpower me by virtue of his superior weight and muscle mass. But he broadcasted tells like an amateur poker player, allowing me to pull out one of my favorite aikido throws. Just as he reached me I darted to one side, reached around, and grabbed his shoulder, spinning him while at the same time I used my straight right arm across his neck to knock him backward.

He hit the ground like a pro wrestler, grunting as the air whooshed from his lungs. I knew better than to dive in after him, but he did hesitate, maybe hoping I was that stupid. I aimed a kick at his head. He rolled clear.

When he reached his feet he stumbled slightly, holding his left hand out for balance. I couldn't decide. Was he running on all cylinders? Or was he playing hurt, hoping to reel me in? No way was I going to underestimate this guy. I'd done that once in my career. Sometimes I still couldn't breathe past the consequences.

I dropped my shoulders, lowered my hands slightly, let him think my guard was down. And once again my adrenaline-induced übervision saved me. I felt, rather than saw, the switchblade flip open in his right hand.

There's always a part of me that knows exactly how much it's going to hurt to die by whatever weapon is aimed at me. *Oh shit,* it whispered, *potential for deep, searing pain here.*

Yeah, the rest of me agreed. *So let's fight this right.*

He struck quickly. But I saw him as if he was moving through a vat of honey. Grabbing his knife hand with mine, I squeezed and twisted in such a way that his elbow and shoulder must've felt like they were coming unhinged. The knife hilt slipped into my hand as he gasped in pain and loosened his grip. He went to his knees.

Still holding his hand, I jerked his arm behind him, holding it high, twisting slightly, letting him know how easy it would be for me to break it. At the same time I pressed the blade against his throat.

"Who sent you?"

"I don't know what you mean."

More pressure. A thin line of blood trickled down his neck. "You people fight too well to be a bunch of pissed-off bigots. And now that I'm mad, you gotta know I'm not going to mind hurting you to get to the truth."

His jaw jerked, and before I could pry his teeth apart he'd keeled over. "Son of a bitch!" I checked his pulse, and when he didn't immediately seize, figured he'd swallowed something less lethal than cyanide. All kinds of drugs could be fit into a fake molar nowadays, many of which could put an operative into a coma for up to a week. So much for quick answers from him. Surely Vayl was doing better. I turned to look.

Yup, the boss had done pretty well for himself. Apparently Jesus Saves had tried to run for it, because they stood about fifty yards away. He gazed at Vayl like a trapped rat, brandishing his cross like a popgun as Vayl circled him. I could feel his power build as his sword danced in the air mere inches from the cross. Jesus Saves could too, and neither his shaking arm nor his bladder seemed to be able to hold up against it.

"You will tell me everything you know about the people who hired you," Vayl said. Being a Sensitive, like me, Jesus Saves was somewhat immune to vamp powers. At the same time he could feel the cold arctic fury that wound around every word Vayl spoke. When the boss moved toward him he screamed like a little girl and ran straight toward the Lexus. Vayl watched him with bemusement for a moment before striding after him. Gibbering like a Blair Witch refugee, Jesus Saves reached the Lexus, saw lights barreling down the highway, and leaped into the road.

"Stop!" he screamed, jumping up and down and waving his arms.

Vayl ran forward. "Are you insane? Get out of the road!"

"Stop! Help me!" yelled Jesus Saves, running toward the lights. Brakes squealed, but semis don't stop on a dime. Jesus Saves died with his cross in his hand, the vampire who was trying to save him watching incredulously from the side of the road.

"Son of a bitch!" I turned away from the carnage as Vayl pulled out his phone to make the call. The Suit moaned weakly. I went to check on him. He'd squirmed out of his belt and was trying to cinch it tight enough over his bicep to stop the fountain that had drenched his shoulder, sleeve, and half his face. "Here," I said, "let me help you with that." I jerked the belt tight, and he yelped in pain. The bleeding slowed to a trickle. "You want to watch who you ambush next time," I told him. "There're a lot worse monsters than vampires wandering the world."

"I know," he whispered, looking straight into my eyes as if he could see my secret life spread before him, a horrific map of violence and destruction justified—*maybe, maybe, maybe*—by the violence and destruction it had prevented.

Vayl came back, leaned over the inert form of Graybeard, whispered in his ear.

"You've only got a few seconds left," I told the Suit. "Soon he'll be crouching over you, speaking in your ear, scrambling your brain. Is there anything you want to tell me before your mind goes as soft as frozen yogurt?" Okay, I was exaggerating. Most likely Vayl was suggesting to Graybeard's subconscious that if he ever tried to kill anyone again, even a vampire, his heart would burst. Maybe the Suit sensed that.

"No," he answered.

"Vayl likes to mess with people's minds," I told him. "Literally. He might go easy on you, leave the memories of your wife and kids, your childhood. If you tell him who sent you."

The Suit was pale, clammy, barely conscious. Which is maybe why he slipped. "He'd kill us," he whispered. His eyes closed. A tear trickled down one cheek. Would you believe I felt sorry for him?

I kept my voice low, trying not to startle him into silence. "Who?"

No answer. I shook him, but he'd passed out, and it looked like he'd be spending the next couple of hours that way.

"Get the car started while I deal with him," said Vayl. "I hear sirens."

Chapter Five

I coaxed the battered Lexus off the highway at the nearest exit and headed south. I'd never used the roads I now took, never even seen them on a map. But I'd get us back to the hotel all the same. Evie liked to tell people I'd gotten a GPS implant. Neat idea, but untrue. My uncanny sense of direction had come to me along with my Sensitivity—after. It made sense in a way. My life as I'd known it had changed in every way it could. It seemed right that the way I perceived life should change too.

"It's still early," I told Vayl. "Do you want to go back to Assan's house?"

Vayl shook his head. "Not yet. We need to learn more about this vampire partner of Assan's. And now that we know about the virus"—Vayl slumped in his seat—"it is clear we need to revise our plan. Perhaps expand our net to include him, or even the vampires he and Assan just met. We must also ensure that our little confrontation does not mean the entire mission is compromised."

"What are you saying? That we should abort?"

"Perhaps another, less clandestine, more fully staffed agency would be the appropriate one to deal with this matter. We must think carefully and decide rightly."

That shut me down. Vayl got quiet too, considering our options, maybe. Or maybe just recharging. In the silence, the banging of our bumper took center stage like an *American Idol* loser, making me cringe. Graybeard and company had really done a number on the Lexus. We'd had to bend the back fenders away from the tires before we could even drive the thing, and I wouldn't bet on the axle still being in mint condition.

By now the three survivors would be strapped in their roller beds, and in another ten minutes hospital personnel would be trying to figure out how one of them could've picked up a sword wound outside of a circus sideshow. Once they'd healed sufficiently, our backup crew would move in and start asking questions. Not that they'd find out much. At least, not in time to help. But you had to try.

"That was a smart move back there," Vayl said.

"Oh, the snake thing? Thanks. Yeah, that did the trick."

"I noticed. Could you refrain from trying it again in the future?"

I glanced over at Vayl. I'd blinked off my night vision, so only the moonlight glancing through the windows showed me his expression. It looked tight, the way men's faces will when they're either feeling or remembering pain. I'd seen it often on Albert after diabetes had forced him to retire, and on David the night we'd stopped speaking. That look went straight to my heart and squeezed.

"You, uh, don't like snakes very much?"

"No."

"Well, quit looking all pinched and aristocratic. I'm not making fun of you."

"I am just somewhat sensitive about my phobias."

"You mean there's more than one?"

He jerked his head toward me. I held up one hand. "Okay, okay, backing off. Um, I suppose this would be a bad time to ask you to talk to Pete for me, you know, about the car?"

His eyes widened. I could almost hear him thinking, *Of all the nerve!* "You were driving," he said.

"But he likes you so much better than me."

"That is because I do not keep wrecking the rentals."

Jesus Henry Christ, Parks, why is it that every time I send you out on assignment something explodes?"

Only Pete called me Parks, and only when he was mad. He called me Parks an awful lot. "The car didn't explode, Pete, it crumpled. In the back. About six inches all the way across."

A strangled scream from the other end of the phone told me Pete might be choking on his own tongue. Maybe if I just waited very quietly at this end he'd suffocate before he could fire me.

"Let me talk to Vayl."

"Okay, hang on."

I took the phone to Vayl, who was lounging on one of the couches, getting a huge hairy kick out of my current predicament. The louse. "Tell him it wasn't my fault," I whispered as I handed him the phone.

"It was not Jasmine's fault, Pete," Vayl said. Just for that I went to the minifridge to get him a beer. I got one for myself too, a reward for spending the hours since we'd gotten back to Diamond Suites trying to untangle this new mystery Assan had presented us with.

"Yes," said Vayl.

At least we'd figured out the identity of Assan's accomplice. He'd made the FBI's Most Wanted Vampires list.

"I know," Vayl said.

The vamp's name, Aidyn Strait, rang bells all over Top Secret Land. He'd spent all of his long, long life trying to solve scientific problems using horribly unscientific methods, leaving a trail of mutilated bodies stretching back to the eighteenth century.

According to his file, which even now stared at me from the screen of our laptop, his latest venture was getting vampires to breed vampires, not through an exchange of blood, but through traditionally human methods.

So how did the vamp version of a fertility specialist end up with the human version of a makeover artist? The connection was tenuous, but visible. Aidyn's funding came from a pharmaceutical company called JetVitale, one owned by a known ally of the Raptor, who had, as we knew, recently hooked up with the Sons of Paradise through Assan. It was certainly feasible to believe Aidyn had come up with this virus for the Raptor. And it wasn't hard to guess where the terrorists fit into the picture.

Vayl took a sip of his beer and gave me a nod of thanks.

"What's Pete saying?" I whispered.

Vayl cupped his hand over the mouthpiece. "He is extremely upset that someone tried to kill us tonight."

"So he doesn't want to fire me?"

Vayl held up a finger, listened for a minute, then shook

his head. "Jasmine," he said, "your job is—how you say—solid. Pete would never fire one of his best agents." *Especially one that I cannot do without.*

I didn't read his mind. I just knew, somehow, that was what he was thinking.

"Oh." I drained my beer, marched into my bedroom, closed the doors, buried my face in the pillows, and burst into tears.

Sometime later I felt Vayl's presence beside me. The bed sank as he sat down.

"Are you all right?"

"I'm great." I turned to look at him, made sure he could see my smile. "Our assignment has turned into a bioterror nightmare. I nearly died tonight. My boss yelled at me for five minutes straight without stopping to take a breath, and in between I spent six hours staring at a computer screen. I think I may get cancer from the radiation. And I feel better than I have in a long time. Weird, huh?"

Vayl brushed a curl away from my cheek with a forefinger, which, oddly, made my insides quiver. "Unique," he said, "which is what I have come to expect from you."

Once in a great while a very private person will get that ask-me-anything look on his face. When you see it, you have to be ready. As soon as those soft brown eyes crinkled at the corners, I pounced. "Look, you've never really explained why you chose to work with me."

"No?"

"Nope. Don't get me wrong, I've enjoyed the ride. And I hope I spend the rest of my career working with you. But I've gotta tell you, I've been racking my brain for six months and I haven't been able to come up with one truly viable explanation as to why a vampire who's been around nearly three centuries needs an assistant. Pete gave me a song and dance that made him look like a gorilla in tap shoes. So . . . why me?"

He waited awhile to answer, shaking his head slightly every now and then as if he was trying out reasons and discarding them one by one. Finally he said, "After what happened to you November last, most people would have simply curled up and died." I stared at him, ready to walk if he even brushed against the heart of my pain. "You did not. You survived, but with Gifts that have only just begun to surface. I felt you needed help to develop those Gifts."

"And?"

"You are correct: there is more. I must ask you to be patient. When the time is right, we will both know."

Nuts. "Okay," I grumbled. I suddenly wanted my cards. I took them off the bedside table, and as I did my eyes strayed to the clock. "It's almost dawn," I said. "Do you need me to help you set up the tent?"

Vayl has never slept in a coffin. Now that I knew he was phobic, I suspected lying in one probably gave him the heebie-jeebies. I don't know what his sleeping arrangements are when we're home. Hell, I don't even know where his home is. But when we travel he brings a custom-made tent that covers his entire bed. The material is impermeable to light, so if someone was to accidentally open a curtain or something, he wouldn't singe. I'd love to have one myself, just because the kid in me thinks it would be a real hoot, like camping out only without the bugs.

"No," Vayl said, "I will be fine. Besides, you must be tired."

As soon as he said the words, I could hardly keep my eyes open. "Okay then," I mumbled as I rolled into my velvety pink pillow. I felt him slip the cards from my hand. Heard him whisper, "Good night, my *avhar*." But I was so tired I thought he said the whole thing in Romanian and none of it sank in.

Chapter Six

You know how sometimes real sounds can invade your dreams? Like one time, I was napping on the couch and dreamed I was interviewing Steven Tyler. Then I woke up and there he was on MTV talking to some bimbette who asked such stupid questions I was glad to wake up and find it wasn't me.

Now I dreamed Vayl and I were discussing the mission. I said, "So what do you think this virus does?" And Vayl answered by making a strange trilling noise, like he had a cricket stuck in his throat.

"How do you think it gets transferred?" I asked.

"Trrrill."

"And what's the deal with the Raptor? I mean, doesn't anybody ever say, 'No, we would prefer not to play with you because you're a big, fat creep.' "

"Trrill."

"Vayl, it's so weird, you sound just like my—"

"Cell phone," I mumbled. I opened my eyes, stared at the glittering handbag on the bedside table, a little worse for wear as a result of its trip to the floorboards during last night's wreck. Beneath the bag, where I'd laid it before we left, sat my personal phone. Ringing. Which meant it was either Evie or Albert, neither of whom did I feel like talking to at—I glanced at the clock—too damn early in the morning.

I said a very unladylike word as I reached over to pick up the phone and my ribs reminded me to fight dirtier next time some hulking bruiser wanted to trade blows. "Do you have any idea what time I went to sleep last night? I mean this morning?" I waited. Nothing. Oops, forgot to press the button. I might actually be glad about that later.

Beep. "Hello?"

"Jaz, I'm so glad you answered."

"Evie . . . have you been crying?"

"It's either that or pound Dad over the head with a mallet."

Crap. I am so *not up to this.* "What's he done now?"

"More like what hasn't he done." Evie really didn't belong in our family. Too sweet. Too anxious to please. It tended to bring out the worst in the rest of us, including Albert.

"Okay, what hasn't he done?"

"He hasn't taken his insulin every day, or followed his diet, or minded the infection in his f-f-foot."

"I thought we hired a nurse to do that for him."

Evie took a deep, trembling breath, but she still started crying again, hard enough that I didn't understand what she said next.

"Evie, all that bawling can't be good for the baby, so cut it out." I knew I sounded stern, but bossiness is the main perk of big sisterhood. And she did calm way down, way quick.

"Now, first of all, where's your husband? He'd be having a cow if he knew you were this agitated over Albert."

"Tim's in Philadelphia on business."

"Okay, after you get off the phone with me, call him. It'll make you feel better. Now, what about the nurse?"

"Dad fired her."

"*What?*" I felt the prickling along my scalp that signaled Big Anger. I wished I was the Queen of Hearts so I could just order my little card soldiers to cut off Albert's head. "When?"

"About a month ago."

"A month! But I've sent him two checks to cover her salary since then."

"Me too." Tears had crept back into Evie's voice. I could just imagine her sitting with her elbows on her little breakfast table, her straight, honey-brown hair sweeping forward to cover her face as she dropped her forehead into her hand. "Apparently Dad's been using the money to buy donuts, beer, and cigarettes. Now he's sick, the infection's spread to his heel and up his ankle. The doctor at the veterans' hospital says he may have to amputate, but he won't know for sure until he examines Dad, and *Dad won't go*!"

"What. A. Dumbass."

"Jasmine!"

"Well, he is."

"No, *I* am, for not keeping better track of him. But we've just been snowed under at work with this turnaround." She was an engineer for Trifecta Petroleum in Indianapolis. Can anybody say free Indy 500 tickets? Yeah, baby. "And by the time I get home I'm so tired I can barely move. But that's no excuse—"

"Yes, it is. The last thing you should be doing is driving to Chicago to look after the original Grumpy Old Man. *He's* the one who's abusing himself, not you, so quit feeling guilty."

"Does that mean you'll call him?"

"Yeah, right after I hang up with you."

"I'm getting ready to go to work, but you can call me back later tonight to let me know how it goes, if you want."

"I'll try. But no promises. I'm in the middle of something big right now."

"Me too. Unfortunately, I'm it." She laughed a little—music to my ears.

"You're so full of it," I said. "I saw the last picture you e-mailed me. You're gorgeous." I meant it.

"Th-thank you."

"Are you crying again?"

"Only a little. And in a good way this time."

"Well, I guess that's okay. Take care of yourself and Evie Junior, okay? You two are the only girlfriends I've got."

"Okay. Love you. Bye."

"Love you too." *Beep.* She was gone, back to the normal, everyday life that I'd give *my* life to preserve.

I dialed Albert's number, but before I hit the last digit I turned the phone off. He was an hour behind me, so he wouldn't be awake until at least ten my time. I set the alarm for nine thirty and went back to sleep.

Psyching yourself up to talk to Albert Parks is like preparing for battle, a metaphor he'd probably appreciate since he'd done that a few times himself during his thirty-year stint with the Marines. You need to have all your resources in place before you make your big move. That's why, before I called him, I showered, dressed in my comfy clothes (maroon sweats and an extra-large black T-shirt), and drank about half a gallon of coffee. Then I gave myself a pep talk.

"Okay, Jaz," I said as I shuffled my cards for the hundredth time, trying to relax to the *whish* of a perfect bridge, "here's the deal. You will not yell at Albert for at least five minutes." I figured the call would be over in two, but I'm one to hedge my bets when it comes to losing my temper. "You will keep your opinion of him to yourself this time, and you won't mention Mom at all."

"Okay, I'll try," I told my closet door reflection, "but I'm not making any promises." I nodded to myself. Then I called Albert.

He answered on the fifth ring. Not a good sign. His voice, when he said, "Hello," sounded faint and weak.

Though he'd gotten himself into this predicament, he would now expect pity. *Ugh!* I grabbed a pillow and threw it across the room. "Hey, Albert," I said, trying to sound pleasant and not overly concerned. "Evie tells me you're not feeling well."

"She's a meddler, that one, just like your mother."

I gritted my teeth. I would *not* argue with him over the fact that what *he* saw as meddling, *we* saw as Mom coming home early from work to find him in the sack with her best friend!

"I heard you fired your nurse."

"Goddamn busybody. Always wanting to know what I was eating, always poking me with those damn needles."

My Rage-O-Meter spiked. I could feel the veins in my forehead throb like war drums as my temper began to shred. It's a fragile thing, my temper. Sort of like the pretty colored tissue paper you find lining gift bags. My inner eye watched it disintegrate into little raggedy-edged pieces that floated away to perhaps reassemble themselves in another place and time as my father whined, "She treated me terrible, Jazzy. And now I *feel* terrible."

"Oh, for chrissake, Dad, you feel terrible because you're not following your doctor's orders. Evie's going nuts worrying about you, and Dave and I don't have time to come coddle you so you'll quit trying to fucking *kill* yourself! So here's the deal. We're hiring you another nurse. You will eat what she says. You will take the insulin shots without complaining. And if you fire her, I will personally haul your sorry ass to the veterans' home and dump you on their doorstep."

"But—"

"Furthermore, you will make an appointment with your doctor *today*, and if he has to cut off your goddamn foot, *none* of us are going to pity you, because you brought it on yourself!"

"Jasmine Elaine Parks—"

"Don't you *dare* pull your Dad voice out on me, old man. I know exactly what kind of game you're playing and it doesn't wash. You weren't there when we were growing up. What makes you think your pitiful health is going to make us come to you now?"

There was a long silence, during which I'm sure Albert was looking longingly at his beer can while I was kicking myself for yelling at a decrepit old war hero. I knew he'd been an awesome Marine. He had a drawer packed with medals and an address book full of phone numbers of men who would *still* willingly die for him. He just never should've had children.

"I'm tired," I said, suddenly feeling even older than his sixty-one years. "I'm working on a big account and it's got me on edge. Evie's call knocked me over that edge and now you're catching the fallout." It wasn't an apology. He didn't deserve one and he knew it.

"I'll call the doctor this morning," he said. I guess if I could make concessions, so could he.

"Good. I'll call you when I find a new nurse."

"Okay."

Another awkward silence. This was the point at which many fathers and daughters would exchange little affectionate phrases like "I love you" and "I miss you." We knew that. We just had no way to get there from here.

"So . . . I'll talk to you later," I said.

"Okay. Bye."

"Bye."

Beep. I found it terribly ironic that lately all my conversations with family members ended in a high, annoying sound.

I threw the phone on my bed, dropped down beside it. Before other things demanded my attention, I picked up the phone, dialed Evie's number, and left a message for her to get me the number of the nursing pool we'd drawn the last woman from. Hopefully I could hire one who hadn't yet talked to his old nurse and learned what an ass Albert could be.

Chapter Seven

I woke to the sound of a doorbell.

"Hey," I told the clock, "I went back to sleep. How cool is that?" Even better was the total lack of nightmares. I started to bounce out of bed, but my ribs turned it into more of a slow roll. Grief accompanied me to the door. Vayl had taped a note there.

> *Jasmine,*
>
> *Before I went to my rest, I ordered you something special, since I know how much you hate to eat out. See you at dusk.*
>
> *V*

I looked through the peephole. Nobody. And the only inhabitant of the hall, when I opened the door, was a serving cart full of covered dishes. I imagined the waiter dashing back to the elevator after he'd rung so I wouldn't catch a glimpse of him and think—*gasp!*—that real people actually ran this hotel. I supposed the employees did a lot of darting into stairwells and linen closets. Were they required to run sprints every morning before work to keep themselves in shape? Hmm, a definite thought. By the time I had the cart inside, the door locked, and the table set for my meal, I'd decided the entire staff met in the attic every morning for calisthenics, and every one of them, maid, cook, and maintenance worker alike, wore matching pink leotards.

I uncovered the lids to each dish one by one, offering each plate a round of applause as it appeared. Number one plate held three small pancakes, a slab of butter, and a minipitcher of syrup. A mushroom omelet spread itself across plate number two, and plate number three held four slices of extra-crispy bacon. Vayl had also ordered coffee and a big glass of orange juice. I saluted his closed door with my mug and said, "To you, Boss. May you never realize how much I truly like you."

As I ate the most delicious breakfast I'd consumed in months, I planned my afternoon. Since anything to do with Assan fell under Vayl's domain, I tabled the whole issue and moved on to our more immediate problem. Four fairly well-informed killers disguised as religious fanatics did not just materialize and try to eliminate two Central Intelligence Agency employees. I wasn't sure how they'd even found us on that highway, but I did have a theory. Someone must have told them we were after Assan, so they had probably watched his house until we showed up. That someone had taken a big risk too, because only a handful of people even knew we existed. That included Pete, the three senators on our department's oversight committee, Bergman, and the woman I was about to call.

Our secure phone sat where we'd left it last night, beside the laptop in front of the unoccupied chair at my breakfast table. I swallowed my last bite and used that phone to call Martha. She answered on the first ring.

"Demlock Pharmaceuticals," she said in her gravelly alto. She hadn't smoked a day in her life, but you'd never know it by her voice.

"I need to establish an order."

"Hold, please."

Moments later Martha was back on a line that was now secure from her end as well as mine.

"What do you need, hon?"

Pete's secretary called me "hon." How cool was that? Of course, she could pretty much do as she liked. She might be a four-foot-eight granny with mocha skin and whipped-cream hair, but she could nail your ass to the floor with a single look. I asked her about it one time. She said it was the result of raising seven children, every one of whom still wilted beneath the Look like old lettuce. Never mind the only one of her kids without a PhD was an MD. All of them acknowledged her as the Supreme Leader of the Evans clan. Luckily she had her soft-spoken hubby, Lawrence, around to make sure her rule didn't run to Fascism. Lawrence spent his weekdays teaching at the Southern Baptist Seminary and his weekends saving souls at Hope Baptist just down the street from my apartment. What a sweet man. And generous too, unlike some guys I was about to name.

"Hey, Martha, I need to talk to Pete. Um, how is he feeling today?"

"Annoyed. But that's typical." She sighed. "This morning I told him the other department heads had started a pool based on the timing of his demise. They're giving two-to-one odds on a heart attack at the office. The man has no idea how to relax!"

Ouch. If he died, I'd have even more guilt to add to the trailer I was already towing. Not a pretty thought. "You should talk him into going on a fishing trip or something."

"I could. But he'd just end up snagging his line on a body or catching sight of some high-level, vacationing drug lord and that would be the end of that."

"Well, we'll think of something. So . . . did he tell you about last night?"

"I heard your car got a little bent out of shape."

"Yeah. But it wasn't my fault."

"It never is, hon. Are you and Vayl okay?"

"Yeah, we're fine."

"Well, that's what really matters." She sighed. Disappointed we'd survived, or just dreading the task ahead? "I'm starting the paperwork this morning, so it should be ready for you to sign when you come back. Do you need a new vehicle? I might be able to get you one from the same company."

The same company. Holy crap, Martha knew exactly what kind of car we'd been driving because she'd made the rental arrangements to start with! She could easily have given Graybeard the details. Of course, Pete would've had access to that information too. The senators? Yeah, they could've found out as well. So much for narrowing down my field of suspects. Only Bergman had an airtight alibi, that being his paranoia. He'd never hire someone else to do his dirty work because he'd be too sure they'd betray him.

Bergman's bow out of the race gave me no consolation.

That still left five other people I liked and/or worked for. No way would finding the answer to this particular riddle make me a happy camper. My stomach churned, spitting acid all over my delectable breakfast, making it want to part company with my digestive system.

"Jasmine?"

"Sorry, I was spacing out." *Out, out, out* . . . I dug my fingernails into my thigh. "Naw, don't worry about the ride. It's taken care of. Pete, however, is another story. Is he busy?"

"Never too busy for you. Hang on."

I didn't have long to wait. Pete's got a thing about telephone charges. He doesn't like paying them.

"What's up, Parks?"

"Last night's fiasco. We seem to have an information leak in our department. There's no other way those jokers could've found us."

"I agree. I'm also concerned about the Assan side of things. If we don't handle this right—" He stopped, because what could he say that didn't reek of drama? We sat in frozen silence, fully understanding the ramifications of a plan that included the words "Raptor," "terrorist allies," and "virus." Then I guess our dwindling phone minutes snapped him back to reality, because Pete trucked right on, saying, "Last night I suggested to Vayl that you might want backup. He said he would let you make that call."

Hell yeah, I wanted to say. *How about the Florida National Guard, for a start*? But in our business, if you pressed the panic button every time you thought the world might be ending, you'd be out of work before you could say, "But we thought—"

However it would be nice to have someone outside the

Agency we knew we could trust, because you never knew what these loons were going to throw at you. And I had an ideal candidate in mind.

"I want to bring in Bergman."

Thoughtful pause while Pete tallied up the potential expense of that request. "You sure you need a tech-head?"

"We've already got plenty of muscle. I know it's gonna cost you, but I shouldn't have to remind you the guy's a genius. Plus he's an outsider." Way out, actually, but I knew how to deal with that. "He made a big difference in the result of our last mission. You said that yourself."

"Okay, give him a call."

"Thanks. And, Pete, I really think we've got to go silent until this is over." I waited for him to protest. If he'd engineered last night's attack, he'd want to keep track of us so he'd know where to send the next wave. His reply, immediate and definite, left no doubt in my mind where he stood.

"I think that's for the best."

Yes! That left one less heartbreak on my horizon. "Okay, talk to you on the other side."

"Parks . . ."

"Yeah?"

"Take care of yourself. That's an order."

"Yes *sir*."

After we hung up I did a little happy dance around the rim of the pit, managing not to fall in despite some spectacular high kicks. Gosh, if I hadn't minded the whole world ogling my butt I could've been a showgirl! I took one more victory lap, settled back down at the table, and called Bergman.

After drumming my fingers through five different sets of prerecorded options and punching a combination of buttons that practically committed me to sacrificing my firstborn if I revealed any detail of our pending conversation to anyone, I had to leave a voice mail. While I waited for his return call I keyed the name of Senator/Suspect #1 into our database and started reading.

Two hours later I'd read all the information I could gather on Senators Fellen, Tredd, and Bozcowski. I'd also done a short background check on Cole Bemont out of sheer nosiness. I felt much better about our spontaneous exchange of affection now that I knew he was definitely one of the good guys.

Wondering when Bergman would decide to crawl out of his cave and reenter the real world, I decided I'd wait more patiently if I could do so standing up. So I moved all the furniture out of the pit and lined it up against the walls like freaked out preteens at the Christmas Dance.

Tae kwon do was the first martial art I ever learned. Mom started sending me to class when I was eight, somehow managing to find me a new instructor every time we moved, so that by the time I hit eleven I'd earned a first-degree black belt. I've trained in plenty of other disciplines since then, but tae kwon do is still my favorite. I started with white belt, worked my way through each form until I reached my present rank, fifth-degree black belt. By the time I'd finished, my ribs were pounding out an SOS on my lungs and my sweats were soaked. So I headed to the shower.

I peeked out the curtain on the way. "Nothing moving

out there. The whole damn state must be hungover." Which was when I realized a new year had crashed on me. Should I make a resolution? Be nicer to old women and cats? Swear less? Learn a new language?

"Got it!" I told my reflection as I went into the bathroom to undress. "My resolution is to learn how to swear in a new language."

If Evie were here she'd be rolling her eyes. "That's not swearing less, Jaz," she'd say.

"Ah, but that is where you are wrong, little round grasshopper," I'd tell her in my Chinese grocer accent. She loves that one because, of course, I do it terribly. "I will be swearing less in English. *And* I will be learning a new language."

I lingered over my second shower and afterward took the time to shave and pluck and cosmeticize myself into some semblance of order. Now wearing black jeans and a long-sleeved purple shirt with prehistoric cave paintings printed all over it, I was ready—to wait some more. These were the times I missed Evie the most. She's one of those people who's easy to be with, laid-back, undemanding, never in your face—like me. I do sometimes think it's good we were military brats. All those moves forced us to become friends with each other because we knew our other friendships couldn't last.

Okay, much more of this mushy crap and I'll have to trade my PPK for a parasol.

I dropped to the bed, turned on the TV, and picked up my cards. While Oprah helped some poor schmuck finally let go of her dead parrot, I shuffled. It sounds lame, I know. But I like the sound the cards make slapping against each other. It's much sweeter than the clatter of my thoughts, looping around my brain like the cars on a kid's racetrack, never winning, never ending, just rushing in circles until I want to lay down on a busy stretch of railroad and hope Dudley Do-Right is busy elsewhere.

Bergman called just as I turned the channel and—what do you know!—Dudley Do-Right galloped across the screen, riding Horse backward because that's how all courageous Mounties ride their steeds in the backwoods of Canada. "Jasmine? Are you secure?"

Hmm, really too many ways to answer that question, and not all of them comforting. "It's safe to talk," I said. "What're you up to?"

"Nothing."

Which meant he had several high-level, top-secret projects on the burner, none of which he wanted to discuss. "Cool. That means you've got some free time, right?"

"Could have. What do you need?"

"Backup. Big-time backup with all the bells and whistles. How soon can you be in Miami with a vehicle?"

Long silence as Bergman did some mental calculating. "How soon do you need me?"

"Dusk would be good." I chuckled, but he got the message.

"I'll leave tonight and call you when I hit town."

"Excellent," I said, and we hung up. Nice thing about Bergman, he likes to leave the details for face-to-face conversations. "Don't worry, Vayl," I said, looking at my wall as if I could see through it, straight into his room, "help is on the way."

Chapter Eight

Nobody could rent me the kind of power I needed in a vehicle, though I only meant to use it until Bergman showed, so I ended up leasing one. That chore accomplished, I spent the rest of the time until dusk rearranging furniture. I reset the pit, using a completely different configuration than the hotel preferred and thinking I'd showed up their designers big-time. Evie always forces me to watch HGTV when I visit, and I felt sure most of their decorators would approve of the cozy new conversation area I'd created. Now I just had to figure out why I thought I needed one.

I was just getting the urge to shuffle cards in response to this new brain teaser when darkness fell. A strange sound from Vayl's room made me jump to my feet. It was half gulp, half gasp, what you might expect to hear from a man who's not accustomed to screaming.

I was through his door before the sound stopped, Grief cocked in my hand.

Vayl stood in front of his tent-covered bed, staring at me as if I had come to spear him with stakes and drown him in holy water. He was naked.

"Whoa!" I covered my eyes and spun around. Redundant, I know, but that two-second view of his magnificent pale bod had activated my conservative Midwestern values, chief among those the belief that you don't ogle naked men who don't already belong to you. "I'm sorry! I heard this noise and it sounded like you were in danger, so I came to save you. I'm outta here," I said, moving toward the door.

"No, stay. There is a, there was a . . ." He stopped, pulled himself together. "I found a snake in my luggage."

I turned back around, following the direction of his pointer finger. His suitcase lay where he'd upended it, on the floor between the bed and the wall.

"What kind of snake?" I asked.

"Big. But not moving. I think, yes, I am almost sure it was dead." Wow, he was doing a great job of not freaking considering how he felt about nonlegged reptiles.

I edged toward the suitcase, toed it upright. "All I see is clothes. I need your cane."

As he went to the dresser for it I said, "You mean to tell me you didn't open the suitcase until this morning?"

"Everything I needed for the party was in the garment bag. And, as you see, I do not wear pajamas."

Actually, I'm trying not to see, thank you very much. I took the cane in my left hand, Grief still ready for action in my right. Flipped over a shirt, a couple of pairs of silk boxers, and there it was. A long brown rattler as thick as a child's arm.

I poked it. Nothing. It didn't curl in response, didn't rattle, didn't move at all. "You're right. It's dead," I told him.

He nodded. “Do you suppose it was alive when it was placed in my bag?”

“Yeah, I kind of think so. I imagine it died either from the rough handling of the bag or the cold temperatures it was subjected to on the plane.”

He nodded again. “Someone does not want us to complete this mission.”

“Because if we do, they’re going to be in very hot water.”

“Or dead.”

“Let me get rid of the snake for you while you get ready. We can figure this out after you’re dressed.” I leaned over to pick up the snake and Vayl yelled, “No!”

“Shit!” It was the first time I’d ever heard him raise his voice, and he nearly had me jumping out of my skin.

“What if it comes back to life?”

“Vayl, it’s not gonna . . .” I met his eyes. Okay, maybe the idea wasn’t beyond the realm of possibility. Since he wanted to play it safe, I unsheathed his sword and cut the sucker’s head off. Then I dumped the parts into the trash can and headed outdoors with the liner.

“We’ll talk when I get back,” I said. Very professionally, I thought, considering the fact that the sight of Vayl’s nakedness was imprinted on the backs of my eyeballs and all I wanted to do was get out of the room so I could savor that picture.

Vayl nodded and headed for the shower. And if I gave that fine muscular behind a glance before leaving his room, I hoped no red-blooded woman on earth could blame me. What I didn’t expect to see were the scars crisscrossing his broad shoulders and back. I winced, wondering if they'd come before or after his change. Either way, damn.

After disposing of the snake I curled up on one of the couches in the conversation area I'd created. Vayl came out of his room shortly afterward. Apparently the new furniture arrangement was less conducive to talk than I'd anticipated, because speech suddenly failed me.

Unless he'd switched to camouflage mode, Vayl rarely entered a room without everyone feeling his presence. His personality could be like mist, drifting gently into your lungs until every breath sent him sliding through your veins. Or, like a violent change in air pressure, it could reach out and slam you against a wall. At the moment, looking at him through eyes I hoped hadn't glazed over, I wouldn't have noticed if a ninja had dropped through the ceiling and started breaking chairs.

He moved with the total body awareness of a professional athlete, and now that I knew what that body looked like, I couldn't take my eyes off it. If a scientist gave a lecture on the alpha male, she'd definitely throw in a few slides of Vayl.

"Vayl, I . . . you . . ." I caught his eyes and stopped speaking. They were the gray-blue of storm-swept waves, snapping dangerously over lips compressed so tightly I could see the outline of fangs beneath them. "Are you okay?" I asked, some instinct making me touch the gun now resting in my shoulder holster.

Vayl descended into the pit and dropped onto the couch I'd positioned on a diagonal with mine. For a minute he just sat there with his elbows on his knees, staring off into space.

"Vayl?"

"Something is wrong with my blood supply."

"What do you mean?"

Vayl jumped up and started pacing. "The blood I brought to sustain me. It is tainted." I felt the familiar bewilderment that used to fog my brain when my math teacher handed me a word problem. How was *I* supposed to know which train would reach Dallas first?

"How could you tell?" I asked.

Vayl grabbed one of the decorative pillows off the couch and began picking at one corner of it. I'd never seen him so shaken, and it was starting to scare me.

"Look, Vayl, just tell me what you know."

Vayl sat down again, avoiding my gaze, watching his fingers worry at the pillow instead. "When I went to get a drink I realized something was wrong. That is, once the blood had warmed, I could smell something in it that should not have been there. Something my nose tells me will make me ill."

"Did you check all the bags?"

"Yes. They are all tainted."

First the God's Arm goons. Then the snake. Now the blood. Who is doing this?

"Did you keep some? We should get it tested."

"Yes."

This is bad, bad, bad. "Vayl, are you thinking what I'm thinking?"

"Of course. But snake venom and polluted blood would not kill me. They would only make me sick."

"Sick, like out of commission? Sick as in vulnerable?"

"Very possibly."

"Then maybe these are just preludes to another attack." I waited for Vayl to agree, but he just shrugged.

The pillow in his hands began to come apart. I was beginning to identify with it, big-time. *Okay, Jaz, keep it together. You are a trained pro. Eventually you will find the ass that needs kicking and that's exactly what you'll do. As long as you keep it together.*

"So let's figure out who's doing this," I said, more to myself than Vayl. "I don't think it could've been Pete. He was too ready to agree with our suggestions."

"That still leaves several highly trusted suspects." He shook his head. "We have been betrayed." He sounded like he'd already had some bitter experience in that area.

"You told me yesterday that we had some evidence the Raptor had a government official on his payroll, right?"

"Yes."

"What if it's one of the senators on our oversight committee? They would have all kinds of reasons for keeping us from completing this assignment if, as a result, it were to come out that they were connected to the Raptor." *And if I'm right, we are dealing with one of the world's major scumbags.*

"Keep talking," Vayl encouraged me.

I shrugged. "I just can't think of anybody else who would know we were here, who could gain access to your blood supply, and who would maybe know of your phobia about snakes."

"I have never told anyone about that but you."

Really? Wow! "No, but anybody who's read your reports might just glean that information, you know, reading between the lines, if you'd had a mission that involved snakes. I don't know; I'm really reaching now."

"No," he said quietly, his eyes on the wall, as if someone had projected some horrifying memories there. "I had a case in 1939. It . . . this abhorrence I feel is directly and probably obviously related to that case."

I waited. When he didn't provide any details I didn't pout, but I did consider swiping his file. Would it still be on Pete's desk? "We have a very nasty problem, Vayl."

"Two, actually."

"Yeah?"

Vayl sank back down onto the couch, looking as bleak as a cancer patient. "Not only is someone trying to kill me, but now I have to find a supply of fresh blood."

I knew that, as we sat there staring at each other, we were sharing the same thoughts. Neither of us wanted to say them out loud, but it had to be done. I started.

"So what are our options?"

"They are limited." Vayl drew in a deep breath, clasped his hands together convulsively. I'd never seen him so agitated. "I cannot hunt. I . . . made a vow." He looked at me out of the corner of his eyes. "I know that must sound stupid and old-fashioned to you—"

"Not at all. Of course hunting is out. We're the good guys."

Vayl's lips twitched.

"Okay," I amended, "we're walking that thin line between good and bad, but we're not kidnapping kids or blowing up federal buildings so I say, if we're erring, it's on the side of good."

"Which is why we cannot raid a blood bank or anything similar to that."

"I agree." Weren't we just two reasonable people? It's

what we spooks do when the alternative is blind panic. "So what *can* you do?"

"I can find a willing donor. Vampires tend to attract them. I know of one in the area I might approach."

Whoa, buddy. Where did you go when I wasn't looking? "You've . . . made some contact? Recently?"

If Vayl had any blood in him, he would've blushed. He avoided meeting my eyes, and he started to fidget like I'd just caught him slipping a frog into the teacher's desk. "I, well, yes." He straightened up and looked me in the eye, realizing, maybe, that he didn't have to answer to anyone, me the least. "I cannot discuss it right now." His look softened. Did I really seem that hurt? "I will tell you later, when we have time."

"You want to save it for the plane ride back?"

He nodded, the corner of his mouth lifting. "Yes. I will make everything clear to you then."

Maybe. "Everything" gave me leave to cover an awful lot of ground. One thing I was sure of, after all these attempts on our lives, I couldn't see me loitering outside some locked door while God knew what went down inside. What if this willing donor of Vayl's was part of the next wave? I voiced my worries. Vayl didn't want to see it my way at first, but I kept talking.

"Vayl, be logical. We are two of the most clandestine people on earth. And yet whoever is after us has found us on a highway, infiltrated your luggage, and tainted your blood supply. You can't do this with someone you can't trust." Our eyes met. I didn't have to say anything. He knew what choices remained to him. Still he resisted.

"I will not. I cannot—"

"Why not?"

Vayl looked at me a long time, his jaw clenching and unclenching as if the words he was about to say needed to be chewed first, ground under his molars until the sharp edges wore away.

"Jasmine . . ." He stopped, thought a minute, tried again. "I do not know what it would do to us. You would be stepping onto a path that could lead you to vampirism."

"Not if you don't drain me. Not if I don't drink your blood."

"You are right. But because you are a Sensitive you could—you probably would—change." I must've looked puzzled because he kept trying to explain. "The kind of—joining—you are suggesting is not one-way."

"So what are you saying, that there's magic in your backwash?"

The tightness around Vayl's eyes eased a little, and a dimple appeared in his right cheek. "You could say that."

"What might happen to me?"

Vayl sank back onto his couch and I sat beside him. "I have never done such a thing with a Sensitive, so it is impossible to predict."

"Could you make it so I can fly?" I asked.

That got his attention. "What?"

I felt a little self-conscious, but figured the time to guard my ego had long passed. "I've always wanted to fly," I confided, "like Superman, only without the ridiculous costume."

"It is not . . ."

"Or how about superhuman strength so when I throw people they sail clear across the room?"

"This is serious!" Vayl's eyes bored into mine, twin obsidian pebbles that looked ready to bury me under a great big avalanche. It ticked me off. Here I was, offering the guy his life, basically, and all he could do was threaten me with metaphorical boulders! "You have no idea, Jasmine. The two of us will mix at a very basic level. *I* cannot predict the outcome. *You* cannot know the risk!"

I considered shaking him 'til his teeth rattled, thought better of it. "Vayl! Calm down! Damn, but you're grouchy when you're hungry!"

That got him. He dug the heel of his palm into the furrows between his eyes.

"You are insane, you know that?"

Ouch. "I'm just being practical. I knew someday I might have to bare my throat to you. Pete and I discussed that very possibility. As for danger and risk taking, that's what Pete pays me to do. And you and I both know he intends to get his money's worth."

"Jasmine, I cannot—"

"Why not!"

"Because you are not *food*!"

I stared at him for a minute; then I started to grin. I couldn't help it. "Vayl"—I tried to keep my face straight—"I'm not asking you to eat me."

Vayl's jaw dropped and I burst into peals of laughter. Eventually I heard him chuckling along with me and I knew we'd be okay. When I had my warped sense of humor back under control I said, "It's just a temporary solution. Until we can figure out something better. Okay?"

When he sighed and his shoulders dropped out of defensive mode, I knew I'd won. Vayl hesitated one more minute. "I will not take much," he assured me. "Only what I need and no more."

No more, no more, no more.

I sighed as I felt his power settle over me, warm and comforting as an old quilt. His fingers grazed my neck as he swept my hair aside. His lips brushed my earlobe, moved down to my throat. He kept nuzzling me with his lips, caressing me with the tips of his fangs until something new rose between us, a force that sizzled and snapped, making the very air churn. I could hear my breath coming in gasps.

"Vayl . . . please."

"Yes," he said, his voice hoarse with desire. For me? For my blood? I wasn't sure there was any difference just then. I wanted to delve further into this new insight, but my frontal lobe chose that moment to completely shut down. Even the pain of his teeth penetrating my skin didn't wake it up.

The air shimmered with power. With magic. My head buzzed with it. Through half-closed lids I watched colored bubbles of light dance across the walls. The darkness came so quickly after that, I never even knew it had taken me until I returned to myself and realized I was lying on the couch with one leg flung over its arm. Vayl sat on the other couch, staring at me like I'd grown an extra head as I struggled to sit up. A tightness on my neck caused me to reach up, but when my fingertips encountered a gauze pad I dropped my hand back into my lap.

"What?" I asked, trying hard not to cry. I don't know if I was more distressed that I'd blacked out or that I'd missed most of an experience that had promised to be unforgettable. "Did I do something wrong?" I asked. "Did I *say* something out of line?" *What the hell just happened?*

Vayl shook his head. "You were perfect. Better than the best. I have never . . . It has never been like that for me before."

"For me either." We smiled at each other. The hard knot of fear that twisted my heart with every new blackout relaxed. Vayl didn't know. My secret was still safe. Now that my attention could wander, I realized the experience had left some aftereffects. "I *do* feel kind of funky though," I commented.

He sat forward, his eyes narrowing with concern. "How do you mean?"

"Umm, like, drunk. But not."

I thought Vayl would come sit beside me, fuss over me a little, but he sat statue still, like a street performer who's run out of gray body paint. Finally he whispered, "I know."

"Know what?"

"It is as if you are an entire spectrum of light that just became visible to me. I can . . . hear your heart beating. I can sense your hunger pangs. I know you are frightened. You are also elated, tired, worried and"—his voice dropped—"excited."

"Oh no," I said. "Oh no, oh no, oh no—" I bit my lip hard, stopping the litany with my own blood. Vayl had kept his word. He'd left me plenty. It trickled onto my chin as I tried to stand, but I moved too fast and lost my balance. Vayl caught me just before I landed in a heap on the floor. As soon as I regained my equilibrium I growled, "Back off."

He stepped away.

"No, I mean with your senses or whatever. You were supposed to give me superpowers. You were supposed to make me fly. You weren't supposed to march through my thoughts like a lumberjack in a rainforest!"

"Jasmine, that is not how it happened! There is no need to panic."

"I'm not panicking!" But I was, and I had no way to hide it. "I don't want you inside my head," I told him, keeping my voice as reasonable as possible, considering I just wanted to stuff my face into a pillow and scream. "It's too intimate, too scary. I'm not ready for that!" I realized I was yelling and covered my mouth.

"I warned you. I told you—"

I raised my hand to stop him talking, trying to swallow my oceanic fear as I did. "I can't have you—exploring me like that. There are things you don't know. Things I can't explain." I stopped, took a deep breath to keep myself from babbling on until he *did* discover my secret.

His lips twitched. "Are you really that bad?"

"Well . . . no, I'm just . . . not that good."

"Maybe that is why I find you so interesting."

"Huh" was my brilliant reply.

He nodded to the couch, urging me to cool my jets. "Jasmine, the change has begun. You cannot let it destroy you."

I sank down and he sat beside me. I said, "No, I can't." *Can't, can't, can't . . .*

"So, please, relax. I promise you, I will not probe. I

will not intrude. Your thoughts, your memories, are still your own."

"Okay." I took a deep breath and leaned back. He turned slightly to face me, his eyes spilling emotions I couldn't hope to catch. Especially not in my current state.

"I have believed for some time that I should do this," he said, "but our joining has convinced me. You must take this." He pulled a gold chain out from under his shirt and unlatched it, freeing a ring from its loop. He held the ring out to me, and I stared at it as it sat in his palm. Intricately woven golden knots formed the band. In the center of each knot glittered a superb little ruby. The exquisite craftsmanship made the ring resemble a magical artifact, like a token of love left at the bottom of the Lake of Dreams by some brokenhearted nymph.

"Oh, wow." I touched it as if it was crafted of spun glass.

"You like it then?" Vayl slipped it onto my finger. Though it sat on my right hand, the feeling still spooked me, as if we'd just agreed to some sort of unmarriage.

"It's gorgeous," I said, holding my arm out to see it better. I dropped my hand to my lap as a thought occurred to me. "I can't keep it."

"What?"

"It's too much, Vayl. Too expensive. Too beautiful. Too personal. Plus Pete would kill me. Remember what he said about not accepting gifts?"

"From clients, not from each other. Jasmine"—frustration furrowed his eyebrows, edged his tone—"why do you always have to make everything so difficult?"

My first instinct was to argue, but I had no basis. Vayl

had made this wonderful gesture. Did I really have to spit in his hand? "It's just, I don't understand why you would give this to me when, you're right, I have been a pain in the ass lately."

"Because it is more than a gift. You wear a ring made by my father's father on the day I was born. It is called Cirilai—which means 'Guardian.' My mother, as she lay dying from the difficulty of my birth, had a vision of *my* death. She knew it would be violent. She knew it would endanger my soul. Cirilai contains all the ancient powers my family could muster to protect me. As long as it exists, I may lose my life, but I cannot lose my soul."

Holy crap, I'd heard fables about such artifacts! But to actually have one wrapped around my finger? Well, to be honest, it made me feel kind of nauseous. "Why on earth would you give something so precious to me?"

If I'd known him for years, maybe I could have read the answer in those amber eyes. He must've spent a minute trying to tell me things with them that words could not express. But too much of the unknown still stood between us to allow a translation. That's what I told myself. Maybe I was just too scared to let myself understand. Finally he said, "I gave you Cirilai because the ring will protect you as well. And because I sensed in you the same power that is invested in the ring. The two of you belong together—with me."

At the risk of sounding like a two-year-old, I repeated myself. "But why?"

Thank goodness, unlike mine, Vayl's patience isn't tied to a lit fuse. His hands clasped together in his lap. "You and Cirilai remind me that, while I am no longer human, I am also no better than human."

"Is that all? We keep you humble?"

"Think of what happens to people who possess such powers as mine when they decide their ideas, agendas, race are superior to all others."

"Napoleon," I whispered. "Hitler. Hussein."

Vayl nodded solemnly. "In guarding my soul, you protect the world. And that is why I need you as my assistant."

Bam! Finally, an explanation for our partnership that made some sort of sense. And one that raised Vayl so high in my esteem that, even though he'd never need it, I'd happily step between him and a bullet. Which gave me an insight into Albert I'd rather not have. But you can't continue to believe your dad's a complete tool when others respect him just as highly.

"I would like to ask you something," Vayl said.

"What's that?"

"Why did you rearrange the furniture again?"

"Well, I wanted to work out and . . . again?"

"Remember Ethiopia? And Germany? And Hong Kong?"

"Yeah. So?"

"So, you have rearranged the furniture in every apartment, hotel, and hut we have stayed in since I have known you. And always the same way. I just wondered why."

"Oh." I laughed weakly, racking my brain for a plausible excuse. "Well, that's the way it always was growing up. No matter what house we were living in, Mom arranged the furniture the same way to make it feel like home."

A damn fine explanation, I must say, and one Vayl swallowed whole.

"I was just wondering."

"Let's go kick somebody's butt," I suggested, thinking it would sure make me feel better. "I feel like I really could throw a bad guy across the room."

"And suddenly we have so many from which to choose." Vayl thought a moment, giving me time to rearrange my brain. Like the furniture, it made no sense to me, but I did recover most of my scattered control. "Do you have any ideas?" he asked.

"Assan comes immediately to mind."

"I am sure it will be a pleasure ending his existence. But he is more valuable to us as he is right now, oblivious and unbruised. First we need to find out where he and Aidyn are storing the virus."

"And how they're making it," I added. "Do you suppose they're keeping their notes at Assan's place?"

"It is possible. Though Aidyn seems to be the creator. We need to ascertain where he is staying as well."

"Sure would be handy if we had a contact on the inside," I said. "But Assan's staff is unapproachable."

"What about his family?"

"You mean the wife?" We shared a knowing look. "You mean the jealous wife who's hired a private investigator?" We both nodded. With the butt-kicking officially tabled, I moved across the pit to a mauve armchair beside which stood an end table with a phone on top, a drawer for the phone book, and a lamp to read it by.

Most men I meet through work tend to avoid that whole live-like-a-normal-guy gig. In fact, most guys I meet through work want to kill me. So when I found Cole's name and number listed in the White Pages I felt a sudden urge to giggle. It went away just as quickly. I'd met a normal guy. Big whoop. That didn't make *me* any more normal.

He answered his phone on the first ring. "Cole Bemont."

"Cole! This is Lucille Robinson. We met—"

"Last night!"

"You remembered."

"Are you kidding? I've been kicking myself all day for not getting your number." We stopped speaking for a moment, homage to the kiss.

"Cole, I have a problem I hoped you could help me with." I kept my voice businesslike since Vayl sat three feet away, and I honestly didn't want to lead Cole any further astray.

"Sure," Cole said.

"Um, don't you want to hear what it is first?"

"Doesn't matter. You saved my hide yesterday. Plus my lips are still tingling. At this point, I'm prepared to do just about anything you suggest."

Yipes! What have I unleashed? I wanted to say, "Cole, despite my actions last night I am *not* looking for a relationship with you. I can't maintain a relationship with you due to the fact that I don't want to. Also, I travel almost constantly and my boss is a vampire who I find disturbingly fascinating. These life choices don't make me a good candidate for pet owner, much less girlfriend." But I needed Cole to help me get information, which meant I needed him interested for just a while longer. *Damn, damn, damn.*

"Can my partner and I meet you somewhere in about an hour?"

"Your . . . partner?"

"It's kind of impossible to explain over the phone."

"Okay. How about Umberto's? It's semiprivate and the food's great."

"Fine." Cole gave me directions and we hung up. I looked at Vayl. "It's set."

"Good. And?"

"And what?"

"You want to say something else, I can tell."

I nodded. "Sometimes this job sucks."

Chapter Nine

When this whole mission ended, I suspected that if I survived, Pete would demote my ride to a used moped. Not great motivation to push the self-preservation button. But at the moment, I didn't care. My local Mercedes dealer had brought me a dark blue C230 Sport Sedan that made even New Year's traffic bearable. The car hummed like a Broadway star. I joined right in, and the two of us sang a duet Stephen Sondheim would've tapped his foot to while we motored down the sparkling streets of Miami.

"I would ask you how you feel," said Vayl, "but it is so obvious."

"It's amazing," I told him. "I just want to hug everyone I know. I want to buy the guy who engineered this car a bottle of champagne. I want to fly. Hey!" I turned to Vayl. "After this meeting let's go hang gliding!"

"In the dark?"

"It's a full moon." I stopped at the light, flying forgotten as a burgundy minivan pulled up beside me. "I have never seen that shade of red before. Can you see all those flecks of gold and black in it?"

"Yes," Vayl answered, his smile more full and natural

than I'd ever seen it. "I take it you are enjoying this part of the change."

"Oh, is *that* what it is?" The minivan activated its blinker and began to inch into my lane. "Looks like he's a little lost," I commented as I waved for him to slip in ahead of us.

"You know, yesterday you would have cursed that man for ten solid minutes for delaying us," Vayl observed.

"Yeah, yesterday . . . I feel different than I did then."

Slight raise of the eyebrow, signaling imminent sarcasm. "No. Really?"

"Will this last?"

"I have no idea."

I followed the minivan for several blocks, then took a right onto the street that led to Umberto's.

"So tell me what you did today other than work activities," Vayl suggested. "How did you spend your free time?" I had to think a minute, dig out my mental binoculars to see past the blackout and the moments before it. Why was it so hard to recognize the woman who'd spent most of her daylight hours clicking through encrypted files, looking for dirt on politicians like some commie-hunting throwback?

Stardust in your eyes, sister. Only now it's time to blink.

So I began talking, starting with the family phone calls. But they required a back story, and that took a while, especially since I kept pausing to point out a fab new color I'd discovered. Eventually I worked my way back around to the research I'd done, specifically the background stuff I'd gathered on our oversight committee.

"Did you come to any conclusions?" he asked after I finally finished talking. I shrugged.

"All the senators are suspect because they all seem *way* too innocent. Doris Fellen gives away tons of scholarship money every year. Dirk Tredd is a true-blue war hero. And Tom Bozcowski was an extremely popular quarterback in the NFL before he shattered his knee." I didn't tell him I'd stared at their publicity photos for hours on end, trying to see behind the facade. It didn't bother me so much that one of them had tried to eliminate us. We knew the risks when we signed on. But to put the lives of the citizens of your own country into the hands of monsters and terrorists—to be honest, the more I thought about it, the readier I was to nail said senator to the wall. With a telephone pole.

"And then there is Martha," said Vayl.

I shook my head. "Man, I hope it's not her."

Vayl put his hand on my arm. "You must accept that someone in your inner circle could betray you."

"Oh, I accept it. I just know, of all our suspects, if Martha's the rotten link there's no *doubt* we'll be coming out of this bruised and bloody."

"You mean you prefer the senators?"

"Absolutely. They can't be nearly as mean, conniving, vicious, and underhanded as Martha."

"She is an excellent secretary, isn't she?"

"The best."

Umberto's is an Italian restaurant located in a miniature pink castle. Only it wasn't exactly pink. It shimmered with shades of silver and rose too.

"I'm beginning to like that color," I murmured as I pulled into the lot, picking a spot where we could exit quickly. I swallowed hard on a spurt of nerve-induced nausea. This whole meet could go south in a heartbeat if Vayl and Cole got to feeling competitive. And it would be my fault for not controlling my hormones better. Damn chemicals. Why couldn't our bodies run on something simpler—like coal?

An image rose in my mind of Vayl and me walking around belching black smoke rings. I laughed inwardly. Wouldn't that change the world though? Everybody would have automatic dental coverage just to keep their teeth from looking like the inside of a chimney. And we'd be recycling our solid waste because sludge makes such nifty ashtrays.

"Would you care to share?" asked Vayl as we headed for the restaurant entrance, his cane hitting the asphalt every other step with a reassuring clink.

"Huh?"

"You are smiling."

"Oh." So I told him what I'd been thinking and we were both chuckling when we came through the door and met Cole, who stood waiting for us there.

He covered well, but I could tell he wasn't pleased to see Vayl and me sharing a laugh. *Dammit.* I know in other places kisses don't mean much. Shoot, in Hollywood they do inconsequential smooching all the time. But to Cole, and most other people in the real world, kisses are significant gestures, not something you play with as I had. I bit my lip, forgot it was still healing from the last bite, and nearly made myself cry. So much for my postdonation high. The express elevator Vayl had taken me on came to an abrupt halt. The jolt left me with a roaring in my ears and a major craving for chocolate-chip cookies followed by a good hour of card shuffling.

"Uh, Cole, this is my partner, Jeremy Bhane. Jeremy, this is Cole Bemont."

Vayl held out his hand. "Pleased to meet you."

"Likewise," said Cole. They shook. I waited for Cole to wince, but Vayl reined in his bone-crushing strength. I sighed with relief.

The hostess showed us to a booth in a corner lit by a couple of candles and a low-wattage, recessed bulb. The decor diverted me enough to make me stop kicking myself and enjoy it. The carpet sparkled with every hue of green imaginable. It contrasted nicely with the white tablecloths and folded napkins. The menu covers felt like real leather. So did the cushioned seats.

Vayl and I sat across from Cole. We ordered drinks—Diet Coke for me, beer on tap for the guys—and the hostess left. "Lucille tells me you are a private investigator," said Vayl.

I expected Cole to squirm under Vayl's icy-blue gaze. He didn't, and I liked him better for it. *Crap.*

"That's right," he said, "although it's not turning out to be what I expected."

"No?"

Cole shrugged. "It's pretty mundane. And I'm not always sure I'm helping the good guys."

I spoke up. "Well, let me assure you that we are the good guys."

"Yeah?"

I looked at Vayl and he nodded. So I took out my ID

and slid it across the table. Cole opened it, studied it for quite some time.

"I had a feeling you weren't just another rich snob," he told me. Despite the fact that he wore white Nikes with black dress pants, his hair looked like he'd just stepped out of a hurricane, and he smelled of citrus gum, Cole suddenly looked all grown-up as he slid my badge back to me. I slipped it back into my jacket.

Our drinks came, we ordered supper, and the waitress left.

"So, Cole—" I began.

"What happened to you?"

"Huh?"

"Your neck." He nodded at the bandage. I'd completely forgotten about it. My hand flew up to it as if I could hide it from him. Vayl bumped his leg against mine.

"Oh that." I smiled, because Lucille would've. "I burned myself with my curling iron. Second degree."

Cole nodded, apparently satisfied. "You were saying?"

"Um, okay, we've been investigating Assan for a while now, and we're sure he's a big hitter in a terrorist group called the Sons of Paradise. We know he's performed surgery on fugitives. We know he has a powerful new partner and a plan of attack that could threaten the entire nation, maybe even the world. We think the documents we need to stop him and his partner are in his house."

Cole whistled in disbelief. "And you think I can get them for you?"

Vayl sat forward. "Possibly. We hope you can at least provide us with information. You do, after all, have a connection on the inside."

Cole locked his hands together and played thumb wars with himself for a few seconds while he processed. "I don't think Amanda knows anything about her husband's shadow life. She sure wouldn't have hired me if she did."

"We need access to her house, especially to her husband's office," I said, hating that I had to push. "But we don't want to spook her. No telling which side she'd land on if she knew the truth. All we want is for you to convince her that, to help further your investigation, you and your partner need to take a look inside his desk, his computer, and his safe."

"My . . . partner?"

I nodded. "That would be me."

Our food came. Cole started stabbing at his lasagna. Vayl and I traded looks.

"What's wrong?" I asked.

"You already have a partner."

Crap.

Vayl nudged me. "If you will excuse me," he said, "I think I will go wash my hands." I let him out of the booth. Cole didn't exactly glare at his back as he left, but I got the feeling he would've liked to.

"Cole." I sank back into the seat. "Last night, kissing you, was the closest I've been to a relationship in . . . a while."

"You make that sound like a bad thing."

Crap in a bucket! We had only traded spit, *that's all*, and now he thought he deserved an explanation. Worse yet, so did I. I took a deep breath. His hands, exhausted from thumb wars, rested on the table. I put mine over them.

"Cole—" I stopped. Had to. Memories exploded out of

the suitcases I generally kept them locked in. Voices. Screaming. Blood—some of it mine. A surging black hatred that nearly swallowed me whole. No way could I put all that into words. No way would I take anyone else back into the hell I still visited in nightmares. So I gave Cole a sketch, knowing he could never imagine the full picture.

"About fourteen months ago, I was a Helsinger. Are you familiar with that term?"

Cole nodded slowly. "Yeah," he said, straightening in his seat as if I'd just called him to attention. "Helsingers are elite teams of vampire killers, named for Dracula's nemesis, Dr. Van Helsing."

"Excellent," I said. He responded to my praise like any good student would, with a smile and a satisfied little nod.

"We didn't start out as a tight-knit group," I told him, "but we ended up that way. There were ten of us in all. I fell for a hard-charging former Navy SEAL named Matthew Stae. My brother, David, was on the team too. That's how he met Jessie Diskov. And when he married her it seemed perfect, because we were already like sisters."

Cole turned his hands so they held mine and squeezed. It was a little depressing holding his hands, because he would soon come to understand why I was too dangerous to touch.

"Some of what happened to my Helsingers on the night my life changed forever is classified. Some I just don't remember. Here's what I can tell you. We'd spent the day clearing out a nest in West Virginia. But we missed the Vultures. That's what we called the leaders. They'd holed up so deep we couldn't find their resting places before dark, and we didn't dare stay longer without our own vamps there to back us up."

Tangents, ah, I love 'em. They keep you at a safe distance from painful subjects. But this was one train I needed to keep on track. "Anyway, they came back for us that night, before we had time to regroup. By the next morning the only crew members left breathing were me and my twin. And David only survived because he wasn't there. He was in the hospital, sidelined with two broken ribs from a previous mission."

"Jesus."

"Oh, you can bet I stopped talking to *him* that night. I lost my team, my fiancé, my sister-in-law. And my brother blamed me for all of it. It was *my* crew after all, my responsibility to see they got home safe after every mission." Like a tired, old dam, my throat began to ache from holding back the torrent of tears that threatened to drown me if I released them. I finished as fast as I could. "So you can see why I can't have a relationship with anyone, especially a nice, normal guy like you. A guy stays with me long enough, he *will* die."

"Unless he's a vampire," said Cole.

Cole stopped my fabricated reply with a raised hand. "I know Vayl's a vamp, Lucille. I can smell it on him."

"You . . . you're a Sensitive?"

"Yep."

"But . . . how? I mean, were you born that way, or—" I stopped because he was shaking his head. His own bad memories were beginning to make his palms sweat. He squeezed my hands and faked a smile.

"I was born in New York," he told me, "just outside of Buffalo. Lived there till I was six, in an old white farmhouse with an actual barn and a pond out back. My brothers and I were skating on that pond one fine January afternoon when I fell through the ice. I was under the water for fifteen minutes before the firemen fished me out."

"So . . . you died?"

"Yeah." He was trying to act casual, in case I began to scoff at his life-altering experience. As if I could after what I'd survived.

"Was it . . . awful?"

He shrugged. "I don't remember. The doctors said kids will do that when an event is too traumatic to bear. I guess it's still too much for me. But afterward"—he leaned forward, eager now that he knew I'd listen—"it was like you hear about in church, Lucille. There was a light, and then my grandpa was there waiting for me, and he had my dog, Splinter, with him. It was"—his eyes shone, making me smile—"absolutely fabulous."

"And when you came back . . ."

"I could sense vampires and other things that ran in the woods east of my house. Between that and the horror of almost losing me, my parents decided for a new, ice-free scene." His gesture encompassed the whole state when he said, "So here I am."

I nodded, my neck creaking under the weight of this new information. I wanted to ask a dozen more questions, because Cole was the first of my kind I'd ever gotten to talk to like this. But he beat me to it. "So why *did* you let him bite you?" he asked.

My hand flew back to the bandage as if it was magnetized. "That's none of your business."

He took the time to blow an orange bubble and pop it

before he said, "No, but it's the price I'm asking if you want me to help you out."

I stared at him, reframing this new picture of him so that it fit with what I'd already seen. "That's very personal," I said.

"I know." Cole dropped his eyes to our intertwined hands, feeling a little guilty, maybe, but not enough to back off. "Tell you what, you give me an honest answer and I'll give you the real truth about why I'm working for Amanda Assan."

Suddenly I felt like it was my bet in a game of high-stakes poker. I looked closely at Cole, trying to interpret his intentions. But his face, usually so much more expressive than Vayl's, gave nothing away. Did he have a straight flush or a pair of twos?

"Okay, Cole," I said, "I'm all in. But if I get my butt kicked on this deal, I'm sharing the pain."

"Fair enough," he said, trying to hide his triumphant little smirk. "So why'd you do it?"

Maybe I could've given him the party line and he'd have bought it. I might've convinced him with the argument that had swayed Vayl. But people rarely ask me for the truth, and when they do I feel compelled to give it to them.

"Part of me just wanted to know what it was like," I told him. "Part of me wanted to feel that vital, to know that without me, Vayl would have lost more than his life. He'd have lost that navigational beacon that lands him on our side of the wall. Because there's nothing more demonic than a starving vamp. And part of me"—*whoa, this is going to be embarrassing*—"just wanted to be close, to be connected to somebody else. Like I said, it's been *a while*."

Cole grinned and brought my hands up to his lips. "Then maybe I have a chance after all."

I rolled my eyes. "Do you *ever* stop?"

He appeared to think about the question. "Not often." His grin said, *I'm wicked fun.* "Women are my passion, my weakness, and my joy. And you"—he kissed my hands again—"are a paragon among them."

"You make me sound like some blue-haired preacher's wife."

His grin twisted. "God forbid."

I took my hands back, settling Cirilai down on my finger from where it had twisted up to my knuckle. "I did my bit. Now tell me why you're working for Amanda Assan."

I thought he'd stall, maybe rearrange the salt and pepper shakers or file the sweeteners by color, but he came right out with it. "I am a PI. But my specialty is supernatural crime. Amanda's brother, Michael, died six months ago in India. He was traveling with Assan at the time. She thinks *he* might've had something to do with it."

"Just because he was there at the time, or . . . ?"

"It was a combination of things. Assan didn't show much remorse for her brother or sympathy for her. Plus the circumstances of his death were odd, and Assan's explanation came out sounding pretty lame."

"In what way?"

"Michael died of a single stab wound to the heart. The weapon, according to the coroner, was an ancient sword of unknown origin. Assan collects swords. Also, symbols were found burned into the skin around Michael's wound."

"What kind?"

"Magical, as far as I can decipher. But I'm no expert and my sources haven't been able to translate them. I'd draw them for you, but—oh." He caught our waitress's eye and signaled her over. She found him a pen and some paper and left us after we reassured her we didn't need any refills.

While he sketched the symbols for me, Cole said, "Assan was in India to give a presentation at a conference on reconstructive surgery. He said Michael, who'd also been a plastic surgeon, had wandered off during one of the meetings, and when he still hadn't returned the next morning, Assan reported him missing."

"He waited long enough, didn't he?"

"Yep. And the meeting Michael left was one he'd discussed with Amanda. He'd told her it would make the entire trip worthwhile."

Yeah, the whole deal sounded about as fishy as a tuna factory. Cole went on. "The icing is that some poor guy who thought he needed an early-morning jog found a torso on the beach last week. Sharks had swallowed a lot of the evidence, but according to a friend of mine who works homicide, the victim had been murdered. By a single stab wound to the heart. And around that wound—"

"Glyphs," I finished. He nodded. "The same as these?"

"Yep."

"Wonder what Vayl will think of them." I ignored Cole's frown as I studied his drawings. Then it struck me that Vayl had been gone *much* longer than even an arranged absence should take. "Where *is* he?" I asked, peering through the atmospheric gloom. Suddenly the hair on the back of my neck stood up in response to the ripple of power that rolled across the room.

"Did you feel that?" I asked Cole. He nodded, looking grave and a little shaken. I slid out of the booth. I think I said, "Excuse me," but I'm not sure. The power called me with an urgency I'd never experienced before. It came from the other side of the restaurant, so that's where I headed, followed closely by Cole.

"Vayl?" I whispered. "Where are you?"

I smelled it before I felt it, a revolting combination of rotten eggs and ash that lashed my inner senses like a lion tamer's whip. The magic snapped past me, leaving me mentally singed, as if I'd stood too close to a burning soul. At least I knew now Vayl wasn't its source. His power had never made me want to shower in bleach water. This came from an altogether different sort of vampire.

I turned, searching for the vamp's target. I found him almost immediately, a spectacled, balding man in his mid-thirties with the soft face and hands of someone who hires out his yard work. He sat at a table with three other people, presumably his wife and sons. They stared at him in speechless shock as he clawed at his throat, his face turning a shade of red I'd never seen before tonight.

"Charlie? What's wrong?" The woman half rose from her chair, but Charlie was way ahead of her. He jerked to his feet, toppling his chair backward in the process. Now the other patrons had stopped talking, had turned to look.

"I think he's choking!" screeched an elderly woman whose ebony cane might've been related to Vayl's. I expected Charlie to nod, but his hands had moved to his chest, pressed flat against it as if to keep his innards from revolting and becoming his outards.

The kids, two blond-headed cuties about seven and nine, sat absolutely still, but I noticed they were clutching each other's hands. Somebody yelled, "Call 911!" and the whole room erupted, everyone talking at once, the woman screaming, "Charlie, Charlie!" and people from my side of the room rushing over to get a better look.

Charlie keeled over, still holding his chest, and I felt the power flare out so quickly I could almost believe someone had pulled the plug. Almost.

I needed to find Vayl. *We* needed to locate Charlie's attacker. But before I could act, Charlie, himself, stopped me. He lay on the floor, his eyes open and yet empty as marbles. I'd seen a lot of dead guys in my time, and Charlie had definitely joined the club. But I'd never seen what happened next.

This dazzling light emerged from Charlie's body and hovered over it like morning mist. Only it looked more substantial. It was as if a Charlie-sized diamond floated three feet off Umberto's carpet, each facet giving off its own unique color. Then, as if some cosmic hand had reached down and turned the wheel of a kaleidoscope, the diamond split, spun, and reformed. Now multiple jewels danced in the air above Charlie's body. A moment later they flew apart like a spectacular Chinese firework.

One shot straight into the wife's mouth, quieting her immediately. One went to each boy, landing gently on their foreheads and then sinking out of sight. Several exited via windows, walls, and doors, and I suspected they'd find their way to his dearest friends and relatives tonight.

The largest one shot straight through the ceiling, destination unknown, but I—jaded, cynical Jaz—was voting for heaven.

"That is some amazing backwash you've got there, Vayl," I murmured.

"What?"

I turned to look and there he stood, not three feet from me, watching the action from a small nook formed by a ceiling-high rubber tree plant and the corner of the bathroom entryway, his power at its usual simmer. Most people would've looked straight at him and never seen a thing. Nobody was looking but me, however, so I was the only one who saw him "solidify." It was like watching a computer sketch fill with color. One moment he was a chalk drawing. The next he was a stern, handsome gentleman admiring the greenery.

"Vayl—" I began, but Cole stepped up, yanking Vayl's sleeve so he would turn and face us.

"Who did this?" he demanded. "Who just killed that man while you stood and watched?"

"It was not my place to interfere—"

"Goddammit, this is not a *National Geographic* special! You're not supposed to huddle in the bushes and film the lions killing the zebras. You're supposed to kill the lions!"

"We *are* the lions," Vayl corrected, "and we must be extremely careful before we challenge another pride. The odds must be in our favor, yes?"

Cole looked ready to go caveman on Vayl's head. "Yes," I said, taking Cole's hand and squeezing until he turned his attention to me. "To kill from a distance"—I shook my head—"that's badass power, Cole. You don't just jump in the path of that. Not unless you want to get seriously maimed."

"Who *are* you people?" Cole whispered.

Vayl and I shared a stony look and a chilling silence. Though John Q. Public knew we existed, he rarely wanted to be reminded. We were thinking Cole would feel the same.

A couple of EMTs arrived and Charlie left on a mobile bed with his stunned family trailing behind. Umberto's manager finally convinced everyone to return to their seats, offering half off their dinners to keep them from bolting. It pretty much worked.

"Cole." I turned to him, took a deep breath, and said a mental goodbye. "Get out." *Get out, get out, get out.*

"Now, wait a minute," Cole and Vayl chorused, looking at each other with consternation as they realized they shared the same opinion.

"Have you ever fought a vampire?" I asked Cole.

"No, but—"

"Then there's no point in staying, is there? Get out while you still have your humanity."

"But what about—"

"We'll call you, okay?" I said, not meaning it, hoping I could talk Vayl out of using Cole's connections, tempting though they were. My little hike down memory lane had reminded me too well how much it hurt to lose good people, and the longer I knew Cole the more I knew he was good people. "Just, please, take off before the vamp that killed Charlie realizes you're with us."

He looked hard at me, trying to decipher my expression. "Okay, I'll go. As soon as you give me your number." I started to argue but, like a magician sliding an ace out of his sleeve, Vayl pulled out our business card and handed it to him.

Cole read it aloud. "Robinson-Bhane Antiquities—Specializing in Eighteenth Century Rarities." He looked at Vayl. "I guess you can do that when you've had firsthand experience." Vayl didn't even raise an eyebrow. I'd begun to think nothing surprised him, not even being outed as a vamp by a PI who looked like he'd just jumped off his surfboard.

"Call us when you have made arrangements with Amanda Assan," Vayl said.

"I will," Cole replied, giving me an I-will-return look.

I nodded, hoping he'd pocket the card, forget where he'd put it, and wash it along with his pants. Then all he'd have left of me would be a wad of crumpled paper with some blurry writing on it.

Before I realized what he was doing, Cole leaned in and stole another kiss. "I'll see you," he said. He turned and left.

"I hope not," I murmured as I watched him walk out the door.

"Jasmine . . ." Vayl's voice had dropped and softened to the point where I barely recognized it.

"Vayl?" He looked like he'd woken up to find some vital body part missing.

He shook his head. "Is the vampire still with us?"

"Yeah."

"Let us take a walk then, shall we?"

"Okay." We headed back to the table, taking the long way around the restaurant. As we walked, Vayl spoke in a voice that only just reached my ears.

"Perhaps you should get out as well."

It took every bit of focus I possessed not to keel over right then and there. "What the hell are you talking about?"

"Your life, Jasmine. Your short, beautiful life." I recognized Vayl's expression. It said, *If you're going to break my heart, make it quick.* The last guy who'd shown it to me had been my high school sweetheart the night I left him behind. Though I could tell he didn't want to, Vayl kept talking. "You wish to protect Cole from the very thing that defines your existence. What does that say to you?"

"*I* define my existence," I told him through clenched teeth. "*I* choose to be here, now. Cole didn't have that choice. He just fell into it. That's a good way to drown." *And he's already done that one too many times.* Vayl let it go.

We made it back to our seats with no extrasensory alarm going off in my head. "The vamp must be in the bar," I said as we sat, hoping my businesslike tone would calm us both. "Move in, or wait?" I itched to deliver some old-school violence to Charlie's killer's table. Action, that's what I needed. All this thinking was driving me nuts. But I knew what Vayl would say.

"Wait."

We waited. We made small talk. We ate. It's all part of the job, in the end, and we try to do the job well.

Now that I knew the vamp's scent, I could differentiate it from Vayl's much better than I had at first. It stayed in one place for another hour. Then it moved. We'd already paid the check, so we moved too. Still we almost blew it. Like most vamps, this one came with an entourage, and the last of the group was stepping into a glistening black limo when we reached the parking lot.

One of the first lessons I learned at the absence of my father's knee was that life isn't fair. Sometimes innocent little kids get stuck with dads who keep leaving and moms who hand out far too many whippings. And sometimes those are the very kids who grow up to learn that everybody leaves sooner or later, by chance or by death, and it's never fair. So, though it wasn't fair at all, it was still true that the one guy still standing outside the limo possessed the ability to spot federal agents at a distance of fifty yards. Apparently he also had the ability to deal with them, because he motioned for his three buddies to leave their seats and join him. They headed our way, the four of them stopping with about fifteen paces left between us—what I like to refer to as dueling distance.

It felt like the OK Corral on steroids. There they stood, making a formidable first impression even without the Tech-9s they held casually at their sides. I felt my skin tighten in alarm at the ease with which they carried those deadly weapons. These were guys who would shoot first and ask questions never. *Why was I ever scared of the monsters I thought were under my bed?* I wondered. *These are the real bogeymen.*

Despite the crisp January breeze, the goon who'd spotted us wore a sleeveless gray T-shirt, exposing massive tattooed biceps. Beside him stood a tall, redheaded man whose mustache grew down either side of his lips to his neck and farther south until it disappeared into his chest hair. He had that look in his eye that said, *I've killed things with shovels and enjoyed it.*

A bright red scar split the third man's right cheek into

halves, the knife that had caused it also leaving behind one milky white eye to remind its owner to dodge a little sooner next time. The fourth man had Chinese eyes, a Russian weightlifter's physique, and an American biker's goatee. He grinned, revealing a couple of gold teeth, and pointed a long, sheath-covered fingernail at my chest.

"You got a problem?" he drawled, obviously expecting me to pee my pants before falling to the ground and groveling like an unworthy subject of the emperor. And that was all it took. A new, screw-you attitude took precedence, trampling my fear under its boots. A highly dangerous approach, I still found it much easier to bear.

"Well, it all goes back to my childhood . . ." I began, but the emergence from the limo of a black, high-heeled pump attached to a shapely, stockinged leg interrupted me.

"I don't like the looks of this," I murmured to Vayl.

He just grunted. He centered on the show now as a second leg joined the first. Silver sequins glittered as moonlight hit the hem of her knee-length dress. One elegant hand came out to grasp tattooed dude's paw and the rest of her finally appeared.

"Hey, look, Vayl," I murmured, "it's Vampire Barbie."

From her waist-length platinum hair to her surgically enhanced boobs, she looked like she'd been plucked from some Hollywood director's fantasy. The neckline of her dress plunged so deeply I hoped she'd used the extra-strength lingerie tape. Her huge violet eyes slanted just slightly, enough to give her the exotic look of some sheik's plaything.

"Get a load of this," I said. "Perfect makeup, perfect nails, perfect figure—it makes me want to shove her headfirst into a steaming pile of horse crap. Why is it you can never find a mounted policeman when you need one?"

Vayl had no answers for me. At all. He'd gone as still as a billboard photo.

"Do you know this woman?" I asked him. When he didn't answer, I shook him. He looked at me, his eyes blank. Dead.

"Who is she?"

"Liliana. My late wife."

Chapter Ten

Not a day goes by that I don't miss my Granny May. Mom, well to be honest, I'm kind of relieved she's gone. But *her* mother's passing still gets to me, even after three years. Sometimes I want to see her so badly it's a physical pain. Now I just wished she was here to prop me up, because damned if I didn't feel dizzy.

I watched Vayl watch Liliana approach us and totally failed to figure out how he felt about it. I, on the other hand, felt very clearly that the world had just begun to spin in the opposite direction. "Your . . . *late* . . . *wife?*" I whispered.

Vayl nodded, just a slight jerk of his head. "She died. Then she killed me. Ergo . . . *late* wife."

That song started going through my head, the only words I remembered being the most pertinent at the moment. *How bizarre. How bizarre.*

Vayl's voice sounded robotic, a programmed conversational gambit offering no meaningful detail as he said, "Whatever happens, Jasmine, do not take off Cirilai." *Who? Oh, duh, the ring.*

Still basically clueless, I fell back on what Granny May used to call my "spider sense." (She was a big fan of

Marvel Comics. Dave inherited her collection, the lucky bum.) She had meant my woman's intuition, and even without my newly honed senses to back it up, it thrummed like a tightly strung web. The rate of thrum increased when Vayl added, "Under no circumstance should you draw your gun."

Grief, a comforting lump under my jacket, contained some Bergman-engineered options that would work beautifully on Liliana. And he didn't want me to pull it? *Nuts!*

"Vayl—"

His look, foreign and glacial, silenced me. I suddenly felt outnumbered.

"This is not something we can escape through violence," he said, thawing slightly as I searched his eyes.

"What about through the *threat* of violence?"

His lips twitched. "One cannot encounter you without sensing that threat. Tonight it should be enough simply for them to *know* you are dangerous."

I disagreed. I hated to question Vayl's commitment to me or to the Agency, but he'd just dropped a big old bomb on me. What else had he been hiding? Should I, God forbid, mark his name down next to Martha's on the suspect list?

I felt like I was looking at a portrait as I gazed into his empty eyes. I'd seen life in them plenty of times, but now I felt stupid to have assumed *his* life had anything in common with my own. He wasn't a monster. I'd seen enough in my time to recognize the difference. But he wasn't a man either. Could I ever *really know*, could I ever *really trust* someone so different from me and mine?

Vayl and I stood staring at each other, teetering at either end of a finely balanced lever. Should I step off? Would he?

"What are you thinking?" he asked.

"That you're up to no good." I sighed. "I hope Granny May was right."

"About what?"

"About trusting my sp—my intuition."

"Grannies are generally very wise in these matters."

Yeah, but mine never met a vampire.

Liliana strode forward, clearly put out that we hadn't unrolled the red carpet for her dramatic entrance. I gave her a look meant to be blank.

"Your kitten is bristling," Liliana told Vayl.

"I would not push her," Vayl replied, leaning just slightly on his cane. "Many before you have found her to be more a tigress than a kitten."

Whatever happened to "Hey, how are you?" "Long time, no see." Apparently you don't have to observe the rules of etiquette when reuniting with a murderous spouse.

"How did you find me?" Vayl asked, his voice absolutely even. I took my eyes off the Bad Boys for just a moment to confirm what I had sensed shaking underneath that husky baritone. Yeah, it was there, in small movements most wouldn't notice. A lift of the shoulder. A jerk of the head. The hollowing of a cheek that said he was biting the inside of his mouth. Vayl was fighting enormous rage, something so big that if he released it he might never get it all back in the box.

Oh boy. I'm in smart-ass mode and Vayl wants to break his ex's neck. If we don't play this right they'll be scraping parts of us off the bumpers of these cars for days.

Liliana flipped a chunk of her long polyester hair back over one shoulder. "These surroundings are rather . . . public, don't you think?" The smile she gave Vayl could've cured frostbite. "Come into my car." It wasn't a request.

Vayl's gaze cut her like an arctic wind. "No."

"You owe—"

"I owe you nothing."

She moved so fast her arm was a blur. Vayl caught it just before her hand connected with his jaw.

"Back off, bitch," I snarled. With no time to draw Grief, I'd resorted to my primary backup, a wrist sheath loaded with a syringe. The needle was halfway into her hip before she could look down to see what was pinching.

A series of mechanical clacks drew my attention to Liliana's goons.

Chinese dude had added a sawed-off shotgun to his arsenal, pulling it out from behind his long black coat like a *Matrix* groupie. The tattooed wonder and his buds had their guns locked and loaded and trained on us as well.

"What is in that syringe?" Liliana demanded.

"Slow, painful death by way of holy water," Vayl told her.

"My men can kill her before she depresses it."

"Then I will finish what she has begun. But perhaps you would prefer to talk?"

Liliana responded with a pretty little pout I was sure she'd practiced in a mirror before she'd gone out for the evening. "All right, then," she said. "You always did like to have things your way." By mutual, unspoken agreement, I withdrew the needle and Vayl pushed her away. The goons let their barrels drop.

"Is that really how you remember our lives together?" Vayl asked grimly. "Because I have the scars to prove otherwise." Good God, had Liliana inflicted those marks on Vayl's back?

"You earned every one of them," she said viciously, looking as if she'd like to hit him again.

"Maybe." For a fleeting moment Vayl's guard fell. His expression became as bleak as a dying man's. Then it was gone, replaced by cold, hard hate. "Who told you I was here?"

"Why, Vayl, it's not like I've been looking for you for the last two hundred years. I could have found you anytime I wanted."

He shook his head, his eyes so dark you could imagine walking right through them and emerging in a whole different universe. "Not true. Someone tipped you off to my whereabouts."

She tilted her head, her hair forming a little river of silver behind her. "What makes you so sure I was looking for *you*? But I did get your attention, yes? You enjoyed my show?" She inclined her head toward the restaurant. "I thought you would appreciate the irony of two sons losing their father."

Vayl's power spiked and the temperature in the immediate area plummeted. But he didn't reply. If he'd tried, he probably would've spit sleet in her face.

"You must admit I have improved over the centuries," Liliana went on. "Once I would have had to sink my fangs into him to kill him. Now it takes only a scratch."

She slid her fingernail against her creamy white forearm to demonstrate. A thin line of blood rose from the wound she'd opened. "And the best part is, I can draw that death out as long as I wish." Vayl stared at the blood on Liliana's arm as she pulled her hands apart as if stretching time. His hand convulsed on the head of his cane as she clenched her fists. Did he imagine poor Charlie's heart squeezing under those lethal nails? She stepped closer.

"Do not let her touch you, Jasmine," Vayl commanded. "Just a drop of her blood mixed with yours will kill you."

Liliana recycled the pout. "Only if I want it to." She gave me a look I recognized right away. It was Tammy Shobeson, the sequel. I half expected her to kick me in the shin and call me a sissy-pants crybaby. Her psychic scent hit me again, and the stench of death and decay backed me up a step. "My dear, there is no need to be afraid. I won't hurt you . . . too much." She darted a flirty little smile at Vayl, but he'd lost his appreciation for cruel humor. And apparently she blamed me for that. When she met my eyes again I felt like that poor goat they'd set out to bait the tyrannosaurus in *Jurassic Park.* And that's when she saw my bandage. Her eyes narrowed instantly. My hand flew upward, a protective gesture I couldn't seem to shake. Her gaze moved to Cirilai.

"Vayl," she said, her voice sort of hollow sounding, as if she was speaking from the bottom of a well, "why is this"—she made an I've-just-seen-a-cockroach face—"*eichfin*—wearing your ring? And her neck—have you marked her as well?"

I didn't like that word, "marked." It sounded too much like a dog raising his leg on his favorite hydrant.

"She is my *avhar*," said Vayl.

It took all my self-control not to turn to him and say, "Your who?" I'd never heard the word before. No, wait. Vayl had whispered it to me last night as he left my room. It hadn't registered then, but now I knew it meant something significant because the news hit Liliana like a wrecking ball. She lapsed into steaming silence, made a dismissing motion with her hand, and the four stooges backed off. Though I was relieved she'd elected to delay the war, I suspected she still meant to wound us. And, like most homicidal maniacs, she followed the profile to the letter.

"Has Vayl fulfilled his end of the bargain?" Liliana asked me, her voice as sweet as powdered sugar. She took my silence for the answer she wanted and went on. "An *avhar* carries a great burden and responsibility," she told me. "Therefore, she also receives certain privileges, one of those being the right to know every detail of her *sverhamin's* past."

My what? I darted a look at Vayl. *You've got some explaining to do, buddy.*

"Liliana," Vayl growled. The panther prepared to pounce.

"So I just wondered if Vayl has told you about his sons—*our* sons—and how he killed them—"

"Enough!" Vayl's voice rang with power. Somewhere nearby a meteorologist had flipped out because the temperature had just plunged from fifty-nine to oh-crap-cover-the-oranges. I shivered as frost coated my eyelashes and my lungs filled with winter. Liliana's gunmen, not being Sensitives, weren't faring nearly as well. They blew

into their hands and stomped their feet, and I heard the Tattooed Wonder say, "I can't feel my nose."

"You four," Vayl barked, "get into the car!" They snapped to attention, did a quick about-face, and marched right into the limo. "And you"—he regarded his former wife like a mongoose facing a cobra—"get out of my sight, for *good* this time!"

She bared her fangs and hissed at him, a fairly hilarious reaction in any other circumstance. "I could offer you an alliance with the most powerful vampire on earth. But you, with your human *avhar*, do not deserve to kiss the hem of the Raptor's robes."

Son of a bitch! She's working for the Raptor! My instinct was to take her down, and I already hated her enough to fuel a charge. But I hadn't done more than twitch before Vayl set his cane across my path. *Nuts!*

"Do not believe this is over," Liliana warned. "You cannot guard her every moment. You cannot see in every direction at once. I have only to wait until you blink."

"Harm one hair on her head and I will burn that laughable wig of yours with *your* head still in it."

I felt a sudden urge to applaud as Liliana muttered an insult I couldn't quite translate, my Romanian being limited to "Yes," "No," and "Where's the bathroom?" But, to my surprise, she did retreat to the limo. The door slammed shut and it pulled away.

"So," I said, "we're just letting them leave?"

Vayl headed for the Mercedes. "No, we are letting them think we let them leave. Come."

We hurried to our car and pulled into traffic a comfortable distance behind the limo. Ordinarily this would be an easy tail considering the make of their ride. But inside our Mercedes the atmosphere was far from relaxed. Finally Vayl said, "I do owe you an explanation."

"Damn straight." *But suddenly I'm not sure I'm ready for one.* "For now, just tell me what I need to know to survive this mission. You can save the rest—"

"—for the plane ride back?" We smiled at each other. "At this rate we will have to fly to Ohio by way of Portugal." Our shared laughter eased the tension, and by the time Vayl spoke again he sounded more like himself.

"I think, first of all, we must consider that you may have been the target of these attacks all along."

"I'll buy the God's Arm attempt," I said. "But why would they expose *you* to snake venom and poison *your* blood?"

"Think about it. They did put me in a vulnerable position, one in which you insisted that I take your blood to sustain me. Most vampires would have drained you."

"Yeah, but you didn't hurt me."

Vayl stopped me with an irritable shake of his head. "You are still looking at this like a human being. Look at it from a vampire's perspective."

Vayl stopped, stared hard out the window, and by the time he met my eyes again I knew we'd made the same leap as we chorused, "The senator is a vampire!"

Chapter Eleven

"It makes perfect sense," Vayl rushed on as I tried to gather my scattered thoughts enough to keep us from crashing into the nearest electric pole. "A vampire would know that, when faced with a deepening hunger, I would turn to the nearest possible source of nourishment."

"You make me sound like a granola bar."

"Jasmine!"

"I'm joking. I know it wasn't like that. Go on."

"Most vampires, at least the ones who scoff at the idea of assimilation, would have drained you without hesitation. This one is, I believe, no exception."

"So do you think Liliana's alliance offer is related to the attempts on my life?"

Vayl shrugged. "It is hard to say. Especially now that she has her own reasons for wanting you dead." He looked at me with regret. "I am sorry. She bloodies everything she touches. I never meant for her to know you."

Or for me to know about her? I shrugged. I'd come to realize it was none of my business, especially since I was keeping some serious information from him too. "So are we really saying that one of the senators on our oversight committee is a vamp who's gunning for me? I mean, that's where we're going with this, right? I saw Martha right before we left. She was still human then."

Vayl nodded. "And still is, I will wager. But that does not clear her. It only makes her a potential partner, or patsy, of the senator."

"A senator though? Are we sure we're sober?"

"Remember I told you at the beginning that something seemed off about this mission?"

"Yeah."

"The committee was supposed to meet with us before we left. They called it a six-month review. Despite Pete's reassurances that he and I were happy with your performance, they wanted to ask you a whole slew of questions. Something about making sure we had made the right decision."

The specter of my past lifted its raggedy head and cackled. The thought that it might always haunt me felt wretched. I wanted to crawl into the nearest bed and burrow under the covers until I was just a lump. Nobody expects anything of lumps. It could be a peaceful existence. Unless you'd just eaten chili. And I liked chili. Never mind.

Vayl went on. "Then, without warning, the senators canceled their interview. They said this new mission was much too urgent to put off any longer. Although when I discussed it with Pete he made no mention of a need to rush."

"So what are you getting at?" I asked.

"If the interview had taken place, the undead politician would have been forced to attend. You are a Sensitive. As soon as you entered the room you would have pegged the vampire."

"A vampire senator." I shook my head. "Scary. But how did they figure to pull it off? People in Washington get kind of suspicious when you only come out at night."

Vayl shrugged. "Technology has befriended the human race; I imagine there are times when it smiles kindly on vampires as well."

Well, maybe. Or maybe our senator had a double. Public figures had done the same throughout history. Or maybe he or she was so newly turned and this plan so quickly hatched that he or she could go a couple of weeks in the dark without raising suspicion. Bottom line, our senator had found a way.

I said, "Okay, so at this point we have a dirty plastic surgeon with terrorist ties allied with a Most Wanted vampire allied with a senator, all of them working under the auspices of the Raptor, who seems interested in offering *you* access to a plot that involves a big, scary virus." A thought occurred to me. "The Raptor's got to know how long you've been with the Agency. Why would he expect you to suddenly change allegiances?"

"His perspective can never be considered unless you include a mind-numbing dose of power. I would assume he feels he has a better deal to offer me. One in which I would find myself at great advantage to my present position." I didn't understand the expression Vayl made next, though instinct told me it was in response to something that had happened in his past. "He cannot fathom a vampire who would willingly distance himself from the *treasures* he offers." He spat the word "treasures," like it tasted vile.

We both fell silent, thinking about the Raptor, a vampire who had become the nemesis of every government of every developed country in the world. If we could get to him—on our terms, not his—to say the safety and stability of the world would increase exponentially would not be an overstatement.

The limo ahead of us slowed, searching for parking. It had led us to South Beach, where the pretty people met to PARTAYYY! Bars, restaurants, two theaters, and a comedy club, all dressed up in Art Deco and neon, shared the neighborhood with the establishment in front of which the limo stopped. The place resembled a Jaycees haunted house, from the rocking tombstones that spelled out CLUB UNDEAD on the fake granite facade, to the glowing skeletons that hung from the second-floor balcony, to the green lights that outlined the entire building.

Despite the fact that many party hounds still sat at home whimpering into their doggy pillows, a steady stream of handsome men, beautiful women, and gorgeous men dressed as women moved up and down the sidewalks. Braving the unseasonal chill, even more revelers sat together at the tables that lined the walk, enjoying the company, the booze, and the cheerful glow that came from twinkle lights lining the frames of their patio umbrellas.

Lucky for us, Liliana and her goons had to wait in line before Club Undead's bouncer, a twenty-first-century version of Frankenstein, let them in. That gave us the slack we needed to secure a parking space in an open lot just down the street. We left the car and joined the crowd, sauntering as close to the club as we dared before finding a spot in a darkened doorway beside a closed deli to make like cuddling lovers.

I stood in the circle of Vayl's arms, fighting distraction.

This whole new spectrum of color had opened up to me, but I couldn't relish it. I felt like a security guard at the Louvre, forced to watch the potential thieves when I really just wanted to stare at the *Mona Lisa*. As it happened, that lovely little side effect was just the first in a series of brushstrokes that would eventually reveal an entirely new picture of my life. The second had just begun to show its shadow, a creeping feeling of immense imbalance, when Vayl interrupted my inner inventory.

"There is something else you need to know." His voice rang loud, almost strident, in my ear. "I did not kill my sons."

"Do I look that gullible?" I asked. "Geez, Vayl, I don't believe half the things *you* say and I *trust* you." I didn't realize he was holding himself rigid until he sighed and slumped against the wall at his back. Hours passed as we kept silent watch. People came and went, none of them of special interest to us. Finally, Vayl began to speak.

"I was nearly forty," he said quietly, his chin just level with my nose. "My boys were almost grown. Hanzi was fifteen. His brother, Badu, was thirteen." Vayl spoke their names as if they were holy. "Liliana gave me five children altogether, but Hanzi and Badu were the only ones to survive infancy. And so . . . we spoiled them." He lapsed into silence. I felt my heart break a little for the couple he and Liliana had been, desperately sad for their lost children, desperate to make sure their living children survived.

Something near the apex of my aching ribs started to quiver. I felt like I was about to get a really grim phone call. And though Vayl was laying out the story of his tragic life for me because some warped vampire rule said

I deserved to know, I knew the feeling wasn't coming from him.

"They grew wild right in front of my eyes," he continued. "And by the time I mustered the courage to tame them it was already too late. They went from teasing dogs with sticks to breaking windows with stones. When they drove into camp one afternoon in a wagon they had stolen . . . I snapped. I raged at them. I whipped them. I forced them to return the wagon with their apologies."

The modern girl in me thought, *Vayl's family was camping? What, were they trying to save on hotel bills?* The next thought, riding a sea of embarrassment, washed over me with the speed of a tidal wave. *They were gypsies.*

"What happened?" I asked.

"The farmer they had stolen it from shot them both before they had a chance to explain."

"Oh, Vayl." I held him tight, and not just because my heart bled for him. That feeling of wrongness had intensified. The little girl in me urgently needed a teddy bear. "That's awful," I murmured.

Vayl made a sound in the back of his throat, a primal distress signal, the kind you might hear from elephants as they mourn over the bones of lost brothers. "I wanted to kill the man because I could not kill myself. I blamed him completely. I heaped my own weakness and self-hatred upon him until just shooting him was not enough. I wanted him to die slowly, over days, even weeks, if possible. I wanted him to sink into horror as if it were quicksand."

"What . . ." I swallowed, sick with this nameless feeling of dread, appalled by Vayl's story. "What did you do?"

"I became the horror." His voice dropped to a whisper. "It was so easy. My family"—he frowned—"my father, my grandparents, you have discerned by now that they held certain . . . powers?" I nodded, Cirilai warming my finger like a living thing. "Though I had never felt the call to take part in their rituals, I had watched them work all my life, lifting curses, saving souls. Now I simply did the opposite."

"How?"

"I took three wooden crosses, profaned by the blood of murdered men, my own sons', in fact. I set them in a triangle and stepped into its center. I called upon the unholy spirits to send me a vampire."

"And?"

"They answered my plea. But they made sure he met my wife first."

"I'm so sorry."

"It was a long time ago, lifetimes ago. There is no need for you to be sorry."

"Well, I am, but that's not what I was talking about."

"What then?"

"I'm sorry I have to stop you telling a story that was so hard to start. But we have to go. *Now*." I grabbed his hand and pulled him out of the shadows, onto a sidewalk lit by streetlamps and some other source my new vision appreciated but couldn't pinpoint. I led him to the corner, where we stood facing a stoplight, the music from a heavy-metal band blatting through the walls of the bar behind us.

"What is it?" Vayl asked as we waited for traffic to clear.

"Hard to describe." I squeezed his hand, trying to stay calm, to separate new shades of neon and the screaming street music from the barely leashed panic that made me feel like jumping out of my skin. "That song," I finally said, "by Lynyrd Skynyrd. Remember the words? 'Oooh that smell.'"

"Yes," Vayl said quietly, his eyes darting around the street, fixing every person, every street sign and park bench in his mind.

"That's it. I'm smelling that smell, the slow descent into misery and helplessness. And on top of that, the scent of vampires. Something foul is going down behind Club Undead." *And I'm afraid to go look.*

But when the light changed we moved. Halfway to an alley that festered like an infected sore behind all those festive lights and decorations, I began to cough. The closer we got, the more the coughing turned to gagging. By the time we reached the first Dumpster I felt like someone had locked me in a hot car with a rotting carcass. I puked beside a trio of dented silver trash cans and wished to God Umberto's had shut down before I'd had a chance to eat an entire plateful of their spaghetti.

I squeezed my eyes shut, more a reflex of the upchuck than a need to see in the dark, and when I opened them the alley glowed, not just green now, but muted yellow and bloodred as well. *God, what's happening to me?*

I stood up, Vayl steadying me as I looked around. Small piles of garbage huddled next to overflowing Dumpsters like a bunch of freshmen who hadn't made the dance squad. Potholes full of greasy water marked a path down the alley only a staggering drunk could have followed. A couple of three-legged chairs leaned against a brick wall under a rusty fire escape. And in the middle of it all stood a vampire who must have spent part of his past battling Neanderthals and wrestling mammoths. Long, dark hair and a full beard hid most of his features. His mountainous frame blocked 90 percent of my view of the alley behind him. But the man lying at his booted feet showed up fine.

Another vamp knelt beside the prone man, gripping the edges of his torn shirt as she pulled him toward her bared fangs. I blew out a disappointed breath when I realized her hair was short, curly, and real. Not Liliana after all.

The moment stretched into another plane, where time froze as we all tried to plan our next move. My attention riveted on the downed man, who's slow-blinking, unfocused eyes and blood-soaked collar bore witness to the attack he'd just survived.

Oooh that smell.

I looked at him closely, trying to pinpoint the source of his scent.

The mountain man saw us and started speaking in Russian. The tone was wary but not yet warning. For all he knew, Vayl had simply decided to duck out of the club for a midnight snack. As Vayl answered, I tried to unravel the mystery of this pitiful human lying on the garbage-slimed pavement one block from where Miami's beautiful people met to play. In the words of Granny May, he wasn't *right.*

Standing this close to him felt like wading through swamp water. If you could distill the scent of maggots on manure, you might come close to his aroma. But it wasn't body odor or bad breath. The man definitely bathed and

Scoped on a regular basis. In fact, for somebody whose pallor reminded me of a mortician with mono, the guy looked remarkable, a male model who'd made one too many round-trips on the express elevator.

The smell of death surrounds you.

His lips moved, though no sound escaped them. He mouthed the words "Save me," then slumped into unconsciousness.

I drew my gun, my forefinger lingering on what I called, to Bergman's delight, the magic button.

"I'll take the girl," I said, mostly because she looked like a runner, and I was highly motivated to put some distance between myself and the man she'd bitten. With my free hand I transferred the car keys from my pocket to Vayl's. "Do me a favor, when you're finished here. Take the guy to the hospital. If I had to do it I think my head would explode."

Vayl nodded, taking all his weight off his cane as he and Mountain Man sized each other up. I pressed the magic button and a mechanical whir signaled my Walther's transformation. The top quarter of the barrel opened to reveal a sheaf of thin wooden bolts no wider than a shish kebob skewer. Metal wings snapped open from each side of the barrel, the action also dropping a bolt into the chamber and cocking the metallic bow string that could send it flying nearly as fast and true as a bullet.

Vampirella gaped at me as I raised my weapon. She said, "You would not dare!"

"Yes," I said, "I would."

"I have done nothing wrong! I have a right to feed!" she responded, her voice shrill. She sprang to her feet, pulling the man up with her. He blinked, tried to focus, gave up, and passed out again. The bloodstain on his shirt spread as the wound on his neck began to bleed again. My hand started to shake as his scent rolled over me.

"You have no rights," I told her, trying desperately to dodge a wave of nausea. It hit me anyway, and the effort it took not to gag brought tears to my eyes. I blinked them away, talking fast, aiming high. "On the other hand, I have several, including the right to shoot vampires with an unwilling donor's blood on their fangs."

Screaming with frustration, she picked the man up and threw him at me. Heavy as a side of beef, he hit me hard and I went down under him, feeling like I'd fall forever, knowing there was no escaping the living death that oozed over me like a flood of yellow pus. I yelled and flailed at the inert weight holding me down, as panicked as if I was truly drowning.

The blackness came in a buzzing rush, and for the first time I reached out to it, thankful, ready to embrace it. Then the man's weight left me. I breathed fresh air tinged with the ice of Vayl's power. The man lay in a crumpled heap twenty feet away. Vayl stood over me, slashing at the male vamp with his cane. I looked for the female, trying to force my brain into motion.

Vayl moved and I sat up, feeling stupid and stunned. I retrieved Grief from where it had fallen beside me. I stood, stumbled off in the direction she must have taken, only years of training keeping me on my feet.

I heard a door click shut. Nothing was automatic. I had to tell my body to move toward the door. I concentrated on the handle, ordered my fingers to wrap around it and pull.

Inside, the thick, hot air pulsed to the beat of Latin dance music. The door snapped shut behind me and I sprang forward, the sudden rush of energy that replaced the nausea propelling me into the dancing crowd. I slid the hand holding Grief inside my jacket and followed the wake my quarry's passage had created. Winding my way between pale young thrill seekers and their immortal lovers, feeling myself come alive again, I could hardly tell the real vamps from the pretenders. And plenty of both filled all three tiers of Club Undead's multicolored dance floor. Leashed power sizzled and popped like cooking bacon, and I knew more than one of these bored rich kids would get burned tonight. In fact, one already had. He probably still lay in the alley like an abandoned lounge chair.

Who was he? What godawful horror crawled through his veins, exuding a stench that could knock me out like a glass-jawed boxer? Could cancer have sunk its claws into him? I didn't think so. Hundreds of people had crossed my path tonight. Some of them must've been fighting the big C. But they hadn't shown up on my radar.

I locked the mystery of the man's existence and the effect he had on me in a mental cabinet so it wouldn't distract me as I moved toward the door. I spotted Liliana and her goons, though none of them saw me. And I saw Assan talking to his vampire accomplice, Aidyn Strait. They stood at the bottom of an ornate wrought-iron staircase drinking and laughing, looking like they'd just figured out a foolproof way to rip off Fort Knox.

I slid past them all without alerting them to my presence and followed Vampirella out the front door. Frankenstein met me just outside. “Hey!” he bellowed as I tried to push past him. “I don’t remember letting you in.”

“You don’t smell like Frankenstein at all,” I said as I pulled out Grief, shoved it against his chest, and fired. “You smell like Dracula.”

A new wave of nausea hit me, but not as hard as before. Lucky for me my gal’s trail led away from Nightmare Alley. I followed her at speed, hoping for an open shot, finding none.

After running hard for several blocks, dodging partiers and pedestrians, she surprised me by stopping suddenly. She stood outside a lamp store, the light from the front windows throwing sparkling highlights onto her hair. Like an A-list actress, she oozed confidence. Somewhere between here and the alley she’d pulled herself together and the realization stopped me in my tracks.

She smiled and I liked her immediately. Her charm could melt glaciers. She might actually be the cause of global warming. I smiled back; how could I resist? Though the spike in her power told me her charisma ran on batteries, I lowered Grief, resisting the urge to drop it.

“That man back there, with the blood on his shirt, who is he?” I asked, wishing I dressed as stylishly as this beauty with her knee-length boots, short denim skirt, and silky red blouse.

“He is a friend of mine,” she replied. “His name is Derek Steele.”

I nodded. “He’s very sick, you know. Probably dying.”

Her smile wavered, seeming to shrink along with the rest of her. “Bad blood,” she whispered. “Aidyn, you son of a bitch, what have you done to me?”

Now I knew where I’d seen her. She’d been the small

half of the couple on last night's helicopter. Aidyn had called her Svetlana. I should've recognized her and Mountain Man right away. I could blame my lapse on Derek Steele's sickening effect on me, but excuses are for wimps. I really should've noticed. Between this, the wrecked Lexus, and the impulsive kiss, I may have just struck out. And I didn't even have a free afternoon to wallow in self-pity. At least I had my new friend.

I said, "I thought all vamps could smell bad blood."

"Not me. Not Boris," she said bitterly.

"So Aidyn set you up, huh? You must be part of his 'final experiment.' But it'll just make you sick, right? I mean, ultimately, you should be fine." I really wanted her to feel better. "Think about it logically. You must mean something to Aidyn. He wouldn't bring you here just to kill you."

"No. That is not why we came." Her voice dropped to a whisper as she worked it out. "The Raptor brought us here to propose an alliance between his Trust and ours. He is becoming such a powerful force, we had no choice but to come. To listen." Her eyes begged me to understand and, of course, I did. Who wouldn't? "But we could not agree to his terms," she went on.

"Terms?" I asked, feeling apologetic for interrupting her train of thought. But I really needed to know. "Alliance? I don't get it. What do you have that could possibly interest him?"

She shrugged and said simply, "Moscow."

Oh.

She went on. "We were fools to think he would let us leave peacefully. Edward must have burned inside that

Boris and I rejected his proposals. But he never showed it. Not once."

"The Raptor's name is Edward?" I asked.

She nodded. "Edward Samos." *Bingo!*

"And he's in Miami?"

"No. We met him on his jet. He flew out as soon as our negotiations ended."

"Do you know where he's headquartered?"

"No."

"Well, Edward sounds like a real shit," I offered.

Her head jerked in agreement. "I need an *avhar*," she whispered.

There was that word again. I had some idea what it meant, but maybe she could give me some clarification. "What would an *avhar* do for you?" I asked.

Her smile returned, switched to high-beam, her fangs making her look more deadly than a pissed-off biker chick. "She would be a dearly loved companion," Vampirella explained. "She would watch over me if I should fall ill and protect me, perhaps even from myself."

She took a step toward me. "*You* could be my *avhar*. I feel . . . so close to you already."

What a sweet thing to say! I waved my hand in front of my face as if the slight breeze could hold back tears. "I'm so flattered!" I said, feeling like I'd just won the Congressional Medal of Honor. Also feeling her power pulse against my skin like a warm waterfall. "But I don't think I'd do you much good."

"Oh?" She cocked her head sideways, her dimples making her resemble a tree sprite. "And why is that?"

"Because I can't be trusted. See, I feel so close to you, like we're best friends. But last year my best friend was killed by a vampire. In fact, I thought she was fully dead until she came to visit me three nights after her funeral. And though I loved her like a sister, and though I was strangely happy to see her, I had made her a promise before she turned. One I couldn't bring myself to break"—I raised Grief and took aim—"which was why I killed her anyway."

I shot Vampirella through the heart before she could move. And as I watched the breeze disperse her remains I whispered, "And that's what I couldn't tell Cole. Why David can't bear the sight of me. Why my brain sometimes gets stuck on replay. With friends like me, there really is no need for enemies."

Chapter Twelve

I pushed the magic button, stowed Grief inside my jacket, and hoofed it back to Club Undead in time to see Liliana and the Liliettes climb back into the limo. Aidyn Strait had joined them, making chummy with Liliana like they were long-lost pals. I started to go for my car, realized it was gone. Vayl had carried Derek Steele off to the hospital in it, leaving me temporarily stranded.

"Derek Steele." I snorted. "Sounds like the hero in a really raunchy Harlequin novel." Only none of those heroes ever found themselves donating blood in dark alleyways. *As if opening a vein in the comfort of your putrid pink hotel room makes you better somehow.*

"No, I'm no hero." A couple of die-hard fun-seekers gave me a strange look as they passed by. *Great. Now I'm standing out in a crowd. Man, am I slipping.*

It did feel that way, like all the layers I'd managed to stitch together to form my so-called life had shifted. Now nothing seemed to line up. I suddenly felt ancient, a tired old antique rusting on the sidewalk along with the metal trash cans. My knees quivered with the effort it took to hold myself up. Drained, as if a bad flu had grabbed me and shaken me till my brain rattled, I decided to find a better place to collapse than on the corner of Washington Avenue. I hailed a cab and slid in, giving the driver, who looked like he'd just gotten off *el raft-o Cubano,* directions to one of our backup hidey-holes. I called Vayl on my cell phone.

"Lucille?" He answered on the first ring. Only people who care answer on the first ring. The thought made me tear up. Which made me consider slapping myself. What had happened to the thick-skinned agent who yelled at old ladies and stonewalled handsome young admirers?

"I'm beat." My bruised ribs and cut lip began to ache, as if even I needed proof before I could give myself a break. "I'm going to crash at the condo until you're finished with your business. Can you pick me up there?"

"Certainly."

"Is everything . . . okay?"

"Fine." Meaning he'd handled Boris easily. *Good.* "We are just pulling up to the emergency room. I will probably see you in an hour or two."

"Sounds good. Drive safe."

He sighed, knowing I really meant, "Take care of my Mercedes."

We hung up and I spent the rest of the drive wondering exactly what kind of world had just opened up to me. It was as if my senses, two of them at least, had undergone a major upgrade. I could see a whole new spectrum of light. And I could sense great imbalances in human health. Now if I could only hear through brick walls I'd make a great sideshow for Barnum & Bailey.

The cab dropped me at the Star One Resort, a multilevel apartment building right on the beach. Most of the apartments were time-shares. So if I ran into anybody in the commons or the elevator, they wouldn't raise an eyebrow at the presence of a stranger.

The lock on the door looked intimidating. A metal-faced number pad with a digital readout prevented easy access, unless you had the right fingerprint. I did. I pressed my thumb on the small sensor pad next to the latch. The tumblers tumbled and I stumbled in, swinging the door shut behind me.

The room looked much better than the Bubblegum Bordello. The walls had been painted off-white. Evie would've called it something romantic like Ivory Lace. The chocolate-brown furniture felt like velvet and the dark gold carpet complemented the gold fleur-de-lis in the red-wine curtains. I opened them and saw a small balcony overlooking the ocean. Nice view if you had the time to enjoy it.

I shucked my boots and socks and plopped onto the couch, promising myself to try out the matching chair and ottoman before I left. And maybe, yeah, maybe if dawn caught us here I'd explore the garden too. It was on the roof and easily accessed from the bedroom by means of a stairway that hid behind the closet door. That extra escape route was what had sold us on the place.

Never mind waiting till dawn. I'll just rest here for a minute; then I'll check out the garden. I closed my eyes, breathing deeply the smells of recycled air (just the right temperature) and apple-cinnamon plug-ins.

I admit it. I blew it. I should've stayed awake, done some brainstorming, solved the mystery, and gotten myself a Scooby Snack. Instead my sleep-deprived bod yelled, "Break time!" and all systems hit pause.

I dream vividly every time I sleep. Even my power

naps remind me of Super Bowl commercials. This time I dreamed of Granny May, not as I remembered her, wearing faded jeans and bulky sweaters that made her extra-huggable. But as I imagined her, winged and haloed, living it up with Gramps Lew who, I was sure, had met her at the pearly gates with a bowl of popcorn and a Frank Sinatra movie.

We talked like a couple of beauticians, and she said a lot of things I couldn't recall later on, though I knew they were important. I do remember a feeling of deep, resounding contentment, the kind you mostly lose after the age of six. Then her face took on a look I recognized, but not from her. Suddenly she resembled my mom when I was about to hear the words "Grounded for life!" The contentment fled and I began to feel a familiar prickling sensation in my fingers and toes.

"It's not your time," Granny May snapped. "Wake up!"

I opened my eyes. I stood. I damn near saluted. I guess it's true that old habits die hard. So do old field agents. As soon as I recognized my magical alarm had not been dreamed, I spun to face the source of the power that had tripped it.

The balcony doors flew open and I could actually see the glass shivering as the doorframe hit the wall. In walked Vayl's former wife.

"You sure know how to make an entrance," I said. I sounded calm, amused. It was a total scam, and the scowl on Liliana's face told me she'd bought it. Good. It might give me a couple of extra steps when I turned to run. Okay, *if* I turned to run. I hadn't made up my mind on that yet.

"It is one of my finer qualities."

"How did you find me?"

"Your trail glows brighter than neon," she said, smiling as she saw the barb hit.

Shit! I was like the Texas hold 'em pro all the amateurs enjoy beating. I'd attracted a shadow I hadn't even noticed. *Is it time for a vacation?*

I think Liliana badly wanted to call me a candy-ass but just didn't have the phrase at the tip of her tongue. So she went straight to the point.

"You have something that belongs to me." She'd suddenly developed an accent. *She must really be pissed.* I snuck a look at my watch. Vayl might be on his way, but he wouldn't get here in time to back me up, much less save me. And I didn't much savor the thought of him scraping me off the carpet. *What to do? What to do?* My nerves were running around like earthquake victims, screaming hysterically and ramming into each other, causing no end of damage and helping me not one damn bit.

"Everything I have is mine," I told her. Wrong thing to say. Her eyes, including the whites, turned the bright red of fresh blood. Her hands twitched and I realized those perfect store-bought nails doubled as covers for retractable claws. They grew, even as I watched, to letter-opener length, and I knew they'd slice through skin just as easily as they'd cut paper.

"That is where we fundamentally disagree." She moved forward and to her left, intending to block my exit. Evidently she couldn't visualize me jumping off the balcony. It seemed like a bad plan to me as well. My adrenaline had already deserted me. *I'm so tired. Almost too tired to be scared. Almost, almost, almost—*

"I don't know what you mean," I replied. As she moved I did too, maintaining the distance between us as I inched closer to the bedroom door.

"Cirilai." She pointed to the ring on my right hand, her claws shaking with the force of her anger. "It is mine."

"Vayl told me his family made it for him."

"*I* am his family!" she spat. "It is my right to wear Vayl's ring!" She took a step forward and I pulled Grief. It was still in gun mode, but it stopped her. For now. So, of course, I egged her on.

"You're not his wife anymore, Liliana. You're not even his *avhar*. The ring is mine, and I'm keeping it."

She screamed. Like a banshee. On uppers. Caught in a vise.

I shot her as she charged. Three times—*bam*, *bam*, *bam*—in a nice tight pattern in the chest. Bright red blood spattered the wall behind her as she fell backward. She hit the dining room table on her way down. It teetered and crashed sideways under the impact. I used the extra time it gave me to turn and run.

Should've nailed her with a bolt, I chastised myself. *Should've pressed the magic button, Jaz.* I should've, but I hadn't, and there was no time now to figure out why.

My bare feet hardly touched the carpet as I sprinted for the bedroom door. Liliana's screams and growls spurred me on. I made it through the door, slammed, and locked it before she could reach me. It was a closer race than I'd thought. Just after the bolt shot home she banged into the door, making it shiver on its hinges. I got a sudden vision of a Liliana-shaped indentation on the other side and laughed. That brought on another scream of rage and a series of attacks on the door that would eventually shatter it. I headed for the closet and the stairs it hid.

I threw that door open and charged up the cold, concrete stairs, taking them two at a time. Another door, sturdy and metal with a bar across its middle that reminded me of the entryway to my high school's old gym, stood at the top. I hit it flying. For a millisecond I thought it might be locked and pictured myself bouncing off the handrail and down the steps like a bird who's just smacked into a third-story window. But the door opened easily, leading me out to the most amazing rooftop I'd ever encountered.

My first, brief impression of the garden was a feeling of bursting into fairyland. White lights had been strung in potted trees and along the latticework walls that divided the rooftop into numerous small rooms. Somewhere running water accompanied the sound of my breathing. It smelled like spring, but my toes curled against the cold night air and goose bumps rose like tiny mountain ranges along my arms.

A quick hunt bagged me a concrete bench whose top wasn't attached to its legs. I lugged the seat to the door and wedged it under the handle so it couldn't be depressed. Maybe it would hold Liliana long enough for me to make a clean getaway.

My escape route required me to cross to the other side of the roof, so I walked through the garden rooms as quickly as I could, avoiding tables and benches where people would sit with their morning coffee when this cold spell snapped, never knowing the story unfolding on this very spot.

Liliana's power snapped at my heels like a pit bull at the edge of its chain. It reminded me of Umberto's, and I sure didn't want to be the next poor slob to keel over in a plate of linguini. I rushed through arbors thick with vines. I slipped past statues of angels, wind chimes that swayed dangerously close to song, an empty concrete birdbath that looked abandoned and forlorn. I'd made it about halfway across the roof when Liliana's power peaked and a sudden, explosive noise halted me.

Liliana's voice hit the air like a jet engine. "I am not just going to kill you!" she screeched. "I am going to tear your chest open and drink the blood directly from your beating heart!"

"That's just gross, Liliana. Didn't your poor dead mama ever teach you any manners?"

I slipped to another section of the roof as she tracked my voice. Hopefully I could play mouse to her cat long enough to find the twin to the door she'd just destroyed. Then I'd run some more. The thought made me want to break something.

I could confront her, of course, maybe even smoke her if she wasn't too fast or too strong. If my aim was true. But I realized, though I wanted to kill her, I couldn't. Vayl should be the one to finish her.

I found the door, framed by hanging baskets, and gently depressed the handle. Nothing happened. It was locked. *Okay, Jaz, you are now trapped on top of an eight-story building with a homicidal vampire. Time for Plan B.*

Liliana's power settled on me like a thick fog. I began to sweat as I waded through it, somehow managing to reach the fire escape without making a noise. When I grabbed the rails to start my descent, I looked down and saw Liliana's limo parked under a streetlight. I only saw the car, but I couldn't believe she'd sent her goons home for the evening. Were they all huddled inside with the heat cranked, still trying to regain the warmth Vayl had stolen from them earlier? Were they guarding my escape routes, waiting to grab me the moment I thought I was free? Why hadn't Liliana brought them up with her? It seemed almost . . . fair.

No, not fair—confident. She was just that sure one puny woman couldn't stand against her amazing superpowers. She hadn't brought reinforcements because she simply saw no point.

I decided my best bet was to circle back to the door I'd come through. I managed to find my way through a maze of potted shrubs and outdoor furniture without making a sound. Part of the twisted remains of a hammock peeked out from beneath the blown door. The opening it had left beckoned. I'd just decided to run for it when her voice froze me.

"I thought you might come back here."

Shit! I wanted to bang my head against the wall, but figured that was a part of Liliana's overall plan and decided to leave it to her.

I turned around, my Lucille mask firmly in place.

She held out her hand, her smile both condescending and triumphant. Three dark blotches on her chest were all that remained of the bullets I'd fired. "The ring," she said, wiggling her fingers to make me move faster.

She had me on strength, speed, and pure evil intent. I'm sure she expected me to cringe and shuffle. Which was why my kick swept right up the center of her body without a block or even a delay. It contacted her beneath the chin, driving her head backward and breaking her jaw, from the sound of it. Off balance and staggering on her too-high heels, Liliana's only move: to reach forward, try to regain her balance. I couldn't allow that.

I kicked her three times in quick succession, contacting her high on the chest, moving her backward several steps each time. When her heels hit the lip of the roof, I jump-kicked her right over the side. She fell loud and long, her body making a spectacular watermelon-under-the-sledgehammer *whump* when it hit the pavement.

Oh no, it wasn't over. People wouldn't be willing to pay such a high price for immortality if it didn't come with some major perks. Her screaming might have stopped when her body met asphalt, and she'd be in no shape to demand anything more of me tonight, but she'd heal. Quickly. Bed rest and fresh blood would put her back on her feet by tomorrow evening. But for tonight, I had won.

I peered over the edge of the roof. The headlights from a couple of stopped cars lit the scene like something out of a Hitchcock movie. Liliana's body sprawled on the street, as twisted and disjointed as a scarecrow's. One driver yelled into his cell phone while the other checked her pulse. Liliana's car pulled up, screeching to a halt from its short trip around the block. All four goons piled out and went to work.

Two held off the protesting drivers with handguns while the others grabbed the unconscious vamp by the wrists and ankles and carried her to the car, reminding me of the deer Albert and Dave used to haul out of the woods after a good morning's hunt. They'd barely gotten her stowed and driven off into the night when sirens announced the arrival of cops who, having seen damn near everything pertaining to the supernatural, would probably believe every detail of the drivers' stories.

Considering the noise we'd made in the room before coming to the roof, I decided even my ID might not stand between me and a visit to the police station. Not a comfy thought with Vayl due any minute and dawn following him like a stray dog.

I ran down the stairs, gritting my teeth against the pounding my poor feet were taking. When I got to the room I went straight to my socks, pulled them on, and wrapped my jacket around my feet before punching into my phone the special combination of numbers that would provide me with some semblance of privacy while I talked. Ignoring the blood spatters on the wall, I stared hard at the drawer pull on the end table next to my chair while I waited for an answer. I got one on the twelfth ring.

"Hullo?"

"Pete? It's Jasmine."

"Don't tell me you wrecked another car."

"Okay."

Medium pause. I heard rustling, probably him checking out his bedside clock, because the next thing he said was "Do you know what time it is?"

"It's after five a.m. here."

Silence. I half expected him to start snoring.

"Get to the point, Parks."

"I didn't wreck the car."

"Spit it out, Jaz."

"Please don't yell at me."

"I'm not yelling!"

"I know. But you might be. Soon."

"If you don't start passing on some real information soon I'm going to yell at my wife. Then you'll have guilt."

"Manipulator."

"Spill."

I ran a hand through my hair and got Cirilai caught in some tangles. As I tried to free myself, I said, "I pushed a vamp off a roof tonight."

"Not part of the mission, but acceptable."

"Not really. The cops are coming up here soon, and they're not going to believe I'm innocent when they see the bloodstains."

"Bloodstains?"

"I shot her first, here in the room. And her goons came and took her away while I was still on the roof, so I have no proof she and I fought."

"Your ID—"

"—could be faked. I don't have the time to talk myself out of this situation, Pete. Dawn's coming."

"All right. Let me talk to them."

"I heard sirens. They'll be here in a sec. In the meantime—"

"Don't you dare sing me a lullaby."

"I wouldn't dream of it. I just wanted you to know, we think one of the senators on our oversight committee might be dirty."

"They're politicians, Jaz. It kind of goes with the territory."

"You're tired. I get it." I told him about our suspicions, wondering how much really sunk in. The guy might actually still be asleep. Dave could do that, carry on a perfectly logical conversation with you in the middle of the night and then not remember anything about it the next day because he'd been mostly asleep the whole time. "Pete, are you awake?"

"Yes, Jasmine, I'm awake. It's your fault too. I want you to remember that."

"Believe me, I will. And, um, we've got the senator thing covered from here, okay? If you get nosy and get yourself killed I'm gonna have to put your kids through college or something, so do me a favor and steer clear."

"You know, last week Ashley was talking about getting her PhD at Yale, so I have to say I'm a little tempted. But don't worry. There's a reason I hire the best."

Wow. Now I have to ratchet it up a notch—keep deserving that remark. "Hang on. Somebody's at the door."

I opened it midknock. The cop on the other side looked slightly stunned that I'd responded so quickly. Even more so when I handed him my badge and the phone and said, "It's for you."

He took it like it might be rigged to blow and held it about six inches from his ear. "Hello?" he said while his partner hung back, his Glock out but pointing at the floor for the moment.

The first cop listened for a while and when he gave me an amused look, I relaxed. When he chuckled, I started to fume. No doubt Pete was telling him all about my tendency to leave a trail of twisted cars and blood-spattered walls that a blind dog with a cold could follow.

"Did she really?" asked the cop. He laughed louder and motioned for his partner to listen in on the call. All told, Pete kept them entertained for another three minutes and twenty-five seconds while I leaned against the wall and timed them. At 3:26 the cop handed me the phone and my badge.

"He wants to talk to you," he said; then he nodded, headed out the door and down the stairs with his partner close behind.

"I take it I'm off the hook," I said as I shut the door.

"Yup."

"Thanks."

"No problem."

We hung up. Since my toes still felt like icicles, I went into the bathroom, shucked my socks, plugged the tub, and ran in enough hot water to soak my feet. I could see the front door from where I sat, so I was aware of the chiseled marble look on Vayl's face when he entered the condo a few minutes later. That all changed when he saw the blood on the walls.

"Dear Christ!" He staggered sideways, caught his balance on the stove, and pulled his phone from his pocket with shaking fingers. "Jasmine, be all right. Please be all right," he whispered as he dialed, his face suddenly very human and extremely worried. He jumped about three inches off the floor when my phone rang. I answered it.

"Make it quick," I said. "There's somebody else in the condo with me and he looks alarmed."

He didn't say a word, just dropped his phone, came over, and picked me up off the edge of the tub. It's a little disconcerting being dangled effortlessly. Plus, I generally equate bear hugs with lumberjacks and friendly purple dinosaurs, not with suave, sexy vampires who savor a daily dose of necking.

"I thought you were dead," he said.

Ah, that explained the momentous show of affection. "So you knew Liliana was coming after me?"

"I . . . had a feeling." I let his evasion stand for now. But in my mind I drew the line. One more and I would raise hell. Or, smarter but less satisfying, ask him to come clean. He let me slip through his arms until my feet touched the carpet. Then he released me completely. I stepped back. Ignored the vast sense of loneliness that suddenly swamped me. Fought the urge to touch him, reassure myself I hadn't just hallucinated that embrace.

"I am sorry I left you. I suspected she would come after you, only not so soon. She has always coveted Cirilai, first because she was my wife and thought she deserved it. Then because our sons were dead and she thought I did not."

"So . . . you've never . . . taken it off before?"

"No. Not for Liliana. Not for anyone. Until now."

Oh God, oh God, oh God. I mentally slapped myself. *Don't panic, Jaz. Every time you panic all hell breaks loose, so do—not—panic.*

"You're right. She came for the ring," I told him. "She demanded it from me."

"What did you do?"

"I shot her. Then I pushed her off the roof."

He smiled. Not the twitchy twitch, but a genuine, full-face smile. "You must have really wanted that ring."

I retreated behind the chair I'd napped in and buried my hands into the back because, frankly, I suspected there might be hyperventilating in my not-too-distant future, and I needed a strong base to lean on. I looked into his remarkable eyes, just now a warm, honey-gold with flecks of amber, and nodded. "To be honest, I did want it.

I do. I'm . . . I can't explain how honored I am to be wearing it. But, also, to be honest, the whole deal terrifies me."

"And that is because . . ."

I took a long look at the stitching on his collar, the urge to cower my way out of this conversation damn near primal. He and I had been tiptoeing around the subject so long I suspected if I made us face it squarely, one of us would be required to cut and run. A perfectly acceptable reaction if you had a place to retreat to. Neither of us did. "I've only been your assistant, your *avhar*, for a while," I finally said, avoiding his gaze. "I'm not exactly sure what I've agreed to, and yet I can't imagine any other kind of life. When you gave me this ring . . . when I gave you my blood . . . it's . . . We've gone beyond anything I've ever experienced with another person. We're trusting the safety of our souls to each other." Just saying those words made me a little dizzy.

He raised my chin with a gentle finger, and I winced as our eyes met. The look we shared pained me in its naked honesty.

"You are my *avhar*. I am your *sverhamin*. The intensity of that relationship has taken us beyond the bonds between coworkers or teammates." He waited for me to speak, his eyes hot with emotion.

And, God help me, I wanted to say what he wanted me to say. But I couldn't. I was still too . . . wounded. It seemed like a strange way to describe me. I'd never been in better physical condition. But it was the most appropriate word I'd found yet.

"After I lost Matt and my crew, Evie kept pushing me to put my feelings into words. She thought, somehow, that would make it all better. But I couldn't tell her I felt like I should be bleeding from every pore. I couldn't say I felt like I'd been flayed alive, that when I looked in the mirror every morning I couldn't believe my hair hadn't turned white overnight. It just wasn't close enough to the truth. So I didn't say anything at all."

"I understand."

I believed him.

"There's only so much a person can go through, Vayl."

He regarded me seriously. "There is only so much a person can go through alone. But I will not ask you to do anything you cannot bear."

"So . . . I can keep the ring?"

"It is yours," he said. "No matter what happens, that will never change."

Chapter Thirteen

I drove Vayl back to the Pink Palace, leaving the room-cleaning chores to the experts. The Agency employs a whole fleet of them for obvious reasons. We made it inside with barely twenty minutes to spare before dawn.

"You look exhausted," Vayl said as I eased my jacket off my shoulders and hung it over a chair. I had something intelligent to say about that, but then I took my boots off and sank onto the couch, and I couldn't think past my body's loud and repeated cheers.

"I know I should let you sleep," Vayl continued, "but I am so relieved Liliana did not kill you, I cannot take my eyes off of you."

"*You're* relieved! When she caught me trying to make my getaway, I thought I was toast."

"And that young man I took to the hospital. His blood smelled so wrong, I was afraid just being close to him had damaged you permanently."

"Yeah, what the hell do you think is up with him?"

"I have no—"

My phone began to ring. This close to dawn it couldn't be good news and I hated to answer it. But Vayl retrieved it from my jacket and tossed it to me.

"Yeah?" I barked.

"It's Bergman. I'm in Florida, but I've gotta sleep. Do you need me tonight or can I meet you tomorrow?"

"Tomorrow's good."

"Where do I look for you?"

"Hang on." I covered the mouthpiece. "It's Bergman," I told Vayl. "Do you know of a good place he and I can meet tomorrow?"

He thought a moment; then his eyes lit. "Actually, I do." He gave me the address and I passed it on to Bergman, along with an agreeable time. When we hung up I said, "So where are we meeting?"

Vayl looked vaguely embarrassed, like I'd just caught him and his pals plotting to stroll on over to the Silver Saddle, where girls dance mostly naked and all the drinks taste like sour lemonade.

"Vayl?"

"The place is called Cassandra's Pure and Natural, after the woman who owns it. It is a small health food store."

"Nice front," I drawled, getting more and more annoyed at Vayl's hesitation. Hadn't we just had a major moment? What the hell was he hiding? "And if you pay Cassandra a little extra?" I asked.

"She will take you upstairs and give you a reading."

"A . . . what?"

"She is psychic. She will touch your hand or read your tea leaves or deal your tarot. Whatever you like."

I slumped onto a couch and started to mutter. "Unbelievable. After what just happened between us . . . no, I don't have any right. None at all. I have to—"

"What in God's name are you babbling about?"

I jumped to my feet. "I'm so sick of your mysteries and evasions I could puke!"

Vayl's eyes went black. He looked like a drill sergeant about to demand push-ups. "You are overstepping your bounds," he said slowly and distinctly, so even we neurotic idiots could understand.

"I don't think so! You work with me for six months before offering a single viable explanation as to why you requested me in the first place. You put Cirilai on my finger and then announce to your *ex* that I'm your *avhar*. You tell me you've met somebody who might be a willing donor and then this psychic—"

"Actually she is the one I was thinking of."

"Either you trust me or you don't, Vayl. I'm fed up with being the last one in the know!"

Vayl sat across from me. "All right," he murmured. "If you will know it all, then I will tell you." He looked at me balefully. "Though I think you ask too much, you are my *avhar*."

"There is a theory," he began, "one I hold dear, that says nothing can truly be destroyed. Everything that was ever present will always endure in some form. That is as true of souls as it is of water and wood." He cleared his throat. If he'd been wearing a tie he'd have loosened it. "I believe my sons exist somewhere today as they did in 1751. I believe they live, physically, somewhere in this world, and so, wherever I go, I find a Seer, in the hope that I will be directed closer to them. In the hope that I will see them again."

"You're saying . . . you think they've been reincarnated?"

He nodded. “I have been told we will be reunited in America. It is why I came here.”

“What . . . what do you . . .” I paused. How to ask this without causing more pain? “So you want to meet them? Make friends? Be . . . a father to them?”

“I *am* their father!” he snapped. “That is the one, incontrovertible truth of my existence.”

I shut my mouth. Then I opened it again, but only to say, “Cassandra’s is fine.”

He stood up. “Ask her about the signs they found on Amanda Assan’s brother’s body. She studies ancient languages the way you shuffle cards.” As in, obsessively. “It may take her some time, but she will not stop until she finds a translation.”

“Okay.”

“Dawn is coming.”

“Yes.”

He shoved his hands in his pockets. At the moment there couldn’t have been a bigger gap yawning between us if we’d been standing on opposite sides of the Pacific. I was sorry for it. And grateful. “Well,” he said, “good night.”

“Good night.”

He moved so silently I wouldn’t have known he entered his bedroom and closed the door unless I’d been watching. If vampires dreamed, and if it would be a comfort to him, I hoped he would dream of his sons.

Chapter Fourteen

I switched my phone to the other ear and shook out the hand that had been holding it. Muscle cramps from clutching the thing tight, so I wouldn't be tempted to punch a wall. "Go on," I said.

"I'm having a hard time getting the wife to cooperate," Cole continued. He'd managed to keep my business card safe from the ravages of the washing machine. That was partly why I felt so violent. He'd kept his word and approached Amanda Assan with our plan and then called me with the results. Needless to say she was less than enthusiastic.

"No kidding?" I checked my watch. I'd only been up an hour and already my day utterly sucked. And not just because of the nightmares that had stalked my sleep, or because Cole had ignored my advice. True to form, Evie had followed through and left the number of Albert's nursing agency on my voice mail. I'd called them and they'd told me I'd have to put him on a waiting list. They had recommended another group in the the meantime, and I'd given them a call. But it bothered me to hire blind like that, not knowing a place's reputation. No choice, though. I sure wasn't going to make Evie do any back-checking in her condition and frame of mind. When I had a spare minute I'd do it myself. Meantime, Albert would be breaking in a new nurse named Shelby Turnett any minute now. I'm not big into prayer, but I did send up a wish that she had thicker skin than mine. She'd need it.

Now this. Trying to gain cooperation without threat leverage always annoys the hell out of me. People are just too willing to say no.

"Did she say why?" I asked.

"She was putting her jewels in the safe last night when he caught her checking out the contents of a small duffel bag she remembered he'd brought back with him from India. When she asked him about it, he told her to mind her own damn business. Then he ordered her to stay in the house for the next week. She had to sneak in her phone call to me. Apparently she's not allowed to talk to anybody either." A spurt of rage made me grit my teeth. I calmed myself with the reminder that soon Amanda Assan would be a free woman.

Cole went on. "She also said one of their houseguests had to go to the emergency room last night and for some reason Assan was more enraged than worried. Long story short, he's on a rampage and everybody in the house is kissing his ass until further notice."

"There's got to be a way to get a peek inside that duffel bag. I wouldn't mind checking out the sick houseguest either. Did she say where they'd taken him? Or was it a her?" He took so long to answer I thought we'd been cut off. "Hello?"

"I just had a thought and I'm feeling like an idiot for not thinking it before."

"What's that?"

"I have pictures of everyone Assan's talked to in the past two weeks." Cole sped up as he began to get excited. "Amanda hired me as the new pool boy so she and I could talk without making Assan suspicious. I might have a picture of that houseguest. And if Assan's meeting with terrorists, I might have the pictures to show which ones!"

Oh baby!

"I'm supposed to clean the pool today," Cole went on. "Why don't you come with me? You could meet me at my office and take a look at the pictures first. Then we could go to Assan's together. We'll both do the pool work; then I'll go to the kitchen, now that I know where it is"—he paused and I could tell he was smiling—"and distract the cook while you snoop around. What do you say?"

"This could be incredibly dangerous for you, Cole." I don't even think he heard me. He rushed on, like a parent-challenged teen planning his first kegger. "You know what else? I saw somebody the night we met. At the party?"

"Yeah?"

"As I was leaving, a door opened and a man looked out. I got the feeling we were having a mutual oh-crap-you're-not-supposed-to-see-me reaction."

"Could you identify him again?"

"No problem. Being purely hetero, I'm a little embarrassed to say this, but he was easily the best-looking guy I've ever seen."

Click. Blocks of information shifted and realigned in my brain as I realized Derek Stinkin' Steele must be the same stud Cole had glimpsed during the Great Bathroom Escape. And his amazing looks suddenly made sense in light of Assan's legitimate profession. It was suddenly imperative to know the man's true identity.

"Forget the pool work for now," I said, "and tell me you're a big fan of the Pink Panther movies."

"I own the whole set."

"Then I assume you also own a few disguises?"

"A dozen at least. I always do Amanda's pool work in disguise. That way they won't recognize me if I need to, say, crash a dinner party sometime." I could tell he was grinning. Despite knowing better, so was I.

"Excellent." I told him to meet me down the street from the hospital Vayl had taken Derek to. "How soon can you get there?"

"An hour."

"Good. See you then."

We hung up, and after a quick phone book search I found Samaritan Care Center in the Yellow Pages. Thirty seconds later I knew Derek was still there, reclaiming some lost fluids in room 429.

I kicked it into gear. I pulled the costumes I'd brought from my trunk. One would transform me into a working-class brunette, the other a truck-stop blonde. I chose brunette.

The hair was straight and shoulder-length. I stuck a red beret on top at a jaunty angle and a new girl began to emerge from the mirror. I called her Dee Ann. She liked to pronounce her name Dee-on and, though she worked as a bank teller, she pretended she could paint better than van Gogh. A man's shirt covered in multicolored parrots, blue jeans, army boots, a long green trench coat, and reflective sunglasses completed the ensemble.

I dressed in my room. My weapons case coughed up Grief and a small black box containing Bergman's latest prototype. It had started life as a Band-Aid. But Bergman had replaced the absorbent padding with a tiny bug. That went on the middle finger of my right hand. I stuck the receiver, a former hearing aid, into my left ear. Theoretically I should be able to attach the bug to Derek's skin, and it would transmit every conversation he took part in for the next two hours. Having had some experience with Bergman's new inventions, I wasn't expecting it to last more than twenty minutes. Hopefully that would be all the time I'd need.

On the way to the hospital I dialed Albert. I often called him in transit. That way I always had a good excuse to hang up. He answered on the second ring.

"Hello?"

"Hey, Albert, it's Jaz."

He chuckled and said, "Two calls in two days. Jazzy, are you turning into a nag?"

I had to slow down so I wouldn't swerve into a fire hydrant. Albert hadn't been nice to me—or anyone else—in years. Was he high?

"Just curious what the doc said," I replied, careful to keep my voice neutral.

"Said I could keep my foot—for now. I gotta tell you, I've never been so relieved about anything!" Ah, so that explained it.

"That's great!"

"So, uh, about the nurse."

"Yeah?"

"I cleaned the house. They're pretty anal about week-old sandwiches on the end tables."

"I imagine so," I said.

It is a strange and unfair phenomenon that children of crappy parents still love those parents. Despite my best efforts, I'd never been able to erase that feeling. So maybe it's understandable that I suddenly felt the urge to park the car and tap dance the rest of the way to the hospital, throwing in some classic Gene Kelly moves as I went. Luckily I managed to resist temptation.

"Did you hire one yet?" Albert asked.

"Yeah. She should be there in the next twenty minutes or so."

"What's her name?"

"Shelby Turnett."

Irritated snort. "What's the story on that, would you tell me? With millions of names out there made just for girls, why do they have to go and use men's names? As soon as you name a girl Bobbi or Terri or Shelby that name is ruined for men for all time!" I should've known the grouch in him couldn't be defeated.

"I gotta go now."

"Work or play?"

"Work."

"Have you noticed that's all you ever do? You should play more." He barked it, like an order, and I instantly wanted to work for the next forty-eight straight. Juvenile, I know, but he brings that out in me. I struggled to keep my temper in check.

"I think I've forgotten how." It was supposed to be a joke, but neither one of us laughed.

"Matt was good for you that way. He always made sure

you had plenty of fun to balance your serious side. You need to find somebody like him. It's been long enough." I knew, for him, that ended the subject. He had commanded me to move on, therefore I would. What a jerk.

"I have to go," I said as evenly as I could, considering I wanted to reach through the phone and smack him upside the head.

"Me too."

Beep. We were done.

Like a couple of Shriners who've veered off the parade route, Cole and I arrived at our meeting place in tandem and parked one behind the other. The minute he saw me he started laughing.

"This is serious stuff, Cole," I said, trying to sound stern.

"Aw, come on, Lucille, admit it: This is fun." He blew a big blue bubble and popped it all over his nose.

"You are so naive," I said, but I couldn't quite swallow the smile that kept surfacing every time I took in a new detail of his appearance. He'd gone with a pair of Drew Carey glasses. A green fishing hat, complete with dangling lure, hid most of his shaggy hair. Fake teeth gave him a slight overbite, and a gray jogging suit somehow managed to make him look wimpy and anemic.

"Check out the socks," he said, wiggling his eyebrows like Groucho Marx. He hiked up the legs of his sweatpants to reveal black dress socks. I couldn't help myself. I started to giggle.

"Those socks really bring out the turquoise in your sneakers."

"Did you notice they match my eyes? The shoes, not the socks." He batted his eyelashes as I pretended to inspect his legs.

I nodded. "I can see that. Now we just need to get you a handbag to complete the look."

He clapped his hands, fingers splayed like a three-year-old's. "Oh goody! Shopping!"

I shoved him toward my car. "Oh, just shut up and get in."

He looked at me brightly. "You mean I'm driving?"

"Yup."

He didn't argue the point, just jumped behind the wheel and started rubbing the soft leather of the seat as if it was his favorite cat. I got in beside him.

"So what's the plan?"

"We go up to Derek's room, pretend we're looking for our father. When he's not there, we both go into hysterics, thinking Dad's dead. You raise hell, I pass out and fall onto Derek. The key is, I have to touch him."

"Why?"

I showed him the Band-Aid.

"Hey, I was just asking a question. You don't have to flip me off."

"I was just . . ." I took note of the finger I was holding up and dropped my hand into my lap, laughing so hard I nearly blew snot all over the windshield. Cole started laughing too, and we sat there for a couple of minutes like two hyenas while deadly serious events moved forward without us. Eventually we would catch up, but for the moment it felt great to just let go. As much as it sucked to say so, Albert was right: It had been a long, long time since I could. Either Cole had come along at exactly the right time or I was going to have to carry him around in my back pocket for the rest of my days.

Cole glanced out his window and pointed at a black SUV that had just passed us. "Hey, I recognize those guys." He looked at me, his face suddenly sober. "They work for Assan."

I nodded and put on my seat belt. "Follow them."

I filled him in on the bug as we drove. Luckily the story only took a minute, because we didn't have far to go. They stopped in the loading lane of the hospital. One guess who they'd come to recover.

"Change of plan?" asked Cole, his eyebrows raised.

"Yeah. Follow my lead and we can still get it done."

"What are you thinking?"

I adjusted my wig in the passenger side mirror so I wouldn't have to look at him. Until now he'd still been on the periphery of this whole nasty deal. Now I was about to dump him front and center. The guilt made my stomach ache. "I think I'm about to get very sick."

Chapter Fifteen

I'll say this for Cole: He's flexible and functions well under pressure. Not a letter of recommendation I'd be happy to write considering what kind of people hire that type, but true all the same. We drove around the block and parked right behind the SUV.

"Come to my side and open the door," I said, feeling the blood drain from my face. "He's nearly here."

"Already?"

I didn't need to reply. Cole was already out of the car. Moments later he opened my door. "Undo my seat belt, and take your time about it," I said, that terrible feeling of imbalance momentarily blurring my vision. Something shook me at the core, as if the Ohio River had suddenly reversed course or all the grass in Browns Stadium had burst into flame.

"We have to meet them near the door," I said. "Be loud. Be scared. Make a major scene. Make sure something happens so I can touch him."

He nodded. "Ready?"

Hoping I wouldn't puke on Cole's nifty velour jogging jacket, I nodded. He pulled me out of the car and helped me toward the door. My blood seemed to jump in my veins, a warning so dire I would've turned to run if Cole hadn't been holding on to me.

"There they are," he said.

I raised my head, forcing my eyes to team up, show me the scene. The men, a couple of clones of the gatekeepers Vayl and I had dealt with the other night, had reached the first set of automatic doors. One pushed the wheelchair. The other strode beside it. Derek slumped inside it, pale and tired looking, wearing a black turtleneck and white jeans. His head was tilted to one side, as if to protect the bandaged area that reminded me forcefully of my last confrontation with his attacker. Then I realized he was watching his reflection in the glass doors.

"Smoke and mirrors," I murmured.

"What?"

"Now. Make it loud."

He raised his voice. "It'll be all right, honey." He clutched at me, gave my arm a comforting pat, and stepped us forward. We'd almost reached the entry doors. He waited until Derek and his entourage emerged. "Don't pass out on me now. It'll be okay."

I obliged and sagged, keeping one hand firm on the back of his jacket. It took an effort not to hit my knees. All I wanted was to puke until my stomach was as dry as an AA meeting.

"Look, honey, a wheelchair!" Cole maneuvered us into Derek's path, blocking his way. "You're leaving, right?" he asked them. "We need the chair, man. My wife's really sick."

"Get out of the way," growled one of the goons. He shoved Cole backward and I let go of him. This time I did fall, right into Derek's lap. I flailed my hands and managed to slap the bug onto the uninjured side of his neck.

"So sick," I muttered. Derek shoved me off his lap, leaving me in a crumpled heap. I considered just staying there. Hell, I was two yards from a hospital. Eventually somebody would discover me here, tuck me into a nice, clean bed, maybe pump me full of tranquilizers. I could legitimately sleep for a week.

Fortunately the person who hauled me off my butt was Cole. My hospital fantasy had barely played itself out before he'd strapped me back into the Mercedes. Actually, the seat felt even better than my fantasy bed. Love those luxury models.

I managed to focus on the road as Cole pulled away from the hospital entrance. The SUV was probably twenty yards ahead of us and gaining. "How close do we need to follow?" Cole asked.

I tried to remember what Bergman had told me about receiving distance. They drew farther ahead of us and, as my nausea diminished, my brain kicked in. "Just close enough to keep them in sight."

We fell farther behind and I sat up straighter, wiped the sweat off my upper lip, ditched the wig and the beret.

"Feeling better?" Cole asked, cocking a raised eyebrow in my direction.

"Much."

"That wasn't an act, was it?"

I shook my head. "There's something so far off about that man that every time I get near him I feel like the earth's about to break orbit."

Cole absorbed my reply with quiet attention. "How come I don't feel it?"

I shrugged. “I’ve become, what you might call, super-Sensitive since Vayl took my blood last night. I think this reaction is part of it.”

“Then we’d better find out what he’s up to. Are you hearing anything yet?”

“No talking. Kind of a steady thrumming sound. Knowing Bergman, this thing is so fine-tuned I’ll be able to hear Derek’s pulse, but his conversation will sound like Charlie Brown’s teacher. Wa, wa-wa, wa, wa.”

“Who’s Bergman?”

I held up a finger. “Someone’s talking,” I whispered.

“—Assan isn’t too happy with you,” said one of the guards. His voice was throaty and strained, probably lined with decades of nicotine buildup. I immediately dubbed him the Marlboro Man.

“I was just following orders.” It was Derek—whining. “It’s not my fault somebody decided to play superhero. You don’t think it’ll hurt my chances, do you? Assan promised to put me in a movie as soon as this was all over with.”

“I’m sure you’re fine. Who interfered with the experiment?”

“A girl with red hair and a man with a foreign accent. He had a cane. Said his name was Jeremy. I don’t remember anything more about her.”

“Well, between them they managed to smoke Jonathon and both your victims.” Jonathon must’ve been the doorman. It seemed strange to think of Boris and Svetlana as Steele’s victims, but that had been her take on the situation last night as well. The final experiment, my mind whispered, transferring the mutated virus from human to vampire. What did that do to the vamp? What did it do to the virus?

"The Tor-al-Degan's ritual is tomorrow. The senator's even coming," chided the Marlboro Man.

"How should I know that?" asked Derek. "I just do what he tells me, and he never tells me more."

"Well, here's what he's telling you now," said the other guard, his voice hard and sharp as an ax blade.

A loud, scraping sound drowned out part of Ax's message. Derek must've scratched his neck, or else gulped loudly, because all I heard was "—Undead tonight, and you're snagging him another vampire so he can finish his test."

"Tonight?" The whine had reentered Derek's voice. I suspected it never stepped very far aside. "I've lost so much blood. Surely tomorrow—"

"—will be too late," snapped Marlboro Man.

Again the interference kept me from getting the complete reply.

"—afterward?" said Derek.

"Leave them to us," said Ax. "We'll make sure of it."

The third time was the charm for the bad guys. The sound that had kept parts of their conversation from me resumed in earnest and when it finished, I couldn't hear anything more. Derek had killed the bug.

I looked at my watch. More time had passed than I realized. Time enough, at least, to ensure that I'd fully recovered for my next meeting.

"What did they say?" asked Cole.

I hesitated, but he was already in it to his neck. So I told him what I knew. "That ritual is going to be the key,"

I said. "If the senator's coming, so are the rest of the bigwigs."

"How do you know that?"

"Dude, that's just how politicians operate." *It's going to be such a pleasure putting a bolt through your shriveled little heart, Senator.* "Are you busy for the next hour?" I asked.

"Not really."

"Then let's chase another lead. Vayl knows a woman who might be able to decipher those glyphs you drew for me."

"Excellent." I gave him the address, and Cole took the next left, heading us away from Derek and his companions. At least now I knew what destroyed my balance every time I got close to the man. The virus he carried must be as lethal as Aidyn and Assan had advertised. Though why those two thought it needed to become a vampire cocktail, I could not fathom. Maybe Cassandra could give us some insight into the whole situation.

Chapter Sixteen

Cassandra's Pure & Natural was a tiny brick storefront in a predominantly Cuban neighborhood. Bins of fresh apples, oranges, and grapefruit sat on the sidewalk beside the door, which was equipped with the most soothing set of chimes I'd ever set off. Inside, the walls and aisles carried a surprisingly wide selection of spices, herbs, vitamins, and natural remedies for everything from erectile dysfunction to the common cold.

I asked the cashier, a petite old woman with gleaming white teeth and blinding red hair, where we could find Cassandra. She directed us to the back of the store, where shelves full of fresh-baked breads, rolls, and sugar-free desserts made my stomach growl.

As soon as Cole caught sight of Cassandra, he yanked off his glasses, spat out his fake teeth, and wrapped them both in his fishing hat, which went into the waistband of his sweats. Literally. He'd probably have to cut the lure to separate them. But at the moment he seemed pretty oblivious. All his concentration centered on Cassandra as she added some bran muffins to a glass case that already contained a full load of fiber-filled goodies for folks forced to make regularity a priority.

A slender beauty with black-velvet skin and hair that fell in braids to her waist, Cassandra moved with the grace of a dancer. She wore a canary-yellow blouse, red flowered skirt, beaded moccasins, and enough gold jewelry to keep eBay shoppers bidding for weeks.

"How may I help you?" she asked in an accent that made my Midwestern drawl sound pale and asexual.

"My name is Lucille Robinson," I said. "This is my friend Cole Bemont." He nodded, doing a nice job of keeping his drool in check. "I—we—need a translation."

She nodded. "I assume you heard of me through a mutual acquaintance?"

"Yes, um, you would probably know him as Vayl."

Instant sympathy filled her warm brown eyes, but all she said was "Yes, I remember him." She leaned aside, caught the cashier's eye, and said, "We're going upstairs, Rita." To us, she said, "Follow me, please."

Cole managed to keep his tongue from rolling out onto the stairs as we trailed Cassandra's swinging hips to the second floor. It made me laugh inwardly to see him smitten, as it were. But I was glad I'd seen the show. It confirmed my feelings for him. I might love him someday, but never in the way I'd loved Matt. Never in the way I could, maybe, if I found the guts, love Vayl.

When we reached the landing at the top of the stairs I was surprised to find the three doors that opened to it, well, open. The one to our left revealed an apartment's living room and kitchen. A bathroom stood directly in front of us, and a gypsy den sat on our right. That's where Cassandra led us, into a large room, the walls of which were covered in silky materials that ranged from bloodred solids to dark gold prints. The new colors I saw within those familiar shades pleased my eye and my spirit. Somehow, despite the fringed pillows on the black couches and the multitude of candles on the large central table, the room maintained an exotic dignity.

Four dark wooden chairs with more curlicues than Shirley Temple sat around the table, which must've been crafted soon after Vayl's transformation. Cassandra sank into one of the chairs and motioned for us to join her.

"I sensed I would be entertaining *three* visitors today," she said, her voice as satiny as the wall coverings. "Are you expecting another?"

"Actually, yes, we are meeting a friend here. He should be arriving anytime now," I said.

Cassandra nodded, the golden studs that lined her ears shining with reflected light. "Rita will send him up when he arrives. Would you like to show me what you need translated?"

I pulled the paper Cole had traced the symbols on out of my front pocket. I took care not to touch her as I handed it to her. Vayl might need the services of a Seer, but I preferred to leave my future a blank. My new senses told me that if Cassandra touched me, she would tell me things I didn't want to hear. I was inclined to believe them.

I'd never doubted Cassandra's abilities. Charlatans don't stay in the biz long when vamps join their clientele. But even if I had come into this thinking Cassandra's upstairs gig was a fraud, her reaction to the symbols would've convinced me otherwise. She dropped the note onto the table in front of her as if she'd been burned. Her face tightened into a mask of fear, and the soul behind her eyes cringed like a spectator at the Holocaust Museum.

"Where did you see these?" she asked, pointing a wavering finger at the symbols but making sure she didn't touch them.

"They had been carved into a dead body," Cole told her. "Actually, two dead bodies on two separate occasions."

Cassandra fingered a crucifix at her neck and muttered under her breath in, well, oddly enough it sounded like Latin.

"What are you saying?" Cole asked.

She looked at him grimly. "A prayer for your protection."

Cole said, "Why do we need God's protection in this, Cassandra?"

"These symbols," she said, "are powerful runes designed to trap the soul after death to keep it from ascending."

I recalled the scene in the restaurant, when Charlie's beautiful blue soul went flying into the wild blue yonder. What if it had remained stuck there, straining to be free? The image made me flinch.

Cole shook his head. "How is that possible?" he asked.

Cassandra made a visible effort to pull herself together. "When people die violently, their souls do not immediately break free," she explained. "During that short delay, the soul can be contained inside the body by branding these runes on the skin around the death wound."

"So"—*ugh, I can't believe I'm saying this*—"then what do you have? Zombies?"

"That is a possibility." Cassandra looked as revolted as I felt. "Another explanation is that a 'rail,' or hell-servant, trapped the soul until his master could arrive to eat it."

I couldn't help it. My mind suddenly supplied a picture of a red-skinned, horned demon picking its teeth with a purple claw as a waiter cleared the dishes from its table.

"How was the soul?" the waiter asked.

"Not bad with butter and lemon," the demon replied. "In fact, I'd have to say it was finger-lickin' good."

I know, I know, *not* funny.

"Aside from the obvious biblical explanations," I said, "why would a demon eat souls?"

Cassandra shuddered. "For the fun of it," she suggested, "or perhaps because it had been called to do so by a vengeance-minded human who was willing to pay the price."

Great, that's what I need right now. It's not enough that I have to stop a megaterrorist from spreading some godawful virus. Now I get to chase down a psychotic netherworlder with the munchies too.

"There is a third possibility," Cassandra said.

"What is it?"

"Demons are not the only monsters who eat souls." She nodded at the symbols Cole had drawn. "The woman who taught me this language told me a story once, of an evil emperor named Tequet Dirani who made it his passion to rule, not only this world, but all the worlds beyond this one. He summoned a Kyron to help him."

"What's a Kyron?" asked Cole.

Cassandra started to look ill as she described something that sounded more like a George Lucas creation than the real deal. "It is a beast built for destruction. Its presence can herald a plague or a nuclear meltdown. And it can rip through the walls that divide universes like a wrecking ball."

"Sure sounds like a demon to me," Cole murmured.

"Not at all. It will destroy for any cause, good or evil. It is, like the djinn, at the mercy of its master's whim."

"Only genies don't scarf down somebody's essence every morning for breakfast," I pointed out. "So how do you master something like that?" I wondered. "How do you beat it?"

Cassandra didn't realize I was waxing rhetorical.

"You control it with food," she said. "Souls, to be specific. Likewise, you might be able to beat it by starving it."

"Is that how the emperor's Kyron died?"

"Oh, Kyron don't die," Cassandra said earnestly. "They simply become weak enough to bind."

Somehow I didn't think she meant bind as in "Yo, Henry, go get me some rope."

"Bind how?" I asked, feeling suddenly exhausted. I eyed one of the couches speculatively. How offended would Cassandra be if a perfect stranger collapsed there for, oh, say three days, more or less?

"According to the legend, a powerful mage bound the Kyron by making her forget her own name."

"That must have been a major bump on the head."

"Indeed," Cassandra agreed. "It would take more than a mild concussion to forget the name Tor-al-Degan."

Chapter Seventeen

"Wait a second," I demanded. "Are you telling me the Tor-al-Degan is real?"

Cassandra nodded, clearly puzzled at my question. Apparently she'd never heard of the Sons of Paradise or their "mythical" goddess. And just as obviously, we at the Central Intelligence Agency were going to have to update our intel on Assan's sect.

"This is important, Cassandra." I leaned forward, trying to see beyond the depths of her dark eyes, into those invisible planes only she could access. "Could this Tor-al-Degan be unbound somehow? Brought back into the world?"

Looking at the door as if she'd badly like to make a run for it, she licked her lips and nodded. "Are you . . ." She cleared her throat and tried again. "These writings and my stories. They have led you to some new understanding?"

For a few *oh-shit* seconds my mind tried to go somewhere, anywhere else as a powerful fist of foreboding sucker-punched me in the gut. I noticed the light dusting of freckles bridging Cole's nose. Cassandra's lipstick was the same color as the dress I'd worn to Assan's party.

And I'd chipped a nail. *Suck it up, girl. This ain't going away.* "Yes," I told Cassandra, "this puzzle is becoming clearer."

The Raptor must have allied with the Sons of Paradise because he needed their goddess, their Tor-al-Degan. Cassandra had described her as a plague beast and their virus sounded that scary.

As far as motive went, the Raptor couldn't get enough power if you hooked him directly to a generator. The Sons of Paradise, led by their new hero Assan, would love the idea of wiping out Americans with some horrifying disease. Aidyn would crow like a proud papa as his killer germs laid the land low. I wasn't sure where the senator fit in, but it probably involved multiple cameras and a toothy grin.

The how and where of their plan escaped me, but that didn't really matter at the moment, because I knew the when. Tomorrow night was the ritual. They should all be there. Vayl and I just needed to go back to Plan A. Grab Assan. Make him talk. Take him and his cronies out. Maybe we could do it in one sweeping gesture. Can anybody say *Boom*?

Before I could ask Cassandra if she thought Kyron could be defeated by a well-timed explosion, Bergman slunk into the room.

"What?" he asked, immediately suspicious as I stared at him, so enmeshed in this new knowledge and how best to deal with it that I wasn't quite able to muster a common pleasantry.

"Nothing much," I finally managed. "Just gaining a little enlightenment." Talk about understatement. That was like saying Vesuvius's eruption was a slight blip in Pompeii's weather pattern.

Bergman looked around the room furtively. If you didn't know him, you'd suspect he'd just robbed a liquor store. He carried that air of guilt with him wherever he went.

"I'll fill you in later," I said. "We've, uh, that is . . . We've found out what we needed to know so, now that you're here, we'll get out of Cassandra's hair."

I stood up, digging in my pocket for a twenty.

"No, please," said Cassandra, "there's no charge."

"My boss blesses you," I said. I leaned across the table and held out my hand, my Military Brat Politeness Training temporarily overcoming common sense. "Thanks for your help. You've been a godsend. Vayl and I will be in touch."

She shook my hand, barely squeezing in response to my firm grip. Then her focus shifted, and I knew I was screwed. I tried to pull my hand back before she could connect with spirits I wasn't ready to face. But her vision had nothing to do with worlds beyond death.

"David is in danger," she said tightly. "You must tell him to stay away from the house with the pink door. It's rigged to blow."

She dropped my hand and sat back in her chair, looking like somebody who'd just debarked from an intense roller-coaster ride. She murmured something that sounded like "Who *are* you?" But I could barely hear her beyond the roaring in my ears. It was as if the explosion had already happened inside my head. The blackness stormed over me like a level-five twister, a miles-wide black-on-black runaway train I could never hope to stop.

But I tried. For David's sake I fought to stand, to simply stay upright and functional while my own wild-eyed psyche tried to bowl me over. This time it worked. The force that had, for so long, squashed my awareness and pushed it down into unconsciousness now tugged at me, pulled me forward so fast I felt dizzy with the rush. I felt supercharged, as if I could see everywhere all at once, be anywhere I wanted to go, do whatever I wished. The way I figured it, this was no time to kick Tinker Bell in the teeth. I wished to be with David, wished hard, like when we were kids and Tammy Shobeson had me down in the dirt, demanding that I call myself and my snake-eating, son-of-a-bitching dad a dirty, rotten coward.

There was a moment when the blackness seemed to offer up a navigational beacon, my own personal yellow brick road on which to set a new land-speed record. Later I would gain the knowledge I needed to slow that trip down, put it into some kind of perspective. But now it seemed instant, a Jell-O pudding trek that put me where I needed to be, in the middle of Desert Nowhere in the dark, in the heat, slamming into my brother, *through* him, screaming, "David! David! David" in a voice so loud and shrill I expected some unseen enemy to lob a grenade my way just to shut me up.

David stood still, a sheen of sweat covering his artificially darkened face. Night-vision goggles covered his eyes, but I knew what they looked like. I faced their twins every day in the mirror. He carried an M4 in one hand and a radio in the other. He looked so fit, so healthy, I just stood there for a second and watched him breathe.

"Jaz?" he whispered.

"You can see me?"

Immediately he shook his head. I could almost read his thoughts. *Nope. Can't see a thing because this was not covered in* Special Forces Booklet 14A. But he reached out his hand, poked it through my stomach and out my back. The same hand went immediately to his forehead and banged on it hard. "What a helluva time to start hallucinating."

He turned his back on me, and over his shoulder I saw the house, a squat little square with dark, dark windows and a pale pink door. His team surrounded it, crouched in the shadows like latter-day ninjas, awaiting his orders.

"David!" I jumped in front of him, holding up my hands, failing to stop his slow advance. "The door! The pink door! It's booby-trapped!"

"Quit freaking out, D." That's what he called himself during his damn-I'm-stressed pep talks. "It's all been scouted. It's all good." The hand with the radio moved toward his lips.

"Goddammit, I didn't come all this way to blow smoke up your ass, Daz. *Don't go through that door!*"

He looked straight at me. "You haven't called me Daz since West Virginia. Not even in my dreams." It was my pet name for him, the one I'd used to remind him he was a part of me despite his hip friends, his athletic prowess, his ability to make even little old librarians laugh.

"You haven't called me at all," I whispered.

He murmured orders into the radio and waited. Neither of us spoke. I didn't want to spook him further. He didn't want to understand how I was, and wasn't, there. I heard frantic whispering.

"You were right, Jaz. The door is wired like a bale of hay."

"Good. Good. I'm glad you listened. Thanks."

"Thank *you*." He shucked his goggles and looked at me then, making sure I saw that he meant it for himself. But he meant it even more for his team, seven men and two women who kicked terrorist ass all over the globe without most people even knowing they existed. "It's . . ." He grimaced. "It's not easy keeping them all alive. I know that now."

It was the closest he'd ever come to apologizing about the rift he'd opened between us.

I just nodded. "I have to go." I had stood in the eye of the storm as long as I could. It was pulling me back, now, blowing me home.

David held on to me with his eyes, which had suddenly filled with alarm. "How did you do this, Jazzy? You're not . . . dead, are you? Because you look awful damn ghostly standing there."

"No." I laughed uneasily. "Of course not. I'm just weird."

Relief cleared David's expression. "Okay, then. I'll . . . I'll call you. Soon. I promise."

"I'm holding you to that one, Dave. Take care."

I let the storm whip me away from my twin and his crew. Back to the gypsy den I flew, dropping into myself at a jarring rate of speed. I gasped and looked around. Lucky me, somehow I'd made it onto one of the couches. Cole, Bergman, and Cassandra hovered over me like emergency room nurses.

"Wow, what just happened?" I asked. "I mean, what did I say?"

"Not much," Cole told me. "You just went white and

started to sway, so we sat you down here. You said 'David' a few times. Is that your . . ."

"Brother," I supplied. "My twin."

Cole looked impressed. "A twin. Wow. I'd have bet money they broke the mold after you."

"Thanks, I think."

Cassandra was wringing her hands, looking more and more agitated. "But, now, surely there is someone you can call? Someone who can stop David before . . ."

"Yes, of course," I said, inserting worry into my voice. No sense in sharing the story of my latest adventure right now. Maybe later, when I could figure out a way to keep it from sounding like a bad episode of *Star Trek*.

I dug my phone out of my pocket. "Is there a place I can talk privately?" I asked.

Cassandra nodded, ushering the men out of the room and gently closing the door.

I dialed a number without even thinking about it. I was probably even more surprised than Albert when he answered the phone to find me on the other end.

"Dad?"

"Jasmine? What's wrong?"

"Nothing, now. There was something, but it's okay." I stopped. Had to. Tears had thrown a hitch into my voice, and the next step was crying on the phone to Daddy. No. Way. Maybe Albert sensed that because the next thing he said was "The nurse came. Damnedest thing, Jaz, she's a he! I mean, Shelby's a fella. He was a medic in the army. Can you believe it? Plays a mean game of poker too."

"Really? That's great!" I put so much bright and perky into my tone a cheerleader would've gagged.

Albert took a second to wipe the crap out of his ear; then he said, "Jasmine, hang up. I'm calling you back on the other phone."

"Okay." I disconnected. I sat on the couch and waited, and when the phone rang I punched the button and said, "Dad, you don't have another phone."

"Yes, I do." He sounded more serious, more like the dad I'd grown up admiring and fearing, than he had in years. "It's safe to talk. I have a scrambled line."

"Did you just eat a big piece of chocolate cake? Because you said 'scrambled line' when I'm pretty sure you meant to say 'scrambled eggs.' "

"I'll make this quick, because Shelby's in the kitchen whipping up a meal he says I'll actually eat and I don't want him getting curious. I have a scrambled line because when I retired from the service I did some freelance work for the CIA. Still consult for them from time to time, which is why I still have the phone."

"But . . . you retired because of the diabetes. Why would—"

"Didn't have it then," said Albert. "What I did have was some expertise in military intelligence the CIA thought they could use. The diabetes, well, that turned out to be a case of life imitating lies." He paused, giving it time to sink in. Then he went on. "I know what you do for a living, Jaz. Have from the start. So when you call sounding like you just dodged a cannonball, I'm naturally going to want to help out. So, first of all, are you really okay?"

I thought about it. "No, but I'm not in any danger." After another second I added, "At the moment."

"Is there anything I can do?" When I didn't answer

right away, he said, "Dammit, Jasmine, don't make me beg. I'm so frigging tired of being a useless old man, I'm ready to volunteer. Yeah, I said it! Volunteer, like some God-fearing, churchgoing, one-foot-in-the-grave bastard who thinks he can save his shriveled old soul by doing five hours of good works a week."

Only my father could have that kind of perspective on volunteerism. Twisted old poop. And yet, since we still didn't know the identity of our leak, I really could use somebody with his contacts. And it sounded like he could use the exercise, so to speak.

Feeling like I was taking a gondola ride through Surreal-land, I said, "Actually, Albert, there is something you can do. Can you check out some senators and one petite secretary for me?"

Chapter Eighteen

It must've been Albert's military background, because, *man*, when he dropped a bomb the entire country shook. I was still as jittery as a hurricane survivor in New Orleans, and I was sure that somewhere in Alaska some poor Inuit had just taken a tumble from his sled for the very same reason. Thirty seconds ago I'd discovered my dad was not only a mostly retired consultant for the Agency, but he also maintained a few connections in Washington, DC, who could make my life much easier and quite a bit longer. Now I'd believe anything. If Cole and Bergman rushed in and told me pterodactyls were circling Cassandra's building, I'd run to the window to get a good look.

Speaking of which, they were about ready to burst in, despite my request for privacy. I could feel their anxiety through the door. I sighed. Already I missed the good old days when being Sensitive only pertained to vamps, and even then their feelings never entered into it. I also thought it would've been convenient to be able to open the door with a simple wave of the hand. Unfortunately my newfound abilities didn't lean that way. Maybe I could buy a really well-trained dog.

Sighing, I lurched to my feet and opened the door. They weren't pacing in the hallway as I'd expected. They were pacing in Cassandra's apartment.

"It's all right," I said as I entered the room. They didn't exactly leap at me. In fact, Cassandra stayed in her tall wooden rocker and Bergman continued skulking back and forth behind her royal blue couch. Cole came and took my elbow, led me to the couch's matching recliner, and gently sat me down.

"You're making me feel old," I told him.

He just grinned. He sat on the granite-topped coffee table that visually connected the seating area to a red-brick fireplace that held dozens of white candles.

"You okay?" he asked, inspecting me closely, perhaps to see if I'd grown an extra appendage during our brief separation. "You look better than I expected you to."

"I feel better than I probably should."

"So things are squared away?"

"For the moment."

"Can I get a ride back to my truck, then? I really do need to clean that pool or they'll think something's up."

"Okay, but no snooping. Call me when you're done too. I want to see those pictures." I checked my watch. "Jeremy ought to be up by then. I'll bring him along." I looked at Bergman, raised my eyebrows. "Follow us?"

He nodded. "Then you and I need to talk." He looked pointedly at Cole. "Alone."

I wanted to snarl, "Well, of course, alone. We already established that Cole would be going somewhere else!" Sometimes Bergman's paranoia made me want to break things. Like his neck. But being a neurotic—I mean sensitive—genius, Bergman continued to benefit from my best behavior. For now.

"Of course," I replied. "I'm anxious to hear what you have to say." I rose and looked at Cassandra. "Thank you for saving my brother. It was . . . wow . . . thanks."

She nodded graciously. "I'll see you later."

"You will?"

"Yes." She didn't elaborate, so I let it go. No sense in chasing more problems. "Until then, I must ask you to be very careful."

"Who, me? Gosh, Cassandra, I guess I should've told you, there's no need to worry about me. At work they call me Safety Sue."

She gave a very unladylike *humph*, which made me like her lots better.

The four of us trooped downstairs and, maybe seeing the way I'd ogled her fresh-baked foods, Cassandra gave us each a free box of blueberry muffins for the road.

"I love girls who bake," sighed Cole as we drove back to his truck, with me behind the wheel this time. He launched into a rapturous monologue that featured, I kid you not, his mom's apple pies. From there he moved to his boyhood, oatmeal-cookie-stealing stories, and by the time we reached his truck I'd inhaled two of Cassandra's freebies. I'd also decided that if I ever met Cole's mom I'd just come right out with it and ask her to adopt me.

I let him off at the corner. Bergman pulled alongside me and yelled, "Follow me!" out the window, so I did. He drove a dark green work van with no windows in back and tinted ones in front. The words "Flaherty's Fine Foods" were stenciled on the side in big gold letters that circled a picture of the sun, complete with curvy yellow beams, Blues Brothers shades, and a big, toothy smile.

He drove to a large deserted park. No kids played on the red and yellow jungle gym. The benches were empty and so were several of the flower beds. He parked beside a pond with a working fountain and I got into the van beside him.

"Thanks for coming, Bergman. I really appreciate it."

"No problem," he said, though we both knew better. "I'm sorry about all the secrecy, but you said to bring all the bells and whistles, and I didn't want anyone else to get a look at your new toys."

I felt a smile chase away my earlier irritation. I *love* new toys.

He reached behind his seat and brought out a silver case with black combination-lock latches. Just the kind of thing inside of which you'd expect to find a top-secret weapon or two. Grinning in response to my excitement, he unlocked the case and set it on my lap. "You open it."

I raised the lid. Inside, cushioned by a casing of black foam, sat three smaller cases, also gleaming silver. I nearly jumped up and down in my seat, but confined myself to a short round of applause.

"You don't even know what they are yet!"

"Look at this," I demanded, bringing his attention to the case with a Vanna White–inspired flip of the hand. "Stuff that starts out looking like this always ends up awesome. Didn't you ever see *I Spy*?"

"Come on," he said, his long, pale face twitching with anticipation. "Open them up."

"If you insist." The first case snapped open to reveal a necklace made with shells, beads, and an arrow-shaped item that looked an awful lot like a shark's tooth. I pulled it out of the case and looked closer. Finally I said, "Okay. I give. Why is this not any other souvenir-store rip-off?"

"I'll show you," Bergman said, the brown eyes behind his glasses gleaming with techno-passion. He took his keys out of the ignition and traded them for the necklace. He stuck the shark's tooth into the keyhole and wiggled it a little. Then he turned it sharply and the van started. To his delight, all I could say was "Whoa. That's cool."

He turned the engine off and handed the necklace back to me. The shark's tooth was now in the shape of a key, but even as I held it in my palm it re-formed to its original shape. "What's your secret?" I asked, although I knew he wouldn't tell me, not even if his feet were bleeding and his hair was on fire.

"Caffeine," he replied, and we both smiled. I put the necklace on and he said, "Oh, yeah, the line everything's threaded on is superstrong. It's been tested to six hundred pounds."

I fingered the beads and the stretchy cord they hung on with wonder. "Cool! Now I can steal some rich old coot's Ferrari *and* go fishing for marlin with the same piece of jewelry."

"Not many women can say that, you know."

"There's no doubt I'm blessed among them. What else have we got?" I opened the second case. It held a couple of hearing aids like the one I'd just used and two round items that looked like mints. "Listening devices?" I guessed.

"And transmitting," Bergman agreed. "The round piece is made to stick to the roof of your mouth. The receiver goes in your ear. The second set is for Vayl. When you're both equipped you can talk to each other without the bother of radios and headsets. The only downside is the sound is a little distorted."

"Yeah?"

Bergman grimaced. "It's like somebody pumped up the bass. I'm working on cleaning that up."

"What's the upside?"

He pointed to two items I hadn't noticed because they were nearly the same color as the box's lining. "Careful," he warned as I picked them up. They looked like the fake tattoos retailers sell to little kids who haven't yet heard of hepatitis. One resembled a line of barbed wire. The other was a long, serpentine dragon. "These adhere to your skin and are indistinguishable from tattoos once they're on. They're transmitters," Bergman explained. "They should allow you to hear each other from a distance of about two miles."

"No kidding? That far?" Bergman bobbed his head, looking like a rooster who's just discovered the henhouse.

I opened the last box. It contained a simple gold watch with an expandable band. I turned it inside out and upside down, but it looked completely normal. So I put it on.

"Snap the band," suggested Bergman.

I did and my hand immediately began to tingle. The face of the watch turned blue, though I still had no problem reading the time. It turned white again and the tingling stopped. "What's up with this?"

"I'm still researching all the possible applications, but at the moment I can tell you the watch absorbs the energy your body movement creates and kicks it back out as an electronic shield. When it's fully charged you can walk through a metal detector carrying a bazooka and no bells will go off. It also masks the sounds your natural movements cause."

"So you're saying all I need to do is snap this band and I'm in stealth mode?"

"As long as the face of the watch is blue. As you can see, it didn't stay blue long because it hasn't had much time to absorb your energy. It also has a limited storage capacity."

"How long?"

"Five minutes at the most."

"Not bad when thirty seconds is all you need."

"So you like it?"

This was the side of Bergman I'd never figured out. The guy could make a lead door do backflips, but he still needed his pats.

"Are you kidding me? This is the finest stuff you've ever given me to work with. You've really outdone yourself this time." Minus the weight of that worry, he sat a little straighter. "Have you got a place to stay?" I asked.

"Yeah." He didn't tell me where, which came as no surprise.

"Great. But look, before you go back there, I have a couple of requests."

"I'm at your service."

I told him about the bad blood and Vayl's need for a clean supply. "So is there any way you can process the tainted blood? See what exactly Vayl's smelling?"

"No problem." Bergman jerked his thumb over his shoulder, bringing my attention to at least forty bags and boxes that filled the body of the van. "I pretty much brought the office with me since I wasn't sure what you'd need."

My next request didn't want to roll off my tongue like the first, but I forced it. "How about a willing donor for Vayl?"

Bergman's eyebrows shot up. "Skirting Agency supplies?"

"For now."

He nodded thoughtfully. "I think I can arrange that by tomorrow. But there's no way I can get him a supply any sooner."

"Tonight's not a problem," I said. I had shed my bandage when I'd donned my costume, but Bergman's eyes still tracked to my neck. If he could see the puncture marks between the gathering gloom and my mane of hair he didn't comment.

"The blood's at the hotel," I told him. "Follow me back?"

"No problem."

I jumped out of the van and into the Mercedes. To soothe Bergman's concern that we might be followed and, I admit, to give myself a few extra minutes behind that smooth leather-clad wheel, I took the long way back to Diamond Suites. Bergman approved of the digs right up to the point when our exclusive elevator opened into our exclusive entryway and we discovered neither was as exclusive as advertised.

"Son of a bitch!" I whispered, pulling Bergman into the corner. The scene reminded me of Christmas at Grandma and Grandpa Parkses'. The smell of cheap aftershave. The trashed living room. The sound of voices coming from the bedroom, two of them, hissing at each other like a couple of pissed-off geese.

I motioned for Bergman to stay put as I pulled Grief from its holster. He nodded at my watchband and held up his fingers, telling me I might have twenty seconds of stealth built up by now. I snapped the band and moved through the open door toward Vayl's bedroom.

"Look in the closet," said one of the intruders, a woman whose accent made me think of those over-crowded trailer parks that attract cops and tornadoes in equal doses.

"Vampires do not sleep in closets," said her male partner in an equally thick drawl. "Besides, I already checked."

No movement or sound came from any other part of the suite, so I decided these two had arrived without reinforcements.

I edged along the wall until I stood next to the open doorway.

"We never shoulda taken this job, Rudy," the woman whined. "Killing the undead is no way to make a living."

"You're the one who wanted to go straight, Amy Jo, not me. I'd be just as happy popping cheating husbands and rich old uncles."

"Now what kind of folks would we be if we kept going around murdering *other* people's folks? Did you look under the bed?"

"Yes, I looked under the bed!" Rudy's voice held that defeated note of exasperation sung by henpecked husbands the world over.

"Sounds like it's just not your day, Rudy," I said as I

stepped into the doorway and took careful aim. I picked the target closest to me, knowing in a moment the shock would wear off, they'd react, and I'd better be ready to shoot. Unfortunately, my target was heavily pregnant, so my own initial shock offset theirs, and we all recovered at pretty much the same time.

"Don't shoot!" Rudy yelled, jumping in front of Amy Jo and, no doubt, scoring lifetime Brownie points in the process.

"Behave yourselves and I won't have to," I said in the most professional voice I could muster considering Amy Jo reminded me strongly of Evie, and she and Rudy both wore black clothing covered with bright yellow fabric-painted crosses. "You guys look like you should be representing the letter T on Sesame Street."

They traded a look that said they'd had the same discussion.

"Who are you?" Rudy demanded, rather haughtily, I thought. After all, he was not only dressed like a letter of the alphabet, he looked like a young Mr. Magoo.

"CIA," I replied, sounding as crisp as a new fifty-dollar bill. "And you two are flirting with a long list of felonies that will put you behind bars until that kid of yours needs knee replacements."

"We're just doing our job," said Amy Jo, flipping her strawberry-blond hair away from her face with one hand while the other guarded her distended belly.

"Who are you working for?"

Rudy squinted his eyes tightly, until all you could see of them behind his Coke-bottle lenses were glittery black pinpoints. "Who wants to know?"

I sighed. "The C—I—A." I said it slow so they

wouldn't misunderstand. Our acronym can be *so* confusing.

Amy Jo jabbed her right elbow into Rudy's left love handle. "She's the one with the gun. Tell her what she wants to know!"

It was Rudy's turn to sigh. "We don't know. They hired us over the Internet, mailed us half the cash and promised the other half after we nailed the vampire."

I lowered Grief until it pointed straight at Rudy's crotch. "You two wouldn't recognize the Internet if a server fell on your heads. So give it to me straight this time, Rudy, before I lose my temper and make sure Junior grows up an only child."

Rudy let out a very Homer Simpson–like yelp and crossed his hands over my target. "All right! All right! This couple came into the bar where we hang out."

"What did they look like?"

"She had big boobs and bright white hair that went down to her butt," said Amy Jo, peeking around Rudy to make sure I heard her right.

"And he had longish reddish hair," finished Rudy. "I think they were both vampires."

Aidyn and Liliana. Should I be surprised? Yeah, I thought so. You don't hire a couple of local yokels to off two of the best assassins in the world. Unless that's not really what you want for your money. Maybe it's well spent if all you want to do is distract said assassins from their original mission. It made sense, especially if you took it as an incident totally unrelated to all the other assassination attempts, which had seemed entirely genuine.

"The vamp you're after is already smoke," I told them.

"What?" the two of them squawked like a couple of irritated blue jays.

"Yeah. Thought he needed a suntan, I guess. Walked right out into full daylight this morning."

"Son of a *bitch*!" Amy Jo punched poor Rudy in the arm because, well, he was there.

"Look," I said, before she threw another jab Rudy couldn't duck. "Tell them you bagged the vamp. He's gone, so it doesn't really matter if you take the credit. Then get out of town. Way out. You'll get the cash and help the CIA at the same time."

Amy Jo looked a little doubtful, but Rudy grinned and rubbed his palms together as if they'd already been greased. "We can do that."

"And, uh"—I motioned to their costumes—"I'd rethink the vamp-smoking biz. The old ones are too smart to allow themselves to be staked in their sleep. Most others keep tougher goons than you around to guard them while they're vulnerable. Why don't you go straight and, uh, open a liquor store or something?"

"Wow," said Amy Jo, "how did you know?"

Because you are me and Evie minus college and Granny May. The words sat silent on my tongue. I just looked at her, and when her eyes narrowed I knew she had me pegged. "You're a Sweep, aren't you?"

I shrugged. "I'm not familiar with that term."

"Like a chimney sweep. You dust vamps and get rid of the ashes. Dust people too, I'm betting," she said, nodding wisely, like an old Chinese monk.

I accepted her metaphor, despite her ignorance of

what actually happens when a vamp goes bye-bye for good. "Yes," I said, "I do." I let her see in my eyes what all my victims had seen in their time. She was already a tough old bird, though I wouldn't put her age past twenty-two, but I backed her up a step. "Someday you might even be as good as me, if a vamp doesn't rip your throat out first. Of course, Junior there might not appreciate that." I motioned to her belly. "There are Moms and there are Sweeps, Amy Jo. You can't be both."

I stopped, mentally kicking myself for falling into lecture mode. Either she was smart enough to figure it out for herself, or she was too damn dumb to waste my breath on.

"Throw the room key on the bed," I told Rudy, too tired to be polite anymore. He fished the card out of his back pocket and laid it on Vayl's crumpled comforter.

"We'll be taking the stairs down." I motioned them out of the bedroom. "You come too," I told Bergman when he caught my eye. He nearly leaped out of our way as we moved to the entryway, a nervous gazelle smelling predator in all directions. To give him credit, however, he didn't rush to his ride once we reached the parking lot. He stood slightly behind me as Rudy and Amy Jo boarded their beige Chevy van, circa 1975, and pulled away. Even from a distance I could see Amy Jo talking into her cell phone, hopefully reporting Vayl's final demise.

"Come on, Bergman, let's get you that blood sample so you can get the hell out of here."

"So Vayl's okay?" he asked as we took the elevator back upstairs.

"Of course. If you've taught me anything, it's to be

perfectly paranoid when it comes to securing sleeping quarters. He's snoozing in the basement."

"What're you going to do now? I mean, now that the bad guys know where you're staying?"

I shook my head as we exited the elevator and reentered the suite. Trashed by trailer trash. How poetic. I started picking up junk and throwing it into a pile. "Find the one place in Miami that won't show up on these jerks' radar." Bergman frowned heavily as he helped me clean up. After a few minutes he squared his shoulders and said, "I know just the place."

"You do?"

He bobbed his head. "Actually, I'm staying there."

I swallowed my spit and it went down the wrong tube. Through the coughing fit that followed I said, "Are you . . . inviting us to stay with you?"

Bergman nodded unhappily. "I figure it's the patriotic thing to do."

"You figure rightly. Thanks!"

Boy, would Vayl's jaw drop when he heard this one. Bergman's privacy, as sacred to him as the Torah, had bowed to the needs of two of the Agency's most notorious members. I'd have to choose the right time to tell him. Definitely *after* he'd climbed off the top of the toilet paper cabinet upon which he now roosted.

After our little confrontation the evening before, I'd expected him to complain when I'd stomped into his room and demanded that he change sleeping quarters so I could leave him during the day without worrying. But he'd just shrugged, grabbed a pillow, and followed me to the darkest corner I could find. I'd covered him with a tarp and disguised the lump he made by placing a row of paint cans along the top edge of the cabinet.

"Sorry," I'd said as I'd turned to leave, knowing he was lying in enough mildew to start a spore factory.

"It is fine," I heard him say. "There is little a hot shower cannot cure."

What a guy. Too bad he'd been mostly dead for centuries.

Chapter Nineteen

Bergman and I sat on a couple of overturned five-gallon buckets in the basement of Diamond Suites, waiting for night to fall. Any minute now Vayl would stir, and he probably wouldn't appreciate the audience, but Bergman's unspoken sense of urgency had rubbed off on me. We really needed to get out before Aidyn and Liliana caught on to our scam and resorted to something more dependable than southern-fried assassins. Like a bomb.

The last vestige of light left the basement. Yeah, creepy. Bergman and I flicked on our flashlights. Somehow that made it worse. And it was no consolation to know there really could be monsters hiding in the shadows between the boiler and the storage closets. I'd been eyeing the edges of Freakoutland for maybe a minute when I heard a huge, gasping gulp that made me jump up and overturn my bucket despite the fact that I'd been expecting it. It was the sound of magic bringing Vayl back to a life he couldn't bear to leave.

When the muttering started, I relaxed. The plastic on top of the cabinet in the farthest corner of the basement creaked as Vayl started to move, his complaints getting louder as he remembered where he was. With our flashlights trained on him, we were mesmerized by the sight of a vamp dressed in blue plastic. We watched him struggle to escape seemingly endless yards of tarp while paint cans dropped off the cabinet's edge like gum balls from a faulty machine. Still enmeshed from the knees down, Vayl flopped off the cabinet before we realized he needed a hand down, falling fast and hard, like a penguin who hasn't bought the whole flightless scenario. Somehow he recovered—so quickly his movements were a dizzying blur—and landed on his feet.

"What are you doing here?" he grumbled, giving Bergman a slight nod to acknowledge his arrival.

"Waiting for you," I replied. "Need some coffee, do you?"

"No." He looked pointedly at my neck and, this is embarrassing, but I'm pretty sure I blushed. Nonetheless, I barreled on.

"Bergman needs a day to find you a willing donor—"

"I told you. I can find my own donors," he snapped. He took a minute to regroup. "I am sorry. Waking is never pleasant for me. What I meant to say . . ." He stopped, took inward stock, and started over. "What I now realize is that I do not need any donors, not tonight anyway. I woke with the same longing as ever, but without the need. Last night . . . the blood I took last night was more . . . potent . . . than I realized."

I cleared my throat. What do you say when you find out your blood is *really* filling? *It's not a Manwich; it's a meal! Nope, not going there.* "Um, we need to get out of here as soon as possible." I gave Vayl the short version of Rudy and Amy Jo's adventures and my distraction theory. I also told him about my visit with Cassandra. His immobile face registered actual shock when I mentioned the Tor-al-Degan.

"I know," I said. "It's supposed to be a mythical creature, am I right?"

"I certainly thought so."

"Well, look, Assan's goon said they're doing a ceremony tomorrow for this Tor-al-Degan. The senator's coming, so you know it's important. I figure we eliminate Assan tonight after we get the details we need to crash their party and"—like the hero and heroine in a really fine melodrama—"foil their plans."

"I agree. But we must anticipate what other distractions they may throw at us to keep us from accomplishing that."

Right on cue, my phone rang. It was Cole. "Lucille? My building's on fire! The pictures! They're burning!"

"Where are you?"

"Here! With the fire trucks!"

Holy crap! "Listen! It's not an accident! Assan is onto you! Look around. Do you see any of his men?"

"No. I don't know. It's . . . There are dark patches. They could be hiding."

Through the phone I heard an explosive popping noise. "Cole? What's that?"

"The windows just exploded! Oh my God, my business!"

"We'll work it out for you, Cole. But right now, you need to run—"

"Hey! What're you doing! Let me go!"

"*Cole*, tell me—"

"Lucille! They've—" The phone went dead.

I shoved it into my pocket and jumped up. "Assan has Cole!"

Vayl laid a hand on my shoulder, probably to keep me from sprinting off into the night like some mad cross-country runner. "We will get him back—tonight. But we need to retrieve Cassandra as well. She is the only other person who has had contact with us. They may know about her. They may use her as the next distraction."

I wanted to say something stupid like "But she's not on the way." I held my tongue. Vayl was right. "I should call her, though. So she'll be ready to go when we come."

"I imagine she already knows."

Bergman and I had already packed everything that could be salvaged into the van. The Mercedes would stay put until the dealer came for it at the end of the week. We didn't exactly tear out of the parking lot, but we wasted no time hitting the road. Bergman drove while Vayl and I sat in the bucket seats behind him, our legs pinned between boxes and trunks. Naturally, since I wasn't driving, traffic cooperated.

"I am sorry," Vayl said, his voice low in my ear. "I know you cherish your privacy, but your emotions are shooting out of you like fireworks. You have every right to be scared and worried, but you cannot let those feelings take you over. Not tonight."

A spurt of anger made me want to slap him, as if I was some diva who didn't get the Double Stuf Oreos she'd demanded before her concert. I took a deep breath and then another. "Okay, rein it in. I understand. I will."

Cassandra waited for us on the curb in front of her

store, two bags in hand, two on the sidewalk beside her. Even after everything I'd seen and done in my life, the Midwesterner in me thought, *Wow, that's just weird.* But weird in a way I deeply appreciated.

Bergman helped her load her stuff, giving Vayl and me each a bag to hold on our laps. She kept the other two, tucking one beneath her feet and keeping the other in hand.

"No speeding," I told Bergman as he settled back behind the wheel. "You hit a bump going over sixty and your exhaust is going to snap off like a LEGO."

"I know, I know, I packed too much. I always do."

He sounded so contrite I backed off. "You wouldn't have brought it if you didn't need it."

"That's why I like you, Jaz. You never make fun of my craziness."

"If you could watch a film of my childhood you'd know why."

He chuckled, the way a person will who's had similar suspicions about insanity in the family. "Where to now?"

I looked at Vayl. "Bergman's offered us asylum. We get to stay on his turf as long as we make our beds and put our dirty plates in the dishwasher."

"Excellent. Take us there, if you please." Vayl looked at Cassandra then. "It is good to see you again."

"Likewise." She looked at me and smiled. "Hello, Lucille. Or should I call you Jaz?"

"Why don't we stick with Lucille? The less you know about me the better."

"But that is why I'm here."

"Really?"

She held my gaze, her eyes like twin wells in the dim light. I nearly kicked in my night sight, but I wasn't sure I wanted to see her that clearly. "When we shook hands, the vision of David came strongest," she told me. "But another crept in, like a shadow, and I could not understand what it meant. So after you left, I consulted the *Enkyklios*."

Vayl nodded as if he knew what that meant, which irritated me. Or maybe it was the fact that Cassandra felt free to nose around my psyche.

"What's an *Enkyklios*?" I asked, the suspicion in my voice causing Bergman to flash me a look of approval.

Cassandra slipped into lecture mode. "It's like a metaphysical library. It's full of the information Seers have whispered to their descendants practically since the beginning of time. For the last several generations we have taken it upon ourselves to travel the world, gathering and storing that information so it won't be lost forever."

"We?" asked Bergman. "Who's we?"

"An international guild I belong to called Sisters of the Second Sight."

"Never heard of it." He sounded as snappish and impatient as I felt.

"No." Cassandra smiled sweetly. "You wouldn't have."

I cut to the chase before Bergman came up with a conspiracy theory even Julia Roberts wouldn't buy. "So what did you find in the library?"

She looked down, hiding her eyes from me. *Uh-oh.* "I think you need to see it for yourself when we get to a safe place."

I sat back in my seat and sighed.

"What are you afraid of?" Vayl murmured quietly in my ear so no one could overhear.

I whispered right back, "She's going to tell me my dad's a demon and my mom was a harpy. She's going to uncover the fact that I'm a monster. I don't guess I'll be surprised to hear it. I've always known at some level. After all, it takes a certain kind of someone to be capable of assassination. You just hate to have your worst traits confirmed by a panel of independent judges, you know?"

I felt Vayl shrug. "I think your perspective is warped. But if you insist on looking at it that way, is it so bad to be our kind of monster? Look at the evil we have averted in our time together." He tucked a stray curl behind my ear. "As long as you do not corrupt any monks or paint eyelashes on the *Venus de Milo*, I would say you have nothing to worry about."

Nothing to worry about. Nothing . . . nothing . . . nothing.

Chapter Twenty

Bergman pulled into the circular drive in front of his hideaway as Vayl and I gaped at the view out the van's front window. Tastefully lit by low-wattage lamps and a couple of well-placed spots, the beachfront two-story looked like it would've been just as comfortable on Cape Cod. The landscaping, the wraparound porch, the white wicker furniture for cripe's sake, it might've come from the latest issue of *Better Homes and Gardens*.

"*This* is *your* safe house?" I asked Bergman.

"Yeah. Why not?" I waited to reply until he got out and opened the side door.

"Well," I said as Vayl and I handed him Cassandra's luggage, "it's just so . . . pleasant." I got out, grabbed a box, and followed him to the front door. "I'd always pictured you in a cave. Or, at the very least, one of those rickety old mansions with droopy shutters and more tunnels than windows."

"I prefer a really excellent security system." He put the bags down, lifted the lion's head door knocker, and thumbed a switch underneath it. The knocker slid sideways, revealing a square of metal and electronics that took detailed measurements of Bergman's left eye before deciding he passed muster. The door clicked several times and stopped.

"Wait," said Bergman as I reached for the latch. Another couple of seconds passed and then I heard a final click. Bergman nodded, so I turned the knob. As the door swung open, Vayl said, "Just remember, Bergman, sooner or later you will have to give us a way to get inside without the benefit of your eyeball."

"No problem. As soon as all our stuff is unloaded I'll modify the system."

I stepped into the front hall and a piercing whistle stopped me in my tracks. Knowing Bergman, if I moved any farther a cannon would descend from the ceiling and blow my head off.

"What is that?" Vayl asked as Bergman came in to give me a critical look.

I held up my hands. "I didn't do anything."

"But you did. That's a wavelength sensor. You're sending some sort of signal."

"Is it the watch?" I asked, snapping the band to see if that stopped the alarm. Nope.

Bergman had run out to the van. He brought back a box, dug around inside, and came out with a handheld wand that looked like a supersized cigarette lighter. Starting at my head, he swept it down my body. As soon as it reached my navel it sent out its own warning beep.

I raised my shirt. "It's your belly ring," Bergman said, adding urgently, "Give it to me."

I took it off and handed it to him. He jumped back into the van, started it up, and raced off. In the time it took us to figure out how to disengage the alarm, he returned. "I planted it on an ice-cream truck. Whoever's following that signal will hopefully zero in on the truck and forget the signal stopped here for a couple of minutes."

"Pete said I had to break it to activate it. That only then would our backup team get involved."

Bergman grimaced. "Somebody activated it remotely and sent your team a false 'okay' signal."

"The same somebody who supplied it in the first place?" wondered Vayl.

"Well, it's not one of mine," said Bergman.

"That's how they found us," I said. "Those God's Arm fakes on the road. Liliana at the restaurant and then again at the condo. Mr. and Mrs. Magoo in the hotel. All they had to do was follow the belly-ring signal." I clenched my jaw, trying not to kick a hole in the wall. "When I get hold of this senator I'm going to rip his ears off and stuff them down his throat."

"What about Martha?" Vayl asked.

I waved an impatient hand. "My gut tells me she's innocent, so until we find some hard evidence nailing her, she's off my list." I'd tell him about Albert's contribution to the evidence search later.

"And the Raptor?"

"I'll leave him to you, as long as you make it vile. *God,* that pisses me off!" The anger wasn't going to help me think clearly though, so I tried to walk it off by exploring the house. Its interior lived up to the exterior's promise. Wooden floors, colorful throw rugs, overstuffed furniture, and antique accessories in twisted iron and oak made the house feel like the set for one of the daytime dramas Granny May used to love to watch. She called them her "stories," and never failed to shake her head sadly when last season's true love became this season's big breakup.

I just about had my emotions back under control by the time we'd unloaded Bergman's van into the living room: a light, airy place with pale blue bead-board walls and a huge fishing net hanging from the ceiling. A long, mahogany bar separated it from the kitchen/feed-a-party-of-thirty dining room. A hallway, painted pastel green, led to three bedrooms and a bathroom. Stairs just to the right of the doorway led to a large family room, a home office, and a master bedroom with a view that made me wish I could sail. I thought there might be some truth to the idea that surroundings influence mood. Maybe I should paint my apartment.

Once everything was in, Cassandra and I started unpacking while Bergman and Vayl set everything up. Several of the boxes held computer components, and before long they'd transformed the dining room table into a communications center. Four PCs sat back-to-back, connected to each other, the Internet, and a central printer through a maze of cords that lay like a big, sloppy coil basket in the middle of them all. Our laptop sat beside them and yet separate, a snooty, secretive stepsister. The table was so long that half of it still remained free for other purposes.

Bergman and Vayl began setting up a minilab on the bar while Cassandra stored the empty boxes in a downstairs bedroom, so I got to work elsewhere.

"Jaz, why did you rearrange the furniture?" Bergman asked a few minutes later, staring curiously at me over a row of shiny glass beakers.

"What do you mean? I'm just—" I looked around the living room and realized I'd done it again. Without any conscious thought, as though an entire section of my brain had switched to blackout mode, I'd reproduced the same design I'd created at Diamond Suites. "What the hell?" I murmured.

Cassandra came down the hallway, took a look at my little project, and sent me a look of trepidation that cut straight to my heart. Vayl's forehead creased and the corners of his lips drooped. For him it was the equivalent of a thunderous frown.

"You deceived me about this, did you not?" he demanded, waving his hand to indicate the new room arrangement. "This is not how it once looked at your house." I shook my head. "I cannot abide liars." His tone, straight out of the Knuckle Crackers Handbook for Schoolmarms, made me grit my teeth. Before I could defend myself, or plan a massive spitball campaign with Jimmy and Susie that would probably get us expelled but would be well worth the trouble, Cassandra spoke up.

"I may be able to explain that better than Jasmine."

She brought out the smallest of her four suitcases and set it on the ottoman I'd moved from its spot beside the couch not five minutes earlier. Now it sat center stage. I sank onto the couch beside her. Vayl, still looking irritated, sat opposite us in a wing chair upholstered in blue twill.

Cassandra opened the case, reached into it, and brought out a foot-high pyramid made of multicolored glass orbs, each about the size of a large marble. I moved the case out of the way and Cassandra gently set the piece on the ottoman.

"Is this what I think it is?" I asked.

"The *Enkyklios*," she said, nodding. "My vision of

your . . . My second vision is recorded here." She touched the top marble of the pyramid and the whole thing shivered in response. "You may want to watch this in private."

"No," I said, challenging Vayl with my glare. "Let's keep this all wide open. That way nobody can accuse me of more lies, and later we can talk about how *I* can't abide people who leap to judgment!" I let the anger carry me, give me the strength to sit in the living room like a regular person rather than lock myself in a closet like a scared kid. It's hard. It hurts to stop hiding. Riding another, and probably my last, wave of anger, I said, "Let's do this."

She pressed on the top marble, which bent but didn't break, like the Jell-O molds Granny May used to make because she thought we liked the taste of rubbery strawberry letters and two-legged elephants.

"*Enkyklios occsallio vera proma,*" Cassandra whispered. Well, that's what it sounded like anyway. She kept going, reeling off a list of words that sounded like Latin but weren't. As she spoke, the marbles shivered again, then began to roll in random directions, though they never completely lost touch. It reminded me of clock gears, and yet no one movement seemed to trigger another.

The pyramid undid itself, rolling into a variety of other forms that resembled the prow of a ship, a sailor's hat, a Harley-Davidson, a strand of DNA.

"That is so cool," I whispered, despite my pounding heart and a nauseating fear of how Vayl would react to the new discovery. Bergman had left his lab/computer center, a miracle in itself, and sidled over to the empty wing chair. He stood behind it, looking as if he wanted to attack the *Enkyklios* with a bat.

At last the marbles stood in vertical rows of three, forming a sort of plateau with a single, bluish gold globe sitting above the rest. "Is that me?" I whispered, feeling a little faint as Cassandra nodded.

"Are you ready?" she asked. I rubbed sweaty palms down my pants.

"Yeah, yeah, yeah, let's get it done." My voice sounded fake in my own ears, a recording in definite need of a remix.

She touched the marble and said, *"Dayavatem."* She pulled her hand away and sat back, making room for the images that rose from it, digital-quality holographs in living color and sound.

I saw myself, fourteen months younger and light-years closer to innocence, sitting in the living room of what looked like an old frat house. The stuffing peeked out of several holes in the couch and love seat, the coffee table had once been a working door that now sat on a double-high pile of cement blocks, and the chairs only rocked because their legs were uneven.

"Look, Jaz," said Bergman, "the furniture in the picture is arranged the same way you did it just now."

"The same way she *always* does it," Vayl said, folding his arms across his chest.

"Since you're so determined to be mad at me, go right ahead," I said. "But the fact is I never knew why I kept moving the furniture around. I wasn't usually even aware I was doing it. Then you said something, and it seemed like such a strange thing to do." I shrugged. "I made up a reason so you wouldn't think I was crazy."

Did I detect a slight softening in Vayl's expression, or was I just fishing? Never mind. The show had gone on. In a room it hurt my heart to see again, my band of Helsingers and I sat around the recycled door playing a card game I knew I'd been good at but could no longer remember the name of.

I could tell we meant to go back out, because we still wore our uniforms. Superman Suits, we called them, featherlight body armor encased in navy blue leather. We were all high on adrenaline and success, toasting each other like German bobsledders, eating pizza, for God's sake. Pizza.

The room tilted and nearly took me with it. But Vayl's hand on my shoulder steadied me. I looked up, grateful he still thought enough of me to leave his chair. He settled on the arm of the couch beside me.

"I only remember bits of this," I said, sensing that explanations might keep me from falling headfirst into the nightmare that, until now, had only played itself out behind my eyelids. "That's Matt on my left. He'd just turned twenty-nine two weeks before. The tan is from the trip we'd taken to Hawaii to celebrate." My throat closed on the words, and for a minute I couldn't speak.

Matt and I sat on the couch, talking softly while the others played out the hand. Brad and Olivia, a married couple from Georgia, sat in the tattered love seat that met our couch at forty-five degrees. They took turns throwing red plastic chips into the growing pile and teasing each other about losing the down payment on their house in a single hand.

Dellan, a muscle-bound vamp who'd been turned in the sixties, sat on the floor to my right, cradling his crossbow, eating all the toppings off his pizza. He threw what was left to Thea, also a vamp and sometimes his lover—depending on how much he irritated her—who sat on the floor to Olivia's left. Tomato sauce made her gag, but she couldn't get enough of that stuffed crust.

We'd go back into the field as soon as the pizza and cards had played themselves out, but for now we were just kicking back and enjoying the company. "That's Jessie, sitting in the chair across from us, the one in front of the fireplace. She was my sister-in-law. She was—" I shook my head, not knowing how to capture in words Jessie's vibrant, infectious humor, her intense loyalty, her deep and abiding passion for my brother. "She was my hero."

Jessie had draped her leg across the chair beside her, as if saving it for David. Having made her bet, she was fashioning an airplane from a couple of paper towels. I knew eventually it would come floating my way and I would be required to throw my napkin back at her, but for now I was content to snuggle with my honey.

It felt a little sick to watch my handsome young lover rear his head back and laugh at one of my wiseass comments, as if I was some grief-crazed widow rolling out the home movies for a torturous walk over the coals of memory lane. But, God, it was good to see him, to see all of them, and remember with a sort of shock how happy we'd been together.

I started talking again, fighting the vortex of pain that had robbed me of everything I'd liked about myself. "Nobody ever heard the knock at the front door. No one except Ron. He was Dave's sub, a rookie straight out of the academy. He was still kind of sick from the slaying, not the vampire bit, the human part that comes before you get to the vampires. Anyway, he'd been visiting the upstairs bathroom periodically." We watched him, a young, spiky-haired version of David Spade, with the physique of a marathon runner and the constitution (at least temporarily) of a tubercular alcoholic. He was coming down the stairs, one hand on the rail, the other on his stomach.

In the living room it was my deal, and I'd just begun to shuffle the cards.

Ron came down the steps slowly, stepping in eerie time to the rhythm of my shuffling. When he reached the bottom, he heard the knock. Nobody else did. They were all yelling at me.

"Get the lead out and deal already!" Jessie roared, throwing her paper airplane at my head.

I grinned. "Just getting the cards warmed up for you, Jess."

A chorus of "Aw, come on!" and "Deal, dammit!" drowned out Ron, who was saying, "Please tell me you didn't order more pizza" as he opened the door.

A blue-eyed, long-legged blonde stood on the threshold, carrying an insulated pizza box container. She smiled coyly at Ron. "Hi. Wow, are you a SWAT guy? I love your uniform!"

Ron grinned. The poor fool couldn't help it. She resembled every centerfold he'd ever drooled over. "Kinda," he said. "Um, how much do I owe you?"

"Sixteen fifty," she said, flashing a couple of dimples, this time accompanied by a tempting bit of cleavage. "Do you mind if I come in?" she asked, looking over one shoulder with just the right hint of fear. "It's kind of creepy out here in the dark."

"Sure, come on in. My house is your house," he said, a chivalric knight taking temporary ownership of federal property to save his distressed damsel. It turned out she was just damned. Ron died with both hands in his pockets, fishing for a twenty while a goofy, I've-bagged-a-Playmate smile played across his face. Pizza Girl had lunged for his throat and torn out his larynx before he understood his mistake had killed us all.

The complaints from my comrades had finally reached a satisfying peak and I'd just dealt Matt his first card when we heard Ron's body hit the floor. Jessie, who had the best view of the entrance, jumped up and yelled, "Vampire!" just as Pizza Girl cried, "Enter and be welcome!" out the front door.

A stream of vamps poured into the house with the impact of a tidal wave. But we were nothing if not prepared, and all of us still wore the weapons we'd used to clear the nest earlier that day.

Brad and Olivia fought shoulder to shoulder, pumping bullets into the vamps. Pizza Girl, her chest a mix of her own blood and Ron's gore, waded through the barrage, lofted the love seat, and threw it at them. They went down in a flurry of splinters and stuffing, and the vamps went after them, swarming like locusts until all you could see were Brad's twitching fingers and all you could hear were Olivia's fading screams.

Dellan smoked two of the vamps who came after him, but with no time to restring his crossbow, he had to resort to hand-to-hand combat. His punches rocked the three monsters who came for him, his kicks knocked them back, and I'm sure I heard ribs crack before they overpowered him. One vamp, who looked like he should've been doling out the cash at First National's drive-up window, picked Dellan up and threw him headfirst into the fireplace, where he lay, limp and broken as a discarded doll. He followed up with a poker through Dellan's heart.

Thea emptied her magazine into the swarm before retreating to the fireplace wall and having at them with the ash shovel. She held her own until Dellan lost his battle. The momentary distraction of seeing him fade to nothing was all her attackers needed. They jumped her like a gang of rapists, only it wasn't her body they wanted. They bled her dry and finally smoked her while Matt, Jessie, and I made a fighting retreat to the kitchen and the back door that entered into it. We delivered bolts, body blows, and bullets in equal numbers. For a minute there was so much blood and smoke in the air you'd swear it was storming plasma.

"Get out, Jessie!" I yelled. She stood closest to the door. "Get help!" She ran to the door and I shot the vamp who tried to intercept her, tore a hole through his brain that would take days to heal. She wrenched the door open and stepped outside. But they were waiting for her, a hungry little horde of newbies so freshly turned their bite marks still remained, livid and glowing to my new-seeing eyes.

Through a haze of grief and unshed tears, though my teeth were chattering like a badly tuned engine, I managed to say, "I don't remember anything at all after Jessie's death."

"I hate for you to have to see this," Cassandra whispered, clutching her hands together so tightly her nails made bloody imprints in her skin. "But it's necessary in order for you to understand the final outcome—to believe."

Oh, I've believed I was God's biggest mistake for some

time now, Cassandra, I thought as I watched Matt and former me trade blows with our adversaries. It seemed like they were everywhere, although I only counted four. They just moved so quickly it was like fighting an army.

"What?" said a voice from my holographic memory, one I now recognized. "Are they *still* alive?"

Aidyn Strait stepped into the room and we experienced a sudden cease-fire. He sneered at us, his fangs dripping with the blood of the other Helsingers. "When you killed my humans, you set me back years in my research. Did you know that?" He snatched a knife from the butcher-block table that stood just inside the kitchen/living room throughway. "That makes me angry. And it's not nice to make Aidyn angry, is it, children?"

The other vamps flinched at their own hidden memories and shook their heads.

One moment Aidyn was sidling toward us; the next he was a blur of motion. He dove at me, the knife he held a glittering extension of his arm.

"Jasmine!" I'd never heard such fear in Matt's voice; it squeezed at my heart. But I couldn't comfort him because I couldn't escape the blade. Unbalanced by the speed of the attack, realizing my fatal vulnerability, I felt this tremendous, oceanic regret that my life should end so soon, with so much left undone.

And then Matt was there, pushing me aside, standing where I'd stood, trying to deflect the blade, trying to defend me. I grabbed at him, attempted to reverse direction and push him out of the way. I was still innocent enough to believe the blade would pause, give me the time I needed to save him. But all my youth and all my will did nothing to slow the blade's descent. I watched it fall and wanted to be the one beneath it after all. But time ran out on me.

Both in that place and in Cassandra's living room, tears rained down my cheeks and I jerked like a marionette as Aidyn's blade pierced Matt's chest. He crumpled to the floor, pulling my whole world with him. An abyss of grief opened beneath me, obliterating every other thought.

I knelt over Matt, weeping uncontrollably. And Aidyn, his knife still in Matt's chest, closed in. One kick, powerfully dealt and directly on target, snapped my neck. I slumped over Matt, so obviously dead that present-day me put my hands to my chest, puzzled and amazed that I could feel my heart beating.

Every eye in the room was on me, but I couldn't tear my gaze from the tragedy that had ended life as I knew it. I shook my head. "I didn't know," I told them. "I don't remember this."

Bergman started to speak, "How—"

"It is a shame we had to kill them, in a way," said holographic Aidyn. "They would have made excellent lab rats."

"We turned at least one of them." Pizza Girl had come to survey the damage. "You can experiment on her." She nudged my body with her toe. "Did you get to see this one's face when she died, Aidyn? I love to see their faces as they die."

Suddenly, like a window opening in my brain, I remembered why I'd missed Christmas. I'd been chasing Pizza Girl. In fact, I'd nailed her with the syringe Liliana had escaped. And my other long blackouts, yeah, those had been revenge trips too. During the past fourteen months I'd killed every vampire in the holograph except Aidyn Strait.

Good God Almighty, if one more insight crashed into my skull today my eyes would stop spinning and just completely pop out of their sockets.

In the holograph there was no movement, no noise, and yet all the vamps jerked their heads up, looked to one corner of the kitchen ceiling as if something hovered there, threatening their very existence. And it did. I could almost see it, like the superheated air over a bonfire.

"Out," hissed Pizza Girl. "Back through the front door. Move!"

They ran like scared kids, cleared out of the house so fast the curtains swirled in their wake.

"I don't see anything," said Bergman.

I felt sorry for him. Because I *could.* My soul rose from my body and stretched, reaching over to touch Matt's soul as it hovered in the air, seafoam green laced with dark blue, a living jewel that suddenly flew apart just like poor Charlie's had. Most of it raced out into the night. But some remained, swirled into my silver-red essence and stayed there, waiting with me, becoming part of me.

A golden light, bright as a meteor, warm as a pair of fuzzy slippers, moved from its spot in that superheated corner of the ceiling and encompassed me, coalescing into human form. Into a man. He could've been one of David's men, his bearing was so upright, so military. But he was as gentle as a lover as he turned my body so my sightless eyes faced his. He laid my hands across my stomach and straightened my twisted neck. He leaned over and lay his lips on mine, passing his breath into my mouth. Then he sat back on his heels.

"What is it that you want, Jasmine?"

He watched my mouth open, heard me say, "To fight." Nodding with satisfaction, he touched the tips of his fingers to my neck and leaned in to lend me one last breath.

Chapter Twenty-one

I've lived through some strange moments. Once, when Granny May took me Christmas shopping, we stopped at a Hallmark store. I was idly eyeing a display of candles, trying to decide if I could weasel twenty-five cents out of her for a gum ball when all the candles suddenly lit. I looked around and caught the eyes of a boy my age who, with a jerk of his head, put them all out again. It's certainly a novel way to meet girls and one I hope worked out for him in the end.

Another time, I was working a case that required me to partner with a coven of witches who got so irate at our target that they cursed him. Before I could actually eliminate him, he stepped off the curb wrong and broke his ankle, ate a hamburger that had been left out overnight and spent a night in the hospital puking it up, found his wife cheating with his boss, and chipped most of his front tooth off when a drunken waiter got too enthusiastic with a champagne cork and let it fly into his face. I think by the end he was probably grateful when an honest-to-goodness piano fell on his head.

I've met psychics and snake charmers, serial killers and geniuses. But nothing in my experience had ever come close to watching my own rebirth. I suddenly understood the supernatural meaning of "weird." I'd always imagined resurrections would be quiet, sacred events. But now I thought maybe Lazarus had screamed just like holographic me did when my soul plummeted back into my body and parts that should never be broken were forced into repair.

My first deep, whooping intake of air echoed Vayl's nightly wakings in a way that made the watching me shudder. The creature who'd brought me back gave me a strange look, a mix of pride and pity that made him seem ancient. By the time I opened my eyes he was gone.

Feeling an immense sense of confusion, I struggled to focus. My first movements were so random I looked more like an infant than a professional vampire killer. A supreme effort brought me around to my hands and knees, and that's when I saw Matt. The soul behind my eyes cracked like roughly used china.

Cassandra touched the orb and the picture faded as my true collapse began. I remembered it all now. The keening, the wailing, the crawling through the blood of my team, screaming for help. Losing, losing, losing my mind. I sent her a grateful glance for sparing me the humiliation of an audience for at least that part of my journey through hell.

"I am so sorry," she said, swiping at the tears that rolled down her cheeks. She kept trying, and failing, to meet my eyes. Maybe she thought I intended to punish the messenger. And, okay, the thought had crossed my mind. *Very* briefly.

"I'm not mad, Cassandra," I said. I struggled to explain. "For me, it's always better to know. There was so much I couldn't remember about that night, so much I needed to understand. Now I guess I do."

"Yeah, but can you believe it?" asked Bergman. "I sat here and watched the whole thing and I'm still trying to wrap my mind around the fact that you're—"

I cocked my head at him. "Alive? Or should I say undead?"

Vayl gave my shoulder a sympathetic squeeze. "Welcome to the club."

Eventually the shock faded, replaced by our pressing need to rescue Cole and my own personal desire to reduce Aidyn to so much vapor. Vayl's focus remained on Assan, as it should. And we hoped to find all three at Alpine Meadows.

Everybody sort of wandered off, leaving me free to do what I needed. So I worked. Packing our gear calmed me more than anything. The familiar movements through my memorized checklist made me feel, well, real. I spent extra time cleaning Grief, making sure it was fully loaded and ready to smoke. I found new pockets for the toys Bergman had provided that I wasn't actually wearing, and stowed the rest of our stuff where it belonged. I came more fully back to myself when I banged my head on the van door while loading it, and finally understood why sometimes people just need to be pinched.

We left Bergman elbow deep in blood tests and Cassandra up to her eyeballs in some musty old books she'd brought with her. If worse came to worse, as I find it often does, maybe she could figure out how to deal with the Tor-al-Degan. She was sure giving it the old college try. She'd read for a while, find something pertinent, and whisper it to the *Enkyklios*. She hadn't gotten the marbles to move by the time we headed for the van, but hopefully it was just a matter of time.

Behind the wheel again, I maneuvered the van through traffic without once swearing at the red Volkswagen that cut me off or the light blue Taurus that hugged my bumper like a lost and lonely child. When it finally turned off our street, Vayl heaved a sigh of relief. "I expected you to slam on the brakes if that man followed you any closer."

"The thought never crossed my mind."

He sat silent and stared at me for so long I started to squirm. "What?" I finally asked.

"Are you going to change now?"

The question took me aback. "Shouldn't I?"

He frowned. Then the mask returned, settling over his face like a shroud. "Of course. Never mind."

"Look, Vayl, it's . . . Reliving the nightmare . . . This new knowledge . . . It's too much, you know? I don't know how to act. Hell, I don't know what to think." I shook my head. "It's too big for me to figure out all at once. So I'm just going to be Jaz Parks, Albert's daughter, Dave and Evie's sister, and Vayl's *avhar* for now. If I need to tack another label on later"—*angel? demon? zombie?*—"I guess there's room there at the end of the list."

Vayl's eyes snapped to my face when I said "*avhar*" and stayed there until I met them with my own. The shroud lifted and he smiled. "I like your plan."

"Is that what it is?"

"Yes."

"How about my idea to rescue Cole?"

"I like that too. Where are the smoke grenades?"

"In the duffel with everything else."

"What about this new communications invention Bergman gave you?"

"Might as well try it out." I told him where to find it and he dug it out, handing me my hearing aid and mouth-mint, putting his own in place. We did a little test and I got goose bumps when Vayl's voice came to me in Barry White bass. They disappeared when he told me mine did the same.

Forty-five minutes later we reached the cul-de-sac behind Assan's house. We would access his property from the back, case the place, figure out who was situated where, and move on to Plan B, which involved heaps of smoke and a well-timed call to the fire department. During the diversion we would execute Cole's rescue, and the Double As, if our luck held. But not until they'd spilled all the juicy details on tomorrow's ritual. Then we'd make them all wish they'd caught their own virus.

Big words for a skinny, redheaded woman who had never felt so overwhelmed in her life. Because, to be honest, I wasn't sure we could pull this off. Yeah, we would put up a helluva fight. But we were going against the most vicious, brutal minds on the planet. People who didn't believe in rules or mercy or the sanctity of life. And even worse, people with the money and the contacts to pull off whatever atrocious plan their devious little minds could concoct. To top it all off, I had no idea how to beat their Kyron. Starve it? Give it permanent amnesia? *You've got to be kidding me!* Hopefully we could wring that information out of Aidyn and Assan as well. Otherwise Cassandra, her ancient tomes, and her New Age library would be holding our last hope.

We parked the van, Vayl retrieved our bag, and I locked it up tight, using a special button on Bergman's key ring to activate its security system. I wasn't sure how it worked, but I wouldn't have been surprised to learn that he'd rigged the van to blow if anyone so much as wiggled the door handle while it was set.

The oval of pavement we'd chosen as our parking lot was well lit but quiet. Each of the six homes that surrounded it looked fit to house a president. But despite the lights glowing behind several of the windows, I had a feeling no one was home. It gave credence to my theory that anyone who could afford such luxury never had time to enjoy it.

We walked into the strip of trees that led to the edge of Assan's property. An artfully landscaped palm grove, it reminded me, despite the lights at my back, of a desert island. But maybe that was because I couldn't shake the feeling Cassandra's little show had given me that I'd been marooned. When we hit the border of those trees and saw Assan's expansive backyard, the feeling grew into a sickening sort of anxiety.

"Vayl," I whispered, "something's wrong."

He nodded. "We will wait and watch." Fifteen minutes later nothing had moved, inside the house or out, and I still couldn't relax. "I was kind of expecting dogs," I said.

"Or at least a patrol," Vayl added. "Let us go."

We made the short, cross-country run to the kitchen door without incident. I started to check out the security system, then realized the door was cracked open.

"Vayl." I spoke so low I thought even Bergman's communicators wouldn't pick me up, but he turned to look at me. I pointed at the door, said, "Trap?"

He studied it and what he could see of the dark, empty room beyond through the window. "It could be," he whispered. He nudged the door open and squeezed through. Snapping my watch band for maximum stealth, I followed close behind. My disquieting feeling doubled. I concentrated on it, tried to pinpoint its source.

"Something's really wrong here," I hissed as we crept past a six-burner stove, an immense island, a three-door fridge. "Somebody's feeling extreme . . . It's hard to explain. They're . . . on some sort of edge."

"Yes, I feel it too. What do you think? Are they waiting for us?" Vayl asked.

"I don't know."

We found the back stair that Cole had used to escape from the guards at the party. Vayl gestured that he would check the rooms along the farthest hall, so I took the three closest, working my way from the back toward the restroom where Cole and I had met.

No one occupied the first room, but Derek's scent lingered, the way it will beside an empty trash bin. The second room had been an office, and might be again. But the file drawers sat open and empty. So too did the desk drawers. And a dust outline showed where the computer had rested.

"They've cleared out," I said. "This room used to hold a paper trail. Now even the shredder's clean."

"So far only two deserted bedrooms over here," Vayl told me. "Empty hangers. Empty drawers."

"*Damn!* So much for solid evidence."

"Maybe not. I hear something coming from the third room."

"I'll be right there." I hurried across the front hall to where Vayl stood, poised to open the third door once he'd satisfied himself it didn't hide an army.

"That's the source of the bad feelings I'm getting," I whispered, "behind that door."

"Did you hear that?" Vayl asked.

I nodded, trying to identify the sound. There it went again, the deep, throaty utterance of a person in pain. And then—"Is that . . . ?"

"Crying? I think so."

"Let's get in there."

For an answer, Vayl tried the door. It was locked.

"No problem," I whispered, pulling off my necklace. I slid the shark tooth into the lock, waited a second, turned it. The door yielded to my funky key with a soft click. I left the key in the lock and drew Grief. Vayl had left his cane in the van, but he was hardly unarmed. I felt his power shift and rise as we prepared to enter the room.

"On three," Vayl whispered. He raised his fingers in quick succession, one, two, three. Vayl threw open the door, shoving his power in front of him like a winter storm. Anyone inside would feel it as a compelling need to do whatever Vayl required before their eyelids froze shut.

I dove inside, staying low, seeking targets. The only one I saw was bleeding too heavily to be any sort of threat.

I holstered Grief and ran to where she lay on the floor of a bedroom so frilly and sumptuous I could not have imagined violence occurring there, except for the beaten woman sprawled on the Persian rug.

"Amanda?"

She moaned, tried to open her swollen eyes. Only the right one obeyed, and that by just a slit. "He said you'd come."

"Assan?"

She shook her head, winced, and fresh tears tracked down her torn and broken face. "Cole," she croaked. I could hardly believe talking was still an option for her.

"Give me your phone," Vayl said. "I am calling an ambulance."

I fished it from my pocket and tossed it to him.

"Too late," Amanda gasped. "I'm . . . you *must* listen." She reached up and I took her hand. It seemed to comfort her. "I thought that . . . since I couldn't sneak you in here . . . I could find some evidence for you."

"Oh, Amanda. Didn't Cole tell you how dangerous your husband is?"

"Yes." She licked her lips. "So thirsty."

"I will get you some water," said Vayl, his call already complete. He left the room.

"Is that the vampire?" she asked.

"Yes."

"Mohammed . . . thought he was dead."

"How do you know that?"

She took a couple of breaths, seemed to steel herself.

"I overheard him talking on the phone. So I confronted him."

"I sure wish you hadn't done that."

"We fought," she went on, her voice bleak. "He . . . admitted he killed my brother. He said Michael was a Son of Paradise too. That the trip to India was his idea, to get some relics they needed to summon . . . But then he tried to back out." In my imagination I could see them fighting over Assan's virulent plans, with Michael dying horribly as a result. But what in the world had he *thought* would happen? It angered me that this family had no sense of self-preservation. Somebody should've smacked them upside the heads years ago and said, "Wake up, fools! You can be hurt!" But even as I raged, logical me wondered why the move to the United States when they already had the Kyron in their pockets in India.

Amanda went on. "He made me admit I'd hired Cole. Then he brought Cole here and made him watch while he . . . beat . . . me." One hopeless sob escaped her swollen lips.

"The bastard's going to die for this, Amanda."

Amanda sighed. "Okay." She was quiet for so long I thought maybe she'd passed out. Or passed on. She stirred. "He burned the files. Took the bag from the safe. Except for . . . He said it was the key, so I snuck it from the bag while he was . . . out."

The hand I wasn't holding had been lying across her chest. Now she raised it, pointed to the bed. I lifted the ruffled skirt, fighting a flash of childhood apprehension as I peered underneath. Even with my enhanced night vision I could barely see the pyramid that sat there, just tall enough to brush the bedspring. I pulled it out. It weighed a lot more than I'd expected.

"What is it the key to?" I wondered aloud.

Vayl, who'd just reentered the room, came over to look. "Something else for Cassandra to research?"

"I guess so. If she has time. If *we* have time."

Vayl helped Amanda drink some of the water he'd brought her. When she'd had her fill, he laid her head back onto a pillow I had taken from the bed. I'd never seen him so gentle.

"Mohammed took everything else with him." Amanda's mind must have been wandering—or shutting down. She was repeating herself. But her next comment was new. "He said the things in his bag . . . he'd used them to summon his goddess and that"—she squeezed her good eye shut and new tears emerged—"that it had eaten my brother's soul." I patted her arm, at a loss to know how to comfort her.

I spoke to Vayl now. "There it is, proof that he summoned the Tor-al-Degan in India. So why didn't it decimate that country? Why does he need to do it again over here?"

"Maybe he did something wrong there. Maybe he timed it wrong," suggested Vayl.

I shook my head, frustrated by our ignorance. "Maybe Cassandra will come up with something."

We heard the strident wail of the ambulance and silently agreed it was time to go.

"We have to leave, Amanda," I said. "The paramedics are here." But she didn't hear me. Sometimes it happens like that, while you're looking the other way, distracted by events and conversations. Sometimes people just go. Those quiet departures sit wrong with me. Death should be louder.

"Wait," I said as Vayl took the pyramid. It seemed disrespectful to leave before Amanda. Her essence rose from her body, violet and blue with large golden crystals interspersed here and there.

"Do you see it?" I whispered. Vayl shook his head. "I wish you could see it. It's so . . ." There really were no words. Maybe just the "ooh" and "aah" that comes unbidden from you when you see an amazing display of fireworks. And then, just as suddenly as the fire fades from the sky, she was gone.

I retrieved my necklace/key from the door and we left the way we'd come, melting into the trees along the edge of Assan's estate just as the ambulance crew reached Amanda's room and turned the light on.

"We've got to find Cole." An unnecessary statement, I know, but I could hardly contain the urgency I felt.

"Where do you suggest we look?"

"I've only seen Assan in one other place—chatting up Aidyn Strait at Club Undead."

"It is as good a place to try as any."

I let Vayl drive. I think he was flattered. To be honest, directing a van down the interstate is, for me, at most a Jell-O-mold-elephant kind of thrill. Plus, I needed to get some updates. I called Bergman first. After a series of annoying beeps and whistles he answered. "Is this line secure?" he asked.

"Safe as a home run hitter. What have you got?"

"Drugs in Vayl's blood supply called Topamax. They

tried to dope him with a huge dosage of an antiseizure medication that's also used to prevent migraines."

I repeated the report to Vayl, who let out a string of curses that would've made Hugh Hefner blush.

"Okay, thanks. How's Cassandra doing?"

"No luck so far."

"Um, would you mind helping her with her research? We really need to find out all we can about this monster." I described the pyramid we'd found and waited for him to jump on the bandwagon. Unfortunately he's afraid of wagons. And bands. There was this pause, during which I could almost hear him cringing.

"Bergman, she's trustworthy."

His voice dropped to a whisper. "I don't know. She's got that funky, supernatural thing going on."

"As opposed to Vayl's perfectly straightforward existence? And mine, come to think of it?"

"She's different."

"In what way?" I asked, wishing I could reach through the receiver and shake some sense into him.

"What if she touches me?"

Aah, now we were getting somewhere. The man who hoarded his secrets like pirate treasure wanted nothing to do with the woman who could divine them anytime she pleased. I said, "I promise she won't touch you. And if you're that worried about it, go find a pair of gloves. Tell her you're cold and get busy helping us out, man!"

"Okay, then," he said after some hesitation. "You'll call?"

"Or come knocking."

"Good enough." We broke the connection. Albert was next on my list. He answered on the first ring.

"Dad?"

"Jaz? Hang on." The background blare of Albert's TV muted. I heard more clicks as he transferred to his safe phone. "Okay, I'm here."

"I know it hasn't been long, but—"

"I've got a lead."

"Yeah?" I guess I sounded, well, shocked, because he said, "Hey, I may be a feeble old Marine, but I've still got connections."

"And?"

"There's something funny about Tom Bozcowski."

"The retired football player?"

"Right. He's had an unnaturally large turnover in interns. Seems they keep getting sick."

"With what?"

"Anemia."

"That *is* interesting. Has the name Mohammed Khad Abn-Assan come up in relation to the senator? Or maybe Aidyn Strait?"

"Hang on, that first name sounds familiar."

He started to mumble to himself, not so you could understand him, and I heard the sound of papers shuffling. "Yeah, here it is. I asked my contact for anything unusual, and he included this little item with the other stuff. Says here Bozcowski had plastic surgery done by Assan right before he ran for senator five years ago."

"Thanks. Keep digging, will you?"

"Sure thing. Oh, and that little secretary of yours? Martha?"

"Yeah?" I kept my voice cool, but inside my heart had jumped several inches to the right.

"She's clean."

Glory hallelujah! "Thanks! Hey, while you're researching, would you see if Bozcowski has a prescription for a drug called Topamax? And look for connections to technology purchasing for the Agency." I described the faulty beacon without saying how I'd carried it. No point in starting a fight I didn't have time to finish. "Also see if he's got any connections to an exotic pet dealer or something similar. We found a dead rattlesnake in Vayl's luggage and we'd like to know who packed it."

"Damn! Okay. Uh, Jaz?"

"Yeah?"

"Are you eating right? Getting plenty of fruits and vegetables and all that stuff? I'm just asking because Shelby's been lecturing me on nutrition. You'd be surprised what good food'll do for you."

"Don't worry," I said, both exasperated that it took this long for the blockhead to figure out maybe he should eat well, and warmed by the fact that he gave a crap about my health. "I'm eating fine." *So's my vampire friend, but we won't get into that. No sense in flirting with a stroke at your age, Albert.* "Why don't you call Evie? She definitely needs a good lecture on nutrition."

"Maybe I will."

I hung up. Vayl glanced over at me and both his eyebrows went straight up.

"What is the source of your evil grin?" he inquired.

"I sicced Albert on Evie."

"I thought you loved your sister."

"I do. She'll worry less when she hears from him, and that's good for the baby. So's eating right, which is all he'll probably talk about."

"I see. Is that the only reason you are smiling?"

"Martha's innocent." That got a big twitch of the lip, which translated to a big grin for Vayl. "And I think we found our senator."

Chapter Twenty-two

Club Undead waved its tacky tombstones at us as we drove slowly by. A new bouncer watched the front, where only the loveliest and palest of partiers lined up for their chance to touch immortality. Beside the bouncer stood a sign on an easel that hadn't been there before. A mix of words traced in neon colors spelled out the message WELCOME TO JAZZ NIGHT, only the colors were arranged so that the words "Welcome Jaz" stood out in glowing yellow relief against the black of the board. An arrow drawn in the same glowing yellow pointed straight up.

"Do you see it?" I asked, leaning past Vayl to get a better view.

"I do."

"Do you think Cole's in there surrounded by goons who're just waiting to shoot me?"

"I would say that is the most likely scenario."

Even with the heater on and my jacket zipped, I felt chilled. But my fear factor didn't matter. Cole needed me. "Let me off at the corner, okay?"

"What are you going to do?"

"Smoke out the innocents downstairs, then meet you

upstairs. I think that's his most likely location. Remember, they believe you're dead. Use it to your advantage."

"I always do." He pulled up to the curb; I got out and waved him off. He'd park in the alley and make his way to the club's upper story from there. I opened my jacket, walked to the line in front of the club, wiggled my butt right up to the new bouncer, and gave him a smile so sweet, if they put me on TV I could've sold chocolate-covered cherries to an audience of diabetics.

Okay, Amanda, wherever you are . . . this one's for you.

"Do you know what I smell?" I asked the bouncer.

"Nope." He looked interested though.

"I smell freshly turned vamp." I reached into the special pocket reserved for Grief and it came to my hand smooth and deadly as a cobra strike. A flick of the magic button, and two seconds later all that remained of the bouncer was a puff of smoke rising from a tiny rain of debris.

The girls at the front of the line screamed and shoved their way to the street. A few others went with them. Somebody yelled, "Gun!" An understandable mistake considering the crappy lighting, and a mini stampede ensued, during which I let myself into Club Undead. The music hit me like a hammer. Who knew jazz could be so intense?

My smoke grenades worked like those little air fresheners you plug in. They had a vent timed to open within twenty seconds of deployment and a fan to spread the smoke within a ten-yard radius. Since Bergman had designed them, I could hold two snugly in each hand and still depend on enough black clouds to make it look like a national forest had caught fire. I distributed them evenly throughout the lower level, avoiding the usual pack of immortal-minded dancers as I moved around the room.

"Vayl, where are you?"

"Approaching the fire escape."

"I'm taking the spiral staircase now." I slid past loud, laughing couples who seemed to think they'd found a permanent resting spot up to the second level, which was just as crowded as the first.

Lit mainly by blue flashing lights and the red and white exit sign stationed above a dark door on the back wall, the cavernous room managed to feel like a damn tunnel. I wiped the sweat off my upper lip as I walked past the dance floor and a steady succession of tables dressed in white cloths. Each held a vase with a black rose in it. Matching black candles flanked the roses, each held by expensive-looking crystal. Men and women leaned toward each other across the tables, trading passionate looks and caresses, making me wonder how they didn't catch their hair on fire.

Speaking of which—

"Fire!"

The smoke grenades popped one after another, sending clouds of black smoke billowing toward the ceiling.

Screaming. Shoving. Flailing arms and pounding feet. The kind of chaos the Sons of Paradise relished. Only this time it was working for me.

I moved quickly toward the exit sign, eyeing the door it highlighted. No telling what lay behind it, and any surprises promised to be nasty. I looked around, hoping to find another way up. What I saw suspended from the ceiling reminded me of a university theater. Lights tilting at every possible angle covered the entire expanse except for the section taken up by the catwalk. It started at a glass-walled booth, perched nearly ten feet above my current position, and wandered across the ceiling in a pattern that allowed access to all the lights. A black metal ladder, nearly invisible against the darker black wall, allowed access from my level. I told Vayl what I'd found.

"I'm going to check it out," I said. "Maybe the booth has a back door."

"Good idea. I am headed up to the third level now. It looks as if the windows are boarded over, so you will have to be my eyes."

"Okay."

I climbed the ladder, which hugged the wall from floor to ceiling, intersecting the catwalk on its way. From there just a couple of steps took me to the door of the overlook. It was open. "I'm in the booth," I whispered. "It's empty. I love smoke."

To my left, a bank of blinking controls stretched from one edge of the window to the next. Two black chairs on rollers parked in front of it. The only other contents of the room were an empty trash can and a full ashtray. There was, however, another door. I eased it open, expecting a sound, a click maybe, that would signal the closing of a trap. I need not have bothered. The trap Aidyn and Assan had set for me was too big for a click. A gong, maybe, but not a click.

My senses told me the room wasn't empty, was actually inhabited by someone feeling deep, repeated waves of misery, and once again they were right. I pulled a long-handled dental mirror out of the kit I'd packed at Bergman's and slipped it through the crack I'd made in the door. I couldn't see any guards, not one. I did see Cole.

He sat in a chair in the middle of a room that reminded me strongly of Granny May's attic. Boxes, old trunks, and abandoned chairs took up every bit of wall space. From the scuff marks in the dust, it looked like they'd been shoved to the sides to make room for the chair. And Cole.

He sat perfectly still, looking straight ahead, breathing through his mouth because his nose had been broken. The only way I managed to contain the fury I felt at seeing him hurt so badly was to promise myself I would damage Assan extensively before I finally wiped him off the face of the earth.

After another look around the room, I decided Cole was its sole occupant.

"Jaz?" Vayl's voice in my ear held the slightest trace of worry.

"I'm here. So's Cole. No sign of his captors."

"These boards are flimsy. I can break through them anytime you need me."

"But you'd rather keep a low profile?"

"Yes, for now. We are going to get only one chance at this surprise. Just be careful."

"I've been hanging with you for the past six months," I reminded him. "Careful, okay, it's not my middle name. But I'm warming up to the idea." I nudged the door wider with my foot while I trained Grief on various sections of the room, both of us primed for attack. The only thing that happened was Cole turned his head and saw me.

He looked like a spring break boozer who'd somehow survived a tumble off the balcony. Black-and-blue bruises covered his entire face, except for where it was red from dried blood. Blood-crusted gashes showed through his torn clothes. His hands, lying limp in his lap, were swollen, the knuckles scraped and cut. He could've gotten up at any time; nothing bound him to the chair, or even to the room, but he stayed put, looking at me with wordless regret.

"Cole?" I stepped forward and he said, "Stop." The word came out slurred, mostly due to his fat lip, but I also noticed a couple of gaps where he'd had teeth the last time we talked.

"We've got to get out of here," I urged him.

"Can't."

"What?"

He shifted his gaze and I followed his eyes to a dark, lifeless TV that sat on top of a round, wooden bar stool. It blinked to life and within seconds I was involved in a staring match with Mohammed Khad Abn-Assan.

Mostly for Vayl's benefit I said, "Assan, what are you doing on TV? Don't you know lowlifes like you have been outlawed by the FCC?"

"Good evening, Lucille. Or should I say Jasmine? We appreciate your quick arrival. It gives us some extra time to prepare."

"For what?"

He chuckled, flashing a couple of gold fillings as he looked off camera, sharing his amusement with his comrades. "Why, the end of the world as we know it."

The fear that spiked through me fueled my comeback. "You know, you could be killed for throwing clichés around like they actually mean something. However, I believe I'll take you out for your other crimes instead. Starting with your wife's death."

Cole made a desolate sound that demanded comfort. But I couldn't give it. Not now, while I was still locked in conversation with Assan.

He laughed again, his absolute lack of remorse making me feel truly murderous. "You are a jewel. How fortunate for us both that my master has created the perfect setting for you."

"Bozcowski's not a master. He's a slave to his own psychotic fantasies." *Come on, Senator, see if your ego can take that blow, even though we both know who's really in charge.*

My comment worked like peanut butter on a mousetrap. No sooner had I laid it down than there came the rodent himself, leaping into the camera frame, red-faced and defiant. I expected him to bluster, but he pulled it together fast. He actually smoothed his thick, stubby fingers through his gray-blond hair and straightened his navy blue suit coat. Ah, the magic of television.

"You are a straight-talking woman, aren't you?" he said. "Well then, I'll give it to you straight. Your actions in the next few minutes will determine whether or not your young man dies. You see, we've strapped a clever little device beneath the seat of his chair. If his weight leaves that chair, it will explode, destroying the two of you, the club, and most of the block it sits on. Think of the loss of innocent life."

"Go on."

"We can disarm it temporarily from our present position, but only for the ten seconds it would take for you to switch places with him."

Scumbag. "You don't mind if I check out your story, do you?"

He beamed at me as if I'd just won him a bet. His jowls quivered with pleasure, reminding me of that bulldog from the old cartoon. Would he come prancing into the room if I yelled, "Oh, Belvedere, come *here,* boy!" I hid a smirk at the mental image as he said, "Of course not. Feel free."

I knelt in the dust of Club Undead's attic and peered under the chair. Yup, definitely a bomb. I had seen similar devices in bomb squad manuals under the heading "Run Like Hell!" Though I felt pretty sure Bozcowski had exaggerated its power—I doubted it carried enough explosive to take out much more than the building's top floor—it would still kill Cole and all the people they'd managed to herd back upstairs. Not an acceptable scenario. I had that sinking-in-quicksand feeling that any escape we attempted now would only make us descend deeper and die sooner.

I stood up again, my mind looping around a single word—*run, run, run, run*–and providing the Pink Floyd soundtrack to back it. A roaring began in my ears, and it had nothing to do with my reconfigured hearing aids. The blackness came next, creeping into my peripheral vision like a feral dog, making my face tingle, making my eyes water. Instinct made me stiffen, resist. It felt so much like losing control, being engulfed in some other, more powerful personality.

I looked at Cole and my heart began its own chant. *Get him out. Get him safe. Whatever it takes. Whatever it takes. Whatever . . .*

I let my head fall forward and closed my eyes. Without

the distraction of sight, I could feel the blackness towering over my psyche like a monstrous storm-filled sky. I resisted the urge to bolt. I didn't invite it in. I just listened. Instantly the roaring sounded less like the Atlantic hammering Florida during Hurricane Barney and more like . . . a voice. All it said was "Let yourself go," but the words carried a richer meaning, showed me exactly what needed to be done. I recognized that voice. It belonged to the golden man who had brought me back to life. To fight.

I raised my head and opened my eyes, catching Bozcowski in such a look of greedy anticipation that I was suddenly reminded of the villain who starred in many of my childhood nightmares, the kid snatcher from *Chitty Chitty Bang Bang.*

"Why me?" I asked.

"Previous experience has taught us we need a willing sacrifice. Taking Cole's place makes you willing. It also eliminates the irritation you've been causing." As if I was a hangnail. But there's power in being so severely underestimated.

I addressed Assan. "So that's why using Amanda's brother in India failed, huh? He wasn't a willing sacrifice. Way to read the fine print, doofus."

Assan's eyes nearly crossed with fury at my disrespect, but something made him look off camera, then move aside. Aidyn Strait joined him and Bozcowski in front of the lens. I fought to remain calm, to mask the fury that whipped through me with stunning force.

"There is no such thing as a failed experiment," Aidyn informed me. "I was working on an entirely different project when I discovered the Red Plague quite by accident. And I could never have developed it without a series of trials helping me refine it to full potency."

The Red Plague? Such a simple name for something designed to be so horrific. I felt sure we were only going to get one chance to turn the tide, so I kept playing along, fishing for information, watching for some slip that would betray their weakness. I said, "That's what I don't get. Why don't you just let it spread the way the flu does? Why all this elaborate human-to-vampire mumbo jumbo?"

Aidyn couldn't wait to brag on his baby. He spoke eagerly, as if I was the science reporter for the *New York Times*. "When I began this experiment I planned for a sexual transmission. You people were so steeped in free love and multiple partners, I supposed sixty-five percent of you would have been dead in six weeks. But the virus mutated into a nonlethal form of pneumonia when humans spread it to one another."

"How frustrating for you," I said.

Aidyn nodded grimly, totally missing the sarcasm. He went on. "I found out quite by accident that when vampires take the blood of a human carrier, however, the Red Plague becomes nearly ninety percent lethal. However, it also loses its contagion characteristics."

I interrupted him. "You mean, it can't be spread?"

"Not by the vampire carrier. I cannot tell you how provoking the entire process has been."

Wow. Did anybody else see a divine hand dipping down to smack Aidyn every time he took a forward step on this one? First his abominable disease turns into a bunny rabbit when he tries to get humans to pass it around. Then he gets the bright idea for vamps to take the lead role, but they're like a bunch of two-year-olds. *No, we won't share!*

Aidyn continued. "However, *One* among us knew the story of a visionary leader named Tequet Dirani and how he nearly ruled this world and those beyond with the help of the Tor-al-Degan. *She* will be our delivery system. She will take the plague from the infected vampire and spread it to the world."

"So what are you telling me, that I should send my damn-you're-an-evil-genius Hallmark card to the Raptor?"

Bang. If we'd been standing in front of an impartial jury I'd have gotten my guilty verdict simply from the expressions on their faces. They recovered quickly, however, and without revealing anything incriminating, damn them.

This would also have been the ideal time for the Raptor, himself, to jump in front of the camera and gloat. He didn't. Svetlana must have been telling the truth about him taking wing, so to speak. Did he want to have some sort of alibi ready when the plague hit? "No, Officer, it couldn't have been me. I was playing racquetball that night." Naw. More likely he had some other power play cooking that he had to attend to before it got all dry and crusty. Dirtbags like him never stayed in one place too long. It wasn't profitable.

All this time Aidyn had been considering me silently. Now he said, "You look familiar. Do I know you?"

His question staggered me. Did he *know* me? I experienced an endless moment of total nothingness, like the shock you get right before the boom of a nuclear blast. In that white stillness I instinctively wanted to grab on to something solid. My emotions were suddenly so mangled I couldn't believe I was capable of coherent thought. *Oh. My. God!* Then I became the explosive, a sleek silver canister containing a mushroom cloud full of infinite death. He'd killed Matt. He'd killed *me!* And I was supposed to keep chatting him up as if we'd met at a conference years ago and were getting reacquainted?

"Jasmine!" It was Vayl's voice in my ear, concerned, maybe even a little panicky. "I can sense your feelings from out here. Something is tearing you up inside. Do I need to come in?" *Hell yeah! Get in here and trash this room! Impale Aidyn's image on that coatrack over there! Save Cole! Save me!*

I took a deep breath. And another. I had to get control. Right. Now. I started to shake. Full-body tremors that made me tighten my shoulder blades and clench my hands. My teeth didn't quite chatter, but it was a close thing, as if I'd been walking in forty-degree weather with no coat for hours.

I closed my eyes. *The killing time will come, Jaz. You can wait for it. The Voice told you so.*

"Jasmine, I am coming in," said Vayl.

"No."

"No?" Aidyn echoed.

"No, you don't know me," I replied, wishing my voice wouldn't shake like that. I tried to get back to the facts. Things we at the CIA would want to know when we prosecuted the ones Vayl and I didn't immediately terminate. "What I don't get is—why kill us off in the first place? The way you look at things, that's the majority of your blood supply moved so far down the food chain even the worms wouldn't benefit."

Aidyn began shaking his head before I'd finished. "No, not at all. We are simply culling the herd, weeding out the weak in order to purify our stock. When they are gone, we will introduce the antidote." I wanted to wipe the smug expression off his face—with a flamethrower. "This will, of course, make the survivors extremely grateful to us. In fact, they will decide they owe us something in return for saving them from the very plague we have begun."

"I suppose that's where you step in, Senator?"

He gave me his classic, CNN smile. So caring, so sincere. *Ass.* "A country under siege needs a strong leader. A popular leader. Someone who can explain the new order to them in such a way they'll wonder why they didn't think of it themselves." His delivery was so smooth I'd have bet he was speaking from a script. One written by Edward Samos, aka the Raptor.

"And that is?"

"Willing servitude, Jasmine dear. Blood for safety, blood for health. It's not such a high price to pay. I'll show them that."

Don't get me wrong. I vote in every election. I figure it's my duty as an American. Plus, I don't get to bitch about the direction the country's taking if I don't do my part to start with. But as I stood beside my injured friend I knew only a politician could face a camera with a pleasant smile as he described how he'd helped set up the mass rape of his own country. I found it hard to speak past the scream that was building in my chest. But I managed.

"So you gain the presidency and your terrorist friends get to see America brought to her knees." Bozcowski nodded graciously as Assan flashed his teeth.

"We'll be dancing in the streets," Assan said.

It wasn't hard to envision. They'd done the same after the Towers fell, and I'd wanted to kill every one of the sons of bitches then. Soon I'd get the chance. But first . . .

I sighed. "All right. Flip the switch. I'm trading places with Cole."

"Like hell!" said Cole, while at the same time Vayl snapped, "You will *not* do this!"

I took Cole by the hands, but I spoke to Vayl too when I said, "You have to trust me now. *Believe* me. I know what I'm doing."

Vayl's voice blared in my ear as Cole tried to shake his head without passing out. "Jasmine! I forbid this!"

"Now!" yelled Assan. "Switch!"

I squeezed Cole's hands as hard as I could, yanked him out of his chair, and took his place. He staggered backward until he collided with a pile of boxes. I thought he'd hit the floor next, but he found his balance.

"Time to go," I told both men before either could argue. "I'll see you again. *Soon.*"

"I'll be back for you," Cole vowed, his battered face combining with his ferocious expression to make him resemble a biblical prophet. *Wild.*

"I'm counting on it," I said. I checked Grief to make sure the safety was on, tossed it to him. "Shoot anyone who tries to stop you. Now get going."

With a final nod, Cole stumbled out of the room. I didn't have time to worry about whether or not he'd make it down the ladder, much less the stairs. The three amigos were still tuned in and I really needed to get rid of them.

"Would you like me to prepare you for tomorrow's

activities?" Assan inquired. "We have such a fantastic evening planned."

Oh goody. I've turned myself over to the Cruise Director of the Beast Boat. "Why don't you surprise me?" I suggested. "You give me too many details and I may just decide to walk away from this whole deal."

"But—you would be blown up!"

"Exactly."

He and Aidyn exchanged a quiet word with the senator. "Very well then. We will leave you in peace." The picture flickered and faded to gray. They'd gone, though I was sure somebody over at Psycho Central still kept tabs on me.

I closed my eyes and lowered my head. Hopefully my watcher would assume I was praying. And in a way, I was. As when I made my out-of-body visit to David, I focused my entire mind on what I wanted. Except this time I had the right words to go with it, words a Voice gave me now in tremendous, booming thumps, as if they resounded from the world's largest drum.

My voice was a quiet murmur, fitting perfectly with the dust and neglect surrounding me. As the words spilled over my lips I began to feel dizzy and disconnected, as if the moment before sleep falls had been magnified a hundred times. My entire body began to tingle, and if I touched someone right now I'd expect to shock them.

I opened my eyes as I felt myself rise. It scared me, actually. I thought maybe I'd truly begun to stand up, and I sure didn't want to end it all with an accidental *Ka-Boom.* Part of me, the gravity-bound bomb sitter, stayed put. But another part continued to move up to and through the ceiling, into the roof's crawl space and through that as well. I started to wonder if anything would stop me from floating away like a hot-air balloon minus its release valve. I tried to direct my movements without luck. Up, up I went, a space-bound spirit with no hold left in the world.

"WRONG!" It was the Voice, still sounding more like thunder than communication. "LOOK!"

I am *looking*! The snippy little reply was on the tip of what now passed for my tongue. It was also a lie. All my attention had been directed inward. Now I looked outside myself. Seven golden cords stretched from various points of the earth up, up to me. I concentrated harder and realized I could tell who the cord was touching simply by the way it vibrated. Actually, the vibration was more of a song. I identified Albert and Evie immediately. Dave, whose cord had just been a yellow blur the first time I'd traveled beyond my body, was there too. Vayl had his own tune, as did Bergman and Cassandra. Cole's was the one I focused on, however. I grabbed that cord of music with what passed for my hands and hurtled down it, delighting in the speed, wondering if this was how it felt to be a skeleton racer.

I stopped just short of ramming into Cole or, more likely, through him. He slumped against the post of a traffic sign, trying to hail a cab. But nobody wanted to stop for a guy who looked like he'd just been mugged and, therefore, had no money for fare.

"Cole," I said softly, whispering right into his ear. "Relax. Vayl's coming."

He jerked upright and spun around, his face a picture of relief and joy. The picture quickly changed to confusion and disappointment. "She's not here, fool," Cole chastised himself. "She's sitting on a bomb. Where you should be."

Okay, I'm invisible. Why is that? Dave saw me.

I let go of Cole's cord and grabbed Vayl's. It took me right into the van, which he was trying, and failing, to start. I settled into the passenger seat as he cranked the key and stomped the gas pedal. Over the sound of the struggling engine I heard him mutter, "Stupid, stupid, stupid son of a *bitch*!" He slammed the steering wheel with both hands, making it shudder on its perch.

"Geez, Vayl, chill, would you? At this rate Cole's going to freak out and walk in front of a bus while you're still deciding whether to flood the van or trash the steering column."

He gaped at me, smiled his dangerous smile, and grabbed for my arm. I think he was hoping for a hug, but his fingers went right through me. The dismay on his face would've been funny any other time. "Um, I guess I should've warned you I'm not quite solid. But I wasn't sure you'd see me."

He shook his head slowly. "Unbelievable."

"You say that like you're impressed, but you're making that face, the one I get after I've made a stupid mistake."

He made a that's-exactly-what-you've-done gesture. "How are you planning to rejoin your body, that is, if it is not blown to bits during the course of events?"

"I thought I'd try just jumping in."

"Are you *insane*?" Now that Vayl had a living—sort of—target for his anger, he had no problem starting the van. And now that he'd asked me the one question I'd feared most, I found I was too mad to care.

"You know what? I probably am! I did walk straight

into a trap so obvious even a woolly mammoth could've avoided it. Because that's my job. Yes, it *is* insane to leave the biggest part of me sitting on an explosive device. But according to my job description, I'm supposed to save innocents, not endanger them. Yes, it's crazy to stick around waiting for a plague beast to eat my soul. You'd think one death would be my limit. But apparently I just can't get enough of it! So can we just agree I'm bonkers and move on already?"

Vayl jerked his head, his version of a nod, and said, "So where is Cole?"

"Two blocks west of here, last I saw him."

"You . . . saw him. You went to him first?"

"His nose is broken," I said defensively. "And, you know what, I don't need an excuse. I might be a couple hundred years younger than you, but I'm still an adult! If I want to show concern for a friend, I will do exactly that!" I nearly stomped my foot, but that seemed a little too junior high to ram home my point.

Vayl steered the van back onto the street as he began to mutter again. I didn't catch it all, but I thought I heard him say, "That will not be all that is broken."

Dammit! If there is any way to screw up a relationship, I will find it. I pictured Cupid sitting in a crappy little bar, drunk and depressed, while he moaned to the bartender, "That Jasmine Parks, *gods*, she pisses me off! Did you see what she just did? Totally blew off this immortal stud to play kiss-the-boo-boo with a fickle little rent-a-cop. Why? 'Cause she's the biggest chickenshit on the planet! I'm ready to toss my bow and pick up a bazooka!"

"Vayl?"

"What!"

"I . . . I'm sorry. I didn't mean to hurt you."

He refused to look at me. Just glared through the front window so fiercely I was surprised the glass didn't crack. "You never do."

Chapter Twenty-three

Meanwhile, back at the ranch, I thought as I floated into Bergman's house, leaving Vayl and Cole to pass the door knocker's muster. From the looks of things, we shouldn't have left the cowpokes to their own devices for quite so long. With Bergman bristling like an irritated land baron and Cassandra throwing off bad vibes like a cornered gunslinger, it looked like we were about to have a good old-fashioned bar fight. Never mind that the bar had never seen a shot of whiskey in its whole upper-middle-class life, Cassandra looked like she wanted to drag Bergman down the length of it, scattering test tubes, chemicals, and bags of contaminated blood all along the way.

I moved over to her, hoping to overhear her low-pitched mutterings. "Lousy, neurotic, egotistical, bigoted, neurotic *bastard*!" She threw a sidelong glance at Bergman as she sat down at the dining room table, unaware she'd called him "neurotic" twice, and that I agreed with her 98 percent. The bigoted part I'd never witnessed, but I was willing to kick his ass once I got my legs back if that part proved true. Then I realized she wasn't referring to skin tone at all. "Thinks magic's for fanatics, skanks, and lesbians, does he?" she muttered. "Why, I'd like to . . ." Her words trailed off as she narrowed her eyes, envisioning some satisfying form of retribution. Then she looked skyward and growled, "What is the *deal* with you? You'd think a thousand years of atonement would serve for one woman. But *noooo*, you've got to torment me even more by shoving me into a gang full of wiseasses and crackpots!"

A thousand years? I suddenly felt like a die-hard stoner. All I could think was, *Dude! She's, like, really, really old! Whoa! . . . Cool!*

Then she saw me. Her face puckered, like she'd just bitten into a not-quite-ripe apple and she sat back so fast her chair went up on two legs. While she fought to regain her balance I tried to figure out this latest mystery. David, Vayl, and Cassandra could see me. Cole couldn't.

"Hey, Bergman!" I yelled pretty loud, because the part of him that wasn't deeply pissed was focused on conducting his experiments.

Nothing.

Cassandra gasped. "Jasmine?"

Bergman looked up, his face so creased with annoyance he looked ten years older. "What did you say?" he snapped.

With all four feet of her chair squarely back on the floor, she twisted in her seat, her frown matching his. "Don't you see her?"

"I would if she was here." His tone suggested that maybe Cassandra had fallen right off the deep end.

"Someday someone is going to pinch off your tiny little head," she told him. He had a comeback ready, and for a couple of minutes they bickered like ten-year-olds. But nothing they said could distract me from the fact that Bergman hadn't seen me either. Bergman and Cole were definitely alive. Well, maybe you could debate about Cole, but since human effort had brought him back as opposed to gold-light, crew-cut guy, I was grouping him with Miles. Vayl, Cassandra, and me . . . well, that was another matter entirely. Another matter that now evidently included David. *Too. Much.*

Cassandra snapped me out of it. She and Bergman had quit slapping each other around conversationally and now she'd moved back to her under-the-breath revelations. "Thinks I can't fight this thing with magic, eh? Well, I'll show him!" She flipped through a book like an impatient client at the beauty parlor.

"Any luck?" I ventured.

She rolled her eyes at me. "I can't find anything more telling about the Tor-al-Degan than I already knew. It is so aggravating! What kind of name is that anyway? I even typed it into Google. You know what I found? Nothing!" She flipped some more, traded books, and continued her search.

"At the risk of sounding overmuch like Sherlock Holmes," said Vayl as he walked in, "Jaz and I seem to have found a rather compelling clue." Cole came plodding in after him and collapsed on the couch.

Cassandra gaped at him, then at Vayl, then back at Cole. "How can you discuss clues when there is an injured man at your heels?"

Vayl gave Cole an appraising look. "He will live. Now tell me what you think of this." He pulled the pyramid from his coat pocket and held it out so they could all see it.

Bergman gave it one hard look and dismissed it. Factoring in his previous comments and Cassandra's complaints, I gathered he wasn't interested because he thought it might be magical. Instead he grabbed the first-aid kit from where he'd stowed it under the sink and went to sit by Cole, where he spent the next ten minutes cleaning, dabbing, patching, and urging him to go to the hospital before his nose healed that way.

Cassandra reacted much differently. She flattened her hands on the open pages of her book, her thumbs and forefingers framing a picture of a horned, winged, fanged version of Cyclops eviscerating some hapless bystander. But her attention wasn't on the picture. It was on the key Amanda had passed on to us. It sat in the palm of Vayl's hand, looking like a kid's toy that had been rolled in the mud.

"I think I've been looking at this all wrong," Cassandra said. "All this time I've been focusing on the Tor-al-Degan when I should have been looking for the key. Not that I really knew what it looked like until just now." She darted a furious glance at Bergman as she grabbed a new book from the pile she'd scattered across the table.

I gathered Bergman hadn't entirely passed on the description I'd given him of the pyramid. Considering the import of such information, I seriously considered calling in some folks with handcuffs and squad cars. Maybe that would scare him out of his idiotic prejudices. But that would be for later. Now Cassandra seemed to be on a roll. She studied the book with more and more interest while the men studied her. About the time I expected her to jump up and shout "Eureka!" or something equally enthusiastic but a lot less geeky, my cell phone rang. After an odd moment when my nonexistent hands itched to dive into my absent pockets, I realized Vayl had it. Our gazes met across the room and he raised his eyebrows as if to say, *Should I answer it?* I nodded.

"Hello, you have reached Jasmine Parks's phone. This is Vayl speaking." He listened intently. "No," he said. "I am afraid Jasmine is not available. Can I take a message? . . . Oh, hello, Mr. Parks."

Holy crap on a TV tray! My dad is talking to my undead boss! Could this get any stranger?

Apparently so. Because when Vayl hung up he said, "You never told me how kind your father is, Jasmine."

Kind? This was the man who cut off little old ladies with his grocery cart so he could beat them to the checkout counter. If you caught him at the park, he wouldn't be feeding the pigeons, he'd be shooting them. Once I saw him punt a Chihuahua twenty yards because it nipped his ankle. *Kind? Huh!*

I whooshed at Vayl, making him blink. "Oh no, you don't," I ordered him. "You don't get to like my dad until *I* like my dad, and I don't. Do I?" I could tell he thought I'd really flipped out. So I tried to distract him. It turned out to be remarkably easy. "What did Albert have to say?" I asked.

"Senator Bozcowski does have a prescription for Topamax. Apparently he suffers from migraines. Also his cousin-in-law owns the firm that made your faulty beacon. And get this: He's on the board of directors for the National Zoo. Not to mention vacationing with his family in Miami at the moment. But you knew that. Did you also know when he is scheduled to return to Washington?"

"Well, I'm pretty sure his dance card's full tomorrow night, so I'll say . . . day after tomorrow."

"No."

"No?"

"He is leaving in the morning."

"*This* morning?" As Vayl nodded I checked out the Regulator clock hanging over the fireplace. It showed close to midnight. *Oh my God, it's happening tonight! Those lying weasels!*

"Um, Vayl?" Bergman ventured hesitantly. "Is there a reason you're talking to the mantel?"

Vayl quickly explained, making it sound like I'd gotten myself into a predicament when I had, in fact, been trying to rescue poor Cole from the sling we'd wound him into to start with! While Vayl talked, Bergman searched the air for clues to my existence, Cassandra smirked at Bergman, and Cole just slouched among the pretty pillows, scowling at the drawn curtains. When Vayl had finished, Cassandra stared at Bergman triumphantly. "Explain *that* with your equations!" Before he could think up a suitable retort she went on. "By the way, while you were playing doctor, I found it."

"Found what, Cassandra?" Vayl demanded. "Quickly please, Jasmine and I have to leave."

"The key!" She pointed to the artifact. "The Tor-al-Degan! I believe I have found the words"—she glanced at Bergman—"the *spell* that activates the key." She held up, not a book, but the *Enkyklios*. "We seem to have a detailed record of this beast after all."

"It sounds as if you are coming with us, then."

Bergman lurched off the couch, went to Vayl and grabbed his shoulder, which he quickly released when

Vayl shot him his don't-touch-me look. But he didn't back down completely. "If she goes, I go," he said, jabbing a finger toward Cassandra.

"Fine."

Bergman blinked a couple of times, surprised at his success.

"You're not leaving me here while Jaz is sitting on that bomb," said Cole. We all looked at him. Despite the fact that he resembled a plane crash survivor, no one ventured an argument as to why he should stay. Finally Vayl said, "All right, if that is what you want."

"It is."

Another moment of silence passed out of respect for Cole's determination and, on my part at least, an attempt to balance myself against a staggering wave of concern. How were we supposed to keep them all safe? I wasn't sure it was possible, but I could tell none of them would entertain my arguments. As I fought a feeling of impending doom, Bergman launched himself into a packing frenzy Cassandra quickly copied. For the next five minutes my little gang looked like they were preparing a full-scale evacuation. All except for Cole, who glared at the drapes so hard I was kind of surprised they didn't catch fire. And I was pretty sure that wasn't Visine I saw glittering in his eyes.

Vayl drove toward Club Undead like a drag racer. Every time he had to stop for a light or a sign, his next move was a flat-pedal takeoff. The first couple of zero to sixties left me so unprepared, I found myself hovering outside the van watching its taillights rush off into the night. When I resumed my place between him and Cassandra for the third time, he sent me an apologetic look. "Sorry about that."

"That's all right," said Cassandra, overriding my objections without realizing I wanted to voice them. "So can I tell you what I have learned about the key?" We both nodded. "It acts as a controller. Remember I told you the Tor-al-Degan can perform good or evil acts? Whoever owns the key can tell it what to do."

"So if they summon the beast before we get there, all we have to do is tell it to go back to where it came from," said Vayl.

"I'm not so sure. In fact, I think the Tor-al-Degan is already here. You said it ate the soul of Amanda's brother. And Cole said the torso they found bore the same markings."

"True. But Jaz said *they* said they needed a *willing* sacrifice."

"Yes. According to my research, the Tor-al-Degan cannot be completely released from its bonds until it receives a willing sacrifice. It can, however, exist in more than one realm at once. Which is why I think it is already here. Most of it anyway."

"Why would they bring it only partway into the world?" asked Bergman.

"I suppose they didn't know any better. They seem to be working from a partial text, or perhaps a copy of a copy of a translation that has left out vital information."

Vayl clutched the steering wheel hard and shifted anxiously in his seat. "We have to get there. *Now!*" He laid on the horn as a light brown Crown Victoria pulled out in front of him, forcing him to brake hard. "Next time take the bus, you old geester!" he yelled as he swerved to go around.

"Geezer," I corrected him.

He glared at me. "Never leave your body again!" He jerked us back into our lane just in time to keep us from getting flattened by a street-sweet Hummer. He tried twice more, nearly colliding with a red Mustang and a dark blue Camry before he finally succeeded in leaving the old fart to stew in his prunes.

"Would you quit driving like a maniac if I went back to my body?" I asked. I'd never seen him so unnerved.

"Yes!" Vayl practically shouted. He took a breath, visibly pulled himself together. "We need to know if you are still unharmed, whether they have moved you, what they are planning. Report back as soon as you discover anything at all."

"Gladly," I agreed. "Your driving is making me nauseous and I don't even have a stomach!" I floated through the roof of the van and looked around. All my golden cords still stretched in their various directions. Was it me, or did they seem slightly dimmer than before? I didn't spend much time pondering. I was too busy looking for the light that connected the separate parts of me. I played the cords one by one, as if they were the strings of a gigantic harp, and delighted to hear one of them sing my own tune back to me. It wasn't as pure as Evie's or as powerful as Vayl's, but I liked it all the same. Especially when it led me straight back to my body.

There I sat, breathing, blinking, looking as blank as the porcelain dolls Evie collected. I shook my ethereal head. *Unfathomable*. I still sat alone and, yes, the bomb still blinked its harsh lights at me when I checked under the chair.

No longer interested in standing at my own side, I moved out, through the door into the control booth, now manned by a bald black man who looked fit enough to break world-sprint records. He played with the sound board, tweaking the music that pounded through the teeming rooms beyond. It hadn't taken long for the smoke to clear and the partiers to return.

Floating out the window and over the humans and vamps who danced shoulder-to-shoulder, I imagined the devastation that would occur if I jumped back into my body and rose from the chair. Hundreds would die. *Still, it's nothing compared to the loss of life our targets have planned.* Something to consider. Seriously. But not yet. At least not until I found them, and it would take precious minutes to search the crowd, time I no longer possessed.

"Help me out here, would you?" I asked, hoping the owner of the thunderous voice hadn't taken a nap. "I've got to find the three stooges." Intuition told me I could sniff out evil now that I'd seen and accepted my transformation, but that ability didn't help much here, with my nose stuck in the attic.

The answer rolled across me like an avalanche, reverberating through me, making me glad I didn't currently possess teeth that might well have shattered against each other in the aftermath. "UNDERGROUND!" I fought a perverse urge to do just the opposite: float back into the atmosphere, chase down the source of that overwhelming voice, and discuss with it the benefits of the whisper. But something told me once I went hunting for my guide, I might never be able to return.

So I dropped from my lofty perch near the catwalk, past the dancers' masklike faces, and through the floor beneath their feet. The wine cellar I entered looked like it belonged under a medieval castle. Dusty bottles lined row after row of custom-made shelves that filled more than half the space. A gorgeous cherry table with four matching chairs stood at the open end of the room, made even more prominent by the ornate Persian rug lying underneath them. Floating next to the table, I could see a set of stone stairs leading upward. But my guide had left strict instructions. So I dove through the wide-planked pine floor into the cancerous bowels of Club Undead.

Chapter Twenty-Four

I fell into a pit, the symbolic significance of which did not escape me. Lit by flaming torches, painted by their smoke, the pit easily measured four times the width and length of the wine cellar standing above it. Uneven stacks of floor-to-ceiling stone impeded the view, so you could never see more than a quarter of it at once. The walls were as crooked as the load-bearing columns, as if some enormous mole had been snacking on various sections, leaving shallow caverns and outcroppings in its wake.

I drifted around the pit's perimeter, hugging the jagged wall like an amateur skater. The floor beneath my non-feet looked muddy, and steaming pools of viscous liquid made me wonder just what a good CSI would discover given the right chemicals.

In one corner a bona fide stream trickled through a gap in the wall and exited via a basin that could've been twenty feet deep for all its blank, black surface revealed. In another corner I discovered portable metal stairs that led up to a door in the ceiling. A quick check confirmed that it opened to the wine cellar, though it was hidden by the rug that lay beneath the tasting table.

About halfway between the stream basin and the stair,

a folding table leaned against the wall. It reminded me of the church buffet suppers Granny May had dragged us kids to on alternating Sunday nights during our summer visits. Eight devoted parishioners could've used it comfortably, or perhaps, not so comfortably after all. The dried stains on the tabletop looked a lot more like blood than beef gravy.

The occupants of the pit stood in groups of two or three, wearing basic black, as if they meant to attend a highbrow cocktail party after the festivities ended here. I counted thirteen altogether, none of whom I recognized as major players. Disappointed that Bozcowski, Aidyn, and Assan, not to mention Derek and Liliana, were haunting some other pit—I mean part—of Miami, I continued my exploration. Still hugging the wall, I moved toward the part of the room farthest from the stairs.

I saw her before she saw me, and though I withdrew into a shallow alcove, I knew she would not miss me once she knew what to look for. The Tor-al-Degan viewed the world through cold, dead eyes, making me feel like a deer forced to drink from crocodile-infested waters. Irises the color of gangrene swam in pus-hued sclera, making any of the acolytes they rested on shudder and back up a step. I'm not sure I'd have held my ground either. And I could understand why no picture of her existed in Cassandra's old books. She was just plain hard to *see*.

It could have been a trick of the lighting, the rise and fall of flame throwing odd shadows so all you got were confusing snapshots, none of which revealed an entire picture. After the eyes I didn't expect to glimpse an ounce of beauty in the beast, but there was a finely sculpted cheekbone, and there, the smooth curve of a shoulder. But

I couldn't blame the fizzle-fade the Tor did next on the torches. I blinked, squeezed my eyes shut before I remembered they weren't physical orbs at the moment.

Must be tough, existing in a couple of different planes at once, I thought as she gained enough definition that I could make out a foot—oh, ugh, make that a big, hairy claw. *Definitely hard on the posture too.* She seemed to hunch, as if to protect something she held close, though I couldn't tell what it might be since she wore a dark, voluminous gown that hid a great deal. Then she turned her head and I saw the webbed tissue that connected her neck to something even larger that moved, *squirmed*, underneath the material that covered her back.

Again, the Tor-al-Degan began to fade, taking on the translucence of fine Japanese paper. She turned her head toward the waiting crowd, which immediately began to chant and sway, reminding me of the snake charmers I'd seen on Discovery Channel specials. Three women, all in their late thirties, all prematurely gray, stepped forward. They kept their backs to the crowd as they knelt on the floor, their knees sinking a good inch in the muck. The rest of the group formed a semicircle behind them and fell to their knees as well. The bottom third of their pants darkened as the cloth soaked up the mystery soup that covered the floor. As I tried to figure out its ingredients, Granny May's strident voice popped into my head. *Well, that'll never come out, not even with bleach.* Frankly, I was glad to hear her. This whole scene gave me the willies. Mostly because I figured my sacrifice was going to be part of the Big Finish.

The Tor's eyes swiveled in their sockets as she opened her mouth so wide her jaw came unhinged with an audible pop. Enormous fangs descended from the pointed teeth surrounding them, and she spit thick white goo at the watchers, making them cringe and retreat, though they continued to chant. Then the Tor whipped her head sideways and slammed those teeth into the wall. The power she might soon unleash became clear as she took a bite out of the trembling earth, leaving ugly black scars in her wake.

As soon as she began to chew she solidified, and I realized how she'd managed to survive in this state for so long. Not only did she gain sustenance from unwilling souls, but she fed on the earth as well. Assuming our Native Americans were right, some of the earth's spirit entered her that way, providing even more nourishment. Though I don't throw trash on the ground and I have been known to recycle a soda can or two, I'd never thought of myself as an environmentalist until that moment, when all I could see were the scars she'd left in her steady consumption of the good earth.

That's enough, I thought. *That's all I need to see. That's all I* want *to see.*

I rushed back to my body and found it where I'd left it, still blinking and breathing, still alone. Out the window I flew, my phantom heart skipping a beat when I discovered the cords connecting me with everyone who mattered in my life had now visibly faded, a hushed octet drawn from the original magnificent orchestra.

Urgency moved me to new speeds and I reached the van within thirty seconds. Vayl jumped in his seat when I dropped through the roof, landing on, or rather in, Cassandra's lap. Muttering a quick apology, I withdrew to my former spot while Vayl informed Bergman and Cole that I'd rejoined them.

"They've started the ceremony," I said. "It's happening below the basement of Club Undead."

Vayl slammed on the brakes and I suddenly found myself perched on the hood of the van as it slid to a stop inches from the back bumper of a dirty green station wagon. Just ahead of us a four-car pileup jammed the street. It must've just happened, because all the drivers involved still sat in their cars and no cops were in sight. I moved over to Vayl's side of the van, standing beside his window as if I really had feet, and told him what I'd seen.

"Dammit!" Vayl never swore. Never. I guess that's when I knew how much he cared. He jerked the van into reverse, but braked hard again as he realized a parade of minivans had him blocked in. He shoved the van into park and let it idle. "This is going to take some time. Go back to your body and stall them."

"What? Vayl, this is not a basketball game! I can't go in there and eat the clock, because when that buzzer sounds the whole top-floor explodes!"

"You have got to do this, Jasmine. We will be there as soon as I can convince these drivers to move."

"How are you going to know where to find me?"

"Give me directions." So I did, along with my last excuse.

"I don't want to go. What if the monster eats my soul?" I sounded like a three-year-old cowering under the covers because we all know what sleeps under the bed. But I was scared, more even than I'd been that night in West Virginia, when I'd been young and dumb enough to believe I could survive anything.

Vayl stared into my eyes, willing me to believe him. "It will not. And if it does, we will hang it by the ankles and thump it on the back until it coughs you up."

I smiled, only because he meant for me to. "Hurry, Vayl. I don't want to die again." I swooped into the air and stalled almost immediately. Only four of the seven cords remained and I had to strain to see them. I picked mine out as the only one leading away from the van and sped along its length, strumming it like a single guitar string, forcing the music to send its faint melody into the cosmos. The cord disappeared entirely as I entered Club Undead, and the prickles at the back of my non-neck reminded me I could still feel enormous fear despite my current lack of adrenal glands.

I slipped into the attic, the scene inside my body's temporary abode striking me as both comical and desperate. There I sat, draped halfway off the chair, "Unconscious and barely breathing!" according to Assan's hysterical assessment, while Aidyn crouched before me, his head and forearms under the chair, his back supporting my legs as he tinkered with the bomb. Apparently their remote shutoff wasn't 100 percent reliable. *Not* a comforting thought.

Assan pressed the shaking fingers of one hand to my carotid while he checked my pupils with the other. "She's dying!" he yelled. "How can she be dying?"

"*Silence*, you imbecile. I am trying to disarm this *bomb*!" Aidyn's spirited reply jiggled my body so that my legs slipped off his back, my feet thumping to the floor to one side of him as my butt slid completely off the seat to land between his shoulders. Assan shrieked like a schoolgirl as my weight shifted.

"Got it!" shouted Aidyn. "Now get her *off* me!"

It's time. I know it's time. Why am I so reluctant to reenter my body? I looked up, imagining the stars twinkling in the night sky, with my guide driving a black Jeep Cherokee between them, singing his own special rendition of "When You Wish Upon a Star." A big part of me yearned for that sort of freedom. *Someday,* I promised myself, *I'll have that. When the price isn't so high.*

Letting go of my hesitation, I slid back into myself, trying to be gentle, unobtrusive even. Still, the rejoining hurt like a full-body charley horse. I woke screaming, startling my captors so much that they screamed as well. Aidyn lurched to his feet, sending me tumbling into a pile of boxes. I laid there a second, stunned and sore, until Assan grabbed my arms and yanked me to my feet, the sword he wore banging into my shins. *Sword?* I thought. *Weird.* And then, *Holy crap, he means to carve me with runes!*

"Bitch!" he squealed, spraying my cheeks with a fine mist as his eyes blazed. "What did you do? *What did you do?*"

I wiped my face and straightened my clothing. "I kept my word," I said, feeling too depressed, too bereft to even consider belting him. I'd gotten my body back, for cripe's sake. Why this sense of loss? It overrode everything, even the anger I should be feeling at being chastised by this rotten little man with his pruny little soul. And then there was Aidyn, who made me understand exactly how Vayl had felt when he found his sons dead. I wanted him to die, oh yeah, but slowly and oh so painfully. Didn't I? Even that rage could not seem to overcome this terrible grief. I hoped I hadn't left it behind. I'd wanted so badly to release it, and now I wondered if I'd be able to muster it in time to ensure our survival tonight. If I couldn't, I hoped it became a little black rain cloud that hovered over these two freaks the rest of their days, sending out hailstones and lightning bolts at inopportune moments.

Assan shoved me toward the door and I stumbled. Aidyn caught me, kept me from falling. "Enough!" he snapped, glaring at his colleague. "We do not need her to break her neck on the eve of our triumph."

What did you say?

I jerked myself out of his grasp, my momentary grief burned away by the heat of a fury so sudden and searing I could barely breathe past it.

"Jasmine!" Vayl's voice buzzed distant in my ear. "What is wrong? I have never sensed such anger in you!"

"How many people have you bled out, Aidyn?" I demanded, my self-control beginning to shear away beneath the force of my feelings. "How many necks have *you* broken? Don't play gentleman with me. *I know better.*"

"What?"

"*Jasmine,* God, Jasmine, get hold of yourself!" Vayl's advice held no more impact than a whisper. But I did hear him.

"Oh yeah, I'll get hold of something." I grabbed Aidyn by the lapels of his Armani jacket. Whatever he saw on my face made his eyes go wide. Assan grabbed my left arm, but I knew I could take them. A simple twist and push would put my hand at Assan's throat, leaving the other free to tear Aidyn's head off, after which I would punt it against the wall. Repeatedly.

Not yet. It wasn't a voice in my head, not really. Just a silvery bolt of reason that started at Cirilai and shot straight into my brain. I dropped my hands as the door flew open and a couple of Assan's goons trooped in.

"What are you doing here?" snapped Aidyn. "You're supposed to be policing the exits. We'll be sealing them any minute now."

One man, whose hair was the color and consistency of motor oil, spoke up. "Liliana has been watching the monitors. She told us you needed help."

Assan snorted and let go of my arm. "Hardly."

Aidyn ran both hands through his hair. "Stick to the plan, people! You two"—he jabbed two fingers at Motor Oil and his smaller, greasier pal—"back to the exits. Liliana, Derek"—he addressed a vent in the wall, which apparently hid a camera—"you should have been downstairs with the senator fifteen minutes ago. Now, *move*!"

The goons scurried to obey as, I imagined, did Liliana and Derek.

"That goes for you too," Aidyn told me, his entire demeanor a Kodak moment in badly disguised wariness.

"Sure." I gave him a Lucille Robinson shrug, knowing that Jaz must be bottled right along with her rage if we were going to pull this off. Knowing also that when the lid came off, payback would be a bitch.

Chapter Twenty-five

The scene in the monster pit had changed somewhat during my brief absence. I had a better view, for one thing. Aidyn and Assan made sure of that. They escorted me straight to the front row while the faithful, with the addition of Bozcowski, Vayl's ex, and Derek "Doomsday" Steele, chanted words in a language I didn't understand, but which my ears heard as "Over llama catcha fur." The Tor-al-Degan swayed to the rhythm of the chant, her eyes half closed as if in a trance. I should've cared more, but my proximity to Derek had doubled me over, and I was close to adding my own mound of puke to the nasty puddles of glop on the floor.

While I leaned against a column, trying to regroup, Bozcowski turned to face his audience, holding up his hands for silence. "Today victory is ours!" he said, baring his shiny fangs as they applauded. "No longer must we watch our goddess hover between worlds, frustrated and impotent. We have found our willing sacrifice!" He presented me to the clapping crowd, a farmer proudly displaying his prize heifer.

I panicked briefly as they surged toward me, but they stopped short, staying at arm's length, well beyond reach of the Tor-al-Degan's grasp. The noise they made swept over me though, their whoops of joy pounding through my head like an ethanol-powered knitting needle. The monster behind me squealed, her high-pitched response making my eyes water.

Assan strode to the back of the pit, taking three large acolytes with him, while Bozcowski continued with the pep rally. I watched Assan's group return carrying the buffet table. They deposited it in front of the Tor and then knelt respectfully.

"No."

Bozcowski interrupted his speech to look at me, his scowl creasing his face like an origami sculpture. "What did you say?"

"No," I repeated. "As in no altar, no pagan sacrifice, no me lying down for it."

"But . . . you agreed."

"Yes, I agreed to die tonight. But I didn't agree how." *Why did I agree to anything? I am, without a doubt, the dumbest woman on earth!*

Assan and his cohorts had risen from their soggy knees to hear our conversation. Now Assan's bottom lip jutted out and his glassy black eyes narrowed to slits. "You have to use the altar. I brought the sacred sword and everything." As if I could've forgotten about the weapon that had cracked against my calves all the way down the back stairs and then nearly threw me headfirst through the trapdoor of the wine cellar when it had gotten tangled up between my ankles.

"Is that the same sword you used to leave little carvings in your brother-in-law's chest?" I asked it in a whisper. My churning gut wouldn't allow anything louder.

"Yes. But we won't need the runes for you. Just a clean, quick execution."

"Oh?" Weren't we being so polite? I could hardly stand it.

"We have no need to hold your soul in stasis because the Tor-al-Degan is already here, prepared to eat it. At least, most of her is here. The rest will arrive soon."

"I'm confused. She looks like she's all here. You can't see through her or anything."

"Looks can be deceiving." I thought about my recent trip outside Physicality and decided not to argue the point. But Vayl had told me to stall, so I reached over the nausea, past the dawning migraine, and plucked out a subject they wouldn't be able to resist.

"I understand what happened to Amanda's brother. But what about the torso? It had the same markings."

Assan pursed his lips and refused to speak. Aidyn was the one who answered me.

"After the debacle with Assan's brother-in-law, we discovered our goddess needed a willing sacrifice. So we petitioned a member of our sect to provide it. He gladly stepped into her jaws, but his soul did not free her. That was when we learned of the second twist, that the sacrifice must be willing, but not a worshipper of the Tor-al-Degan."

Wow. Whoever had trapped the Tor had gone to great lengths to ensure she remained trapped. Leave it to a bunch of vampire/terrorist punks to foul a perfectly good binding spell.

"So, uh, what happens when the Tor-al-Degan gets your plague-laced vampire blood?" I asked.

Aidyn's eyes rolled upward, drawing my attention to

the club above our heads. The club whose exits had just been sealed. "She will walk among them, transforming them into living, breathing versions of herself." I thought he'd give me more details, but he stopped, smiling at his fantasy vision.

Liliana had been quiet up to now, sizing me up like a tigress waiting in the weeds. To look at her you'd never guess she'd taken a dive off a roof recently. Unless you made the mistake of meeting her eyes. The memory stood there, poisonous and pissed. Suddenly she pounced. "Where is your *sverhamin* now, you mortal cow?" she asked, sidling up to me as if we were about to share a juicy secret.

Though Derek's scent made me want to curl up in a ball and pretend this was all a bad dream, I straightened and held her off with a raised hand, as if I were a running back in a slow-motion replay. "Back off, Liliana."

She grabbed Derek's forearm and pulled him, stumbling slightly, to stand beside her. He looked much worse than the last time I'd seen him. His jaw was slack, his eyes unfocused, his skin bright red with fever. He kept reaching out with his hands, making pinching motions with his fingers like a kid at a 3-D movie.

I raised my hand higher, leaning my back against a column.

"I have found your kryptonite, haven't I, Wonder Woman?" she asked, giving Derek a rag-doll shake.

"I believe you're mixing metaphors there, Lil." I stood up, realizing if she'd found my weakness, I'd discovered a new strength. It came from Cirilai, responding to the words Vayl spoke into my earpiece, spreading cool vigor up my arm and through my body, pushing Derek's stench off to a bearable distance. I realized now why Vayl hadn't been exactly clear on how the ring would protect me. Maybe I wouldn't have accepted it had I known it was a conduit, a way for him to share his power with me from a distance. Any other time I might've bucked at the intimacy that implied. Right now—right on!

"Give me the ring," Liliana hissed, doing such a good imitation of Tolkien's Gollum that I laughed.

Screaming with frustration, she grabbed my neck with both hands.

"Liliana, stop! Are you insane?" It was Aidyn's voice coming from somewhere beyond the shadows that had dropped over my vision as Liliana squeezed away my blood supply. I thought dimly how strange it was that she didn't just scratch me. She'd have had me so much easier. But she'd flipped out all the way, and logic didn't fit into the place she'd gone.

I grabbed her wrists and squeezed back. She cried out in pain. I yanked her hands off my neck, held them wide away from my body and head butted her so hard my vision rimmed everything in gold for the next ten seconds. It was worth it.

She grunted in pain. I stomped her foot and followed up with a kick to the knee that made her scream as the entire leg gave. She swiped at me as she went down, collapsing like the Wicked Witch of the West, only there was no melting this iceberg.

"Please do not kill her." Unbelievable. Not one, but two pleas for mercy kept me from smoking Liliana right then and there. Aidyn said it to my face. Vayl whispered it in my ear.

"I would kill you if I could," I told her. "I don't care

who begs for your life. You're an evil creature and you deserve no pity, not one drop."

Though the Tor-al-Degan hadn't even cleared her throat, everyone suddenly attended her.

"I like this woman's soul." *Holy crap, what a freaky voice*. It crawled across the skin like a colony of spiders. I had to bite my lip to keep myself from begging for mercy. Led by Bozcowski, her little congregation fell to its knees like a fanatical group of synchronized swimmers. The Tor-al-Degan was looking at me like I generally regard a big plate of cheesecake. "She will taste of spice and vigor," said the Tor. "Let us begin."

I braced myself to fight whoever tried to manhandle me onto the buffet table. But I wasn't the one Assan's assistants grabbed.

Derek had collapsed beside Liliana, watching through bleary eyes as she squirmed with pain. Now four Deganites lifted her out of the muck and carried her to the table. She sat on it, her legs dangling over the side, the one I'd kicked still slanted strangely. Derek crawled toward her and the Deganites helped him to his feet.

"Say it!" urged Bozcowski from his perch in the muck. "Say the words!" Aidyn had moved to stand by the table, but the senator wasn't talking to him, or Liliana and Derek. His urging was for Assan, who had retrieved a gym bag from wherever he'd left it. From it he pulled a bubble-wrapped object about the size of a standard flashlight. When he unwrapped it and sat it on the ground between the Tor-al-Degan's feet, I saw its base was made from a human skull—a small one, maybe a child's? Three primitive stone daggers protruded from the top of the skull, and on their points sat a shallow stone bowl.

At Bozcowski's urging, Assan had begun chanting. Every time he paused, the congregation echoed him. It reminded me, ridiculously, of Girl Scout camp and the song I still knew by heart—*The other day (The other day) I met a bear (I met a bear) Out in the woods (Out in the woods) Away out there (Away out there).*

I realized my mind was beginning to play tricks on me, trying to remove my consciousness from this scene and send it back to better days. That way it could protect my frail sanity from moments like this that could well snap it. What a great idea. Too bad I couldn't allow it. I made myself watch carefully. Somewhere among this devilry, *please, oh please*, was the key to their downfall.

Assan had unwrapped and placed three of his grisly statues in a tight triangle around the Tor. But Liliana had gone on without him. She held Derek between her legs, the fall of her hair hiding his neck as she prepared to drink from him.

For Vayl's sake I said, "Liliana, if you take his blood, you'll die. It's tainted with the Red Plague. You heard Aidyn say that, right?"

She threw me a smirk. "I am the Raptor's mistress, you dolt. He would never allow this unless his pet scientist had created an antidote for vampires as well." As she leaned to drink from Derek, my gaze tracked to Aidyn. What I saw in his face looked an awful lot like Liliana's death sentence. Samos must've found himself a new girl.

"It is time." I shivered as the Tor-al-Degan's throaty growl scratched at my senses. "Bring her!" Assan had stepped back beside Bozcowski, and though the chanting continued, I could see the change it had brought. The Tor looked more vibrant, more lethal, as if the ceremony had filled her with venom.

"Vayl," I whispered. "Where are you?" No answer. *Damn Bergman's prototypes!*

"Your mewling little eunuch cannot save you now," snarled Aidyn. He grabbed my arm and jerked me forward. We walked past Derek, who had collapsed, blood on his collar once more. No way would he live to see his antidote, much less a leading role. Liliana lounged atop the table as if it were a gigantic, vibrating mattress.

"Not *her*, you imbecile," snapped the Tor, making Aidyn flinch. "The vampire!"

I nearly laughed to see Aidyn's insults thrown back in his face. He didn't take it well either. His expression would've sat comfortably on a preacher who's just discovered his theology's full of holes.

He let me go, left me standing just feet from the Tor while he fetched Liliana. Her complexion pink from gorging, she rose languorously from the table and followed him to the first skull, not even limping from our last encounter. With a casual flick of the fingernail, she opened a vein in her wrist and let Derek's blood, now transformed by her vampirism, drain into the bowl. I watched the blood flow, a thick red weapon designed to kill ninety out of every one hundred people it contacted. Whole families, whole towns, would be decimated if Vayl and I couldn't stop this tonight. Our entire country would become a funeral, with Senator Tom Bozcowski providing the eulogy.

The chanting rose in volume and urgency. The Deganites, including Bozcowski and Assan, swayed to their own rhythm, their faces a collective mask of fanatical bliss.

Derek, still on his knees, drenched in his own blood, had joined in.

The second bowl was full, and it looked like my cavalry was still stuck in traffic. Assan reached into the duffel, pulled out another package that he would soon discover was not the key. Then all hell would break loose. Maybe literally. With no key to control her actions, wouldn't the Tor run rampant?

Not without a willing soul.

I could run, but I wouldn't make it far. And that would still leave the Tor poised to wreak havoc. As the first drops of Liliana's blood hit the third bowl, I did one more quick study of the Kyron. Her inability to maintain a solid front made her seem vulnerable despite the energy that came off her in waves.

One clean shot, Jaz. That's all you're getting and then you're done for. I took a last heartbreaking look at the life I could've had and let it go.

I began to cave myself inward, as if my soul was a collapsible laundry cart. Turn and fold, turn and fold, until the only portion left of me could've been punted, like a paper football, over goalposts formed by four fingers of a sixth grader's hand. It was the only fortress I knew how to build, and my sanity huddled at its center where, if I survived, maybe the blood and the horror of what I was planning could only leave a faint stain.

"Aaahh! Aaaahh! *AAAAAAHHH!!!*" It was Assan, too freaked to scream with words, holding a wooden statue of a closed fist with the middle finger raised. I couldn't connect that F-you statue to Amanda's frilly room, which was how I knew it must've been her brother's, maybe from his med school days when he still felt confident enough to flip off the world. It looked as if Assan had gotten the message.

Strings of box tape and bubble wrap streamed from his fingers like thick cobwebs, jigging to the rhythm of his shaking hands. His eyes had gone buggy, and he kept glancing from the Tor to Bozcowski to Aidyn, as if at any moment one of them would tear him limb from limb. And maybe they would if the angry mob the Deganites were becoming didn't lynch him first. They converged on him, pushing, shoving, yelling spit-laced curses. Aidyn, still mesmerized by the slow trickle of Liliana's blood, looked around, confused. So did Vayl's ex.

I rushed to the nearest torch and tore it off the wall, breaking the tip off its wooden handle so that its jagged end threw splinters onto the murky floor. A small sliver of wood floating in an oily puddle gave me an idea. I touched the torch to it and it flamed nearly waist high, grabbing gases from the air that burned green and stank worse than a rotting skunk in the middle of a swamp.

With only seconds to spare before somebody figured out their sacrifice had grown a spine, I sprinted from puddle to puddle, lighting them up like road flares behind me. When I was done, a fence of noxious flame trapped Liliana and the Tor. Both of them screamed at Bozcowski, Aidyn, Assan, the crowd, not one of whom had thought to stock the dungeon with a fire extinguisher.

I had one more moment to grab a second torch from the wall before the bad guys reorganized. Behind me, the Tor and Liliana cringed against the back wall as putrid green flames licked the air and pronounced it kindling. I held the torches out in front of me and the crowd backed up. I took a step forward. They retreated another step, their shoes squelching in a puddle of mire large enough to hold fifteen pairs of feet.

"I'll bet you guys didn't know I went through college on a track scholarship," I said, glaring into their flushed and wary faces as they tried to figure out how to surround me. "For javelin."

I tossed the right-hand torch up in the air, caught it in an overhand grip, and launched it at their feet. The puddle ignited instantly, catching a woman's skirt and a man's sleeve.

The crowd stampeded, throwing their burning brethren into the muck as they went, stomping bones along with the flames. They reached the stairs as a herd, scrambling over each other to reach the top. Men cursed, women screamed, people fell, got up, and jumped back on. Bozcowski, Aidyn, Assan, and I watched, spectators at a train wreck. Then Assan shook his statue at me.

"You're dead," he croaked, advancing on me slowly.

I nodded grimly. "You don't know how right you are."

He stopped, not sure what to make of this. Aidyn and Bozcowski tried to flank me. I waved the torch at them. "Don't. Move."

Behind them the crowd's roar doubled. The men turned to look, so I risked a peek as well. The Deganites were backing, tripping, falling down the stairs in the face of a pair of space-age guns held by Cole and Bergman. As those two cleared the stairs and began to round up the Deganites, they were joined by Vayl, carrying his cane, and Cassandra, holding the key in one outstretched hand. In her other hand, the *Enkyklios* was transforming, its marbled parts rolling into the shape of an hourglass. She was already chanting, and I risked a look behind me to see if the Tor had heard her call. Evidently she had. Despite the heat of the fire that trapped her, she'd pulled away from the wall and risen to her full height, her eyes glued to the key.

The screech of buckling metal drew my attention back to the stairs. Cole and Bergman had made it to floor level with their prisoners. Vayl and Cassandra had reached the fourth stair when the whole structure collapsed. Vayl tried to balance Cassandra, but she lurched out of his hands and onto the floor, averting her face just in time to miss the taste of mud and flammable gases. A portion of the stair glanced off her head and shoulder, the artifacts flew free, and her chant ceased.

My heart froze as I looked back at the Tor. She'd fallen to her hands and knees, was lapping Liliana's tainted blood out of the offering bowls, one after another, taking into her being the plague that would rip the skin from our country and leave behind it a mass of festering sores if we didn't stop her. Right. Now.

"Cassandra!" I yelled. "Hurry! Get control!"

Assan chose that moment to attack, rushing me like a crazed linebacker. I never could've met that mad charge full-on, but then I never meant to. I faked a run to the right until he committed to that direction; then I came back left and connected with a leg sweep that sent him sprawling. I moved toward him, meaning to follow up with a bone-crushing kick to the skull, but Vayl's voice stopped me.

"Jaz! Behind you!"

I spun around in time to see Liliana launch herself over the wall of flame, which was vastly shorter now than it had been a moment before. The Tor's chuckle of triumph told me she might've had something to do with that. I tried to dodge out of Liliana's path, but stepped into deep, thick mud. It grabbed at my shoe, slowing me just enough that Liliana's nails grazed my neck as she landed, reopening the wounds Vayl's fangs had made.

"Now I've got you!" she exulted, keeping her distance as I desperately jabbed the torch at her. Assan struggled to his feet and drew his sword. His eyes were on the trickles of blood running down my neck as he said, "Now, Jasmine. Now is your time to die." *Son of a bitch!*

Liliana began to circle me, her expression a study in satisfaction. Assan followed suit. "It looks as if our rat is finally cornered," she told him. "Shall we play a bit before we take her soul?" He grinned and nodded, licking his lips as if he was about to sit down to a luscious feast.

As I turned to keep Liliana and Assan in full view, I could see Vayl and Aidyn over their shoulders, struggling for possession of the key Cassandra had dropped. The *Enkyklios* sat forgotten, half buried in guck. Something about the scene it played called to me, and I narrowed my eyes, trying to discern details I was too far away to see. Vayl distracted me, shooting the sheath off his cane just as Aidyn threw a punch that connected with his shoulder. The missile flew off course, missing Aidyn completely, but hitting Assan in the back of the head, taking him directly to his knees and over onto his side.

Liliana didn't even spare him a glance as she said, "You must admit I have the upper hand, Jasmine. Perhaps *now* you would like to hand over Cirilai? No? Well then." She held both hands out, as if she meant to grab me by the shoulders. Then she closed her fists.

The vise gripped my heart so suddenly, so painfully,

that I screamed. It felt as if she'd actually sunk her claws into my chest and squeezed. But that wasn't the worst of it. The worst part was that I couldn't catch a full breath, just shallow pants that made me even more desperate for air. A moment's release allowed me one whopping inhale; then the vise closed again, bending me backward, bringing tears to my eyes. Through the numbing wall of blood and panic that pressed against my body I heard the sharp crack of a rifle shot. The Deganites screamed and the clamp around my heart dropped away.

I looked up from where I'd been crouching, one hand on my chest, the other on my thigh, trying to prevent a full-body muck bath while the torch sputtered on the ground beside me. I had a moment to be grateful nothing else had caught fire as I searched for the source of the shot. Cole was swinging his gun back around, training it on the Deganites, though he spared me a look that could've meant anything. I read it as a command. *I've done my part. Now stand up and do yours.*

Liliana stood swaying, hands out for balance, the hole in her chest a bloody blob of muscle and bone. I grabbed the torch. It flickered to life as I raised it and leaped toward her. She held her hands out as if to resist me, but the injury left her too weak to maintain even token resistance. At the last moment I flipped the torch in my hand and rammed the jagged handle into the opening Cole had left for me. Liliana clutched the torch and staggered backward, the shock and denial on her face lit by yellow and orange flames. Then her face was nothing more than a ghostly shadow made of smoke and steam as the remnants of her physical being fell to the floor, a heap of clothes and fake hair with a few particles of dust and ashes mixed in.

I moved past Bozcowski, who was digging in the mud, apparently under the impression that we were in the middle of trench warfare. "Where is it? I thought I saw it fall over here. Where is the key?" he kept asking himself. I was pretty sure he was excavating the wrong spot, so I went to help Vayl, inwardly cheering as he delivered a smashing uppercut that lifted Aidyn completely off the floor and threw him five yards back. A black slash at his throat revealed how close Vayl had already come to taking his head. Then Assan rose to block my way.

"Oh, no you don't," he muttered, holding his sword out before him with both hands. "I still have plans for you."

"It won't work, Assan. I'm not a willing sacrifice."

"But you were once, and like most contracts, supernatural or otherwise, the word given to seal the deal is the one that counts."

I felt an immense, fiery hatred for this minuscule pile of bones and trash that had dared to masquerade as a loving husband, a charitable soul. I would disarm him with a couple of well-placed kicks. Then I would disembowel him with his own sword, which, as I eyed it, seemed more and more familiar. Where had I seen it? And recently too.

He jabbed at me, forcing me to back up, to close the distance between the Tor-al-Degan, still trapped behind a knee-high wall of flame, and myself. Then I suddenly had it.

"The *Enkyklios*," I breathed.

"The what?"

The scene that had played out just beyond my vision had

involved the sword. Someone, a tiny blurred figure shining with sweat, covered with blood, had fought the Tor-al-Degan with Assan's sword.

"I need that sword," I told him.

"Don't worry. You'll get it." His smile, white and gold teeth gleaming from a face half caked with mud and grime, made him look purely demonic.

"Then come give it to me," I demanded.

"I was never one to turn down a beautiful woman's invitation."

I'll bet. I glanced over his head. Vayl had Aidyn down on his knees, one hand at his throat, the other holding his wrist, pressing hard, trying to squeeze a dagger out of his grip. He leaned over, inhaled deeply, opened his mouth, and breathed icy air into Aidyn's face. I saw Aidyn's skin begin to crackle and darken. Meanwhile Bozcowski had moved to another mud hole in his desperate search for the key. Then Assan demanded my full attention.

He charged straight at me, sword held high before him. "Run, bitch!" he screamed. "Run from your fate!"

"Now why in the world do you think I'd take your advice?" I asked him. Utter disbelief crowded the rage from his eyes as he saw I meant to stand my ground. But he didn't stop. He came steamrolling toward me, mud flying from his ruined shoes, sword cocked and ready for a killing blow. Still I let him come, and just as he began to make the cut I jumped at him, coming in under the arc of his swing, giving the blade only air and a small slice of my calf, not even enough to sting until later.

Remembering every tip I'd ever heard Albert give David during his high school football days, I went in low, head up so I could see, catching Assan just above his right hip, driving him backward into a pillar. When I heard the air whoosh from his lungs, I grabbed his right wrist and twisted while I drove my other hand hard into the back of his elbow. His agonized scream told me I'd done the move right. From there it was easy to tear the sword from his grip and drive him to his knees. He hit the mud one last time, cupping his broken arm with his whole one. I swung the sword hard and straight, taking his head so cleanly that it stayed on his neck for a teetering moment before it toppled off, hitting the mud a second before his body followed.

Twenty feet beyond my left shoulder, Vayl had also found a use for one of the pillars. He slammed Aidyn into one and the resulting crack surely signaled a fractured skull. Then he looked at me. "This is your kill, Jasmine. I have been saving him for you. Come—" Words failed him as his eyes tracked away from mine, *behind* me, and the horrified expression on his face reminded me *nothing* ever goes as planned.

I turned on one heel to find the Tor-al-Degan standing inches away, her reeking breath making me feel like I'd just entered a sewage pipe. I jumped back and she smiled, revealing at least three rows of graying teeth, all of which looked shark sharp.

"Cassandra!" I yelled. "Center stage, girl! Reel this monster in!" I risked a look back and wished I hadn't. While Cole guarded the prisoners, Bergman struggled to help Cassandra sit up. She looked ill, like somebody had slipped raw eggs into her morning juice. Vayl fared only slightly better. Aidyn had taken advantage of his momentary distraction to disarm him. Now they were duking it out like old-school boxers, standing toe-to-toe, delivering blows that would've sent most men to their knees.

Only Bozcowski continued as before, a frustrated pirate digging for treasure.

I looked back at the Tor, a wave of despair dulling my vision, making my mouth taste of metal and grave dust. I felt my shoulders slump, watched my sword arm drop.

"This is how it will feel when I eat your soul," the Tor whispered. "Everything that was good and glad in you will nourish me, bring me full into this tasty, luscious world of yours where I will eat, and eat, and eat . . ." She subsided, glassy-eyed, smiling hellishly at the prospect of such a meal.

In that moment she reminded me strongly of a balding, thick-lipped serial killer Vayl and I had recently dispatched. He'd worn that same expression right before we blew his brains all over the wall. I wanted to call it an omen, but it was too late for that. I laughed bitterly.

As soon as my laughter hit the air I felt better and knew she'd been bewitching me. I'd just been so focused on Cassandra and Vayl I hadn't noticed my magic meter spiking.

"You laugh," said the Tor. "Why?"

"Because you won't be able to squeeze enough joy out of my soul to qualify as an anorexic's dinner." I shoved the sword into her and she screamed, her rotten-egg breath burning my nostrils, making me gag. She staggered backward and I pulled the sword free. As she turned to run, I struck again, slicing into her slithering hump, my sword sliding through it easily until it lodged in her spine. She screamed again, but when she turned to look at me over her shoulder, she wore an evil grin.

"Gotcha." In that one word her voice tipped the scale from old hag to nether being. At the same time her ripped gown fell to her feet. The whole room got a nightmare glimpse of sagging, pustule-covered skin and then all hell broke loose.

Chapter Twenty-six

Surely if Dante could've seen the rock-lined pit under Club Undead he'd have thought it an accurate depiction of at least one of his many hells. Lit by torches and burning bits of floor, the Tor-al-Degan's current residence stank of flammable gases, blood, vomit, and outright evil. It also rang with the voices of her worshippers, who'd agreed it would be a bright idea to summon her fully into our realm—a big, bad carnivore who saw the entire world as her Little Red Riding Hood.

The Deganites, who probably passed as upstanding citizens by day—bankers and insurance agents and definitely lawyers—screamed like a bunch of U2 fans as their goddess began to change. The rest of us just watched, stunned speechless, as a yellowish red substance the consistency of hair gel oozed out of the Tor's wound.

I let go of the sword hilt and backed up, fear and confusion warring with panic and horror to see which could gain control of my mind first.

In defiance of gravity, the ooze rose, growing over the top of the Tor's head. It spread downward as well, until it looked as if she had stepped inside an enormous tank of pink Vaseline.

Oh God, oh God, oh God. I looked back at my friends. Cole still had the crowd corralled, but they seemed cheerful about it now. Everything else had gone from bad to worse. Somehow Aidyn had escaped Vayl long enough to deck Bergman, who lay crumpled on one of the floor's few dry spots like a worn-out bloodhound. Aidyn had then grabbed Cassandra, who still looked spaced out, and now held her in front of him like a shield. The *Enkyklios* lay at their feet, replaying another fight scene featuring some long-dead hero and the Tor. This one had, not a sword, but a two-handed battle-ax. Time after time the Tor suffered blows that would've felled a crazed elephant, and yet she kept coming back for more. Kept . . . healing.

"Give me the key!" Aidyn screamed. "Give it to me now before I break this Seer of yours over my knee!"

"I do not have it," said Vayl. "One of us must have kicked it into a pool while we were fighting." He said it casually, a weatherman mentioning the cold front that was about to whip through the region. But his eyes kept darting to the Tor, as did Aidyn's.

In the short time I'd looked away from her, she'd changed dramatically. She'd grown to twice her height inside that viscous shell. Her hair had clumped and then formed into tentacles. Spinal plates grew out of her back. And where there should have been an extra protrusion in the shape of a sword hilt there was, instead, a jiggling tumorous mass that reminded me alarmingly of a giant egg sac. Only I had a gut-wrenching feeling its contents heralded, not birth, but death. No doubt about it, she had fully ingested the plague. But she still hadn't completely entered the world. I kept reminding myself of that as the transformations continued, happening so fast I could hear the squeal of bones stretching and the wet, ripping sound of skin opening to make way for new appendages, including two vicious-looking pincers that emerged from the Tor's bleeding jaws.

She stretched, rising to a height of at least eight feet. Her new muscles rippled beneath skin the color of a bad sunburn. Her eyes had brightened to violet, the same color, in fact, as Liliana's. I had never seen anything so immense, so unearthly, so unbeatable. Tammy Shobeson's voice squealed in my head, *Loser, loser, loser!*

"Time to play," the Tor growled as she shook the gel from her new body (if only Jenny Craig had her recipe). She moved toward me. Even though I knew deep down this was the end for me, I stood my ground. There was no other option.

"Move!" she demanded.

"No."

"What do you hope to gain by standing in my way?"

I thought about it. Even now, in the final moments of my life, smart-ass me was ready and available for service. "I'd like a title. Maybe Idiot of the Year. Is that one taken?"

She leaned over me, the putrid tang of her breath making my curls wilt. "Are you trying to save the lives of your puny friends?"

"What if I was?"

"Then you would, without question or debate, qualify as a willing sacrifice."

Shit! I turned and ran, mowing through the mud like a sleek little ATV. I waved my hands and screamed, "Run! Run! She's going to kill us all!"

As soon as I passed Vayl, I heard a shot. One glance back showed Cassandra diving off to the right while Aidyn began to topple backward, a dark and gaping hole in the middle of his forehead. Vayl closed in on Aidyn fast, a sword-wielding juggernaut that didn't stop until Aidyn's head flew from his body and the smoke of his remains stained the ceiling.

The Deganites milled around, showing the whites of their eyes as Cole swung his gun back toward them, having done all he could to pull the odds back into our favor. He looked ready to bolt, but he stood his ground, which made me enormously proud. I gestured for his gun and he immediately tossed it to me. I sprayed the wall just above the Deganites' heads. "Run! Run! Run!" Like good little sheep, they obeyed, surging toward the stair wreckage in a babbling mob. Even though it looked more like a tornado victim than a means of egress, people were still finding a way to climb up toward freedom.

I turned the gun on the Tor and opened up. I'm not sure, but I think I might have been screaming while I shot her so full of holes she looked like a puzzle with several missing pieces. Moments later Vayl joined me, firing Bergman's weapon. He caught my eye and I realized we were both grinning, a couple of crazy hyenas tackling one badass lion.

The Tor backpedaled fast, squawking and bellowing by turns. She grabbed Bozcowski from his latest fishing expedition and held him in front of her like a shield. His body bounced like a marionette as our bullets struck him.

"Put me down, you freak!" he demanded, his voice rising up the scale to a shriekish whine. "Let me go, you disgusting piece of swamp rot!"

She conceded, in a way, by throwing him against a wall. The sound of his spine snapping oddly resembled the crack of a split log. He fell to the floor in a heap, moaning piteously, picking at his twisted legs as if they had somehow betrayed him.

And I thought we had her. I honestly did. That's how badly I wanted it to be true. Then she lunged.

Even in the midst of battle, when moments move like hours, the Tor was a red blur. Fangs the size of my hand sank into my right side. It felt like two flaming skewers had pierced me through and through, sending bolts of electric pain shooting through the rest of my body. I felt myself sinking into the agony, as if it was a tar pit from which I could never escape.

The Tor shook me. My feet left the ground and, even as a red haze of torment settled over my brain, I thought distantly that I must resemble an old dog toy, frayed around the edges and in desperate need of retirement.

I pressed my gun against her skull, shot until my magazine was empty, and she would not let go. Dimly, a mere echo in the booming crush of sound that was my blood rushing, my ribs breaking, my lung collapsing, I heard Vayl yelling, urgent, adamant orders I knew I must obey if only I could decipher the language he barked them in.

Then I was outside, above, watching from a place so quiet, so warm, so *safe* that all it would take would be a plate of chocolate-chip cookies and a tall glass of milk for me to feel as I had every time I'd visited Granny May. I realized I'd split from my body one last time, only all the golden threads were missing. I searched for them, feeling a wave of grief at their loss. Then I found a new thread, one imbued with every color of the rainbow, and was amazed I hadn't seen it before, it was so large, so gorgeous, pulsating to some basic rhythm that might well have been the heartbeat of the universe.

I moved toward it. Who wouldn't? But something stopped me, tugged at me, pulled me back. I looked down, perplexed, and then I saw the problem. The Tor had grabbed on to a trailing ribbon of my essence with one of the tentacles that flanked her jaw. I watched her reel me in, panic beginning to eat at the edges of the brief peace I'd found. But I was aware of more, as if I could see everyone and everywhere at once.

The last of the Deganites had reached the door and was climbing through. Cassandra had crawled to Bergman and was rolling him over. He winced and grabbed his side, saying something to her that caused her to turn him farther and grab at something he'd been lying on.

Cole had moved to Vayl's side, where they both fought to force the Tor to release my body. Cole delivered a flurry of blows to the Tor's midsection, at least one connecting soundly enough to break her arm, eliciting a high-pitched scream. Vayl leaped onto the Tor's back and sank his fingers into her throat. Frost crackled up her chin and across her face. He dug deeper and the frost turned to ice. No more sounds escaped her throat, not even when he broke her jaw with one powerful blow of his fist.

My body dropped to the floor, bouncing slightly before it settled into the ooze. Cole immediately went to work, inspecting wounds, searching for a pulse. But Vayl stayed put, hacking away at the Tor's tentacles with bloody fists. I realized even though he coudn't see me, that he knew . . .

The Tor-al-Degan was eating my soul. Slowly. With the relish of a connoisseur. And when she finished, nothing could stop her from leaping onto the throat of the world.

Once I'd thought maybe I was crazy, and the fear of losing my sanity, losing *myself*, had dogged every breath, dictated every action. Worse than an infestation of cockroaches, a cancerous tumor, the loss of my family . . . the feeling had left me unwilling to rest, unable to find peace. That had only been fear. This was real.

Second by second, the Tor was ingesting the best—and the worst—parts of me. I was losing myself inside the horrifying red hell of the Tor's gaping maw. I struggled. I fought. I prayed. I tried desperately to tear myself free. But the slow torture of my ultimate destruction went on. And though I had no voice, I began to scream and scream and scream . . .

A voice rang across the room, Cassandra's deep, rich tones washing across me like warm, clear water. She'd come forward to stand by Cole as he worked furiously over my cooling body. In her right hand she held the pyramid, the key. And in her left she held the *Enkyklios*, echoing the words as she heard them from the small vision of a Seer who had stood in a long-distant past and saved the world for a time.

The Tor bellowed and shook her head, denying the

power that had suddenly appeared, demanded her allegiance. But Cassandra would not relent. And moments later I was free. Flying. Soaring toward that stained-glass rainbow of a lifeline and following it straight to the top.

Chapter Twenty-seven

"You know, I thought I was headed to heaven," I said as I looked out the window. The skyline of Las Vegas glared back at me. I stood in a lavish suite, definitely high-roller territory, surrounded by plush furniture, satin curtains, and so much marble the room could've doubled as a mausoleum.

"Some would tell you you're already there," said my companion.

I would've pegged him as a fighter from the start, even without the crew cut and the upright bearing. I recognized those eyes, had grown up around men with the same look. Only battle will do that, only pitched battle and the death of men you love like brothers.

I also recognized him from our last encounter, when he'd mended my broken neck on the blood-stained floor of a house that should never have been called "safe."

The guy, this warrior, had smiled when I'd showed up and he'd said, "There you are," as if we'd prearranged my appearance in the middle of his hotel room. He'd left his perch on a black leather bar stool and come to shake my hand. "Hello, Jasmine. My name is Raoul." Spain bronzed his skin and flavored his accent, but his manner was pure American military.

"I'm dead, aren't I?"

He'd cocked his head to one side, as if sizing up the new recruit. "That remains to be seen."

I'd gone to the window then, confused and somewhat depressed, pretty sure I'd been relegated to the eternal Between. Below me, Sin City sparkled like a desert queen's tiara. Too bad the stones were fake.

"I guess some people would like to spend eternity gambling and watching showgirls strut across the stage," I said. I turned from the window and dropped onto a couch that made every bone in my non-body sigh with pleasure. "Shoot, I wouldn't mind spending a couple of weeks doing that myself."

Raoul settled onto a matching couch that met mine at a forty-five-degree angle. I suddenly realized this room was arranged the same way I'd done the furniture in Diamond Suites and Bergman's safe house. Yes, and in that long-ago place where Aidyn had destroyed my life.

"Have I been here before?" I asked.

He nodded.

"And David? Has he been here?"

"In a way."

"Oh."

"You're not supposed to remember."

"Hmm."

"Are you okay?"

"Should I be?"

He smiled again. "Probably not."

"So, why am I here?"

He looked surprised, as if I should know. "You're a hero."

I was beginning to get the idea. "Look, *I* didn't save the world back there. It was Cassandra."

"Despite the fact that it's a very catchy phrase, there is no such thing as an army of one."

"What exactly is it that you want?"

He gave me that don't-play-dumb-with-me look that you just hate to see when you're stalling. But to my surprise, he gave me an answer. "You're sitting in headquarters, Soldier. It's time to re-up or retire. It's your call, of course, but we'd like you to continue your work."

I jerked my head toward the window. "Funny place for a headquarters."

"We try to stay close to the front."

"Then you should be in Miami."

"The battle there has been won."

"But not the war?"

"You did not defeat the Raptor."

"Will I be done when I do?"

"If you like. But he is a canny beast. You won't catch him easily." Raoul pursed his lips and shook his head. "However, I digress. You need to make a choice."

I nodded. It was time to move on, then, one way or another. I could retire. The word "rest" hovered out there like a green velvet dressing gown. But I'd seen what it had done to Albert and there was no reason to think I'd be any more content. Plus, my retirement would leave Evie to cope with the cantankerous old man on her own. I'd never see her baby girl. I'd never hear Dave's story, which must be as remarkable as my own. Bergman and Cassandra would probably kill each other. Cole would become a bitter old man. And Vayl . . . Vayl would wander the earth alone, longing for his sons. Longing for me.

I looked Raoul in the eye. "I'm in."

"Excellent." He nodded at me and a mystical wind rose in the room, knocking over lamps, shattering vases, forcing me to squeeze my eyes shut tight.

When I opened them again, Cole's face was inches away, his breath still warm in my mouth, his fingers pressing against my neck. When he felt the blood move once again inside me, a blissful look of triumph settled over his face.

"She's back," he said, looking over his shoulder. Cassandra and Bergman hugged and gave me the thumbs-up sign. Vayl knelt beside me, a wide smile stretching his face to new limits, making him look happy and pained at the same time.

"Jasmine, I am so glad you're here."

I thought about it a minute and nodded. "Me too." But something troubled me. Something beyond the pain would not allow . . . I searched as much of the cavern as I could, considering the only body part I was willing to move was my head. There, still sprawled against the wall. Bozcowski. Everyone had forgotten about him but me.

He met my eyes. Even without telepathic abilities I could read the thoughts raging inside his damaged mind. He had a good lawyer and a genius publicist. If he kept his mouth shut he might be able to ride this one out. Why not? Politicians had a rich heritage of wriggling out of tight situations. And after all, people loved him. Shoot, he might even make vampirism the newest nationwide fad!

The sick thing was, I could actually envision a situation or two where his fantasies came true. I looked at

Vayl, let my eyes stray back to Bozcowski so he'd understand. *Finish the job.*

He stood up, strode over to the senator, grabbed him by the collar, and dragged him to within a foot of where I lay. He dangled from Vayl's fist like an obese seventh grader who needs help finishing his first push-up. "Cole, do you still have Jasmine's gun?" Vayl asked.

Cole reached into the belt of his pants and pulled out Grief. "Release the safety and push the magic button," Vayl told him. While Cole readied my weapon, Vayl and I spent some time in each other's eyes. More and more for us, key moments required no conversation at all. Vayl would've preferred to off Bozcowski himself, because he knew this was about to cause me pain. He also knew I needed to do this. Bottom line, the senator had betrayed his own people. It was right that one of his own should end him.

Cole put Grief, now altered to shoot as a crossbow, in my hand. Vayl raised Bozcowski another inch to give me a clear target.

"Jaz, please," Bozcowski blubbered. "You don't want to do this!"

"Actually, yes, I do." I raised the gun and fired. Bozcowski's body wafted away like the smoke from a newly doused fire. Vayl brushed off his hands and took Grief from me. I closed my eyes.

"Better?" he asked.

"Yeah," I sighed. Now I could rest.

Acknowledgments

I should first recognize my husband's part in this whole scheme since, when I finally confessed to him my secret love of all things vampire, he didn't laugh and say, "Good Lord, Jen, how old *are* you?" Nope, he said, "Then maybe you should write a vampire novel." To which I replied, "It's all been done already." And he said, "Not by you." So, thanks babe, without your encouragement, I'd never have dared this book. Big thanks to my agent, Laurie McLean, for taking a chance on me and giving me the kind of full-out support and honest feedback I have come to deeply appreciate. Thanks also to my editor, Devi Pillai, whose humor, patience, insight and constant barrage of questions have helped me elevate this work to a level I couldn't have imagined when I first sent it to her. For their insights into weaponry and military information I must acknowledge Ron Powell and Ben Rardin. Any mistakes I've made in either arena are my own. And special you-brave-soul hugs to my readers for taking on the daunting task of reviewing a raw manuscript and offering honest feedback to its nail-biting author. Love to you all: Jackie Plew, Hope Dennis, Ron Powell, Katie Rardin and Erin Pringle. Most of all, thanks to you, Reader, for climbing out to the edge of this limb with me. I hope you enjoy the view!

extras

meet the author

Jennifer Rardin began writing at the age of 12, mostly poems to amuse her classmates and short stories featuring her best friends as the heroines. She lives in an old farmhouse in Illinois with her husband and two children. Find out more about Jennifer Rardin at www. JenniferRardin.com.

interview with Jaz Parks

We sat in my sunroom, though dark had fallen hours before. I thought Jaz had chosen the spot for Vayl's sake. So he could watch. I knew she'd brought him, as she had many times before, but we had yet to meet. I wasn't sure why.

The tape recorder sat on the coffee table between us, mutely turning, as if constantly shaking its head at the story she'd been documenting for the last few weeks. I could hardly believe it myself.

JEN: "You've told me things I'm sure some people would keep from their priests. But that's still left me with some pretty big questions." Jaz sat forward in her white wicker chair, her red curls framing her pale face so perfectly I felt I should take a picture. She could be any lovely coed on any Big Ten campus, except for the shock of white hair spiraling from her forehead around her right cheek to her chin.

JAZ: "What do you want to know?"

JEN: "Are you haunted by the people you've killed?" Her eyebrows shot up. I could see her thinking it was none of my damn business. But she wasn't ready to shut me off. Not yet.

JAZ: "That would presuppose that I felt guilty about killing them, wouldn't it?" She thought a second. "The ones that bother me are the ones that didn't go down as quick or painless as I would've liked. But I'm not haunted. My job is to take out bad guys. If you think that makes me a bad guy . . ." She shrugged. "That's your problem."

JEN: "Actually, I don't. But I do think it makes you unique. How did you get into this line of work?"

JAZ: "After the big blowout with my dad, I'll tell you about that later, the military was just out for me as a career path. But I still wanted to serve my country." She paused. "What, no smart-ass remark?"

JEN: "No."

JAZ: "Sorry. Even now I get a little defensive. You can love a man or a kid or a piece of damn pie and nobody has a problem with you. But love your country and in some places you get booed right out of the joint."

JEN: "Go on."

JAZ: "Anyway, the CIA recruited me straight out of college. After the Helsinger tragedy . . ." a pause here while Jaz looked out the window, and then down at the lovely gold and ruby ring on her left hand, "I was a wreck. But I kept it all buttoned up good and tight. So after a couple months at a desk, I got an interview with Pete, and he hired me." Her laugh managed to completely lack humor. "The job killed me, and then it saved me. Ironic, huh?"

JEN: "Why are you telling me all this?" She answered quickly. Too quickly.

JAZ: "I guess I want to leave something behind me when I'm gone. A legacy."

JEN: "You could just as easily have said you wanted the historians to get their stories straight once this is all declassified."

JAZ: "Meaning?"

JEN: "Either way, your story's bullshit." She smiled, then. She appreciated honesty, I think because she so rarely saw it in her world.

JAZ: "All you hear any time you turn on the TV is, the world is ending. Some scientist with too little data and too much funding is in the microphone of some anchor who's only interested in scaring the hell out of her audience because that's how you get ratings, man. Nobody seems to recall that people have been screaming about the world ending for the last two thousand years. They're scared out of their minds. They live in fear. Every move, every decision, is based somewhat on how terrified they are at any given moment. People need to know there's hope. That people like me are out there fighting for them, making sure the world keeps turning, so they can occasionally let go of that fear and find a moment or two of happiness." She sat back. Grimaced, like she'd eaten something sour. "And if you ever tell anybody I said that I'm going to kick your ass."

I liked her. God help me, I felt a real affection for this dangerous woman sitting in my old farmhouse while her vampire lover hovered somewhere among my gardens or my fields. Even though I knew the only reason she'd picked me was that she'd read one of my stories in a magazine and liked it, and she knew I'd keep her secrets until she told me it was time to tell. What a weird old world.

JAZ: "Things are stirring. I won't be able to stick around much longer. After I'm gone you'll have plenty of time to write up the Tor-al-Degan story. In the meantime, let me tell you what happened next."

JEN: "You mean after you got out of the hospital?"

JAZ: "Of course. God, they had me on the strongest drugs. Couldn't remember a thing that happened that first week. Took me a while to heal, of course, but I want to tell you about the mission. It involved this Chinese vampire named Chien-Lung. Dragon fanatic. If he'd been a teenaged guy he'd have had dragon posters plastered all over his bedroom walls, tattoos, T-shirts, the works! Anyway, let me start at the beginning . . ."

introducing

If you enjoyed ONCE BITTEN, TWICE SHY,
look out for

ANOTHER ONE BITES THE DUST

Book 2 of the Jaz Parks series

by Jennifer Rardin

Holy crap, I've had another blackout! But as soon as the suspicion hit me I knew otherwise. I hadn't experienced the usual warning signs, and I'd never before left my mind in a daydream while the rest of me got busy. This was something new. Something scary. Because after the knock-down-drag-out with the Tor-al-Degan, I thought I'd kicked those nutty little habits that made me seem, well, nuts. Okay, the card shuffling kept up without much of a break. And sometimes words still ran loops around my brain until I forced them back on the road. But those moments were rarer now. And the blackouts really had stopped, along with the dread that someone I knew would find reason to recommend an asylum and a heavy dose of Zoloft.

Familiar laughter caught my attention. The couple from the beach, they were here, just entering an elevator. Without conscious thought I'd followed them to their hotel and booked a room. I checked the receipt. At least I'd used my personal credit card. If I'd had to explain this to Pete, well, maybe I could've come up with something. But I probably would've just resigned.

I shoved the stuff the desk clerk had handed me into my back pocket and strode outside. I needed to do something concrete. Something to bring me back to myself. So I phoned my sister.

"Evie?"

"Oh, Jaz, I'm so glad you called."

"You sound tired."

"I am. E.J. has hardly stopped crying all day. This doesn't seem right, does it?"

Hell no! But then I'm the least qualified to say. "Did you call the pediatrician?"

"No. I know he'll just say it's that colic." Her voice started to shake. "I just feel like such a terrible mother that I can't make her stop crying!"

Now here was something I could deal with. "Evie, you are an awesome mother. This I can tell you from experience. I've seen you in action. Plus I have had a crappy mother. So I know whereof I speak. You rock. I know it's tough on you guys having a baby who cries all the time. The lack of sleep alone is probably making you a little crazy. I know I'm still kinda grouchy and I've only been gone, what, a couple of days? But listen, you will figure this out, okay?"

Big pause. "O-kay."

"Did I say something wrong?"

"It's just . . . usually you tell me what to do. Then I do it, and things get better."

"That was before you started playing out of my league," I said, smiling when I heard her soft laughter. "Just . . . trust yourself, okay? You and Tim know E.J. better than anybody, including the pediatrician. And get some sleep, would you? You're going to have bags under your eyes you'll be able to store your winter clothes in."

"Okay. How are things going with you?"

Well, let's see. I think my vampire boss should pose for his own calendar and I'm having a crazy-daisy relapse. Otherwise—"I'm doing okay. Call me when you can, okay?"

"Okay. Love you."

"Love you too."

Feeling somewhat rebalanced now I'd touched base with the most stable person I knew, I walked around to the back of the building, which faced the festival site. As I wound my way through the first tier of cars in the parking lot, a green glow near some fencing that disguised a large garbage bin distracted me from my inner teeth-gnashing. It didn't mesh with the white of the lot lights. I drew Grief and chambered a round. The glow brightened, changing color from pine needles to ripe limes.

I closed my eyes tight for a couple of seconds, activating the night-vision contacts Bergman had designed for me. They combined with my Sensitivity-upgraded sight to show me a greenish-gold figure standing beside the fence. It faced me, but leaned over every few seconds, fully engrossed in whatever lay at its feet. Oddly, a black frame surrounded it, as if someone had outlined it with a Sharpie.

I moved closer, sliding past the dark hulks of parked vehicles, taking quick glances every few steps, trying to identify the thing on the ground that acted as both the source of the green glow and the subject of the outlined figure's interest. When I finally caught a glance, I bit my lip to keep from gasping. It was the body of the security guard, the one who'd been hanging out with the two-faced man. *His* face, a twisted photo of his last tortured moments, warned me not to look any further. But I had to. One of the suckier parts of my job.

Okay, enough with the procrastinating. You're at a possible murder scene with a potential suspect. Look at the body already.

Blood, everywhere, as if someone had tapped a geyser. Exposed ribs. Dark, glistening organs. Someone had ripped this guy's chest open from neck to navel! The smell, damn, you just never get used to it. And thank God we were outside, otherwise I'd be puking like a bulimic after an Oreo cookie binge. Above it all hovered a jeweled cloud I could only think of as his soul. I wanted to regard it as untouched. The one part of the man his murderer could not soil. But I couldn't. Because this is what had his killer's attention.

No doubt, the one who'd taken his life stood right next to him still, and had been all day, posing as a man with only one face. "Man" was the wrong descriptor though. That outline—nobody I'd ever met had that. And when he leaned over, the outline split at his head and his fingers, allowing some of the greenish-gold of his inner aura to seep through.

His mouth opened wide and from it unrolled a huge, pink tongue covered with spike-like appendages. He ran it along the length of the dead man's soul. It shivered, frantically trying to fly apart, to meld with his family, his friends, his maker. But the spikes released some sort of glue that forced the jewels into immobility. At the same time the soul cloud bleached to pastel.

The two-faced man looked up, his eyes closed, ecstasy lifting the corners of his flabby lips. And then a third eye opened on his forehead, a large, emerald green eye that darkened at the same rate at which the dead man's soul lightened. *Coincidence? I don't think so.*

I'd had enough.

I stepped forward, skirted the bumper of an El Dorado coupe, and trained my gun on the monster's face.

"Dinner's over, pissant."

The two-faced man opened his regular eyes, which were blue, took one, long look at me, and growled.

"Give me a break," I drawled, sounding oh-so-bored, though my stomach spun like a roulette wheel. "I know special effects guys who can produce scarier roars than that." Okay, I don't really *know* any, but I've watched *Resident Evil*, haven't I?

This time he bellowed, and I admit, it gave me something of a chill. But it didn't freeze me like it was intended to. I was ready when he charged, leaping over the body like some meat-hoarding gorilla, his hands stretched wide, a full set of lethal-looking claws appearing and disappearing as he moved. If he raked those vein-poppers across my throat while they were just fingernails, would they still leave stitch-worthy gashes?

Not something I wanted to find out. I fired, five shots

in quick succession. They staggered him, though I could see the black outline had worked as a shield, preventing them from delivering any fatal wounds. Five more shots backed him up, almost to the body. Thanks to Bergman's modifications I still had five left. And I intended to make them count.

As he moved on me again, I concentrated on the breaks in his shield. They came and went in rapid succession, but I noticed a pattern based on his movements. It helped that he approached more warily this time. Apparently it still hurt to be shot. I should be thankful, but small favors sometimes suck.

I watched his face, waiting for the blur and the accompanying break in his shield. There!

I fired once, but the shield had already closed. I would have to anticipate the breaks, rather than wait for them to reveal themselves. Four rounds left. I took careful aim and fired. One. Two. Three. Four. Damn! The timing just missed with every shot. And now I'd used the last of my ammunition. If Grief didn't work in gun mode I didn't anticipate much success from it as a crossbow. I holstered my weapon.

But I was still armed.

Unlike Vayl, I don't use blades as a rule. Generally if I have to get that close to a target, something's gone terribly wrong. Same deal defensively speaking. Still, I keep one on me. My nod to the wisdom of weapons redundancy.

My backup plan started life as a bolo. It had been issued to the first of my military ancestors, Samuel Parks, before he marched off to war in 1917. Handed down father to son since that time, the ugly old knife had lost its appeal for David after Mom threw it at Dad upon finding him on top of her best pal. Since it had sailed clear through the bedroom window on that occasion, I'd discovered it on the lawn the next morning. Thus, it came to me.

I carry the knife, sheath and all, in a special pocket designed for near invisibility by my seamstress, Mistress Kiss My Ass. I call her this because it's the response she gives me every time I call and say, "Sherry Lynn, guess what, I just got a new pair of pants!"

Reaching into my pocket, I grabbed the artfully disguised hilt and pulled. A blade the length of my shin slid out. Originally meant more as an all-purpose tool, the bolo had been refined to my needs thanks to Bergman. Now it was sharp enough to cut metal or, better yet, defend my life.

The creature circled me, looking a lot less intimidated by great-great grandpa's knife than I would've liked. *Well, screw it.* I ran straight at him, yelling like a pissed-off soccer mom, waving my blade like a samurai warrior. I faked left, right, left, watching as his shield opened wider and wider. It could not keep up with his bobbing head as he tried to avoid getting his throat cut. One more feint and I jumped forward, burying my blade in the shield gap his movements had caused.

He died instantly.

I pulled my weapon free and cleaned it on his stolen uniform. Glad the bolo had saved me. Sorry the same family had subjected it to nearly one hundred years' worth of blood and guts. We seem to spawn killers, no doubt about that. I found myself hoping hard that E.J.

could break that chain. Maybe when I got a free second I'd give her a call and make that suggestion. Never mind that she was less than a month old and would spend the entire time trying to eat the receiver. It's never too early to start brainwashing your young.

BLACK SHIPS

Jo Graham

An extraordinary tale of a young woman who becomes an oracle—in an age when an oracle held more power than a king.

In a time of war and doubt, Gull is an oracle. Daughter of a slave taken from fallen Troy, chosen at the age of seven to be the voice of the Lady of the Dead, it is her destiny to counsel kings.

When nine black ships appear, captained by an exiled Trojan prince, Gull must decide between the life she has been destined for and the most perilous adventure: to join the remnant of her mother's people in their desperate flight. From the doomed bastions of the City of Pirates to the temples of Byblos, from the intrigues of the Egyptian court to the haunted caves beneath Mount Vesuvius, only Gull can guide Prince Aeneas on his quest, and only she can dare the gates of the Underworld itself to lead him to his destiny.

In the last shadowed days of the Age of Bronze, one woman dreams of the world beginning anew. This is her story.

"Haunting and bittersweet, lush and vivid, this extraordinary story has lived with me since I first read it."
— Naomi Novik, author of *Her Majesty's Dragon*

ISBN: 0-316-06800-4 / 978-0-316-06800-0